Friends with bite

and

the curse of the vampire

M. J. Wallenda
W. T. Wallenda

Friends with bite

and

the curse of the vampire

Impressum:
Imprint:
©2024 by W. T. Wallenda and M. J. Wallenda

Proofreading: T. Wallenda
Cover Image: S. Wallenda
ai-generated-8697984_1280
romantic-8840815_1280
https://pixabay.com/de/service/license-summary/

Cover design, Production and
publishing: BoD – Books on Demand,
Norderstedt
ISBN: 978-3-7597-6746-2

© S. Wallenda

Chapter One

It's the middle of the night, midnight to be exact. I'm woken from my sleep by a mega thunderstorm outside. It is the first time I wake up in this house. We've moved to a small town called Greenfield. It is in Franklin County, New England. More specifically, in Massachusetts, on the border of New Hampshire.

Before that we lived in a mini village in the middle of nowhere. A road led into the village and out again two minutes later. There was nothing to do there except hang out in your room. Pretty boring for a 16 year old kid.

I never made any real friends in the village. Only farmers live there, most of them related to each other. New villagers are treated like strangers and watched for years before they somehow become part of the stepchild existence. At least that's how it seemed to me. No matter. Now we're gone.

My father applied for the vacant position of sheriff of Greenfield/Massachusetts and got the job. No wonder. He was a really good cop in Boston before that. I would have given him the sheriff's job, too.

It's a cool thing to be the son of a police chief. My mom also got a job offer from Greenfield and took it. She is a doctor and now works at the Greenfield Baystate Medical Center Hospital.

As for me, I'm also saving a lot of time every day. I no longer have to spend as much time on the school bus as I did in that godforsaken farming town. Recently, I've also been able to sneak around in my car. Secretly, because I don't have a driver's license yet. My parents have two cars. A white BMW and a black BMW - the whole family has a thing for German cars. Sometimes I affectionately call the German cars Black and White.

There's another car here right now. It's Uncle Joe's sports car, a white Porsche, of course. He has it with us because Joe is going on a long trip with his wife and is afraid his car might be stolen. Of course, no one is allowed to use the Porsche. The thing is sacred and any scratch on it would be a disaster.

Dad currently works from Monday to Friday until about half past four or five in the evening. Mom does the same. But she also has to cover different shifts.

Since they leave the house before me and come home after me, I can drive the Porsche to school. That's super cool. Now I can hear the rain pattering on the roof and drumming on the window. I usually like it when it's pouring outside, with lightning and thunder. That's when I sleep best. But today is different. Today the raindrops are somehow louder and heavier. The rumble of thunder sounds very close and therefore very scary.

Is it always this loud here? Or is it just today?

I imagine huge puddles forming outside and more and more water pouring down.

Water. At this thought I feel how dry my mouth actually is. My tongue almost sticks to the roof of my mouth. I'm thirsty. So I decide to go to the kitchen to get something to drink. Before I go downstairs, I look out the window. We live on the edge of town, right next to the forest. When it's stormy, it looks really dark, even mysterious. The trees sway in the wind. When there is lightning, their outlines take on eerie, dancing shapes. Almost like little monsters, they jump and leap back and forth, chained to their roots.

I look down from the treetops. Another rumble of thunder pierces the night, followed by a long, jagged flash of lightning and another clap of thunder. For a moment I thought I saw something in the shimmering light of the flash. I stared intently into the darkness of the night.

Someone's standing there with their car, it rushes through my head. I start, jump. Then I catch myself. Curious, I use the next flash to find the spot where I made my observation.

Yes, a car.

The headlights are off. Only the interior lighting comes on for a moment as a person gets out of the car.

A man.

At least that's what I assume, because the figure looks strong. I recognize the make of the car.

Wow, a Mercedes. Are there more German car enthusiasts in Greenfield?

The figure slams the car door, slings something over his shoulder, and runs quickly into the woods.

What's that guy got? A rug?

"Something is wrong here," I say quietly.

Is he carrying a dead body?

My thoughts race wildly.

What is this strange guy doing in the woods in the middle of the night?

I step back from the window and sneak out of my room so as not to wake my parents, who are sleeping on the same floor. Instead of turning on the light, I grab my flashlight and go down to the kitchen. I close the door behind me and turn on the light. Then I take a few sips from the faucet and wipe my mouth with the dishcloth that was lying around.

My mom would tell me again that the dishtowel is only for washing up and that I should use a glass, blah blah blah. My dad just had a couple of days off. Actually, he got them because of the move, but I hope he still has enough time to finally fix my computer. Unlike me, he knows his stuff. When it comes to swapping out graphics cards, upgrading the ram, and stuff like that, I'm completely clueless. Apart from that, tech nics is my thing.

I take another sip and go back to . I'm very careful with the first step. It creaks. After that I can walk normally. In my room, I turn on the light and go to my bed. I fluff my pillow, put the flashlight back in my nightstand drawer, lie down and cover up.

Click

I reach for the light switch and it's dark again. My eyes quickly adapt to the darkness. My eyes wander around the room. Past my posters, along the bookcase, down to my school bag and finally to my guitar. My parents gave it to me for Christmas the year before last.

The storm outside is still raging. I look at my watch and watch the fluorescent second hand make its rounds. It is now 00:15. When I was younger and woke up at this time, I was always afraid. But not anymore. Now it's just a time like any other and no longer a witching hour.

My eyes fall on my satchel again. Tomorrow is the last day of summer vacation. After that, school starts.

The day after tomorrow, I'll be the new kid. Then I'll attend Greenfield High School and it will soon become clear whether I'm the new kid on the block or the alien new kid like in the farm town. The alien in the country, so to speak.

I know that first impressions determine whether it will be a good or a difficult year. So it's up to me to be cool or uncool to my classmates.

I have a plan for that, too. I want to drive my uncle's Porsche to school. Just for fun. But I don't want to say anything about the car so I don't seem like a show-off. I just want to look casual. My mom will be at the hospital and my dad will be out running errands. So I can sneak the Porsche out of the garage and make my plan a reality.

Great thing.

With these thoughts I fall asleep. In the background, the rain is still drumming hard against my window. But the rumbling thunder is becoming less frequent. The storm seems to be losing its power.

I am rudely awakened. Someone is loudly slamming the front door. I rub my sleepy eyes and turn over again. But I can no longer think about sleeping. Too many things are running through my head.

Who left the house now?

Mom and Dad don't have to work today.

Hm, maybe the wind?

There was quite a storm last night. Or has my father been alerted? After all, he's the sheriff.

I turn to my alarm clock, which reads 8:23. Although 9:00 a.m. is my standard time to get up on vacation, I want to know who left the house and slammed the door in such a hurry. Also, my bladder is clenching.

Too much water at midnight, I think.

So I get up and go to the bathroom. Then I shower and get dressed. I make my bed and saunter down the stairs. Mom is sitting at the breakfast table reading the newspaper. "Good morning," she greets me.

"Good morning," I mumble.

I made myself a hot chocolate and sat down at the table. "Where's daddy anyway?" I ask.

"He had to go to the office."

"Why? It's his day off. Did something happen?" "He got a call from one of his deputies. Somebody found a body in the woods. Terrible," she says excitedly, her hand shaking a little as she lifts her coffee cup to take a sip. She sips just a little and puts the cup down.

I can tell immediately that she is very excited. "A body?" I ask, immediately thinking of the man carrying something into the woods.

Mom clears her throat and looks at me. "A very strange thing. The strange thing is that the body is completely drained of blood. As if it had been sucked dry."

"Like a vampire or slaughtered like a butcher?" I add, not really believing what I've heard.

"Like a vampire. That sums it up perfectly. That's what they told Dad on the phone. Funny, isn't it?"

I frown at him. "Hm, yeah."

As I make myself some peanut butter toast, I consider telling them about my observation, but decide against it for now.

My mom clears the dishes and goes upstairs. The song on the radio is replaced by a commercial, then the host chats. Finally, the news comes on. Trivial chatter that doesn't particularly interest me. But suddenly I pricked up my ears.

"...and now our reporter on the scene. William Holden reporting live from Greenfield, Massachusetts. A bloodless body was found there this morning. William Holden, do you read me?"

It cracks, then the reporter speaks.

"This is William Holden, your local man. You're listening to NFC Radio Franklin County, your station for everything! A tragedy must have happened here in the woods of Greenfield. The question is, are there vampires? But first, let's get to the facts. According to the spokesperson for the local sheriff's office, joggers discovered a dead woman in the bushes early this morning. They immediately called the sheriff's office. An emergency physician confirmed the death of the victim, who was about 20 to 25 years old. The body was taken to the Institute of Forensic Medicine. The cause of death will be determined there. The case is already a mystery. According to initial findings, the body is completely drained of blood. There are two small wounds on the neck. Otherwise, the body shows no signs of injury. The new sheriff of Greenfield commented: ..." Now I hear my father's voice.

Wow.

"Mom, Dad's on the radio!" I call, and then I listen to what Daddy is saying.

"We have to find out who it is. We will begin an investigation immediately and check all missing persons cases."

The reporter asks, "Sheriff Allington, are you turning this case over to the FBI?"

Addy replies: "No. The crime falls under my jurisdiction and there is no need to involve the feds at this time."

Reporter: "I have one last question. The body is said to be completely drained of blood. What do you think about that?"

The father replies, completely relaxed: "Let's wait for the results of the autopsy, then we can talk further. Now, if you will excuse me, I have a murder to solve."

A commercial, followed by an oldie, blares from the speakers. Again I wonder if this man I saw last night could have something to do with it.

Was he really a vampire? What a load of rubbish.

I mean, vampires don't even exist.

Or do they?

I clear the table and head for my room.

Miss Piddy, my neighbor at the time, used to tell me stories about vampires and that she knew where one lived. She also gave me a small stone with a beautiful red glow. She said it was very valuable, but not in terms of money. She said it was very valuable, but not in terms of money, and that I would need it someday. Since then that stone has been lying in my room.

After a while, my mother did not want me to meet her anymore because everyone thought she was crazy. I followed my mother's instructions. The old neighbor was so creepy and I never really felt comfortable around her anyway.

Vampires, I thought. *Was she right after all?*

I make a decision. I have to find out more about these bloodsuckers. There has to be a library in Greenfield. I go to my office, sit down at my PC and turn it on. Then I type in the search term Greenfield Library. Moments later, I arrive at the Greenfield Library's home page and see the address and hours. A quick glance at Google Maps and I know the fastest way to get there.

I'm in luck. The library is only an estimated ten minutes walk away. I want to go right now.

"Mom, I'm going to go explore the neighborhood," I call out as I pull on my sneakers. While she's still saying, "Okay," I scurry through the door and pull it into the lock.

Google Maps was right. It takes me about ten minutes to reach the library. It is housed in an old brick building and is larger than I expected. The signage for the different sections is good. I quickly find my way around and head for the section I'm looking for.

Local History.

Excited, I walk past the rows of books.

Damn it! Not what I'm looking for.

I try Fantasy and Science Fiction again.

Another flop. Everything is just fiction. No non-fiction or anything.

But it's also somehow logical. Vampires don't exist. At least not in the way we think of them. But it's all just an invention of Bram Stoker, I think.

I decide to stop searching for the time being and go to . I look at my watch outside the library.

11:00 a.m. and I haven't really done anything today. I feel like a real adventurer, taking every chance to experience something exciting. But what can you do in a city where you've just moved and don't know anyone?

Suddenly I had an idea. At first it flew through my head and I almost dismissed it, but with each passing second it returns and takes shape.

I go to the scene of the crime and look around.

I mean, what could be more exciting than visiting a fresh crime scene where a vampire might have killed someone and drained them? I'm sure my dad is already done with the forensics, and when the crowd at the edge of the forest has died down, I can have a look around undisturbed. Convinced that this is a good idea, I set off.

On the way to the forest I get a little worried. What if the guy is lurking there?

After all, they say that the killer always returns to the scene of the crime - . Goose bumps. They start on the back of my neck and I can feel the hairs standing up there. Then it goes down my back to the tips of my toes. Despite the looming fear, I keep walking. I tell myself not to go too deep into the woods and to watch every step I take.

There are still two police cars parked at the edge of the forest. One of them is parked right where I saw the suspicious Mercedes last night.

But the driver of the police car didn't cover any tracks, I think. *The heavy rain did that. It washed away everything that would have indicated the type and size of the tires.*

The forest looks quite mysterious. Suddenly I'm not sure it's as safe as I thought.

I entered the forest. It smells of leaves and rotten wood, mixed with a breeze of healthy, fresh forest air, if you can even smell it as such. The ground is still quite wet and it's noticeably cooler in the forest. I'm still wondering if I should close my leather jacket when I hear soft footsteps. Leaves rustling and a branch breaking. I'm startled and quickly scurry to the side to hide behind a thick trunk.

Splat

Something cold hits my neck.

How disgusting. Water is still dripping from the trees. At least I hope it's a drop of water.

Oh God, don't let it be bird droppings, I think and reach for it.

Phew, lucky me. Only water.

I am relieved.

The footsteps come closer and closer. I recognize two men in uniform.

They are deputies. But I stayed behind the tree, because I had no business here. My father had told me that a thousand times when we watched crime shows on TV. The deputies were talking.

"The crime scene is taking forever again today. The new sheriff seems to know a thing or two about it."

"He was a homicide detective in Boston." "And then he moves here to the sticks and becomes sheriff?" "His wife works as a doctor at the hospital."

"Then it makes sense. Besides, being sheriff is a great job." "Then why didn't you run for sheriff?"

They both laugh.

"Forget it. Come on, let's hurry. The boss told us to get coffee and donuts for all the emergency services."

The voices die down. Finally I hear the slamming of car doors and the hum of an engine.

There are definitely more police there, and it sounded like it was going to take quite a while. So I decide to turn around and come back the next day. I'm sure no one will be here then.

Back home, I disappear into my room and play on my parents' laptop. I borrowed it because my own PC still isn't working properly. When my dad comes home later, I immediately quit the game and run downstairs. Curious as hell, I immediately start bombarding him with questions.

"Hi, Dad! Did you find out anything? Was it really a vampire? What kind of evidence did you find?"

Dad looks at me questioningly. "What a greeting. Well, James, I can't tell you anything, of course, you know that. Police investigations are secret and not for everyone." I make my miserable face. "Daddy," I whine. "I'm not for everyone and you have to say something anyway. I heard your interview on the radio today. They'll be lining up to talk to you soon, and you can tell me what you're telling them. Or do I have to wait until tomorrow and buy a newspaper to find out what my father is working on and what a dangerous place we've moved to?

Dad scratches the back of his head. A good sign. I know my old man.

"That's right. Why not?"

He walks into the kitchen and sits down. Mom joins him. "You two take good care of this. I mean, who you talk to about it and everything." He changes from a lecturing look to a concerned one. "I also want you to be home when it gets dark. Then I won't have to worry, because in the near future I'll probably be in the office more often and have to work some overtime."

"What's wrong?" asks Mom.

"We discovered another body while searching the area where the body was found. It has been there for several days and has also been taken to the forensic department. The pathologist will have to do a thorough autopsy on both of them. I'm waiting for the report before I go public with this, so please don't talk to anyone about it.

We nod.

"I don't believe in coincidences. It's also striking that the second body is also completely drained of blood - at least that's what the doctor at the scene said."

"Oh my God," Mom says. I get goose bumps. What kind of murderous town have we moved to?" I immediately think.

"It's possible - and I'm being very, very careful about this - it's possible that this is a serial killer. If that turns out to be the case, I would have to turn the case over to the FBI, because that would be federal jurisdiction. But the investigation is still in its infancy, and I will be leading the case myself for the time being."

"A vampire?" I ask.

"You've been reading too much crap. Vampires don't exist. At least not these fictional or mythical creatures or whatever you want to call them. You know that yourself. But I'm assuming a mentally disturbed perpetrator or a ritualistic group of perpetrators," he speculates, thinking about what he just said. Then he nods. "Yes," he says finally. "Maybe there were two ritual murders. But as I said: We're at the beginning of the investigation. I have a press conference in two hours and will announce what I've told you. Then we will wait for information from the public and the evaluation of the evidence".

I think about telling Dad about last night. But I decide to keep it to myself for now.

"And what did you do today?" my father wants to know. "I, um, nothing really."

"Were you here the whole time?" he asks.

"No, I was in town briefly. In the library too. I was looking for something to read, but I didn't find anything."

Mom gets up and goes to the stove. She picks up a pot and pours some water. "Dinner's ready," she says. "You can set the table."

I have pasta with tomato sauce. I eat quickly. My detective instincts are aroused.

I really need to know what the Mercedes driver had to do with the body.

After dinner, we cleared the table together. "I'm going to relax a bit by looking at your computer," says Dad, when suddenly the guitar riffs of *Hey Joe* and the voice of Jimi Hendrix can be heard.

It's the ringtone on Dad's cell phone. He pulls it out of his pocket, looks at the screen, and answers it.

"Hello," he says, listening to the caller. His features turn stony. "Again? ... Where? ... Okay, I'll be right there." He puts the cell phone back in his pocket. He looks at us with a stern and worried expression. "They found another body. It's down by the creek and it was slightly buried there. The heavy rains washed it out. Don't wait for me. It's going to be a long night.

Chapter Two

Beep, beep

The annoyingly shrill beeping of my alarm clock jolts me out of my sleep. I hate that noise because it means both that I didn't sleep in and that I have to go to school. A hand slips out from under the blanket. With my eyes closed, I press a button on the alarm clock.

Only two more minutes, I think sleepily. I turn over again, snuggle back into my pillow, and doze off.

Beep, beep

That stupid alarm. That's what I call the repetition of the alarm. My hand slaps the alarm monster again.

Off!

It's very tempting to stay lying down, but I pull myself up and stand. I immediately think of the first day of school and my super-cool plan to drive Uncle Joe's Porsche there. Dad is busy with the murder cases and drives Black. Mom will drive white to go to the hospital. So I should have free access to the Porsche.

Half lost in thought, I make my way to the bathroom. After a shower I get dressed. A faded t-shirt, ripped jeans and my look is complete. Now I put some wax in my short hair, fiddle with it with my fingers and look at myself in the mirror. Satisfied, I hang my lucky stone necklace around my neck. I got it from my grandmother and I could really use some luck today.

Everything will be fine, I think. One last look at the gel. *It fits. I'm going to breakfast.*

"Your father's gone again," Mom says and asks, "Do you want me to drive you?"

"No," I mumble, my mouth still full of jam toast. I wash it down with freshly squeezed orange juice and add, "I'll take the bus."

"That's good. I'm already late. Are you sure that won't be a problem?"

"No, it's fine. I have no problem with that."

"Okay. See you tonight and have fun!"

"Bye, Mom."

I've won! My plan is working.

Shortly after Mom drives off in the white BMW, I slip into my leather jacket and sneakers, grab the Porsche key, and walk into the garage.

My heart is pounding as I put the key in the ignition. Uncle Joe has the automatic version of the speedster. That suits me just fine, as these models are easier to drive than the clutch versions.

The sound of the 400+ horsepower engine is awesome.

Wromm, wromm

I step on the accelerator and literally shoot out of the garage onto the road.

"Wow, he's got power under his ass!" I exclaim.

Only the most awesome cars in the world make noises like that, and the Porsche 911 GT3 is definitely one of them.

To be honest, I have to say that I've only driven a black car once, and that was in an old jalopy. It belonged to a friend of mine and we drove around meadows and country roads. But I've never driven on the road. But I've never driven on the road. Especially not in such an expensive car. I have to get out of here before the neighbors notice and ask my parents about it.

I turn to the right and carefully step on the gas.

Fuck! I have to change gears. The speedometer reads kilometers, not miles. What the hell was that? 100 km/h is about 62 mp/h.

I glance at the speedometer and then quickly back to .

I have to slow down.

The speedometer needle has shot up to 100 in a matter of seconds and is slowly coming back down to 80.

Still too fast. Much too fast.

I almost hit a car, manage to brake just in time before a red light, and almost hit a pedestrian on the hood of a car. The older man gives me the finger and yells something behind me that sounds like "You bastard! I continue through the green light. But much slower. Gradually I get a feel for the accelerator and two streets and a traffic light later I'm in control of the Porsche. At least I am convinced that I am in control. It's like taming a wild horse. I am the greatest.

I park in the teachers' parking lot in front of the school, press the gas pedal once more in neutral, to be on the lookout for a lot of people.

Wromm, wromm

Only now do I turn off the engine.

I calmly slam the door shut and push the button to lock it. I push my sunglasses up a little, adjust my leather jacket, and traipse toward the school entrance. To avoid looking fat and like a totally arrogant snob, I move normally. I don't strut around like a supermodel or puff myself up like a rocker.

Hundreds of looks come my way. Most of them from the lower classes, of course. A few teenagers who, judging by their outfits, must feel pretty casual, stare at me regularly. I give them a quick nod, enter the school and look for the blackboard with the lists of names. There I look for my name. I find it and see what class I'm in. I memorized my room number and floor and began my search.

It takes me a long time to find my classroom. In the meantime, the hallways are full of students and, bang, all the doors are closed and I'm standing alone in the hallway.

Pro: I can read the room numbers. Disadvantage: I am definitely late.

Finally, I'm standing in front of the door to my new classroom. Our teacher is Mrs. White. I smile because I remember the white BMW. Then I take a deep breath. This is the moment of all moments.

If I blow it now, I'll be the rag forever.

I open the door. Silence reigns. All eyes are on me. The teacher, I think it's Mrs. White, doesn't look very friendly. She has the look of a startled wild boar and the figure to match.

Oh dear, I am screwed, is my first thought.

That's typical James again. I have the plan of the year and it fails because I'm too scatterbrained to find the classroom. While I'm still searching for the right words, Mrs. Boar-White's death stare hits me again. I open my mouth to greet the class, but she beats me to it.

"Young man. Who are you and why are you late? Think about your answer. One thing in advance: I don't tolerate back-talk, I'm not here to make friends, and if you don't behave in a disciplined manner, it will show up in your GPA and in detention!"

That did the trick.

Stupid cow. Wild boar.

My first instinct is to apologize, but I suddenly make a decision I never thought I was capable of. I need the perfect answer to avoid ruining that all-important first impression and looking like a loser. A sentence that will earn me respect in front of the class and not ruin it for me with this snipe.

"I'm new to school and couldn't find this classroom. My dad wanted to drive me here, but he has to deal with the serial killers. Oh, you don't know that yet, well, it'll be on the news later. Well, I had to take my own car and of course it ran out of gas. So I set out and had to find a gas station and then the school. I'm really sorry that I haven't found the classroom yet. It won't happen again. I've memorized the way."

I think what I've just said is brilliant.

She frowns. She was expecting something, but not this answer.

"My name is James Allington," I add.

"Sit down," comes the curt reply. "I'll let it go this time. But if it happens again, I don't care if you or your father save the world. You'll get detention. Do you understand?"

I nod and move to the only empty seat.

"And if I hear expressions like 'cursed' or something like that again, you'll have extra homework."

This statement leaves no room for doubt. She means it. I sit down. My neighbor shifts a little to the side. As the teacher chats, I look around the classroom. I pay special attention to the girls. My gaze lingers on a really cute one. She has long, straight blonde hair and is wearing tight jeans and a tight black top.

It's amazing how this girl looks.

She is beautiful. She is perfect. I think I've fallen in love for the first time in my life. Well, a crush is an exaggeration, of course, but I have to find out her name.

When I arrived late, she even smiled at me a little. At least I think she did. She keeps whispering to her neighbor and they both keep winking at me. I conclude that the neighbor is her boyfriend and that I'm considered interesting.

Now she's smiling. It looks really cute and is the perfect counterpoint to Mrs. White's babbling.

The lessons are reeled off according to the syllabus and then, after what feels like 100 hours, it's finally recess time. The boy sitting next to me makes a sound for the first time and introduces himself: "Hi, my name is Kieran."

"My name is James," I answer and offer him my hand. He takes it.

"You were talking about the bodies found earlier. It's all over the news channels." "Yeah, really intense."

"Do you know more? I mean because your dad is the new sheriff."

I look at Kieran. He's a nice guy and I like him immediately.

"Supposedly it was a vampire. Well, if you want to explain the bloodlessness," I suggest and wait for Kieran's reaction.

"Do you believe that shit? They're just made up."

"Maybe they are. But maybe they really exist," I say mysteriously and jokingly at the same time.

"You don't really believe that vampires exist, do you?"

"Want me to tell you something?"

Kieran seems very curious. "Like what?"

"I've seen him. The vampire. In the woods, hiding one of his corpses," it slips out and I curse myself for telling you about it. But no matter. Now I've said it. So I wait to see how my maybe new buddy reacts.

"You're fucking with me now."

"No!"

"Don't take me for a fool."

"Kieran, we haven't met yet, but I can tell you one thing. I'm not lying. I swear to you, I made an observation the night before last and I've never told anyone about it."

"Not even your father?"

"Not even him."

Kieran looks at me. He seems to be thinking. Then he nods. "Okay, James. I think you and your kind are kind of cool. I believe you."

"I'm really not lying."

"Well, how about we meet in the woods today and check it out together?" he suddenly suggests.

Bam, that was right on the button. How should I react? Can I trust Kieran?

I'm so stupid. Why can't I just keep my mouth shut?

"Fear?"

"No," he says immediately. "I'm with you. Fuck that! We are going to see the crime scene. I'll tell you exactly what I saw last night."

"That's what we'll do. And in between, I'll explain to you how life works here in Greenfield and at this school, and who's friends with who."

"Good idea. You seem really okay," I say, not realizing the dangerous consequences our planned evening could have.

As spectacular as my arrival at the school was, I want to leave. But this plan goes down the drain. After my last class, I have to go to the office to get some forms for my parents to fill out. When I finally leave the school, all the students have already left. I get into the Porsche and drive home. Relieved that Black and White are not in front of the house yet, I slowly roll into the garage.

Mom arrives less than ten minutes later. We have a snack and I tell her that school is fine. Then I give her the packet of forms and say goodbye.

"I'm meeting a new buddy. See you later."

My mom is still talking to me when I close the door. It's warm. A pleasant temperature. The air is clear.

Not too hot, not too cold. Perfect for a leather jacket, I think and walk towards the woods.

I can see Kieran from a distance. He's already waiting at the meeting point. I'm excited to see how my friendship with him develops.

"There you are at last," he says. "Are you ready?"

"Of course!" I reply.

"Then go."

As we walk, I talk about my observation. It's good to talk about it with someone. I also feel safer than I did yesterday.

It's just better with two people.

We reached our destination quickly. At the edge of the forest, we look for the place where the Mercedes was parked and have no trouble finding it, as some of the deputies' paraphernalia is still lying around. Mostly small boards with numbers stuck in the ground and scraps of caution tape lying around.

"They could clean up better too," Kieran grins.

We start looking for clues. My new buddy is very meticulous. He examines the place very carefully, looking for footprints in the grass and on the ground. He looks for footprints and tire tracks. It almost seems to me that he is sniffing like a dog. I stifle a grin, but also admire his accuracy.

"Not good tracks. The tire tracks here in front of us are from the sheriff's department cars and the ambulances," he observes.

"I agree," I reply, agreeing with his opinion.

"Shall we?" he asks, pointing to the path that leads into the dense greenery of Greenfield Forest.

"Of course," comes the determined answer.

The forest is somehow eerie. Dark. But maybe it's also because it's noticeably cooler under the shady trees. We go straight ahead for a while, then turn right and leave the path. Eventually we reach an area secured with tape. The tape is marked and prohibits access to the area. There is also a warning sign. There is also a warning sign.

Crime Scene
No Trespassing!

Greenfield Sheriff's Department

We ignore the barriers and warning signs and continue. I've never disregarded any barriers before, especially those of the police, I think for a moment, but my curiosity and excitement quickly push my concerns aside. We take a good look around.

"Everything looks normal here," I say after a few minutes. "That's right. I'm sure they've sealed off the area. Let's go."

I nod and follow Kieran as he slowly walks ahead. After about 15 minutes we reach a cabin. It's not very big and I guess it's an old hunting lodge. A window shutter has been torn from its moorings and hangs crooked. Although the wood of this ramshackle hut is covered in moss, it still looks quite habitable.

"Do you know this one?" I ask, pointing at the hut. Kieran says no. "No. I've never been to this part of the forest." He starts to think and has an idea. "Maybe it belonged to old Sam Parker. He used to be a hunter and trapper. But Parker's probably been dead for ten years."

"Or maybe some rich lawyer from Boston had a hunting preserve here once," I add.

"Could be. It doesn't matter. Come on, let's take a closer look at this thing," Kieran suggests.

We approach the small hut and walk around the outside. We look in through the window where the shutter is broken. The panes are milky but completely intact. "Nothing!"

"No one's been in there for years."

"Not even the sheriff's department."

"Why would they?" I say.

We go to the door. Kieran grabs the doorknob and turns it. It creaks and there is a faint metallic click. "Not locked."

"Open it," I urge.

Carefully and very slowly, Kieran opens the door. We are greeted by a musty smell. We look in curiously.

The cabin is sparsely furnished. A desk, a small bookshelf, a chair and a bed frame without a mattress. In the corner is a small stove with a kettle on top.

"Judging by the dust, there hasn't been a fire here in a long time," Kieran whispers.

The books haven't been eaten by mice, I wonder. "Everything's pretty dusty, not just the stove." I slide into the doorway next to Kieran. There are lots of cobwebs everywhere.

"Do you think we should go in there?" I ask, but at the same moment Kieran lets out a "Cool!" and enters the hut. I follow him. As I look around, my new colleague walks purposefully to the desk. There are some papers and pens lying around. Next to it is a small inkwell and a kerosene lamp.

Kieran opens one of the books.

"This is handwritten. Looks like a diary," he says, flipping through the pages. "Squiggly handwriting, almost indecipherable," he adds, lifting the book to show me.

December 18, 1781

For Oloisius

You will kill all people who have knowledge of this cabin in a period of 13 days.

You must kill people who enter it on the seventh day.

If you refuse to do so, or if you cannot meet the deadline, you will die. For you are bound by our contract for all eternity!

Astrigo

Suddenly a page slides out and fluttered to the floor. I bent down and picked it up. It's a touching feeling to hold such an old document.

"What is this? Can you read it?" asks Kieran.

"Looks like a letter or something," I say. I take a closer look at the yellowed and slightly brittle paper, holding it very carefully so as not to damage it.

"It's written legibly."

"What are you waiting for?" my buddy urges.

"Okay," I reply and begin to read aloud.

We look at each other. Goose bumps spread over my back. I feel quite uncomfortable and a bit scared.

"Do you think he's still alive?" asks Kieran.

He doesn't seem impressed at all.

Didn't he hear the part about the date? That part is over two centuries old.

Kieran looks at me questioningly. He seems to be serious.

"If this Oloisius or this Astrigo are still alive, they're vampires or some other kind of creature," I answer, trying to make fun of Kieran a little. The joke also takes away my fear.

He shrugs. His eyes get wide, then narrow. I can't quite put my finger on it, but somehow Kieran suddenly seems very uncomfortable.

"Let's get out of here!"

He puts the book down on the chunky desk. I want to put the note down next to it, take a step forward and am startled.

Crunch

The floorboards under my feet creak audibly and loudly. "Hey, take a look," I say, pointing down. "The desk is on a trapdoor."

"Let's get out of here!" Kieran demands nervously. He seems excited. I, on the other hand, am getting curious and my initial fear has completely disappeared.

"Oh no! I want to see what's down there. Can you help me move the table to the side?"

"Forget it. I'm leaving," Kieran says and leaves the hut.

Hm, what's wrong with him?

As if fear is like a yo-yo, it comes back to me. The moment Kieran is at the door, it hits me again. This queasy, goosebump-inducing feeling spreads quickly.

"Kieran?"

I look at the door.

He's gone. My buddy is gone. What a chicken!

The yo-yo effect strikes again. The fear is gone, the curiosity is back.

Am I crazy? James, what are you doing? I ask myself as I push the desk aside.

Even though I feel rather queasy, I have to know what is hidden under this trapdoor.

Once again, my curiosity wins over reason. I glance at my grandmother's lucky stone, then grab it. I grab the iron ring and pull the trapdoor open. It takes some effort, but I manage it. I look towards the door, hoping for help.

Crap.

No sign of Kieran. Then I look down into the dark hole below me.

My thoughts jump around.

I didn't think Kieran would be such a coward. It's really dark down there. I'd better get out too. I don't even have a flash-light or anything.

Just as I'm about to close the trapdoor, I remember something. *Of course I have a flashlight. The app on my phone.* I quickly take it out of my pocket and tap the screen. One more swipe and I use the app. I shine the light into the basement of the cabin. A ladder leads down. At ten, everything is quiet. Nothing can be heard.

At that moment, I feel like Indiana Jones, comparing myself to the brave and fearless adventurer from the Hollywood movies.

"Kieran, if you're out there, please wait a minute! I'm just going to take a quick look around," I call, hoping that my buddy is still out there waiting for me to come out of the hut. Maybe I want to give myself a little courage. In any case, I feel safer when I'm not alone. But I don't wait for an answer. As soon as I've spoken, I take another deep breath. Relieved to see that it's not rotten, I climb down the old ladder.

Step by step I take the rungs. They hold. When I reached the bottom, I lit everything. It smells very musty and damp.

It's not a cellar, it looks like a secret passage. A tunnel leading away from here in two directions.

Contrary to my original decision to just have a quick look around, I consider going a few meters into the tunnel.

Maybe an old gold or silver mine, I think.

I take a quick look at the ground.

Damp clay, I notice.

Then I jump back. Besides my own shoe prints, there are other footprints on the floor. You can even see the tread on one of them.

These tracks are not from 1781, but from today. There used to be no treads on the soles of shoes. Someone must have been here recently.

This is how Robinson Crusoe must have felt when he came across the cannibals' footprints in the sand.

What should I do now? Continue or go back upstairs and tell Kieran about my discovery?

I quickly gather the facts. I'm in a tunnel. There are wooden beams at regular intervals along the ceiling and side walls.

The whole thing is probably not from modern times, but probably from the 18th century, I realize soberly. Everything looks a bit like a canal into which one descends.

Even the ancient Romans had secret catacombs under their Eternal City.

As soon as I finish thinking about it, I know that I'm going to go in one direction, adventure-wise.

Fuck Kieran and the fear. I want to know where this tunnel leads. I'm not sure which way to go.

Right or left? Or should I follow the tracks?

I illuminate the ground. I am confused. The footprints go both ways, but only one way for a few meters, then the ground becomes rocky and you cannot see anything.

In any case, the person who walked here definitely walked in both directions. So it doesn't matter which way I go. In cases like this, like when I'm in a foreign city, I usually go around to the right, so I'll go that way now.

I remembered that I still have the drawing application on my phone. I've been meaning to delete it for a long time, but I never got around to it. Or rather, I've always been too lazy, which seems to help at the moment.

A modern Hansel and Gretel game. Instead of scattering breadcrumbs, I draw my path.

I laugh briefly, turn on the program and the phone light, and then I start walking. The light from the phone is enough to illuminate the path reasonably well. I quickly get used to the damp, musty smell. I walk slowly, stopping now and then to listen for footsteps. At short intervals, I swipe my fingers across the screen so that the route is recorded in the app. I feel safe and unobserved.

It is always straight ahead.

Fortunately, there are no side streets leading away from the main tunnel, so it's impossible to get lost.

But only 50 meters further on, I am proven wrong. I come to what looks like a crossroads.

What a mess! It would have been too easy.

"James Allington, you're not a lucky man after all," it slips quietly from my lips.

I slowly approach this fork in the road and am suddenly astonished to find myself at a dead end. On the left and on the right there are doors. Heavy oak doors. I quickly examine both sides. Looking for traces or clues.

Nothing.

At least I don't notice anything. I wonder if the doors are locked.

Thoughts race through my mind. One part tells me to turn back immediately, the other urges me to open the doors. I wonder who made this tunnel. I wonder who made this tunnel. It must have taken a lot of work.

Where did they put all the excavated material?

More questions arise.

What are these doors for? Do they lead to more corridors or are they rooms? And if so, are they hiding places like those of the ancient Romans, or are they secret treasure chambers? Was there gold here in the past?

I concentrate, pluck up courage and decide to open one of the doors. This time I deliberately choose the left side. My hand reaches for the iron doorknob, almost trembling, and I turn it to the right. It moved easily. It was as if someone was oiling the lock at regular intervals.

Crunch, clack

My pulse is racing. The goose bumps on my neck again. The door opens. I push it open very slowly and shine my cell phone into the dark room. I wonder what I will discover, I am curious. And then I see ... nothing. Instead, the musty smell intensifies.

That's the musty musty smell, I insist, breathing only through my mouth so I don't have to smell the musty stuff. In front of me is a 20 square meter, completely empty room. Or should I call it a cave? It is, after all, a windowless underground cavity secured by a heavy oak door.

What was this room used for?

As I ponder, I make a drawing on my phone. Then I look at the picture and am satisfied.

This is exactly what it looks like.

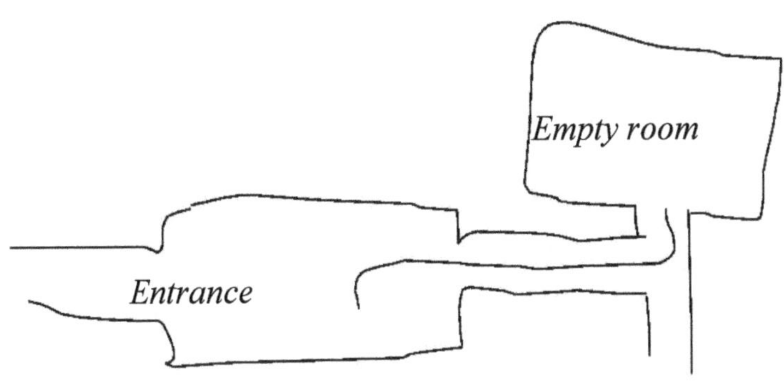

I decide to open the other door as well. No sooner have I pulled the oak door back into the lock than I stand in front of the second door and turn the knob.

Click, click

This door opens easily as well. I go through the whole process a second time. Very slowly and always with my cell phone on, I push the door open. Earlier I thought the mustiness could not be topped, but now I realize that there is a new record for stale, musty air.

Wow, this place smells old. Worse than my grandmother's bedroom.

I carefully open the door all the way. When I look inside, my blood literally freezes in my veins. I jump, want to run, but I can't move because of the shock. The room is as empty as the other one, but in the middle of this dark cave is a coffin.

If you were to compare my face to milk, my complexion would definitely be paler. I'm really scared.

A second look follows. The lid of the coffin is closed. If Kieran were here, I might open it to see what - or rather who - is inside. But since I'm alone, I prefer to make my exit and retreat.

Quietly, as if I don't want to wake anyone, I close the door. I turn around and run back to the entrance as fast as I can. I quickly reached the ladder.

Shock. The trapdoor is closed.

Was it Kieran? Did the thing close by itself?

I get scared, want to call for Kieran - but what if it's not my new buddy, but the guy who dumped the bodies in the woods who closed the trapdoor? Panic sets in. I climb up the rungs. Push against the trapdoor.

Bloody hell! Too. What idiot closed the hatch?

I push against the trapdoor with all my strength. Every muscle in my body is tense. I can feel blood rushing to my head. It lifts maybe two millimeters. Someone has pushed the desk onto the hatch.

"Kieran, if you're up there, let me out! This is not a good joke!" I yell.

No answer. I listen. Silence. I don't hear a sound. I think.

Think, James!

I vacillate between courage, desperation, and pure fear. Thousands of thoughts race through my mind like .

Bloodless corpses. A coffin. Oh my God, what if there really is a vampire sleeping there?

I feel almost sick with fear. I quickly realize that I have to act. Staying here would be the stupidest decision ever. My whole body shakes as I climb back down the ladder. Hoping to find another exit, I turn left. This tunnel passage is identical to the other one. Rocky floor, walls and ceiling supported by wooden beams. After only twenty meters I come to a crossroads. The tunnel forks into three directions.

"That one too," I groaned, and had to make a decision. On the far left, above the tunnel, there is a picture. It's covered in dust. A clue, I am glad to see, and walk over to it. As the light from my cell phone falls on it, I recognize the outline of a skull. Startled, I back away. I quickly light the two tunnel entrances.

Nothing.

Instinctively, I choose the right side again. As I walked a-long the corridor, I noticed something I hadn't noticed before. At least, I hadn't noticed it. There are torch holders attached to the walls at regular intervals. Some of them even have half-burned torches in them. I can also see dark soot stains behind them and on the ceiling in the cone of light from the cell phone lamp.

Kind of creepy, I think. *Indiana Jones, you'd be proud of me.*

I hope. I see a door. My steps quicken. Standing in front of it, I reach for the knob and turn it. It's locked.

"Great," I mutter softly.

Seeing no way to open the door, I turn around. When I reached the fork in the tunnel again, I chose the middle passage. After a few meters it forks again. This time I choose the middle one.

The golden middle. Finally get me out of this web of tunnels and corridors, it shoots through my head and off I go. After about twenty meters I find another fork.

"Now it's getting complicated, damn it. I can't get lost now."

I record my route on the app. Of the two options, I choose the one on the right again. A glance at the phone's battery level reassures me. Still almost 70 percent. I won't run out of light that fast. I count the steps. And right after number 30, I stand in front of a door. I put my hand on the doorknob again, turn it, and the click gives me hope.

Open, I breathe a sigh of relief.

But instead of being on my way out, I find myself in some kind of library. The entire cave is lined with wood. Walls, ceiling and floor.

That makes the climate a little more pleasant and probably drier, I think. *Maybe to keep the books from rotting.*

In the middle is a clumsy, simple desk. It is made of roughly cut wood. Behind it is a chair of the same kind. There is a kerosene lamp on the desk and a half-burned candle. Although it is tempting to enter the room and browse through the books, I close the door and walk back quickly. I head straight for the left tunnel that I left out earlier. After exactly 30 steps, I stand in front of another door. This time I jump slightly. It is ajar. I only have to push it lightly and it swings open with a squeak.

"This can't be right," I exclaim as I find myself back in a wood-paneled room. This time there are various paintings and drawings hanging on the walls, then a shelf sparsely filled with books. However, it is pushed away from the wall and protrudes into the room at a right angle.

Something is different here than in the previous room.

Cautiously, I take a step forward. I let the cone of light from my cell phone circle around me and walk to the shelf.

A draft.

I can feel it very clearly. There must be some kind of air shaft here. I shine the light on everything and discover a shaft behind the shelf. It's almost right under the ceiling. I have to stretch to put my hand in front of the entrance to the shaft. I can clearly feel the draft. I took a closer look at the entrance. It's wide and big enough for me to crawl through.

This is the way out. The draft proves it. This shaft leads outside.

I am sure of it and am happy to have finally found an exit. I turn around and look into the room.   Only now do I notice that all the pictures, whether paintings or drawings, are of men. I go to the first wall and illuminate the pictures. I almost recoil in horror as I recognize long, pointed canines in the mouths of three of the five paintings.

"They are..." I stammer, "They're... vampire teeth!"

Goosebumps spread. From the top of my head to the soles of my feet, they run cold down my back and make me shiver.

Vampires, I repeat in my mind, and it fills me with fear. All the bodies in the forest, my observations the night before and in the cabin. Then there's my discovery in this tunnel system. I know I'm on the trail of something really big, and what's worse, it's incredibly dangerous.

If these are real vampires who are up to no good, they will come looking for me and drain me. If they're psychopathic maniacs, a bunch of idiots, they'll come looking for me, torture me to death, and drain my blood. I am lost. I have to get out of here. Right now!

I go to the shaft, clench my cell phone, which still serves as a flashlight, between my teeth, and try to pull myself up. Then I think of an easier way. Then I think of an easier way. I lean against the wooden shelf. It moves. It's not easy, but I do it. With the courage and strength of desperation, I manage to push the shelf against the wall. Now I can use the shelves as a ladder, which has the advantage that I can light the shaft before I crawl in.

I climb onto the first shelf and test if it can hold me. It fits.

I put my right leg on the next step, shine the light into the shaft and pull myself in.

Just when I thought that the musty smell couldn't be topped, I'm proven wrong. It smells almost cloacal. I am relieved to see that the shaft is dry. There are cobwebs everywhere. One of these fat, disgusting creatures flees from me and runs into the tunnel at lightning speed on its eight legs. I have to take a deep breath, overcome my aversion to spiders, and try to think away an emerging claustrophobia by weighing which is worse: staying in the tunnel and falling victim to a vampire, or crawling out through the spider shaft.

Freedom.

So forward. I begin to crawl, but my progress is slow and painful. This is also due to the fact that I first try to remove the many cobwebs with my left hand before I crawl through them. Every now and then one, two or even three of them run over my arms and hands. Fortunately, they are not as big as the first one I shooed away.

Better on my hand than on my head, I told myself. Meter by meter I crawl upwards. At one point I stopped for a moment. Some animal is running away from me.

I hope it's not a rat's nest, I think.

When I didn't hear any more noises, I started crawling again. I don't know how long it took, but after my long, dark journey through the shaft, I finally see daylight. I can literally smell the fresh air and push my way forward for the last few meters. Finally, I slip through a small hole that I can barely fit through and into freedom.

I lie down on the leaves and suck in the oxygen. Suddenly I am overcome by an indescribable feeling of happiness. I have done it. I have escaped from the tunnel system. After a few minutes of rest, I sit up. I am in the middle of the forest. The entrance to the shaft is barely visible. It is hidden under the gnarled roots of a huge tree. If you discovered it by chance, you would immediately think of a fox or badger's den. The best camouflage.

But I am preoccupied with another question.

Where am I?

I have no plan and get up. I remove the cobwebs and dusty dirt from my hair and clothes as best I can. Then I look at my cell phone.

No reception.

So I just walk in any direction. It's already dusk, and soon it will be dark. I follow the sun and the mossy side of the trees and try to go straight. The silence of the forest is not very relaxing when you are looking for civilization. I am all the happier when, after a good half hour, I hear the sound of engines. Sometimes they hum low and loud, sometimes they roar high and fast.

Relief. It sounds like a road, a busy road. I go straight on and reach *Route 91*. In a good mood, I follow the highway for two kilometers, and at sunset I'm standing in front of the town sign of Greenfield.

Another twenty minutes later, I'm standing outside our front door, exhausted but happy.

The Black and White is parked in front of the house, so my parents are home. I open the door and am probably more excited to come home than I've ever been in my life.

"James, it's late. What took you so long?" my mom calls from upstairs.

I'm only half an hour late, an hour at the most, but mothers always have to exaggerate.

"I was with Kieran, my new boyfriend. The time went by so fast," I reply.

I wash my hands, go to the fridge and drink what feels like a pint of orange juice to wash all the dust out of my mouth. Then I go upstairs to my room. Of course, my clothes are all dirty. I change and throw the dirty clothes in the laundry basket. Then I sit down at my desk, pull out my cell phone, plug it into the charger, and open the drawing application. I immediately try to draw a detailed plan of the tunnel system. When I'm done, I look at my work with satisfaction. Questions arise. My brain rattles.

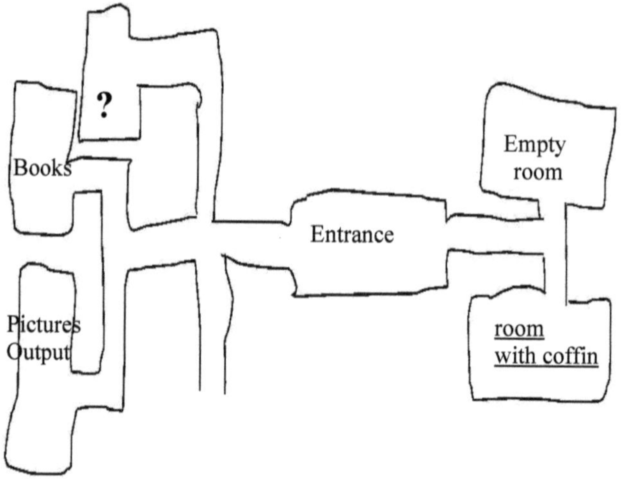

What is behind the closed door? Where does the tunnel marked with a skull lead to? Is there someone in the coffin? Who locked the hatch in the hut and pushed the desk onto it? Was it Kieran? Who built the tunnel system and why? What about the contract we found in the cabin? Is there a connection between my discovery and the bodies we found? Are the guys in the paintings a secret brotherhood, or are they actually vampires?

I go to dinner with these unanswered questions. Mom and Dad talk about Uncle Joe and his trip. They are probably avoiding the hot topic of the body finds for my sake. Of course, it could be that Dad just wants to get some distance. He looks tired and exhausted. That's why I say nothing about the bodies.

After dinner I help to clear the table. Back in my room, I turn on my laptop and search the Internet for anything I can find about vampires. I find an interesting site. It not only mentions the origins and the first documentary facts, but also describes the characteristics of a vampire. However, I already know them from various movies and books.

"They are pale, possess supernatural powers or strength, and have razor-sharp teeth," I repeat while taking notes.

But I also found something I didn't know before. According to this, vampires are said to possess a very special kind of ruby, the radiance of which allows them to walk outside in daylight without being burned by the sunlight. They must wear the stone on a chain close to their heart. I look at a picture of a ruby from Tansania on the Internet as an example.

I immediately think of my own little gem I got from Miss Piddy. It looks very similar to the ruby on the Internet. My red stone is in a little box in the nightstand drawer, right next to Grandma's charm necklace.

It could easily be the same one.

I quickly start to combine, get Miss Piddy's stone and compare it to the one from the Internet. I go to the window, hold the stone up to the moonlight and look at the red color. Then I put it on the windowsill and go back to my desk.

Aha, so if I see someone wearing a necklace with a red ruby, it's possible that person is a vampire. Good to know.

I finish my research, click on my game and play some more GTA.

When I lie in bed later, I let the day pass by once again. First I relive the adventure in the tunnel, then I think about the girl from my new class. Unfortunately I can't remember her name. There were too many names to remember. I think of her sweet blue eyes. Tomorrow I'll ask Kieran what her name is and what she looks like. I fall asleep.

Chapter Three

For everyone, there is one sound that they describe as the ugliest in the world. It's your own alarm clock. When you hear it, you automatically jump up. I don't like the sound of my alarm clock at all, and that's why I chose it.

Ugly, but effective.

This time I wake up before this ear torment. I tap the alarm in the dark to silence it and turn on the light. There's less risk of falling asleep again in the light. I gather my thoughts. Yesterday's adventure still dominates the movie in my head.

I have a lot to discuss with Kieran today.

At some point my thoughts drift to the school and the pretty girl. Five minutes later I'm in the bathroom and half an hour later I'm already in the garage with the Porsche key in my hand.

I limit my breakfast to a glass of orange juice, because my craving for a ham and cheese bagel gives me the idea to stop at the Greenfield Bakery and buy a sandwich bagel and two donuts.

The sound of the engine is music to my ears.

Wrommm

The radio is playing an old song by an old rock band. The guys are called the Rolling Stones, my dad has some of their records. I step on the gas and feel great, cool and free. Lost in thought, I don't notice how fast I accelerate to 40 mph and race toward the crosswalk. Almost too late, I spot an old woman with two shopping bags trying to cross Pleasant Street. She sees me, realizes I'm coming at her at high speed, drops the bags in shock and jumps to the side.

I sketch out the situation, brake, swerve, roll over one of the shopping bags, and see in the rearview mirror that the woman is holding her clenched hands.

He is holding his fists up in a threatening manner and is cursing and swearing loudly.

I slow down, get scared, and speed up again.

Take off!

I quickly turn into the next side street, drive an extra lap around the block, and hope she hasn't written down the license plate number. My heart is pounding with excitement. I immediately decide not to use the Porsche again.

As soon as I park in front of the bakery, however, I decide that I'll still drive it, just not as fast as a complete idiot. I'm happy with this compromise and buy my breakfast. Then I drive very slowly to the school. After parking, I look at the Porsche.

Phew, lucky. No scratches.

Relieved, I lock up the sports car and walk into the building. Of course, I try to look casual again. We have math with Mr. Chear in the first period. I'm late, but I manage to get to the classroom before our teacher. I nod at Kieran and sit down. At the same moment, Mr. Chear enters the classroom, closes the door and quickly starts the lesson.

The topic suits me. I watch the class. Kieran seems to understand the material as well. He leans back and relaxes, while a few other boys are frantically taking notes and seem quite tense. I watch the pretty girl. Her name is Riley and she looks really good. Today she has her blonde hair pulled back into a horse tail. The look really suits her. I really have to meet her later and have a few words with her.

Finally a break. I get the bag from the bakery out of my backpack, eat my bagel and grab Kieran. "Come with me! I have something to tell you."

"I have to go to the snack shop. I don't have anything to eat," he replies and starts to leave.

"Here, will a donut do?"

"What kind?"

"One with chocolate filling, one with nut filling." "Both?"
"You're quite a glutton."

"You can also give me half of your bagel, then one donut will be enough for me."

I look at my ham and cheese bagel and hand the bag to Kieran. "Eat the donuts."

Kieran takes it, pulls out the first donut and in three bites it's gone.

"I've never seen anyone eat a donut that fast."

"Hungry," he says, barely intelligible, before shoving the next one into his mouth.

"Yesterday was hell. Why did you run away?" "It was too scary for me. Besides, we wanted to go to the places where the bodies were found. I went ahead once, but you didn't come back. When I went back to the cabin, the hatch was closed and the table was back in its old place. I thought you'd gone out and gone home."

"Now watch out, you glutton. Listen!"

I tell my buddy everything I experienced yesterday and don't miss a single detail. Kieran just stares at me. He even forgets to eat the last half of his donut.

When I'm done, he frowns thoughtfully.

"If it wasn't me or you who locked the hatch, then who was it?"

I shrug. "The killer?"

I get that sinking feeling in my stomach again. "That would mean he might have been in the tunnel at the same time as me."

"Possibly. But he knows at least one thing." "Which one?" I ask.

"That someone discovered the entrance to the tunnel." The break is over.

"Let's talk later."

We puzzle over the next few breaks and decide to keep our secret for now. I learn from Kieran that on his way back from the hut he discovered a path and followed it. It leads directly to the place where we entered the forest.

School is over. Unfortunately, I didn't have time to get to know Riley because of the explosively important topic. I get into the Porsche and drive home. I see White standing in front of the house and know that Mom is home.

Damn, this isn't my day. First the grandmother at the crosswalk, then this.

Even as I carefully pull the Porsche into the garage, I know I am in for a very unpleasant conversation. She sits in the kitchen. Before I can say a single word, her voice booms out at me: "How dare you drive the Porsche to school?"

"Sorry. I was late and I thought..."

I am abruptly interrupted and the second verbal barrage hits.

"Sorry? You don't even have a license! You're the sheriff's son and you're making a mess! Uncle Joe will never trust you again, and Dad will ground you for the rest of the year. What kind of fuss do you think there'll be if you get into an accident? No insurance will pay, you'll be ruined for life. My God, how can you be so stupid?"

She catches her breath for the third word attack. "Your father will..."

She uses the word father. Oh dear. She's really angry.

"...will be more than disappointed in you. Go to your room, I don't want to see you again!"

Luckily, the incident with Grandma and the shopping bags ended well and the Porsche wasn't scratched. Dad will be furious, of course, but with a little luck and some understanding on my part, I'm sure I can get the punishment reduced. As always, when I'm stressed with my parents, my hand automatically reaches for my grandmother's good luck stone. I'll never forget the day I got it. It was the day before she died. She smiled and I carry that smile in my heart. My fingers clasp my neck.

Oh, did I forget to put on the necklace? I go to the night-stand.

It's empty. Shock. Goose bumps. Panic.

The box where I keep the stone is open. I go into the bathroom and search.

Nothing

Back in the room, I try to remember the last time I wore the necklace.

It was yesterday. I definitely had it on. I reconstruct the whole day.

I had it on in the tunnel, because before I opened the hatch in the hut, I ran my fingers over the stone. What happened in the evening?

I get hot and cold. I didn't take the chain off. So there's only one possibility.

I lost the chain. Probably in the tunnel. And maybe in the narrow shaft when I crawled out.

"Fuck!", it rolls off my tongue. My mother must never know about this. This is her mother's stone. She's told me a thousand times to take better care of it than my most precious toy.

I must find the lucky stone again.

I know it is very dangerous to go back into the tunnel.

At least alone.

But when I consider which is worse, going to my mother or facing her wrath when she finds out I lost the stone, the tunnel is the lesser punishment. I can save myself the trouble of asking if I can go now. The answer is clear. The answer is a resounding *NO!*

So I sneak downstairs. Mom is in the basement doing laundry. A good moment. I grab my sneakers and jacket, walk out the door and close it almost silently. I quickly slip into my sneakers and jacket and run.

My thoughts turn to the lost rock.

I'm sure I won't find the entrance to the shaft anytime soon. I don't have much time, so I have to go back through the hut and into the tunnel.

I reach the edge of the forest at an easy, steady pace. When I get there, I wonder if it wouldn't be better to call Kieran. I'd feel safer with two people and I could show him around.

Nonsense. When I say that I'm only going back to look for the stone, he calls me crazy.

So it's a done deal. I'm going to do this alone. I enter the forest with a slightly queasy feeling. I remember Kieran telling me about a path. Now I look for it. After about 50 meters I see the almost hidden path. It winds through dense undergrowth away from the main path. I follow it and make really fast progress. Just before I reach my destination, I stop. The hut is in front of me, maybe another ten or fifteen meters. A sound from the direction of the old wooden house makes me jump.

Something was there.

I scurried behind a tree, leaned against it and took a deep breath.

Look, my inner voice tells me. I move my head carefully to the side. I have a direct view of the entrance. At that moment, the door opens. My heart races. Instinctively, I push myself closer to the trunk.

Whoever's in there can't see you, James, I reassure myself and continue to watch.

A man leaves the old cabin. He is dressed in dark clothes, shirtless, strong build. I can't tell his age. He closes the door behind him and walks straight into the woods.

Phew, not my direction, I breathe a sigh of relief and try not to lose sight of the guy, but suddenly he's gone.

He was just there. Where did he go? He can't have vanished into thin air!

I decide to stay in my hiding place and wait a while. Silence falls. Only the sounds of the forest could be heard. A small crack here, a chirp there. Somewhere a bird flutters.

After a few minutes I decided to go to the hut. The closer I got, the more anxious I became. I kept looking around.

He's gone and didn't see you, I tell myself.

Then I open the door and enter the cabin.

He was in the tunnel.

My first thought gives me a slight shock. The desk has been pushed aside, but the hatch is closed.

How much time do I have before he comes back? If he wasn't coming back at all, he would have put the desk on top of the hatch.

While I'm still thinking, I reach for the ring to open the hatch. Goosebumps spread like lightning when I heard someone climbing the ladder below me. Heavy panting and creaking wooden rungs confirm my worst suspicions.

I must leave immediately!

Driven by fear, I rush to the door, pull it open and try to pull it into the lock as quietly as possible, then run as fast as I can to the path and throw myself behind the nearest large tree in a panic. I've never run so fast in my life. This would have been my best time in sports. I'm panting like crazy, fighting for oxygen. My chest rises and falls wildly with each breath. Gradually I calm down and look around the tree towards the cabin.

Another man is leaving the house. He is a little smaller than the first man, but just as darkly dressed. A wide hat hides a broad hat hides most of his face, but I can make out gray hair and register that his complexion is more than pale. Almost white. Except for the mouth. There I thought I saw a red color, as if a child had eaten spaghetti with tomato sauce and was completely covered in it. I quickly pushed the thought of spaghetti out of my mind. Instead, a second one pops into my head. It makes me shudder again. I think of blood.

I hope the guy didn't hear me.

I immediately put all my discoveries together and come to a small conclusion. It is possible that I just saw a vampire. Everything points to it. And because of the red ruins it doesn't mind the daylight.

I feel my knees start to shake. If I'm right, this vampire would have some kind of superpowers. Then I would be lost.

As soon as he can scent me, smell me, see me - however they do it - he will hunt me down, kill me, and drain me.

I'm scared to death because you can't run from a vampire. I don't even dare to breathe. Nevertheless, I push my head to the side and continue to watch the guy. He doesn't even look in my direction, but walks in the same direction as the other guy before him.

I wonder what I should do. Leave or go back in? Or come back tomorrow with Kieran as backup?

"Get the stone, you wuss," I whisper to myself, pluck up all my courage and venture back into the hut.

This time I go to the window first and look in. The desk is back on the hatch.

Very good! To all appearances, none of these creatures are still at it. I certainly have some time.

A mixture of curiosity, a thirst for adventure, a test of courage for myself and a good dose of fear of my mother if she found out about the loss of the stone urged me to go back to the hut and into the tunnel.

As always, I hear the creaking sound when I open the door. The hut still smells musty. I go to the desk, push it aside and grab the hatch ring.

Do it!

I open it, use my cell phone flashlight and climb down the ladder. The musty smell intensifies. I stop and listen to make sure I'm really alone.

Silence. Very good. Now all I have to do is find my lucky stone necklace.

Just to be sure, I check the map on my phone again. Then I walk along the marked path. I illuminate the path as best I can. My eyes are staring at the ground. My necklace must be here somewhere.

But nothing. No matter which way I go, the cold ground is empty. Not a single stone or chain to be seen. I finally reach the wooden door behind which the coffin lies. This is the room I dread the most. I had hoped to find the stone first, but there is no choice. I have to go in and take a look. My knees trembled again. I listened, heard nothing and grabbed the doorknob. I slowly turn it to the right. I hear the lock click.

Click

I push the door open. The mustiness is enormous and it smells like thousands of old, wet rags.

Not only my knees, but also my hands, my whole body trembles as I open the coffin.

Closed.

I breathe a sigh of relief. The cone of light from the lamp moves across the room. To the left of the coffin, something is reflected on the floor. I recognize the silver necklace.

My pendant, I silently rejoice and go to pick it up. I bend down when, at the same moment, a heavy, slurping sound makes my hair stand on end. Even as I reach for my necklace with my left hand, I see out of the corner of my eye that the coffin lid is being pushed aside. I grab the chain, turn around and run for the door. But before I reach the door frame, a strong, ice-cold hand grabs my neck. I know I'm going to die. Here and now.

A scream, as shrill and loud as I have ever screamed in my life, leaves my lips: "AAAHHHHHH!"

The grip is rock solid, impossible to break. I have no choice but to turn around. I expect anything but what I see.

In front of me is a boy my age, maybe a year or two older. He is dressed in jeans and a T-shirt. His skin is whiter than my mother's sheets, and his eyes are narrowed, as if a wild animal has sighted its prey. The boy opens his mouth and I see sharp vampire fangs. I am speechless. I'm in shock and squeeze the charm tighter than ever. I know that in the next second I'll get the death bite and then I'll be the next sucked corpse they find. I am paralyzed and cannot react. I can't say anything, I can't fight. I just stare at this vampire. His teeth get closer and closer to my neck. I close my eyes and wait for the bite. I hope for seconds that it will be painless and quick. Questions arise.

Am I really going to die? What was that again? If you get bitten but not sucked out, you turn into a vampire? Is that true?

I hate blood. I would rather die than feed on blood. My short life flashes by in my mind.

Oh man, I'm an idiot. I could be sitting in my room right now playing GTA, but I had to come here alone again. James, you've done another great job. Congratulations!

Suddenly, the vampire lets go of me and starts laughing heartily: "Hahahahahaha! Hey, I made a fool out of you." I stare at him in disbelief. He's let go of me. I'm shaking like a leaf.

Should I be happy or cry? What is he up to?

Humans must be flight animals, because I turn and run for the door. A few hours ago, I was thinking about what vampires' superpowers looked like and wondering what they could do, but this look shows me what they look like in real life.

The bloodsucker was just behind me and I'm only two steps away from the door and, poof, the monster with the oversized fangs is standing in front of me again, grinning stupidly.

"You want to escape, human child? Then I will suck you dry. Your last hour has come!"

Only now do I realize that he speaks my language. He sounds like a normal boy, but I don't like what he says at all.

"Fuck, no!" I quickly reply, "I just wanted to close the door so it wouldn't be so drafty.

Tell me, am I stupid? What the hell am I talking about?

He laughs. "You're really funny. What's your name?"

"J-James," I stammer.

"I'm Devon. How are you?"

I take a deep breath. "Shit! I'm really scared of you. Scared to death, to be honest."

"Relax man, I already ate."

"Reassuring," I reply sarcastically, rolling my eyes. "Then you're going to play with me before I become your dinner, or what?"

"What a load of rubbish. I have no idea what you know or have read about vampires, but believe me, it's definitely different."

"How different?" I ask, feeling a little more confident than I was a minute ago. The grim look in Devon's eyes is also gone. He looks completely normal now.

"It's not safe for you to be down here. My father would have killed you for sure, but I don't see it that way. Assuming you can keep a secret."

"I swear that..."

Devon waves off. "You can save yourself the trouble of swearing. Either I trust you or you die. It's that simple."

What a stupid situation. I've never faced a vampire in my life - how could I? And now I'm supposed to show Devon that he can trust me.

"Listen to me. I'm here because I...", I begin to say and explain everything I've experienced in the last two days. I don't leave out a single detail. "...and then I saw the necklace lying next to the coffin. You know the rest. You were there." Devon frowns. "It all sounds very plausible. You seem to be telling the truth. I am most impressed by your courage. You didn't tell your father, even though he's the sheriff, and you had the guts to come back here to look for your necklace. The only thing that worries me is that Kieran. You let him in."

"Kieran may be a bastard for leaving, but he keeps his mouth shut."

"I trust you, James, and I'll spare you. It's lonely down here and the conversation does me good."

Suddenly, Devon turns his head to the left. "I sense danger. Someone's coming."

"No one knows I'm here."

The vampire puts his index finger to his mouth and whispers: "It's definitely my father. You need to hide!"

I recognize the panic in Devon's eyes and know immediately that the situation is dicey for me. I look around. He immediately points to the coffin.

"In there!"

"Forget it! I'm not going to lie down in a coffin."

"Then he'll kill you and suck you dry."

My eyes wander from the vampire boy to the coffin. I assess the situation, scratch the back of my head and say: "That box doesn't look so bad."

With considerable trepidation, I walk over to the death chest and look inside.

"Hurry up," Devon urges.

I take a deep breath, clench Granny's good luck charm in my fist, and climb inside. "I hope you're not kidding me again."

"Shh!" he points, putting his index finger over his closed mouth again. "Keep quiet. I'll do the rest."

The lid closes. Darkness surrounds me. Something like claustrophobia envelops me and crawls through my body. I want to jump up in panic, push the lid aside and flee. I push myself to find inner peace.

Imagine something beautiful.

I think of Riley, but her image quickly fades and is replaced by my mother's. She looks really pissed.

She's going to quarter me when she finds out I'm not home. But that's the least of my worries right now. I hope I can trust Devon.

I've lost track of time and don't know how long I've been in the coffin when the lid is pushed aside with a creak.

Trembling, I wait to see the face of the person standing before me.

Is it Devon or his father?

Relieved, I see the teenager.

"I've never been so happy to see a vampire in my life," I blurt out.

"Quick, you have to leave right now! My father will be right back. He shot a deer in the forest and only got a tub for the dead animal."

"Don't you ever drink human blood?" I want to know. "Only the wild vampires do. They are renegades who don't follow our rules. We weren't allowed to do that a long time ago. But there are exceptions. A few of us are allowed, or have to, kill intruders and drain them." "Intruders? Do we have to suck out everyone who comes here? Why?"

I feel sick thinking about how close I came to death.

"The hut in the forest is one of the few secret entrances to our protective realm down here. Treaties are signed and guards are appointed. My father is one of the guards. He has to kill people who enter the hut or have knowledge of it, and then he can consider them prey.

"I have seen such a contract. There is always a time limit. 13 days or something like that," I say. "That's right. That rule is from the old days." I head for the door.

"My dad isn't my real dad. He's my stepfather."

"Why are you telling me this now?" "Because you're my chance." "Huh?"

"You're my chance to finally get rid of him." "What do you mean?"

"He is the guard and he doesn't know that you have entered the hut and know our secret. I want to take advantage of that fact."

I am astonished.

Devon puts his hand on my shoulder. "Look," he begins. "We vampires rarely die of natural causes. So when one of us kills the father or mother of a family, he automatically takes their place. My stepfather, whose name is Oloisius by the way, killed my father and mother. Then he locked me in this hole and I cannot get out because of a curse. This curse has been on me for almost 200 years. You are the key to my freedom.

"Me?" I gasp, startled, and stare at Devon. "How did you come up with that?"

"I'll explain it to you another time. You must visit me again. But now get out, go! You must hurry before Oloisius comes back."

I nod, thinking to myself that I'm definitely not coming back here, and go into the tunnel.

"Keep the secret to yourself. It's vital for both of us," he calls after me.

Then I disappear into the corridors of the tunnel system. Finally, I'm at the exit. The hatch is open. I listen for a moment, hoping that Oloisius has not yet arrived at the hut with the doe.

Nothing. Everything is quiet.

I climb up, leave the hatch open and walk into the woods. I follow the path and only when I'm out of the forest do I breathe a sigh of relief.

At home, I manage to sneak into my room unnoticed. Later, I get a second big scolding from my parents and am told several times how stupid and reckless I was. I vow to do better and have to promise never to borrow the Porsche again. Then, unexpectedly, I don't get a fine. I just have to think about my mistake and wash and polish the Porsche thoroughly by hand. Oh yes, and of course in black and white.

Half relieved, I go to my room and close the door behind me.

The next day I ride my mountain bike to school. It's Friday and I'm looking forward to the end of the week.

I'm just parking my bike when Riley arrives with her bike. "Hi," I grin.

"Hi," she smiles back. She points at my bike and says, "Not out with the Porsche today?"

I grin sheepishly and think about giving her a cool answer, then look into her eyes and decide to just be myself.

Either it works or I've lost.

"To be honest, it's not my Porsche. It belongs to my uncle. I wanted to use it to, uh... Well, I..."

Riley laughs. "It's much nicer to ride your bike in this weather anyway."

"I thought so, too."

I wait for her to lock her bike.

It looks so cute the way she holds her folder with both hands.

We walk to the school building together and chat casually about the class. We take our seats in the classroom and Kieran winks at me.

Later, during the first recess, he gives me a friendly tap on the shoulder. "Hey, mate, things seem to be going well. Is Riley into you?" I feel some color shoot into my face. "We traipsed over there together. Nothing else."

"Of course," he winks.

I decide not to tell anyone about Devon for now, and so it's just another school day.

I eventually catch up with Riley and we walk back to the bikes together. We talk about this and that, but I don't have the heart to ask her out this weekend. Next week I decide. I'll ask her then. Right now it's too early.

Finally the weekend. I love Friday afternoons. School is over and the whole weekend is ahead. Two late nights and lots of free time.

At home, I start the weekend by sitting in my room and playing a good game of Call of Duty.

If my parents caught me doing that, I'd get rid of the laptop, too.

My dad is really strict about age restrictions.

"It's just a game," I said once when I wanted to buy it.

"The makers had something in mind when they made it 18," I was told.

After that, the matter was settled. Well, officially settled. Of course, I secretly got the game. But I only play when I'm sure I won't get caught. As I'm about to shoot, I suddenly remember Miss Piddy's words: "If you come across a vampire nest, you must tell me!"

I stop and get shot in the game. I don't care. Totally different thoughts are buzzing around in my head.

What did she mean by that? Does she have any experience with vampires?

Everyone always thought that the good woman had a full-grown vampire, but she couldn't have been that crazy, because I found out for myself. Apparently, vampires are real.

Does she know a bloodsucker?

I haven't talked to her in what seems like forever.

Maybe she knows something and can help me.

New questions arise.

Can I trust Devon? He could be lying, trying to lull me into a false sense of security so that I can become the next treat for him. I don't know how many times a vampire has to drink blood to get sated.

"Miss Piddy," I whisper to myself.

I lean back. Almost everyone thought she was crazy. And now, after my experience, I think she's as normal as my dad, Riley and me.

My God, what must that woman be going through? Whenever she leaves her house, everyone avoids her. She must be very lonely. Yet she has a smile for every child. Unfortunately, the children are afraid of her. I really feel sorry for her. I make a decision. I have to tell her about my encounter with Devon.

Damn it! I can't say anything. Everything must remain secret.

I'm in a dilemma.

https://pixabay.com/de/service/license-summary/

wanderer-5297457_1280

Chapter Four

I wake up in the middle of the night. I feel a draft and I shiver a little. When I went to bed, I left the window open. At first I snuggled under the covers, but then I decided to get up and close the window. As soon as I get up, I am startled. A scream echoed through the night. Loud and high-pitched. Just once. I look intently into the darkness to see if I can make out anything at the edge of the forest.

Nothing. Damn! Should I wake Daddy?

I decide against it. The scream could have been anything. An animal or guys screaming and staggering home from a pub crawl.

And if not? James, take a look!

I hate those two voices inside me when I don't know what to do. If I don't do anything, my conscience will torture me, so I decide to take a look for myself and get my binoculars. Back at the window, I open it, listen, and search the entire visible area with the binoculars.

Nothing.

As I put the binoculars down, I think I see a movement or something and lean further out of the window to increase the angle of view to the right.

It's a car, I think, and I lean out really far. At the same time, something rumbles on the roof.

Click, click, click

"Shit!" I hiss as Miss Piddy's stone rolls across the tiles towards the gutter. I instinctively reach for it. In the process, I overbalance and lose my footing, falling out of the window and sliding across the roof. I grab the stone and make a fist. With my other hand, I reach for the gutter to hold on to, but I can't, and I fall ten feet straight down. My mouth opens and I hear myself scream loudly. The impact is hard. At the same time, a dark darkness surrounds me. I feel no pain or anything else.

When I open my eyes, I'm in a hospital room. White, bare walls, cold, bright light. It smells sterile. My mother is sitting next to me.

"Where am I?" I ask.

"In the hospital, James. You need a lot of rest. Boy, what are you doing? You could have been killed! What makes you climb out the window in the middle of the night?" "I..." I try to answer.

"It's a miracle that nothing happened to you. There's no fracture, not even a cut."

"I wanted to..." I start a second try.

"We think you have at least a concussion. We'll see tomorrow."

I realize there's no point in talking to Mom now. So I decide to spend the rest of the night in the hospital without protesting.

Tomorrow I will tell you everything.

While Mom is still babbling at me, I feel myself and realize that absolutely nothing hurts. I move my fingers and toes. Everything works. I'm just tired, but otherwise fit as a fiddle. I have fallen so far.

"Dr. Higgins, my colleague from the night shift, talked to me. He says you can leave the hospital tomorrow - if you don't have a concussion, of course."

She pauses, thinks, and then probably remembers what else she wants to say: "Oh yes, your binoculars were next to you. I brought them into the house. And you were holding a rock in your fist. You didn't let go of it until you got here. Your fist was really tight. It's on the nightstand next to you now."

"It's okay, Mom. I'm going to sleep now, okay? I'm tired." "All right, James. Good night."

She kisses my forehead, smiles, walks to the door, turns off the light, and leaves.

I immediately turn on the night light above my bed and examine the stone. I was shocked to see that the color had changed. It is no longer red, but gray. But it is definitely my stone. I would pick it out of hundreds of stones and recognize it because of its unique shape. It looks like the fossilized tooth of a dinosaur.

The next morning I make it through the doctor's visit, my mom is there of course, and I'm sent home with the words that I must have had a guardian angel because I was completely unharmed.

I also made up my mind about the binoculars and told Mom that I couldn't sleep and was looking at the moon and stars with the binocular glass. I slipped and fell out. She believed it.

I wait until lunch, then I think about whether I should go to the forest. Something had happened there. I heard a scream and I think I saw a car.

Should I tell Dad about the scream?

I lean back and think. Since two corpses have already been found here and another one in the immediate vicinity, it is quite possible that the entire area is being watched by plainclothes policemen.

If that were the case, they would certainly have informed Dad.

I try to think several steps ahead, like in a game of chess.

Or is he just keeping quiet so as not to jeopardize the investigation? What will happen if they catch me in the woods? Nothing will happen. I am just the curious son of the sheriff. On the other hand, stupid questions could be asked. What I was doing there and so on. That would be the biggest bummer, because then I wouldn't be able to visit Devon. He kind of saved me instead of killing me. In retrospect, he's like a buddy.

That's really cool. I have a vampire for a buddy. Crazy world.

My decision is made. I remain silent and wait to see if the deputies find another body in the woods.

It wouldn't work for me today anyway. My parents are both at home and they wouldn't allow me to leave after I fell out of the window. So I decide to leave the body search to the sheriff's office for now. This decision turned out to be absolutely right, because Saturday turned out differently than expected.

My mom is redeeming her last birthday coupon. Dad had given her a lobster dinner on the coast. And it was in Newbury-port. A nice little town on the coast, about 110 miles from here. Mom thinks it's the right time because I survived the fall unharmed and something like that deserves to be celebrated.

An hour later we sit in the car I call Black and we drive off.

The day is great. We return home late. Beautiful weather, excellent lobster and a long walk along the sandy Atlantic beach make me fall into bed exhausted and sleep for ten hours straight.

The smell of freshly brewed coffee lures me into the kitchen on Sunday morning. Mom and Dad are in a good mood. There were eggs and bacon.

"They're in a really good mood today," I say.

"I'm going fishing. I've been planning it for weeks, and my old buddy Mike Tanner called me this morning. They're going fishing and have a spot open. I'm taking the Sunday off and I said yes."

"And I have to fill in for Dr. Higgins and take his Sunday afternoon shift. In return, I get the week off and can go to the hairdresser's."

Dad looks at me. "Is that okay with you, James? Can we leave you alone today?"

I see a relaxed GTA day ahead of me and nod. "Of course, I know what I'm doing."

Mom points to the refrigerator. "We still have pizza in the freezer. Or would you rather go to Burger King?"

While I'm thinking, Dad pulls out his wallet and puts a 20 Dollar Bill on the table. "Whatever you want to eat, James, buy it yourself. Just don't climb on the roof," he winks.

We laugh.

"Definitely not."

Then we talk about this and that and I have long since caught the good vibes. Whistling, I go to my room after breakfast. I love these days of having a storm-free pad.

Wow, the weekend starts like shit with house arrest and as soon as you fall out of the window, everything is forgotten.

Suddenly all sorts of thoughts are swirling around in my head.

What happened the other night?

I review the whole event and stumble over one thing every time. As I fall, I reach for the shimmering red stone, grab it, fall from the roof, and land on the ground unharmed. Afterwards the stone is gray.

Does it have a meaning? What is it about the stone that looks like this stone from the Internet that supposedly keeps the sun away from vampires so they don't burn?

Questions abound. Only one person knows the answers. Miss Piddy.

After my parents have both left, I realize that fate has opened a door for me. Suddenly, I am no longer grounded and have the whole Sunday to myself. I have twenty dollars in my pocket and the opportunity to fill up the Porsche and drive to Miss Piddy's.

The decision is made and I know what I have to do.

To be on the safe side, I wait a full hour to make sure Mom or Dad haven't forgotten anything and come back unexpectedly. Then I get the keys to the Porsche. I feel very guilty about the fare evasion, but I also know that I can solve a lot of mysteries by talking to Miss Piddy. Maybe I can even help solve the murders. I'm sure Dad will understand.

That eases my conscience and I go to the garage.

Wrooom

There's hardly a cooler sound than the roaring engine of a 911 Porsche under your ass when you're behind the wheel.

I pull out of the garage, get out, and close the garage door. Then I take a deep breath, get back behind the wheel and drive off. This time I follow all the speed limits to the letter. I drive very carefully and pay close attention. I don't even turn on the radio.

If something happens to my car today, I can emigrate. I leave Greenfield and take the highway east. When I arrive in my old town, my heart beats with joy. Not the joy of reunion, but the joy of getting away from this dung stain. I follow the main road, pass Ike Duddlies Barber Shop and turn into the street where Miss Piddy lives. I pull up to her house and park. My heart is pounding.

I hope she's home.

I get out and open the back door. It squeaks and the fence needs another coat of paint. The original white is peeled and weathered. My palms are damp. I haven't been this nervous in a long time. Lots of onions and bunches of garlic leeks hang on the porch. A cat jumps up and runs away.

I look in vain for a doorbell. So I knocked on the door. After the third time I hear: "Wait a minute! An old woman is not an express train.

Slurping footsteps follow. The door opens slowly and squeakily. Miss Piddy stands before me and looks at me for a while with a stern expression. She has grown older. She looks like a grandmother out of a fairy tale book. Gray hair tied back in a bun. She could easily play the role of a witch, at least the way she looks now. I wouldn't be surprised if she had a big knife or a shotgun behind her back. She seems to recognize me. The stern features relax. Finally, she begins to smile, and the shotgun that has been haunting my thoughts turns into a crochet hook.

Now she looks like Mother Hulda, I think.

She steps aside. "Well, well, well. You're the little Allington boy. Why don't you come in?"

I squeeze out a "Hi, Miss Piddy" and enter her house.

Creepy

Strange things are hanging everywhere. Stacks of fresh and dried, loose garlic cloves braided into pigtails. Holy water jars and crucifixes complete my initial suspicion that the old lady is protecting herself from vampires. It smells strong, like garlic, but the place is clean. No cat poop or anything like that. She goes into the kitchen. I follow her.

"Would you like some tea?"

"No, thank you."

"I'll make us a cup."

Did I not make myself clear? A cold Coke would be something, but some stupid hot tea...

"Sure," I reply, trying to be polite and thinking to myself: *I hope it's not fruit tea.*

"I have fresh fruit tea. I'm sure it tastes good."

I am a born loser.

Finally, we sit down at the table. There is a steaming cup of fruit tea in front of me. I pick it up and take a quick sip.

"Hmm, it's delicious," I pretend, trying to ignore a taste that reminds me of curried chicken skin with apple slices and cherries.

Miss Piddy grins. "It tastes awful. It's a mix from the Indian place, and I don't like the taste of it at all. I'm happy when guests come and drink it," she laughs.

I keep a straight face and take a second sip. "Actually, not that ..."

"Good," she adds.

I laugh. She does too.

"Boy, let's have a Coke and talk about what you came here for."

I like the old Lady.

She's really cool.

I sip a Coke with ice and lemon. It's really good now. The disgusting taste of tea disappears.

"You're not here by accident, James. What brings you to me?"

I think about how to begin. "Well," I stammer, "I'm sure you remember when you were telling me about vampires and..."

"Stop!"

She raises her hand and looks deep into my eyes. Her gaze is almost sinister. The kindness in her face is gone. "Did someone follow you?"

I shrug. "I have no idea. I don't think so. I borrowed my uncle's car."

"Black?"

"No, the Porsche is white."

"You idiot. If you don't have a license. Driving without a license is a criminal offense."

The old lady is in a good mood. "Yes, then I drove here illegally. I don't have a license," I admit.

"Okay. So you've met vampires?"

"How do you know that?"

"Tell me, boy. Please don't leave anything out. I need to know everything, you hear me? Really everything."

I drink my Coke, put the glass down, watch the slice of lemon twist around an ice cube, and begin to tell the story. I talk about my observation that stormy night, about the cabin, the tunnel, and finally my fall from the roof. "…and now I'm sitting here with you looking for answers. I haven't told a single person yet. I thought I'd talk to you first," I finish, pulling the stone out of my pocket and showing it to Miss Piddy.

She has been listening intently the whole time. Now she looks at the stone, stands up, staggers to a cupboard, opens it and comes back with a bottle of whiskey. "I need a drink for this shock."

She opens the bottle, pours some into her coke and drinks from it.

"There you go, my boy. The stone I gave you was a magic stone, of course. It should protect you. But it only works once. Don't ask me why, I can't explain it. It's just the way it is."

"Okay," I say. "Where do you get rocks like that? I think I could use some more."

"James, I have loved you since you were a little boy. You always laughed so happily and were never afraid of me. Everyone in this town thinks I'm crazy and a weirdo. Never you. Let me tell you something."

"You always told me so much. Even about vampires." "That's true, but unlike you, I haven't met one yet. But I have another secret. I met a witch once in my life."

I must look pretty stupid, because Miss Piddy stops her story and looks at me questioningly.

"James, are you all right?"

"Uh, yeah. Sure. I expected anything but a witch."

"Yes, yes," she waves her off, "they do exist. A few survived the great witch hunt. One of them, her name is Astaria.

Cast a spell on your stone. That's why it protected you. I also know of the existence of vampires from Astaria."

"That sounds interesting."

"Shut up and listen to me."

I nod.

"I met Astaria in the winter. She broke down in her car while passing through and I helped her. She spent the night with me and we talked half the night. We talked about this and that, and we talked about scary encounters. So I learned from her that vampires exist. And of course there are witches. The next morning, she gave me the stone, explained that it offered magical protection for a single dangerous situation, and left with the advice to always stock my house with crucifixes, holy water, and garlic. I also melted down some silver jewelry, had it consecrated, and formed it into small shotgun pellets that I loaded into my old shotgun. I gave you the stone because I like you. Unfortunately, I don't think I can answer any more questions about vampires."

"And Astaria?"

"I never heard from her again."

I look at my watch. "I'd better be going."

"Take care, James."

I stand up and say goodbye. "Wait."

She grabs one of the bundles of garlic and hands it to me. "Put this in your car."

"Sorry, Miss Piddy, but then my parents would kill me first and then my Uncle Joe. I'd rather have a vampire in the passenger seat," I joke.

She laughs. "Get home safe, James."

I drive home as carefully as I drove to Miss Piddy's. I drive the speed limit and avoid detours.

I didn't find any solutions or further clues at Miss Piddy's, but the visit was still worthwhile. At least now I know that there are witches as well as vampires and that a witch can also make magic stones or whatever you want to call this magic stuff.

"I think I'm crazy," I suddenly hear myself say. I've never been interested in this Harry Potter stuff. The magic crap has completely passed me by. And suddenly it goes bing, and I'm confronted with this stuff in real life.

James Allington, if you ever tell your parents about this, they will put you in a mental hospital.

I laugh at my thoughts.

Then I'm walking around in a straitjacket and everyone thinks I'm chafing.

I'm thinking about Miss Piddy.

Poor woman. She's been through it all, with the witch and all, and everyone thinks she's had a complete breakdown. That won't happen to me, I tell myself.

I finally reach Greenfield and drive home.

I really want to learn more about vampires and witches. I click almost to death on my laptop, but find nothing that gives me more or better information. At some point I also search for werewolves and zombies.

Werewolves are possible, zombies are completely invented. At most as voodoo spells, but that's going too far. At some point my head is empty and I start playing some casual shooting games. I decide to go back to the library soon and look for suitable research material on.

The next night I have a kind of nightmare.

I wake up in the middle of the night. I look at my alarm clock: midnight. I get up as if hypnotized and go to the window. It's a full moon. I watch as a Mercedes pulls up to the edge of the forest and a man gets out. Hunting fever and curiosity gripped me. I must follow him and discover the ssecret. I quickly get dressed and run out of the house towards the forest. I'm almost there when I realize I don't have a flashlight or a cell phone.

Anyway, I have to follow him.

The closer I got, the better I recognized the figure. Suddenly the moonlight seemed as bright as day. As if a camera is zooming in on the man's face, he appears huge in front of me. The gaze is cold and terrifying. Blood drips from the corners of his mouth. Sharp, large, razor-sharp teeth are visible. The color of his face is ashen. He reminds me of a dead man. Goose bumps spread over my body. I want to run away, but I'm paralyzed. His gaze literally pulls me in. I can't move. I open my mouth to scream, but no sound comes out. I feel like a fist is grabbing me from behind. I can feel the cold. Mortal fear spreads. The vampire comes towards me. He stares at me. I can't escape his gaze. I cannot even blink. He twists his mouth, seems to grin.

Only now do I realize that he is carrying a person. It is a woman. Her hair is white and tied back in a bun. I can't see her face yet. The closer the vampire comes, the greater my fear. Suddenly I see who the woman is. The vampire is wearing Miss Piddy.

Sweat runs down my forehead, sweat of fear. My whole body shakes as he stops in front of me. He drops Miss Piddy to the floor. She remains motionless. I want to look down to see if my old friend is still alive, but I can't take my eyes off the vampire.

He greets me: "Hello, James. Nice to finally meet you."

The voice sounds eerie and slightly distorted. He grabs me, pulls me towards him, opens his mouth and I smell horribly stinking breath.

I wake up. I'm shaking, on the verge of opening my mouth to scream as I slowly return to reality. It was just a dream.

I take a few deep breaths. Then I look at my watch.

Just after midnight.

Can vampires sneak into dreams? Do they have a sense of who is following them and was that a threat or is it all just a figment of their imagination and Miss Piddy is in no danger?

Of course, falling asleep right away is out of the question. I try to think of some nice things to thank other people for, but it's not that easy.

Tomorrow I really have to tell Riley how I feel about her. Or rather, that I really like her.

And if she doesn't like me, what the hell, I want her to know that I think she's really great.

I am determined to do this.

I'm putting all my eggs in one basket. All or nothing.

I can't help thinking about Miss Piddy.

Is she in danger? Hm, why should she be? She hasn't had any experience with vampires yet, and yet she protects her house with garlic. What about the witch who was with her? Is it just a coincidence?

I remember the letter from the cabin. Suddenly I realize that I wasn't alone in the cabin. My buddy Kieran was in the hut too. Is he in danger too?

Damn, I really need to talk to him about everything. Either we work more closely together in the future or I won't tell him anything anymore.

Then I think about taking notes. Like a kind of diary. Just in case something happens to me, my dad could march into the tunnel system with the deputies or the National Guard or the FBI and level everything.

I hate Monday mornings during the school year. You have the whole week ahead of you and almost no desire to study. I am convinced that about 95 percent of all students feel the same way like me. A few nerds and weirdos make up the remaining five percent. But Monday is by far the worst day of the week.

When I get to school, Riley's bike is already there. I look around and see that she's about to enter the school building. I park my bike and run after her. I catch her at the top of the stairs.

Luckily, she's alone. Not a friend in sight. The opportunity is perfect.

I tap her on the back, smile, and say a little breathlessly, "Hi, Riley! Good morning."

She turns and smiles back. "James, hey!"

I've practiced the best way to say it about a thousand times from last night until just now, and now that she's standing in front of me, smiling at me, I can't bring myself to say it.

"I... uh... Well, I wanted to..."

She laughs. "I don't know you like that. You usually talk like a waterfall."

I notice I'm blushing a little and force myself to grin. Then I close my eyes for a moment and say: "Do you have any plans this afternoon?"

"Wow, do you want to ask me on a date?"

Shit, why are women so complicated?

All of a sudden, I find my pick-up line pretty stupid and my behavior clumsy. I want to sink into the ground. I'm even more surprised when Riley follows up with a sentence that sounds like music to my ears.

"If that's the case, then of course I have time. You're a great guy, James. I like you."

I'm happy inside. I could jump in the air, do a somersault and yodel at the same time.

"Great, that makes me happy. What do you suggest?"

"You're asking me out on a date and you want me to suggest something?" She laughs sweetly.

"Uuh..., I wanted to ask, when can you start?"

Now she smiles. "Let's say from 5 p.m.? I can't stay late tonight. We're having guests, and I promised Mom I'd help. My brother never helps, or rather, he always acts particularly stupid."

"Sounds good. I'll pick you up," I say and find her brother pitiful. I would do the same.

We enter the classroom.

"I'd say 5:00 at the ice cream parlor. I mean downtown. Right near the movie theater."

"And that's where I want to invite you."

"Be on time! I hate waiting."

I wink at her. "You can count on it."

As she sits down, I run my fingers over her hand. She turns her hand and holds it briefly. It feels cool. Cool, but gentle. A few classmates have been watching, and I walk proudly to my seat.

Yes, James. You got your first date right.

During the breaks, Riley is surrounded by her friends and they seem to talk about only one thing: me. At least the girls from her clique keep looking at me, giggling and whispering and then moving on.

I grab Kieran.

"Hey Kieran, you and I really need to talk." Kieran leans against the wall. "About what, you old girl teaser? You want information on Riley?"

"No. Well, actually, yes, but..."

"She's very popular. Some people like the cool blonde, but she's never let anyone get close to her. I'm surprised you got a date right away."

"How did you know about the date?"

"Boy, the walls around here have ears. Someone hears something, passes it on to someone who knows someone who is very interested, and in a matter of minutes, the news spreads. Either verbally or via WhatsApp."

"Riley never had a boyfriend?" I ask.

"Let's just say not that I know of."

"Thanks for the info. Makes me a little proud." Kieran winks. "You're lucky I'm not into her, otherwise we'd be rivals by now."

"I wanted to talk to you about something else entirely."
"About the cabin in the woods?"

"That's right. Anything to do with it is dangerous."

Kieran sees some guys from the football team and says hello. They wave and one of them calls out: "Hey Kieran, are you coming? We want to talk about this weekend's game."

"I'll be right there, guys," he replies, giving me a quick look: "Sorry, I have to go."

"I wanted to tell you ..."

"The game is really important. We're hosting Turner Falls and we'll pass them with a win!"

"Take care of yourself! And if anything seems strange or dangerous..."

And he's gone.

Another time then.

"Why aren't you playing football?" Thomas Moore asks me. Moore is a bit of a nerd. He gets almost nothing but good grades, looks like a Christmas elf with glasses and red hair and freckles, but he's not a slimy creep, he's just nice. Just smart.

"I play soccer. It's not as legendary here as football or base-ball, but I love the sport."

"I play chess."

I frown at him. "Great."

"You know, I've replayed all of Magnus Carlsen's world championship games, and I think I know his way around."

Riley's clique passes us. "Albert Einstein is trying to get James into the chess club," one of them laughs.

Thomas says: "Mandy, you're too stupid to even put the pie-ces on the board properly. Besides, Albert Einstein has nothing to do with chess. He was a physicist."

While the redhead is still talking, I take the opportunity to leave.

Gosh,this guy is boring. This Mandy saved me.

I can't remember ever spending so much time in front of the mirror before a date with Riley. I even showered again, styled my hair properly with hair wax, and used some of Dad's perfume. Not much, just enough for Riley to smell in case she gets really close to me. I can't stop thinking about her. Until two weeks ago, I laughed at everyone who talked about love stories or saw them on TV or in the movies. Now it's hit me for the first time. Man, what a thing. But this Riley really is a great girl.

What should I wear?

I would love to have a brother like Felix from Orphan Black. He may be gay as a post, but he's also incredibly casual and mega cool. Felix would probably be the best advisor I could imagine. I stick to jeans and a t-shirt. A leather jacket over it, my Mustang sneakers and that's it.

"James, are you still leaving?"

I'm surprised that Mom is already home. But then I remember she took the Sunday shift. Perfect. "Yes, Mom. I'm meeting a friend from school. We are going to the ice cream parlor. Do you have any money?"

Mom walks up. She sees me and looks like she's never seen a boy on a date before. "Did you use Dad's cologne? It smells like it."

I bend down and slip into my sneakers. "Mom, do you have a few dollars for me now?" I repeat.

"Sure, here," she says, handing me 20 Dollar. "In case you want to invite the girl."

"You're the best mom in the world," I say, hugging her and take the money. Then I look at myself in the hall mirror.

That's how she knows you, that's how she wants to meet you, I tell myself, and I hurry out of the house.

I am very punctual. I arrive at the ice cream parlor twenty minutes before the appointed time and wait. The weather is perfect. Not too hot and not too cold. It's dry and after the ice cream we can walk around the city. I am excited.

Riley arrives shortly before five. She has changed her clothes, too. At school she wore a light blouse, but now she's wearing jeans, a t-shirt and a denim jacket, just like me.

"Hi," I say, probably grinning so stupidly that you can tell I have a crush like never before.

"Hi, James."

She leans her bike against a tree, locks it up, comes over and gives me a kiss on the cheek. I am so out of here. "Shall we go inside? I love ice cream and Luigi's is great."

I'm glad Mom slipped me the money. Besides the 20 Bucks, I still have 10 Dollar of my own money. That is definitely enough. "Let's go inside. I'm curious how that thing tastes."

The house cup is actually a hell of a device. It costs $9.90 and you shouldn't be full when you order it. Riley's eyes twinkle like stars as the Italian ice cream maniac serves the two sundaes. Sparklers shoot sparks.

"Buon appetit!" Luigi says and leaves.

"I eat a house cup at least once a month," says Riley, unbuttoning her denim jacket to remove it and place it on the bench next to her. "I used to come here a lot with my brother Ian, but since he started medical school, he hardly has time for me anymore," she laughs, enjoying looking at the miracle candles.

I take off my leather jacket and set it down next to me. When the sparks have fizzled out, we pluck off the burnt candle sparklers from the ice cream scoop and chase the spoon into it to finally enjoy the delicacy.

I shove the spoonful of ice cream into my mouth and look at Riley, my eyes wandering along her body. When I see the pendant on her necklace, I stop. I choke and cough. She notices immediately and reaches over. She takes the pendant and makes a fist around it.

"What's wrong, James?" she asks, getting right to the point. "What's wrong with my pendant? I saw you were a little shocked."

Even though I don't have to cough anymore, I'm still faking it. She has followed my gaze and knows that I have seen and recognized him. She is wearing the vampire stone.

My Riley is a vampire girl.

"Tell me what's going on right now or I'll get up and leave!" She's serious. I have to make a decision in a split second.

Can I trust her?

Well, I owe my life to the boy in the tunnel. He also told me that vampires live normally among us, and if the girl I've fallen in love with is a vampire, then I have the choice between being unhappy and maybe having to kill her before she sucks me dry, or trusting her and just telling her everything I've experienced in the days since we moved here.

"All right, that's it then. It's a shame, because I really like you," she exclaims, reaching for her jacket.

"Wait!"

Riley looks at me. Her look leaves no room for doubt. She's leaving and it's all over. I have to make a decision right now. Well, the decision has already been made.

"Let's eat the sundae in peace. I'll tell you all about it."

Her gaze softens. She seems to be thinking. The smile I like so much about her returns. Demonstratively, I dip my spoon into the ice cream and put it in my mouth.

"Mmm, delicious," I mumble, grinning at her.

"James," she admonishes.

I want to defuse the situation and grin even more. "Delicious. Very tasty indeed. Almost as tasty as blood."

Now it's Riley who is faltering. "Bl-blood?" she stutters. "How did you come up with blood?"

"Riley, I like you too. I really do. Well, I'm not exactly a hero at expressing myself formally and..."

"You have a crush on me?"

"Uh... yeah."

"That fits. I have a crush on you too, you little show-off with your borrowed Porsche."

I am relieved.

"But you don't tell me anything. I want to know exactly what's going on, otherwise there's no point. You can't build a friendship on lies and secrets."

"Riley, can I really trust you?"

"You can. Absolutely."

"I recognized the stone you wear around your neck."

"It's just an ordinary piece of costume jewelry and..."

"Oh, nonsense," I interrupt. "You are wearing a very special ruby. It probably comes from Tanzania and has the power to protect vampires from the sunlight that would otherwise kill them. Let's keep this brief. Riley, are you a vampire? Or do you say vampireness?" I frown thoughtfully.

I speak so quietly that she can hear me, but none of the other customers in the ice cream parlor can hear me. She looks at me as if she's hit a brick wall.

"Vampire?" she asks, acting completely clueless and innocent.

I decide to tell her some details of what happened to me. I start with the night I woke up during the storm, tell her about my observations at the edge of the forest, leave out the part about the cabin, and go straight to Miss Piddy's story. I also leave out the part about Devon and the tunnel. I can always do that later on. Then, of course, I tell her what Miss Piddy told me about the witch, and finally I tell Riley all about my research on the Internet, including the part about how I found the stone that protects vampires from the light of day and allows them to live normal lives. At the very end of my story, my girlfriend also learns the story of how I fell off the roof and, of course, that I've come to believe in all this stuff since that experience. "And now you can either call me crazy, get up and leave, or tell me honestly what you and your necklace are all about."

Riley is stunned and leans back. Her sundae is empty.

Bull's eye, I think.

Valuable, exciting seconds pass. She puts the spoon in the sundae, waves her index finger at me, and whispers: "James, bend over the table."

I comply, expecting her to whisper something in my ear. Instead, she kisses me on the lips. "I'm your girl. And because you've been so honest with me, I'm going to tell you my story. But again, absolute secrecy, no one must know. Do you promise me that?"

I nod. "I promise on my grandmother's grave."

"Then watch out," Riley breathes, looking deep into my eyes to see how I react.

My hands slide across the table and take hers. I squeeze them tight. "You can trust me. I promise."

Then she begins to speak.

"I think you're the first mere mortal to know about this. If you say a single word about it, we'll both be damned."

I nod silently.

"All right, then, watch this."

I can feel her shaking. Her handshake gets stronger.

"James, I'm scared. Terribly scared. There's a terrible curse on my family.

I return the handshake, wanting to give Riley security and strength.

"Nearly 200 years ago, a powerful sorcerer named Hostang came here. He called the elders of our family together and asked them to do the impossible. He gave us exactly 200 years to fulfill his demands or we would die. And that meant my whole family. Hostang seems to have very influential friends in . We have tried again and again to find out something about him, but it has not been possible. We don't know where he is or how he has so much power and knowledge about us. The only thing we know for sure is that he's up to no good. James, the time of the curse is coming to an end and we are at a loss.

Since I have already learned from Miss Piddy that witches exist, I have no doubt that warlocks also exist. Probably there are weak, strong, good and bad ones. This Hostang seems to be a really bad one, and his power is enough to wipe out Riley's vampire family.

"What's impossible?" I ask.

"Hostang gave us a task and exactly 200 years to solve it."

"Plenty of time," I interject.

"So that can't be the problem. What's the weak point of the whole task?" I ask, trying to look at the problem from a logical human perspective.

"According to an old legend, the first vampires who came to America hid three magical coins. They had stolen them from a vampire-pirate count in ancient Europe. Each coin is valuable and useless on its own. However, if you possess all three coins, you become the supreme ruler of all vampires and gain enormous powers. Supposedly, you can live normally among humans without any help. In any case, the three coins were hidden in safe places. Through meticulous research, my family actually managed to discover the three hiding places."

"Good, then what's the problem?"

"Of course, their hiding places were also magically protected. This protection is like a giant safe. So you can't get to the coins even though you know where they are."

"Now slow down, Riley. You know where the coins are, but you can't get to them because they're magically protected. Is that right?"

She nods. "They're in three different caves. All of them are locked. They can only be opened when a certain constellation comes together and..." she pauses.

"What kind of constellation?" I interject.

"The respective doors or gates only open when a vampire, a mortal human and a werewolf voluntarily place their hands on a gate stone together. In addition, you have to be prepared for deadly traps, i.e. overcome these traps."

"Like in the old Indiana Jones movies?"

She smiles for the first time. "Yes, sort of."

"You're a vampire, I'm a human. Now all we need is a werewolf." As soon as I say that, I lean back. "I've heard about the existence of vampires and witches. I didn't know about werewolves until now. Do they exist and how do they relate to you vampires?"

"Of course there are werewolves. They're almost as old as we vampires. And the relationship is," she hesitates, searching for the right term, "let's say... strained. We're not exactly best friends. We used to fight to the death. For a few decades now, we've been trying to live peacefully with normal people. We respect each other and avoid each other in a kind of truce.

"I am beginning to see where the weakness is. You don't trust humans or werewolves, but you should get one of each species to lay a hand on the stone with you. And if you don't, you'll die, which would be a big inconvenience for the humans if they knew about you and the werewolves. Can you put it that way?"

"That's the big problem."

Riley begins to shake again. A tear runs down her cheek. "James, I'm desperate."

"I'm willing to help you, all of you."

"That's fine, but we need a werewolf and we'll never get him to help us vampires. James, we used to kill each other. We're the werewolves' archenemies."

"But not for a couple of decades. At least that's what you said."

Riley remains silent.

"I see a well-founded hope in that. Do you know any werewolves?"

"No. Like I said, since we live side by side in peace and the fighting has stopped, we've been hiding. Every man for himself. Vampire to vampire and werewolf to werewolf."

"I'll start researching werewolves today."

"Thank you, James."

Luigi comes to the table. "Did you like it?"

"Great."

"Wonderful."

"Can I get you anything else?"

Riley looks at her watch and shakes her head. "No, thank you. I have to get home in a minute."

I pull out my twenty. "I'll pay. That's right."

Luigi takes the bill, smiles, winks at me, says, "Pretty girlfriend," and leaves.

We get up and leave the ice cream parlor. We walk hand in hand. I'm proud as a peacock. We kiss at the door. I don't even notice that Riley is a vampire. She feels completely normal. Her lips are warm. Okay, her canines are probably a little longer, but I really didn't notice that before. I don't care at all. As long as she doesn't kill people and suck their blood, she can be a vampire. She likes ice cream. So she won't just feed on blood.

Oh, James, these are all things you will learn from your girlfriend, I think.

Almost as if we'd agreed, we both pull out our cell phones and chat on . Then we exchange numbers.

"See you tomorrow."

"See you tomorrow, Riley."

As she rides off, I look after her for a long time. "I promise I will do everything I can to save you."

Werewolves. Damned, cursed and pooped on! Where the hell can I find werewolves? If I tell just one person about this, I could end up in the loony bin.

My first thought is of Miss Piddy. Before I even get to that, I call her. No luck. She promised to try to find this one witch who used to stay with her, to ask her some questions, but I think that's more of a false hope. I have to find out for myself where these critters live and how to get to them.

A new task awaits me. I, James Allington, friend of a vampire lady, have to find a werewolf. Crazy, but true.

https://pixabay.com/de/service/license-summary/

couple-6548045_1280

Chapter Five

When I get home, I immediately sit down in front of my laptop. It boots up pretty fast. I open the browser and type in *werewolf.* Result: Over two million pages.

Shit, I think, but immediately realize that 90 percent of it is pure fantasy and related image settings. I narrow down the search by specifying certain parameters that I have set up beforehand. My fingers literally race across the keyboard.

Characteristics of a werewolf.

Within seconds, Google spits out the results.

Just under 40,000 pages.

A huge difference. Still, it is a lot of work. All pages to read are as high as a mountain.

Higher than Kilimanjaro.

I skim through a few fantasy blogs that are still around and finally get stuck on an interesting encyclopedia about werewolves. I don't like what I'm reading at all. These things aren't cuddly mutants, but according to one theory are descended from demons and therefore evil.

That's nonsense! Evil creatures don't live among humans, I realize.

I continue to search. Another page takes a more understandable path for me.   It leads to Greek mythology. A tyrannical king named Lycaon incurred the wrath of Zeus, the father of the gods, because he wanted to present his own son as a brat at a banquet. Zeus condemned the king to live as a wolf among wolves. And whenever he had to satisfy his bloodlust, he turned into a vicious wolf. I lean back, thoughts running through my head again.

There is often a grain of truth in Greek mythology. This could be the origin.

I concentrate and read on. These creatures first spread to Europe and from there to the rest of the world.

They are usually vicious and bloodthirsty. After their transformation, they are as quick as an arrow and have incredible strength. Their senses are similar to those of a normal wolf, they have excellent smell, hearing, and so on. I begin to take notes and delve further into the world of werewolves. I discover that they are part of the lycanthropy phenomenon that is currently widespread in Africa.

This is also where the gems that have power for or against vampires come from. The circle is complete. So lycanthropes are people who believe in werewolves, but also vampires, witches and all that stuff. What do you mean "believe in"?, I laugh.

I've met these creatures and learned to love one of them.

My Riley. What a great girl.

For a moment my thoughts wander to my friend. Then I return to reality and continue reading.

Werewolves are said to live among us as normal people and turn into bloodthirsty monsters at full moon to satisfy their hunger and bloodlust.

You can kill them by shooting them with at least three silver bullets or by shooting a silver bullet through their heart. You can also kill them by decapitating them or stabbing them with a silver knife, inflicting several serious stab wounds that will quickly become infected due to the silver. However, there is a risk that you will be injured so badly that you will die or become infected and turn into a werewolf yourself.

Fuck, that's crazy, I wonder.

Then I read a few more things about how werewolves have mingled with ordinary mortals, how they can live to be hundreds of years old, and how they are not as bloodthirsty as they used to be. I think this is where truth and fiction get mixed up.

To summarize. Werewolves breed with each other and form families. But they can also infect humans and turn them into werewolves. So it's a bit like vampires.

That's the next keyword. Now I'm looking for *Werewolf vs. Vampire.*

While Google suggests the pages, I draw a first conclusion. I can confirm or refute a few theories in advance and thus eliminate them.

W erewolves are neither servants of vampires nor are vampires descended from werewolves, i.e. they are not mutated werewolves. A werewolf is a person who transforms into a mystical creature, i.e. a wolf, during a full moon, when he is in danger, or when he is not in control of his transformation. A vampire is an undead, also a type of human, who can live among us quite normally with the help of certain gems that he wears as a necklace.

Witches and warlocks are people or creatures who possess magical power or the knowledge of how to use magic. They can be good or evil. How old they become cannot be researched. But I think they are usually mortal, or if they are, they don't get too old.

Maybe 100, I think.

It is also a fact that all of these creatures are extremely allergic to silver bullets or silver in general and can be killed as a result. They also cannot tolerate sunlight, fire, and of course decapitation. Although the latter speaks for itself. It's hard to live without a head.

It would rain down my throat too, I grin.

I also know that werewolves and vampires are mortal enemies, or at least they were.

My head is spinning. I finish my research and let all the new information sink in. I need to digest it. My father comes home. The front door slams audibly into the lock.

"James, are you here?"

"Yes, Dad. Upstairs!"

"Can you clean and vacuum the inside of the BMW? It's pretty filthy."

My desire to vacuum the car is close to zero. But I know I have a lot of catching up to do and I don't want to upset Dad. "Okay," I reply and head straight downstairs.

"I went to the car wash. It's just the inside," he adds.

I take the car keys, somewhat relieved. "All clear."

While I'm vacuuming and wiping the car with a plastic cleaner, Mom comes home. She parks *White* in the driveway, gets out and says, "Good idea, James. I'm going to leave the keys in the ignition. You can start right here."

Ass card.

I try to keep a grin from my face and mutter to her, "All right, Mom. "Excuse me?"

"I'd be happy to, Mrs. Allington. Your valet is always at your service."

She laughs. So do I.

"I think we can relax the house arrest a bit, too."

I didn't think that cleaning cars could do so much good.

In a much better mood, I clean first *Black*, then *White*.

When I'm done, I go to the garage and vacuum the Porsche as well. I almost forgot, but Uncle Joe would have noticed a few crumbs on the doormat. Satisfied, I go into the house for dinner.

Later, my cell phone rings. A glance at the display tells me it is Miss Piddy calling. I answer it.

"Hi, Miss Piddy."

"James?"

"Yes, who else?"

"A Mr. *Hi*, that's how you got in touch. You always say your name on the phone because the caller can't see who he's talking to."

"Miss Piddy, yes, this is James Allington," I say, suppressing an annoyed tone.

"I thought about werewolves for a long time, and then I remembered that I once had a neighbor who always acted strangely when the moon was full. I was just a kid then, so I believed it, that she had once been all hairy. My mother thought I was dreaming, but I know I was wide awake. I remember exactly what her name was. She has a very unusual name. I didn't hesitate for a second, I went to the town hall and found out where she had moved to.

"Interesting."

"She moved to Boston. I've only been to Boston once, as a young woman. But it's not for me, you know, the big streets, the skyscrapers..."

The initial silver lining on the horizon immediately turns pitch black. Boston is a metropolis of millions, and the chances of finding someone who moved there umpteen years ago are close to zero. Still, I politely let Miss Piddy finish, but I'm thinking of Riley because I can hear Miss Piddy's voice, but not what she's saying.

"And then I found her number."

"Uh, sorry, Miss Piddy. I was... well, my dad was just talking to me, I didn't get the middle part. I'm sorry. Can you repeat that?" I fib to her to cover up my rudeness.

"Because Mrs. Pennewoogletea has such an oddly unusual name, I memorized it and called information. There is exactly one such name in the Boston phone book."

"That's amazing."

"I'm not one hundred percent sure if she's a werewolf or not. Don't forget that."

"It's at least a lead."

"What should I ask her on the phone? Maybe: Hello, Mrs. Pennewoogletea, this is little Angie Piddy. You were my neighbor 60 years ago, and I'd like to ask you if you're a werewolf."

"You're right. The situation is pretty silly."

"If you had specific questions, maybe I could confront them."

I think about it.

"Miss Piddy, would you like me to talk to her?"

"That seems like a better solution, too."

She gives me the phone number, wishes me good luck, and hangs up.

My heart races with excitement as I punch in the numbers and a bell rings.

Tüüüüüt ... tüüüüüt ... tüüüüüt.

"Pennewoogletea."

It is a woman's voice. It sounds anything but old. More like my mother's. I want to hang up, but Riley is in danger.

"Excuse me, Mrs. Pennewoogletea, this is James Allington of Greenfield."

"I don't know you, goodbye."

"Stop! Greetings from Miss Piddy. Miss Angie Piddy," I shoot off in a flash.

I hear her panting. She hasn't hung up. "From whom?" she asks.

"Angie Piddy. She was her neighbor about 60 years ago. In a little town called..."

"I know where I lived! What do you want?"

"I need your help."

"Get to the point! I'm about to move. Lucky for you, the phone will be disconnected tomorrow."

She's moving again. Her voice sounds anything but old, and she knows Miss Piddy. Werewolves get very, very old. She is one. Don't screw this up, James.

"Just listen to me, please."

"You have one minute, then I'm hanging up."

"I know you are a werewolf. But I don't want anything from you, and your secret will stay a secret. I live in Greenfield, Massachusetts. My girlfriend is a vampire and I need to know if there are werewolves in Greenfield. Please help me. My friend's life depends on it."

Heavy panting. I even think I heard a growl or a grumble. But maybe it was just my imagination. "If you vampires are so stupid as to think that we are - wolves betraying our packs..."

"I am a human. My father is the new sheriff of Greenfield. Bad things have been happening here. Murders! And, oh, hell, I'm desperate. My girlfriend, her whole family, is cursed, and if they don't solve a quest, the curse of *Hostang* will kill them.

I just did something I never wanted to do. I told a complete stranger over the phone what Riley had confided in me. It's only in hindsight that I realize this. I was driven to do it because I was afraid of betraying Riley.

"What's your name?"

"Allington. James Allington. I'm 16 years old and we just moved to Greenfield."

"How do you know Miss Piddy?"

"We lived there. She also gave me a magic rock that saved my life," I gushed.

"Slowly, very slowly. What do you want to know about me?"

"Whether you know any werewolves in Greenfield or the surrounding area. We need to befriend one to break the curse." Laughter.

"Werewolves and vampires never become friends, you dumb-head."

"Please!" I beg.

"We werewolves look just like you and all the other normal mortals. You don't recognize us. We live among you. Everywhere. So there must be some of us in Greenfield. You'll have to find them yourself." She pauses, there is a loud gasp. Then she continues: "If you think you're going to find me now, you're wrong. My moving van is at the door. I am gone. You will never find me."

"Do you have a name for me? I don't know where to look."

"They live among you. Look closely and you will recognize them. And, boy, I want to warn you urgently. You are playing with your life. You already know too much, and I'm surprised you're still alive. By the way, I heard about the murders from afar, and I also read something in the newspaper. Everything looks like of an imminent war. I'm leaving. Listen to me and go too. Leave Greenfield and leave things as they are. Try never, listen …" she warned urgently, „… never to have anything to do with us or these vile vampires. And stay away from witches and wizards. They are dangerous too. That's all I can tell you. Goodbye!"

She hang up.

My hands are drenched in sweat. My whole body is shaking and I sit down on the bed.

I take a deep breath.

You've taken a small step forward.

I organize the new information, think of a few words, then tap WhatsApp. The message box opens on the screen. I type a message to Riley.

Hi, I actually had contact with a werewolf. She said there are some living here in Greenfield. Now we just have to track them down and then we'll make friends with one. Trust me, we can do that, sweetie!

A little chat begins. Riley is happy and we encourage each other. Then we purr like lovers. We write that we miss each other and then arrange to meet tomorrow fifteen minutes before our usual time. We want to go to school holding hands and show everyone that we are a couple.

The next morning goes almost exactly as planned. Riley and I meet in front of the school in the bike parking lot, greet each other with a kiss, and walk hand in hand into the school building. Suddenly Kieran appears out of nowhere.

"Wow, that looks like love," he grins cheekily.

I'm a little embarrassed, but Riley counters in a flash. "You're just jealous because you're forever single."

"I just like girls with black hair and yellow-green eyes. I can't go for blonde hair and blue eyes, or even worse, red-haired girls."

"Then you can take care of my Riley when I'm not around," I interject.

Everyone laughs.

"I think little Amy Willings would be just right for you. She's got really long black hair," Riley says. "Yeah, something like that."

"You like her?"

"James, that's not what I meant."

"I can talk to her sometime. We were in the same gym class together."

"No!"

"Really, I'll talk to her," Riley repeats.

"Guys, stop messing with me."

"But if you have a crush," I laugh.

Kieran pokes me in the side. "I'll never say another word about girls if you're going to use them like that."

We enter the building laughing and in a good mood. Half the school now knows that Riley and I are dating. I admire her courage and composure. Her family is threatened and she jokes around like it's nothing. She plays her role well. I'm sure she's desperate inside.

Riley and the other girls have an hour longer school than the boys because of a lecture from their course. I go with Kieran to the bikes. The weather is gorgeous and I spontaneously ask him if he wants to get an ice cream.

"Good idea. We'll get a scoop at Luigi's."

"I thought of that too. I went there yesterday with Riley."

"Let me guess. House cup?"

"Bingo!"

Kieran laughs. "That wasn't hard."

At first we talk about some trivial things, then I deliberately steer the topic in a certain direction.

"We still haven't made any progress with the dead in the forest. Should we go back there? We don't have to go to the cabin if you're scared."

Kieran stares at me with big eyes. They are yellow-green. I notice that they look exactly like his future girlfriend's.

"I'm not scared."

"That's not what I meant at all. Let's start again. The bodies were found drained of blood. Do you think they were vampires? Do you even believe in vampires and werewolves and stuff like that?"

"That's bullshit!"

"Drained," I repeat.

"Did your dad find out anything in pathology?"

"He didn't tell me."

"Can you find out?"

We arrive at Luigi's and stand in front of the ice cream counter. The choice is enormous. But I stick with one of my favorites and get a scoop of hazelnut. Kieran chooses vanilla. We pay, go outside and sit on a bench in front of the ice cream parlor. The weather is perfect. A warm fall day in New England is just beautiful. Soon, the sea of leaves will turn red and colorful, attracting millions of tourists to enjoy the *Indian summer*.

We already live in a wonderful piece of good old America, I think, licking my tongue over the delicious ice cream.

"So?" I ask Kieran.

"So what?"

"Do you believe in werewolves and vampires?"

"Oh, stop it," he waves it off.

"What if I told you I met one?"

My buddy looks startled. His pupils dilate slightly, then he narrows his eyes. His gaze suddenly has an animal look to it, but he quickly relaxes.

"Who did you meet?"

"A vampire."

"You've got to be kidding me, dude."

"We're like best buddies, aren't we?"

"We barely know each other."

"But you already have a secret and trust us."

Kieran thinks about it and nods. "That's true."

"And we like each other."

"If I didn't know you were with Riley, I'd think you were gay."

"Oh, man."

"It was a gag!"

"Never bring it up in front of people."

"Don't worry, buddies don't make fun of each other in front of people," he insists. "But tell me, what's the story with the vampire?"

"Kieran, what I'm about to tell you must remain our secret. I need your word of honor!"

We look at each other in silence for a while. Behind Kieran's brain shell there seems to be something clattering, clicking, working. He frowns, smooths it out again, finally nods, holds out his hand to me and says: "I give you my word of honor. Whatever you tell me will remain our secret."

That takes a load off my mind. I could really use a comrade-in-arms and something like a best friend right now. I do something.

"The linchpin of my story is the hut where we both stayed. There I discovered a system of tunnels. Changing paths, doors, some you can open, some you can't." Kieran listens intently. I tell the story up to the point where I found the exit, returned home and discovered the loss of my stone. "So I decided to go back."

"You must be brave. I wouldn't have dared. At least not alone."

I continue my story. I stop right where I met Devon. I ask for Kieran's word again and without a murmur he gives it again and I continue my story. "And then an ice-cold hand grabbed my shoulders."

Kieran shows me his goosebumps. "Dude, that's more than awesome! I have total respect for you just listening to you," he searches for the right words because he doesn't want to come across as a coward and a scaredy-cat.

I grin. "The guy is a real vampire boy who was locked into this tunnel system by his stepfather and has been kept there for umpteen years."

"Sort of a modern day Rapunzel, only not on a tower, but in a tunnel. And not a hot chick, but a vampire."

"You can say that in ghetto slang. Especially if you keep saying *dude*."

He winks. "Sure. I can talk normal too. Thought you'd like it."

"Sometimes this, sometimes that."

"So this Devon guy needs your help. You're supposed to help him get his stepfather out of the way, so to speak." "Now hold on tight and listen to me carefully." Kieran is as quiet as a mouse.

"Do you remember the contract we found in the hut?"

"I do."

"This stepfather I told you about is none other than *Oloisius*."

I emphasize the name *Oloisius*.

Kieran drops the last piece of ice cream from his hand. "O-O-loisius?" he stutters.

"Right."

"That damn treaty is 200 years old. They're not even alive anymore," he counters.

"Yeah, that's about the right age, but vampires don't just live to be 80 or 90, they can live to be a few hundred, right?"

Kieran doesn't seem to be listening to me at all. His look still seems a little frightened. "You remember what it said, don't you?"

This time I nod. "He has to kill everyone who enters the hut within seven days and those who find out about it within 13 days."

"That's..."

"Tomorrow."

"And this Devon now knows that you and I found the cabin?"

"Inevitably. I was with him."

"It would be great if you didn't give me away, i.e. who I am and so on. You really are a true friend. It was nice to meet you. How often do you want me to visit your grave, buddy? I also put fresh flowers on it every month. What kind do you like?"

"Don't make those jokes. I have no desire to be sucked dry by a vampire."

"Me neither!"

"Then let's get active!"

"How?"

"We have to go back to the hut and watch Oloisius. If he's responsible for the murders, we need proof. With that, my father can put him behind bars."

Kieran laughs out loud. "Lock up a vampire? At night, he bends the bars, sucks out a few fellow inmates and strolls off to freedom!"

"Not if we make sure there are plenty of consecrated silver crosses and garlic everywhere. Then he will sit in the corner like a heap of misery and blubber. And if he has to give up his protective stone because jewelry is forbidden in prison, he won't survive the light of day. Either way, we would have won. But we need proof, and we can only get it if we can prove that he committed the murders.

"And if you tell your father?"

"You can visit me in the psychiatric ward," I answer immediately and unequivocally, "because that's where my father will take me."

"Gosh. You're challenging me. I don't know if I can do this."

"I didn't know that about myself before I got into it. I'd prefer vampires and stuff like that to be fictional characters and just on the big screen or in books. But no, they have to exist in real life and they have to cross my path.

I won't tell Kieran about Riley and the curse on her family for now. Maybe later. For now, we need to keep Oloisius at bay. I wonder if Devon's stepfather is part of Riley's family, too, because that would add him to the cursed, which would be good for us. Anyway. I can't speculate. I need a clear plan to save Kieran, Riley and myself.

Kieran stands up. "Speak up, buddy. I'll keep my mouth shut and stand by your side. When are we going to the cabin and what do I need to bring?"

"Silver would be good. Silver and holy water or something like that."

Kieran grimaces in disgust. "Sorry, we don't have anything like that back home."

"Never mind. So when do we meet?"

Kieran looks at his watch. "Three-quarters of ten, at the fork in the road by your house, towards the woods."

"See you then."

We say goodbye and on the way home I wonder if I should talk to Riley about Devon and Oloisius.

Does she know about the tunnel system at all? How many vampire families live in Greenfield? Are all Greenfield vampires humanized, i.e. do they live peacefully among us, or are there also those wild revolutionaries that Devon told us about?

It is questionable if Oloisius even knows that Kieran and I were in the cabin. If he did, Devon would have told him about it. I don't think he has, because right now I'm probably his only hope of rescue. Whatever happens tonight, we need to make contact with a vampire. Either we find Oloisius and follow him, or we need to visit Devon so he can tell us everything he knows. We need information.

I write a few notes in the memo on my phone and then plug it into the charger. I want to start the adventure with a full battery.

We are having hot dogs for dinner. I'm putting a mega portion of pickle slices and fried onions on the sausage when the phone rings. "Who could that be?"

Mom looks at Dad. "The sheriff's office?"

"I don't think so. I told the boys they could reach me on my cell if anything came up," Dad replies, getting up and answering. "Allington?"

Mom and I look at him. While she leaves her hot dog on the plate, I close mine and look forward to the first bite.

Dad is still listening to the caller, grimacing and mumbling three times in a row: "Yes. Yes, that's him. Yes, he's blended."

Mom and I look at each other. Her fear that a victim has already been discovered and Dad will have to leave has evaporated, and she reaches for the ketchup.

Dad closes the intercom and whispers: "It's Uncle Joe. He wants to know how his Porsche is." He looks at me and says coldly, "James took care of the Porsche."

I'm about to bite into the hot dog when I feel hot and cold running down my spine.

"Dad!" I whisper, admonishing and pleading at the same time. If he exposes me now as a Porsche thief, I can run from Uncle Joe and his revenge until the last day of my life. Then Oloisius and Hostang would just be cheap Mickey Mouse figures. Uncle Joe is a real adversary.

"No, Joe. He didn't touch the car roughly ... I know that could damage the paint. He just carefully vacuumed the inside and went over the leather with polish. Not that it would get brittle or all dusty."

Dad winks at me. I breathe a sigh of relief and finally take a ravenous bite of my hot dog. Then I show Dad my extended thumb. "Super done," I mumble with my mouth full. "Really great"

"Don't talk with your mouth full and don't gobble like that," Mom scolds.

"All right, Joe. I'll tell him. Well, have a nice vacation. Bye and best wishes from all of us. Enjoy the days!"

Dad sits down. "What do you think would have happened if..." "I don't want to know, and it didn't happen. I never officially drove the Porsche."

"I hope for your sake that Uncle Joe didn't tamper with the speedometer."

Shit. Bloody, bloody, miserable chicken shit! "He didn't really, Dad. Did he?"

He laughs again.

"Mr. Allington, Sheriff of Greenfield, that's enough. Your son is dying of fear," my mother warns.

"He didn't," Dad reassures me.

"That's okay. I promised anyway. I don't drive a Porsche anymore."

"Good, that's what I wanted to hear."

"As long as I don't have a driver's license," I add, laughing. Everyone laughs.

"You're sixteen now. I could imagine paying for your driving license training."

"But only if you do well in school."

"Yippee, you're the best! I would never have dared to ask that after borrowing the car for a short time."

"That was a load of crap!"

"A whole sewage plant full of crap, Dad."

Immediately after dinner, I start making preparations for my planned nighttime excursion. I oil the door lock and handle so that nothing squeaks or rattles when I leave. I leave my shoes outside the door on the porch. I put my jacket there too. I charge my cell phone. Since I can't get my hands on any silver bullets or other vampire weapons, and we don't even have any fresh garlic in the house, I stay pretty much unarmed. But I don't care. We don't want to fight, we want to get information. What we need is solid evidence that can be used in court. If we actually manage to convict Oloisius, we'll be one step closer to finding a werewolf that Riley and I can befriend without being hunted by a vampire.

In an emergency, I write a WhatsApp text that I can send with the push of a button. I want to send it to Riley in case of danger. If I don't come back, she should let my dad know. I've also left a note for Dad on my desk with the coordinates. If I don't come home or Riley asks him for help, I know he'll find the note and start his search at the coordinates I wrote down. This double and, in my opinion, sufficiently coded precaution should be enough.

Even if something happens to me and I am unable to inform Riley, Dad will eventually find the note with the coordinates and will definitely go to the place.

At 21:40 I sneak out of the house unnoticed. I slip into my shoes and jacket outside the door and start walking. The expensive evening with Kieran can begin.

I don't have to wait long. After a few minutes he comes back with a flashlight in his hand.

"Come on," I whisper to him and lead the way. "But leave that thing off." I point to the flashlight.

"I only carry it for emergencies. Where are we going anyway? Do you have a plan?" he asks me.

"To the cabin, we discussed that." "And you don't think it's too dangerous?" "Are we starting that again? I thought you weren't afraid." "I'm not, but I'm extremely careful!" "Yes, yes."

Off we go. A look up. Half moon. The starry sky mel is clearly visible and it is correspondingly cool. I close the zipper of my jacket. The edge of the forest looks especially menacing in the dark. I can feel my knees getting weak, but I don't want to show it. When an owl lets out its call and the echoing ooooooo, we stop. Kieran moves his head from side to side and then back again. His hand is on my shoulder, his index finger on his mouth. He gestures for me to be quiet.

After a few moments he whispers: "It's okay, let's keep going."

I have no idea what he wanted to hear, but Kieran makes me feel safe. I'm glad he's with me. As we enter the forest, the last doubts come back. The feeling of being watched from the forest by thousands of people is simply unpleasant.

This time it's Kieran who shows his coolness. He walks along the path without fear or doubt, moving smoothly and calmly, not stepping on any branches lying around, while I'm more like a clumsy animal, trampling on anything that seems to make a noise.

Snap, and another branch. I could slap myself. *How does Kieran do that?*

That last crack was pretty loud. Kieran scolds him: "Now be quiet and look where you're going! If you keep stomping around like a bull in a china shop, we can approach the hut with a flashlight and cowbells around our necks."

"All right, I'll be careful."

I try to place my steps exactly where Kieran has gone and follow him closely.

"Scared?" he breathes to me after a while.

"No, man. I'm just trying to be really quiet."

"Well, as an Indian you would have failed."

I have to laugh.

"Stay serious."

We turn onto the path that leads to the cabin. We walk along it for a few minutes. Suddenly Kieran stops. Of course I bump into him, startle and curse: "You idiot, can't you help me..."

"Shh!" he hisses. "I heard something."

I fall silent immediately. Kieran's hand grabs my arm. He pulls me aside into the brush. "There's someone there!"

Those stupid goose bumps again. I used to think I had more balls than my buddy, but now it's the other way around. And then I start to think.

What does he always hear? I haven't heard anything.

I know that not even a minute has passed when I nudge him. "I didn't hear anything.

"Be quiet, someone is coming," he shouts at me.

I am suddenly silent and listen intently. Time doesn't seem to pass and I doubt my friend's words, want to stand up and call him an overprotective coward, when I also hear a loud crack.

How is it possible that he can hear it and I can't? I really need to see an ear specialist. I'm probably headphone-impaired.

I crouch as low as I can. The only sounds I make are my heartbeat and pulse.

Crack

Someone step on a branch. Leaves rustle. Kieran was not wrong. It's not an animal. Someone is in the forest and is now traipsing along this path, which runs exactly two meters in front of my nose and leads to the hut.

My knees start to shake. I look at Kieran. His eyes are narrowed, he's sitting in a crouch. It almost looks like he is about to jump up. He is very centered and seems anything but afraid. His eyes are fixed on something. I follow his gaze and recognize a figure in the faint light of the moon and stars. Tall and strong. The man seems to be carrying something. Something big. I get even more scared when I think of a corpse.

Shit, I see the killer. If he discovers us, we can say goodbye to the world.

The figure approaches. The corpse turns out to be an adult doe.

The animals weigh about 100 kilograms, I think. *And the guy carries it around like a light stuffed animal. He has uncanny powers. He must be a vampire.*

I'm dying of fear as he stops at our level and curses, "Bloody hell! Stupid animal!"

Then he puts the animal aside and walks on. I quickly realize that the guy is between 180 and 190 centimeters tall and very broad-shouldered. I can't make out his clothes, but I can see he's wearing a baseball cap.

Is that Oloisius?

I look at Kieran and am almost scared to death. My buddy is sitting there like a dog, or rather a wolf, ready to pounce. His muscles seem to be tense. His eyes are glowing yellow-green, really sparkling, and his mouth is slightly open.

Am I wrong or have his ears become pointed and slightly hairy? Shitty lighting conditions here.

Kieran looks at the possible vampire. I concentrate on my friend's eyes. Now I can see them clearly. They are small and yellow-green! I can't believe it. I swear to God. I have seen this look many times in books about wolves and in my research. It is the eye of a wolf.

Kieran is a werewolf!

I immediately look the other way, confused and not wanting to embarrass my friend.

"We're following him!" I hear.

When I look at Kieran now, everything looks normal again. I wonder if I was wrong or if what I suspect is true. The whole way he behaved in the dark, how well he hears, how he acts, supports my theory. But I still don't want to ask him any questions. Not yet. I have something like a great hope in this moment.

Maybe I can save Riley. If it's true about Kieran, it can work.

But I don't want to bring up this explosive subject too soon. I still need more information.

"What's the matter, James? Did you pee on yourself?"

He pulls me out of my thoughts. "Me? Of course not, you ass."

"What, you don't want to follow him?"

"Yes, I do!"

"What now, you pants pisser?"

"No, I didn't pee myself, and yes, we're following him."

"But be quiet, your heartbeat was louder than the school bell," Kieran grins.

We get up and head back to the trail. Kieran marches off. I follow him, staying close behind my buddy. When the vampire reaches the clearing where the cabin is, he turns right and doesn't go to the cabin. So my theory that it was Oloisius who was supplying Devon with the fresh blood of the doe is also shattered.

When we enter the clearing, the guy is nowhere to be seen. Nevertheless, Kieran continues on. I trust his instincts and stay close behind him. We walk back into a dense forest. There is no path anymore and so we move slowly over rustling leaves. After about 100 meters, Kieran stops and points through the thicket. "It's stopped," he whispers to me.

I can't see anything, can't even tell where the vampire is, but I trust Kieran. "What is he doing?" I ask.

"He's lifting something up. It looks like a trapdoor. Now he grabs the animal and goes down."

"What are we going to do?"

"Wait."

We must have been waiting at a safe distance for twenty minutes. I remain calm. This time the excitement lasts and it's anything but boring. Kieran is very attentive and reports every detail he sees. Then it gets exciting.

"He comes back up, closes the trapdoor and puts leaves on top," Kieran describes each of the man's activities.

"And now?"

"Now he walks away."

"Towards us?"

"No. He just goes into the woods."

"Let's wait another five minutes, then we'll see what's down there."

I think about it and say: "Yeah, sure. Let's do that," even though I'm not sure I want to do all that. To be honest, I have to admit that I'm scared.

While we wait, I look at Kieran. I can't see anything that would indicate a werewolf. Maybe I was wrong.

"Now!" he says suddenly and runs off.

I have no time to worry, so I get up and follow my buddy.

Kieran immediately finds the spot and pushes the foliage aside with his feet. "Trapdoor!" he cheers, bending down and grabbing the ring to pull it up.

"Isn't that too dangerous?"

"Do you think the doe has turned into a zombie and wants to eat your brain?"

"You ass."

"I like you too," my buddy grins.

"So, shall we? Or was it just you who invented the cabin and you don't have any balls in your pants?"

That did it. "Lift the lid already!" I say gruffly.

Kieran opens the trapdoor with a creak. I pull my phone out of my pocket and activate the flashlight app. A wooden staircase leads to a room about twenty square meters in size that looks and smells like a small butcher shop. The doe is hung up to bleed out. The blood drips into a basin. On one wall are hatchets and knives. The meat is presumably being cut and packaged as steaks or roasts. Opposite are bottles that appear to be filled with blood. In any case, there are funnels for that.

"Okay, let's get out of here. We have seen enough. It's a poacher who hides here. He'll..." I say.

"We're going in!" Kieran interrupts me.

"Why?"

"Because I want to take a closer look. This room must have a purpose. I think a normal poacher would grab his deer and throw it on his truck. Staying here in the woods is pure nonsense."

Kieran's argument makes sense to me.

"I'll go first."

He climbs down the wooden steps. The cone of light from his tavern lamp flies through the room. It smells of iron, of dead animal, and somehow of blood. The smell of butchery.

"It's a kind of blood storage for vampires. In the back, under the stairs, there are many bottles. Large ice blocks provide cooling. The system here must have been built back then."

"When?"

"200 years ago, around the time of the treaty we found."

Now I also go down the stairs. The smell, which I describe as a butcher's odor, becomes more intense. Something inside me resists, but my curiosity has long since overpowered my fear. Kieran lights a shelf of large containers. The light from my phone sweeps over the dead doe and the collection tray. Suddenly a thought pops into my head.

Get lost!

I feel it bubbling in the pit of my stomach. My inner alarm bell rings. "Kieran, he's coming back. The blood must not clot in the tub or it will be useless for him. Let's get out of here now!"

"In a moment, look over here," he answers, waving. "This is definitely the secret food cache of the vampires of Greenfield. If they knew we were here, we wouldn't be alive much longer."

I go over, see jars with labels, read a few names. Kieran goes to the stairs and climbs up.

"James, someone is coming. Get up, we need to get out of here as soon as possible!"

I run to the stairs in a panic and jump onto the second step.

Crack

The rotten wood breaks. I slip through with my leg up to my knee and get stuck.

"I'll help you," Kieran hisses and starts to come down. Then he stops. "Shit, he's almost there!"

"Get out, get help!" I yell and regret it at the same time, because I know I won't make it out of here on my own. My leg is trapped and I can't pull it out fast enough without hurting myself.

"James, I..."

"Go away!" I repeat.

Kieran disappears in a flash. I turn off my phone and shove it into my jacket pocket. Then I face my fate. It takes less than a minute for a figure to appear, stop in front of the trapdoor and look inside. My heart slips into my pants, I start and jump.

I am so dead.

"Well, who have we here?" he says.

The voice is deep and anything but polite. "Who are you and what are you doing in the forest in the middle of the night?"

"I..." I stammer.

He descends the stairs. "How did you find this cellar? Are you spying on me?"

"No, I... By accident!"

"I can feel your fear and I can feel that you're lying, child!" His hands grab my arms. He pulls and I can free my foot from the hole in the stairs. He lets go and I can stand.

Painless, I breathe a sigh of relief. *My leg is not injured.* I think feverishly if I can get past the guy and make up for it before he grabs me.

No chance, he would catch me right away.

"I hear? And don't try to lie to me, or you'll be hanging right next to that doe."

I feel almost sick with fear. My thoughts race and then I spit out an answer that I quickly weave together from half-truths and lies. I hope he buys it.

"I'm the sheriff's son. I wanted to be a hero and catch the guy who dumped all those bodies in the woods. I know it's stupid, but there was this thirst for adventure in me. I just wanted to be someone that people looked up to. We just moved here and it's really hard to make new friends.

He broods. I can clearly see how it works underneath his brain shell.

"I got lost in the dark and then I saw you. I was curious. I thought you had a body on your shoulder. I didn't know you were a hunter!"

"Haha, hunter," he laughs out loud. "You little snoop! Didn't your father teach you not to mind other people's business?"

"I'm sorry! I certainly won't tell, even if you are a poacher."

Another roar of laughter. "Poacher, a good joke!"

He grabs my shoulder and turns me around. This guy has bear strength. He goes through my pockets, finds my cell phone and puts it in his pocket.

"Hands behind you!"

I obey. In a flash, he has my hands tied together with a rope.

"I'm going to let you in on a little secret."

I'm scared to death, I hope Kieran can get help fast enough.

"You are dangerous. You found me."

My whole body is shaking and I curse my idea to go into the forest. "Are you going to kill me?" I ask, finding the question stupid even as I ask it.

"Don't worry, you little snoop. You won't end up like the others."

I breathe a sigh of relief.

"I'm going to do things a little differently with you. Your father will stop looking for the murderer, otherwise he'll get you back bit by bit. We don't need snoopers in Greenfield."

Kidnapped and taken hostage. A hostage the vampire later eats for dinner. I'm the biggest loser ever.

"Sit down!"

I obey. The vampire lights a kerosene lamp. Then he takes the vat of blood, lifts it with ease, and places it on the countertop. He then stirs the blood with a large wooden spoon and pours it into several large glass containers. He takes a small bottle from a drawer, pours some of the contents into each blood-filled bottle, and closes them with a cork. He sees my questioning look. "I use this to make it durable and tasty."

"You don't have to kidnap me!"

"Shut up, or else..." he points at the doe. I am immediately silent.

After he finishes his work, he grabs me, scolds me about the broken wooden step, and pushes me up the stairs. "If you try to run away, you'll be very sorry!"

I believe every syllable he says. I think of Kieran. I'm secretly hoping he's still there, jumping out of a bush, beating the vampire never-ender and setting me free. Nothing happens.

After the trapdoor is closed again and covered with leaves, I have to go ahead of the guy. He leads me to the exit of the forest. I see a dark Mercedes.

Shit, it's him! I'm in the hands of the killer.

I immediately calculate how fast I can run with my hands tied.

Not fast enough. Damn, where is Kieran with the rescue team?

"What's your name?"

He opens the trunk and points inside. "Get in or I will squeeze you in!"

I get in.

"One peep and you're dead."

The trunk is closed. The driver's door slams shut. The engine starts. The car moves. I count silently. One, two, three ... and try to estimate the approximate distance we will cover. I miscount at 157, start again and finally give up. This trick works for Hollywood stars in action movies, but not for a sixteen-year-old boy being kidnapped by a vampire.

Eventually, the journey comes to an end. Doors slamming. Footsteps. Things are pushed around. A few minutes later, the trunk opens.

"This still applies. If I hear a single sound, you will die instantly."

We are in a garage. He pushes me to a door, opens it and turns on the light. I tried to remember as much as I could. The room is not large and has one small window. It is about 1.80 meters high. If I'm lucky, I'll fit through, but it might be too small.

"You will spend the night in my little workshop. I'll think about what to do with you until tomorrow. And so that I can spend the night in peace, I'm going to gag you.

"That's not necessary, I'm definitely not going to..." I say and, poof, I have a smelly, oily rag over my mouth. The vampire grabs some duct tape and secures everything by wrapping it around my mouth and head.

"Are you getting enough air through your nose?"

I nod. The question also calms me down a bit.

He doesn't want me to die. Not yet.

"Sit on the ground. Here!"

I have to sit next to a massive workbench. He puts a chain around one of my ankles and locks it with a padlock. Then he hands me an old blanket. "If it gets cold, you can cover yourself."

How? My hands are tied behind my back, I think, because I can no longer speak, or at least make myself understood.

He took my smartphone out of his jacket. "You don't need it," he says. "Without this stuff, your generation feels naked," he laughs and puts it on the workbench.

Then the vampire turns off the light and leaves.

It takes a while for my eyes to adjust to the dim moonlight streaming in through the small skylight.

I wait until I can hear nothing more from outside. When he seems to be gone, I first try to determine the range of the chain. I can't reach the wall. I can't reach the wall where all the tools, from pliers to heavy hammers, are neatly hung. There's nothing lying around on the workbench. This guy is very neat. I sit up and concentrate on the room.

Where do I see something I can use to get out of here?

Finally, I spot a small screwdriver. It must have fallen off the workbench and rolled into the corner. I immediately try to reach it with the tip of my foot. I reach out as far as I can and manage to touch the screwdriver, but instead of rolling it towards me, I push it away.

Damn it!

I think about it.

If only my hands were free, I could throw the blanket and pull it over me.

Then I have the ultimate rescue idea. I take off my shoes, pull down the sock of the free foot with the toes of the chained foot, and try again to get to the screwdriver. I can touch it with my big toe and get it in the right position so I can grab it with my toes. It creaks. I pause. The sound is like a squeaking door. *Footsteps! He's coming.*

I immediately pull my legs up.

The workshop door opens. He turns on the light. "I've become curious. At first I wanted to talk to you tomorrow, but now I have a few more questions." He looks at my feet. "Why did you take off your shoes and socks?"

"Hm ... hm ... hmmm," I mumble unintelligibly through the gag.

He laughs and pulls the tape off my mouth. Then he takes out the cloth. I inhale sharply. "Thank you. I don't get enough air. I took off my socks to loosen the gag with my toes," I lie, finding the excuse very successful.

"It's a good thing I came back. I have a question I'm really interested in anyway."

I think I saw his vampire teeth. *Hopefully the half-dead man has already eaten.*

The man looks at me questioningly. "I noticed a few things. You weren't alone in the woods."

"Yes," I shoot back.

"Nonsense! I knew it right away. It smelled like a wolf when I was in the cellar."

"You must have mistaken it for the dead deer. I'm not a wolf, I'm a man."

"You're going to tell me who was with you in the forest, or I'm going to be very unpleasant."

"I was really alone."

"My daughter goes to your school. She told me on the first day of school that some poser with a Porsche had just arrived at the school. She also said he's the sheriff's son. And since we only have one sheriff, I know it's you. Well, James Allington, I know your name, who you are, and what grade you're in.

My thoughts immediately turn to Riley. *Is it her father? She's a vampire. I don't know any other vampires.*

"My daughter also told me that you're good friends with a guy named Kieran and that you're very interested in Riley."

Phew, lucky me. It's not Riley's father. So there's another vampire girl in my class. Where did I end up?

"So, James. Were you in the forest with Kieran?"

"What's your daughter's name?"

"I ask the questions."

"I was alone. Honest!"

He comes very close to me. He radiated cold. I see a leather strap around his neck. His stone is attached to it. He has an unpleasant smell coming from his mouth, not to say that he stinks. *Should I give him the tip for the mouthwash? Better not. He doesn't seem to be in a good mood.*

"Either you tell me who your companion was by tomorrow morning, or I'll just grab all the boys in your class one by one and ask them myself!"

I wrinkle my nose in disgust.

He laughs. "You don't like the smell of stale blood. I just took another sip."

"I was really alone," I point out.

He walks to the door and turns back. "I'll do without the gag, but if I hear a single sound, you're dead," he warns me. Then he comes back, walks past me and stops beside the screwdriver. He bends down, picks it up and says, "There it is. I've already missed it." With a big grin, he hangs it on the tool board. "You'll tell me the name in the morning. Good night!"

He leaves, turning off the light.

I curse inwardly. He has destroyed my hope for liberation.

Why does this idiot have to come back and see the screwdriver again?

I lean against the workbench and think. This will probably be the worst night of my life.

Either I die tomorrow or I betray my friend.

You lose all sense of time when you're tied up in a mini-workshop and the only light is stale moonbeams fighting their way through the skylight. Just as dim as the light in this room are my chances of ever getting out of here again.

I don't know how long I've been sitting there staring when I hear the door creak again. This time the noise isn't like before. It sounds more like it's constantly interrupted. As if someone was trying to be very quiet. I am expecting something.

Is this guy trying to torture me with sleep deprivation and noises like this?   If so, he's succeeding.

Now he is standing in front of the door. He opens it. Not as fast as before, but very slowly.

"What do you want from me?" I say angrily. "I already told you that I was alone in the forest! Is that so hard to understand? No matter how much you tortured and hurt me, I was alone. There's no name I can give you."

A figure enters the room. I realize immediately that it's not the vampire who kidnapped me. He's taller.

"You're a great buddy. Sounds like you didn't betray me," I hear Kieran's voice.

I am relieved. A whole bag of worries and fears falls away from me at once. "I'm here. The guy chained me to the work-bench."

Kieran turns on his flashlight, sees me, and comes quickly to me. He looks at the lock and chain, then the beam moves to the tool.

"How did you find me? I thought you went for help."

"I hid in the thicket and followed you to the car. I stayed put because I was afraid the vampire would kill you. In that case, I would have attacked him."

"You're a real friend!"

"Hold still, I'll saw through the chain. It's faster than picking the lock."

"Doesn't it seem strange to you that vampires exist?"

Kieran doesn't answer. He grabs a hacksaw and starts working on a chain link. "I recognized the Mercedes. It's Cassie's dad's."

"Cassie Anderson? The snooty one from the snobbish clique who always walks around all snooty?"

"That's right, Cassie."

"Your dad is a stinking vampire and almost admitted to the murders. At least he knows more about them. But there's no hard evidence."

"Does that mean your dad can't arrest him yet?"

"I don't think there's enough for prosecution. Dad could easily get him for kidnapping, but then Mr. Anderson would definitely say I broke in."

"That can be good. It´s best not to tangle with Mr. Anderson. He's a ruthless businessman who buys up bankrupt companies, fires the employees, and sells them to other companies on the cheap. He makes a lot of money that way. Most of the people in Greenfield hate him. He is powerful and has a lot of influence. Judge Adams is one of his friends. That means we need a lot of evidence to charge Mr. Anderson with the murders. If we implicate him and he doesn't go to jail, we can get our way."

Rattle

"The chain is through."

"The hands!"

Kieran also uses the hacksaw to cut the handcuffs. I rub my wrists and immediately put on socks and shoes. Then I grab my Smartphone.

"Get out!"

Kieran goes first. I grab the small screwdriver that Mr. Anderson cleaned earlier and follow my friend. We walk through the garage. At the Mercedes, I use the screwdriver to puncture the front tire, then the rear.

"So, ass, have fun changing the tires."

We exit the garage through a side door. Kieran points to the house next door. "The lights are on there."

"Anderson heard something. Run!"

We run as fast as we can. Kieran is a great runner and overtakes me in quickly. He sets a tremendous pace. We hear the screeching of tires. Anderson pulls the Mercedes out of the garage. The headlights catch us. Then the car stops. We hear the plop, plop of the flat tires and then loud cursing. I stay two blocks behind Kieran, then I run out of breath. After I've fallen noticeably behind, Kieran slows down and waits for me. We laugh and high five each other.

"Done, but it's not over yet. You now have probably the most powerful enemy you can have in Greenfield," Kieran says.

While I'm huffing and puffing like an ox that's pulled a school bus ten miles, Kieran doesn't seem to mind the run.

He has the stamina of a werewolf, I think with a grin. He's my best hope for Riley.

"I never liked the Andersons, but I would never have believed that the old man was a vampire and a murderer. What did he want to know about you?" asks Kieran, eagerly awaiting my answer.

"Who I was with in the forest. He said it smelled like a wolf in the cellar."

Kieran is silent, looking at me. "So?"

"I answered that it smelled like a dead deer and that I was alone. Then he threatened me with the worst. He also mentioned that his daughter had told him that we were friends and that I had a crush on Riley."

"That bitch!"

"He didn't find out about me."

"The fact is, you are in grave danger from now on. And he's on my trail, too. We need a battle plan."

I yawn. "But not today."

Kieran looks at his watch. "Almost two in the morning. Let's go home. Tomorrow we'll figure out how to fight and what we can do."

I shake Kieran's hand. "Thanks, you saved my life!"

"We're friends after all. Friends save each other's lives when they have the chance," he grins and chimes in.

Chapter Six

The night was short. When I wake up, the first thing I think about is whether it was all just a dream or whether it really happened last night.   A glance in the mirror immediately tells me that it was.

Not a dream. I look like an overworked tomato, and I also have slight streaks on my wrists.

On the way to school, I'm already thinking of a plan to get Mr. Anderson. He scares me. I still feel safe because he has nothing on me. If I'm lucky, he'll see the situation as a draw and stay calm. It's like a chess game. Everyone is waiting for the other's next move to react and checkmate him.

Riley is waiting at the bike stand talking to a girl. When I realize who she is, my stomach turns. She's actually standing next to Cassie Anderson, joking with her. This can't be a coincidence. I wink at Riley, put my bike down and hug my friend. A kiss follows.

"Hi Cassie. Are you okay?" I ask.

"Yep," she replies, examining me from top to bottom before turning back to Riley. "So what's up Riley, are you interested in the makeup class or not?"

"Makeup class?" I ask, frowning.

"You don't know anything about it and you'd better stay out of it, James," Cassie salivates at me.

"Well, Riley is naturally beautiful and doesn't need to show off to cover up a pimple face."

"Oh, that's outrageous!" Cassie exclaims, promptly turning and walking away.

"That wasn't nice," Riley says.

"Do you care about her?"

"Cassie? We went to kindergarten together, started school together, and got along really well. It's only been since the beginning of the school year, we haven't been together as much as we used to. Maybe it's because *Sandy Wyler* has become friends with her. I can't stand her."

"I don't like Cassie. She's conceited."

"Like it or not, what you said wasn't nice. Besides, I think you'd change your mind if you got to know her better."

I want to tell Riley about Cassie's father right away, but spontaneously decide to wait a little longer. "I'm just the kind of guy who talks straight about what's going on and stuff, and I don't mess around," I say instead.

Riley laughs. "Whatever! Come on, school's about to start."

"How often do you hang out with Cassie?"

"Jealous?"

"Bullshit."

We joke around a bit.

When the class starts, my thoughts are everywhere but on the subject of the class. Of course, I am called upon.

"James! ... James?"

Caught. Damn, what did he ask?

"You should pay more attention and stop daydreaming."

"Sorry."

"The American Civil War is in itself a subject of interest to boys."

"It is, Mr. Opener."

"Well, then you can tell me how old George A. Custer was when he became a general in the Yankee army."

"He was twenty-three years old, Mr. Opener. Custer was born in New Rumley, Ohio, in 1839 and died at the Battle of Little Big Horn in 1876. He became the most famous general of his century."

"Just pulled your head out of the noose again, James. Very good. Now let's get on with it ..."

I fall back into my thoughts.

Riley will know that Cassie is a vampire as well. I guess the whole vampire world knows each other. I guess they just don't know who's a werewolf. Pretty tricky.

I look at both girls. Riley is paying attention, her eyes following Mr. Opener as he writes some numbers on the board. Cassie takes a small file out of her purse and starts doing her fingernails. Try as I might, I can't see this stupid stone.

Well, maybe she's not wearing it as a necklace, but it's in her clothes. But that would cause problems in the gym. Do vampires actually swim?

I guess a lot of what I know from the Dracula movie will be different in reality. But one thing is for sure. Riley will definitely be able to give me information about Cassie and her family. Sooner or later I'll have to tell her.

Probably sooner than later.

The day drags on. I spend my breaks with Kieran and the boys. We talk about soccer, basketball and I try to bring up soccer, but it doesn't work with the others.

It's still an unusual sport here, which surprises me because the USA has even participated in the World Cup.

School is over.

"And don't forget to read pages 17 and 18," Mrs. Hopper, the substitute English teacher, tries to drown out the bell. We get up and walk out of the classroom. Cassie has joined Riley and is chatting with her. They're both laughing. I catch up. When I walk next to Riley and glance at Cassie, she blinks. "You again."

"I said something stupid this morning. Sorry."

Riley winks at me. Cassie stares at me like she's hit an invisible wall. She ponders me. "Where are you from? What's the name of the nest?" she finally asks.

"It's so small, you probably don't know it. But if you put your nose to the wind when it's coming from the west, you can smell it. Cows, pigs, chickens. The people there are a disaster.

Both girls laugh. I did it.

"Riley, how did you come up with that clown? James, you're funny. Okay, I accept your apology."

I still try to find out if and where she wears the vampire protective stone, but give up after a few glances so no one thinks I'm hot for Cassie and keep trying to stare at her cleavage. Joking and in a good mood we walk on. We meet Kieran at the bikes. I kiss Riley goodbye. "Are we writing?" I ask.

"Yep!" she winks at me.

She rides off with Cassie. Kieran and I push our bikes along the path to the road and discuss last night again.

We, especially me, are definitely in danger. Anderson is not to be trifled with. I could arm myself with garlic, consecrated silver crosses and the like, but that would also scare Riley away.

Together we go over all the details again, trying not to leave anything out.   From the discovery of the cottage to Devon to the appearance of Mr. Anderson. In the end, we always come back to the same thing.

"We have to tell Devon. He's a vampire, and he knows the vampires of Greenfield. Either he can negotiate some kind of truce between Anderson and me, or at least give us some tips on how best to deal with him."

"But there's also this Oloisius," Kieran twists his eyes. "Wow, what a shitty name. How can you be called that?" He shakes his head.

"Okay, let's think about how and when we can get in touch with Devon. We can talk on the phone later. For now, I've got steamed cabbage."

"All right, see you then." We go our separate ways.

I'm home alone. Mom left a note for me at.

There's chili con carne in the refrigerator.

I heat it up in the microwave. A few minutes later, I'm sitting at the table with a Coke and the best chili north of Mexico, eating.

My brain is buzzing all the time. Of course I'm scared. Especially of Mr. Anderson. I trust him with everything. The big shock comes with the last bite, which I wash down with Coke. It's been exactly one week since we entered the hut. I cough and choke.

Today is the day Oloisius is supposed to kill us. What if Devon was just messing with me and told his forced stepfather about me? Then I will die today.

I feel sick to my stomach again. I haven't had a quiet day since we moved to Greenfield. I sit back and try to collect myself.

Don't get nervous, James. Just think calmly and take care of yourself.

My next thoughts are about Devon. *Can I trust him? Is it true that he's being held prisoner there? Or is this just a tactic to make me feel safe so that he or Oloisius can strike in peace?*

I decide to meet Kieran right away and write to him on WhatsApp, he's online anyway. I stare at the hooks.

Blue, he has read it.

I see that he's writing.

Come over. I am alone the whole night.

I put the dishes away and go straight to him. When I get there, he's already at the door. He waves. "Come in."

"Hi!" I greet him, park my bike and follow him into the house. I hang my jacket on the coat rack and take off my shoes. Kieran's room is upstairs next to the entrance. Everything looks normal. Nothing but absolutely nothing about this werewolf house is different from ours. Except maybe that it's bigger.

I wonder if I should tell him that I strongly suspect he is a werewolf. I have to bring it up sometime. I don't think he's going to come out on his own.

Knowing that today is the day that we, the people who entered the hut, are supposed to die and that Mr. Anderson is probably hunting me, it almost slips out of my mouth by itself. "Kieran, I'm just going to say it. I think you're a werewolf."

Whew, done.

Kieran freezes and stares at me with wide eyes. "Please what? What am I supposed to be?"

"I don't just think it, I think I know you're a werewolf," I repeat.

"You're right!"

"You don't have to deny it. I know because of various observations I've made. I also talked to a werewolf on the phone. It was Miss Piddy's former neighbor," I blurt out.

Silence. Kieran takes a deep breath. His eyes sparkle a little. "This is a game with fire and you can get burned," he warns.

"Believe me, I've learned things in the last week that I thought were impossible."

He sits down on his bed and points to a chair in front of his desk.

"You're my friend, and I trust you, or I never would have told you," I say.

"We are friends. Best friends. What we've been through together is amazing."

"It is, isn't it?"

He nods. "I trust you. Yes, I am a werewolf. But this must remain our secret. Every normal person who finds out is a danger for us werewolves and the old ones don't hesitate for long. Actually, that makes you..."

"Doomed to die?" I add questioningly.

"Yes, or let's say silenced."

"Great, then not only are the vampires after me, but the werewolves of Greenfield as well. Believe me, Kieran, I have no interest in being hunted by the wolves as well."

"Go ahead and give me your word of honor."

He gets up and comes over to me. I take a swing. "Word of honor," I say.

"I think you're the first normal person to know this secret."

"Kieran, this thing we've gotten ourselves into is much deeper and more dangerous than you think."

"In what way?"

"It's not just about the bodies and the fact that we found and entered the cabin, it's about much more." "Much more? About what else? You mean Devon's release?"

"Even that is only a small additional part. I need your help!" I say firmly, my expression more serious than ever. Kieran recognizes immediately that I'm scared and that the story I'm about to tell him requires a great deal of trust.

"You make it very exciting. What's it about?" he wants to know.

"I really need your absolute trust and your iron silence. I'm keeping another secret and I've also promised a person not to tell anyone about it."

"I understand."

"I'm probably in the stupidest predicament you can get into."

"James, you know my secret, and that is the greatest proof of trust I can give you. No matter what you tell me now, it will always be our secret. I give you my word of honor!"

I take a deep breath. "And I can rely on that?"

"I'll keep it like my own secret."

"It's about Riley."

Kieran smiles. "Don't tell me she's pregnant or something."

"No. Worse."

Kieran stops grinning. His face literally freezes. "She's terminally ill and needs a donor to match her bone marrow?"

"She's a vampire."

Kieran doesn't say a word. He turns pale and then bright red. His eyes narrow slightly and sparkle yellow-green.

"Do you know that there is an eternal war between us werewolves and the vampires?" he says, slightly agitated.

"Which can be described as a truce at the moment."

"True. But we don't like each other."

"So far I don't get the feeling that Riley hates you and you don't like her. So stop spewing that crap about us hating each other."

Kieran calms down again.

"That's right. When you look at it that way, you're probably right."

"Young people, you are the new generation. If you can keep the peace, maybe there will always be peace in the future. And when a whole race of werewolves and vampires want peace, a few old revolutionaries won't succeed."

"That would be nice."

"Are you ready?"

"Start already."

I go back a long way and start my story from the beginning, even if Kieran already knows half of it. I just want him to see all the connections and find out how I got into this whole situation. Finally, I squeeze him one more time before telling him about the curse on Riley and her family. When I'm done, Kieran stands up, comes over and pats me on the shoulder.

"I'll keep my promise and not tell anyone about this. And I give you my word again that I will help you and Riley. We will be the first to unite vampires, werewolves and humans as friends and ensure a peaceful, shared future."

"And lift the curse from Riley's family at the same time," I add with relief.

Kieran laughs. I join in.

My friend suddenly falls silent and pricks up his ears, almost like a dog. He looks at the window. "There's someone there." The young werewolf's voice catches my attention. Kieran goes to the window to see who is on the porch.

"Maybe a raccoon?" I ask.

At the same moment, Kieran lets out a startled scream. "Ahhhhhh!"

Mr. Anderson is standing outside the window. He is holding a baseball bat and smashing it against the glass. It shatters into a thousand pieces.

Kieran backs away. I freeze in fear. The bat moves along the window frame. Anderson removes the last sharp shards of glass from the wood.

"Thought I'd find you here," the vampire's deep voice pierces the room.

"I can smell it. It stinks like a werewolf."

We jump to our feet and try to escape through the door, but Anderson is lightning fast. Smooth as a cat, he jumps through the window frame without hurting himself and is suddenly standing in the doorway in front of us. "You don't stand a chance!"

We stop, back away, but Anderson grabs each of us by the neck. His grip is as tight as a vise. He has powers that cannot be adjusted. My hands grip his arm. I fight for oxygen.

Kieran growls. He begins to transform. His primal instincts are awakened. His hair sprouts, his hands turn into claws, and his mouth turns into a fanged mouth. "A cute little dog," Anderson laughs. "You want to play?"

"How did you ... know we were ... here?" I croak out.

The grip loosens a little, and I suck oxygen into my lungs.

"All it took was one look at my daughter's school yearbook and I knew where to find you. There's only one Kieran in her class. And now you're both going to die."

He pushes us to the window. The doorbell rings. I try to scream, but I can't make a sound. Mr. Anderson immediately squeezes hard and I'm afraid I'm going to suffocate.

"Are you expecting another friend?"

I squeeze out a "No" and blink at Kieran. He's completely mutated into a werewolf now.

Anderson changes direction again and pushes us towards the door. "Let's have a look then!"

My eyes go back to the window. I see someone climbing through. It's Cassie. Her father didn't notice her.

That traitor. She told her father where to find us, it shoots through my head.

"Dad, no!" she cries, stabbing her father in the back with a syringe.

Anderson gasps. He stops. His grip loosens. I take the chance and free myself. Exhausted and relieved, I sink to the floor. Anderson collapses like a wet sack. Kieran rolls over. He pants, then gradually regains his human features.

Cassie can't believe what she sees. "Kieran's a werewolf?"

I nod and grab my neck. I don't seem to be hurt. "And your dad tried to kill us. We found the blood stain in the woods. We saw him bleed a deer," I explain. Then I point at Mr. Anderson. "What about him?"

"I saw him snooping around my room. I know him and I was worried. So I followed Dad."

"Did you... I mean, is he dead?"

"No. I injected him with a serum. It's a kind of silver legion that knocks him out for a few hours but doesn't kill him. I'm going to take him home and there he'll have to tell me everything or I'll have to report him to the elders. But that's too much information for you.

She looks at Kieran, who now looks completely normal again - and also rubs his neck.

"You're a werewolf?"

"And you're a vampire," he replies.

"We'll keep that quiet, right?" Cassie suggests.

Kieran and I look at each other and nod in agreement.

"Absolutely," I say. "But you need to keep your father under control."

"I'll talk to him. He has some explaining to do."

"Cassie, thank you so much. We probably wouldn't be alive right now without you."

"It's okay, guys. Give me a hand. I've got to get Dad into the Mercedes somehow."

We get up and go to work. Cassie grabs Mr. Anderson's shoulders, Kieran and I each take a leg.

"Cassie, you're a really great girl. I owe you an apology. I always thought you were a conceited, arrogant, stupid cow."

She grins. "Maybe I am."

"But you're heavy."

"Are you saying I'm too fat?"

We all laugh.

"No, not at all."

We carry the vampire to the front door. There he plops down on the floor again as Cassie opens the door. "That's going to be a bump."

"He's lucky that's all it is. If it hadn't been Cassie who came here, but my parents, it would have been a fight to the death."

We carry him to the porch and look around to see if the air is clear.

"No one in sight. Where's the car?"

"Just outside the driveway."

"Keys?"

"I took them out of his pocket earlier."

A *beep* and a *thud* follow. The hazard lights flash briefly. The Mercedes is open.

"Trunk?"

"Nonsense, back seat. Leave him there until he wakes up.
I'll put the car in the garage."

"Do you have a driver's license?"

Cassie laughs. "Almost. I have a car and I can drive. Is that
enough?"

We've had enough. We get to work. It takes some effort to
heave the heavy body into the Mercedes, but the three of us manage it.

"I'm going now. And remember, boys, not a word to anyone."

"Word of honor," comes the refrain.

We go back to the house and look at the battle scars in the
room. Kieran gets some plastic sheeting and duct tape. "It's
going to be a fresh night," he says, starting to stick the plastic
into the frame.

"Then grow some fur." We laugh.

"What will you tell your parents?"

"That you were here and we played soccer. Then the ball
hit the window."

"And who did that? You or me?"

Kieran points at me. "You, of course."

"You ass!"

We laugh again.

"No, I say it was me. That's okay. It wouldn't be the first
time."

I am reassured.

"Cassie is really cool. Sending her vampire daddy to the
land of dreams to save us."

"She's very smart. If we were both dead, or even just missing, not only the entire sheriff's department, but the entire werewolf community would have been looking for us, and thus the
culprit. They would have and there would probably have been a
war between vampires and werewolves. She prevented that."

"I hadn't thought of it that way."

"I think it's very good that we're doing this together now, without any secrets. You wouldn't have a chance on your own. All you need is a werewolf," Kieran grins.

"And some of those needles Cassie used wouldn't be bad either."

"I've got something better." "What is it?"

"My grandfather gave it to me. It was when I was young and playing in the forest. He said that the transformation doesn't always work, and that it takes a long time to learn and use it properly. We only turn into wolves automatically when we're scared to death, like before. And because I was often alone in the forest, he gave me a bow and arrows one day. Some of the arrows were normal, and five of them had a colored tip. He told me that the five arrows were like *magic arrows* and that I should use them when bad people with sharp teeth came at me. Later I found out that they are silver arrows that kill vampires. They are treated with a special varnish so that we werewolves don't endanger ourselves with them. Once an arrow enters a vampire, the varnish dissolves within seconds and the silver kills the vampire." He goes to his bed and pulls out a large cardboard box. As Kieran lifts the lid, the described weapon appears in front of him.

"The bow was made by an old Indian and is almost indestructible. The arrows are also included."

I see about fifteen arrows in a quiver. The feathers are all different colors. Kieran carefully pulls out an arrow with the same feather color.

"That's them. Yellow on the front and back. Deadly silver underneath. The other arrows are for practice."

"Great. We should take this with us when we go into the vampire tunnel system and solve the riddle to free Riley from the curse."

I look at my watch. "If this Oloisius guy wants to kill us, he still has five hours."

"I don't think he knows we were in the cabin."

"Let's hope so. One vampire attack a day is enough."

"I'm sure my parents will be home soon. They're in Boston. My father has an appointment at the port, he has to inspect some goods for his company. Mom is shopping all day. I'm just waiting to hear exactly when they're coming back. It's better that I'm alone when I tell them about the window."

"I don't want to be there either."

We say goodbye and I head home.

Already on my way I notice my inner tension. I'm constantly looking around for possible pursuers. My thoughts also turn to Riley. I have to talk to her and tell her that I've talked to Kieran, that he's a werewolf and that he can help us. I'm already searching for the right words when she happens to be riding her bike in front of me as I turn onto Cherry Street. I pedal harder and catch up. At the next light, I come to a stop beside her.

"Hi," I gasp, laughing at her.

"James," she exclaims in amazement and delight. "Where did you come from?"

"I was with Kieran and you?"

I see her gym bag on the luggage rack. "Cheerleading practice."

"I'm glad I met you. I really need to talk to you."

We push our bikes across the street as the light turns green.

"Hurry, I have to be home on time."

I immediately start stuttering. At first Riley's face wrinkles with worry, then she looks horrified and wants to push me away, saying, "That was a secret and I trusted you!"

Finally, she hugs me and breathes, "Thank you, James."

"We're going to make it and defeat the curse."

"I'm ready for the fight. When do we leave with Kieran?"

"As soon as possible. I'll call him later."

"Please let me know very soon."

"I will. Bye, baby," I say, giving her a quick kiss, getting on my bike and turning off.

Riley continues on down Cherry Street.

When I get home, the first thing I do is check the windows and doors as inconspicuously as possible. I want to know that no one has entered or tampered with them in any way. When I'm sure everything is okay, I go up to my room.

"Not hungry?" "No, Mom."

"What were you looking for?" asks Dad.

"Uh, nothing."

"You didn't check the windows for termites, did you?"

"Dad, you don't have to explain everything!"

"We're going to the movies tonight. Will you come with us? The change will do us all good."

"What movie?"

"The new one with Julia Roberts."

"No thanks, I'm not in the mood for a boring, disgusting movie. I would have gone to an action movie."

"Are you staying home?"

"I think so."

In my room I take my cell phone out of my pocket and immediately call Kieran at .

"Hi, are you okay? Did the window work?"

"No, my parents are staying in Boston for the night. The carrier ship from China that my father was waiting for arrived late. He has to go back to port tomorrow morning. They're taking a hotel."

"My parents are going to the movies. Shall we take advantage of that? I'd stay with you then."

"Come over here."

I quickly pack a few things and go downstairs. "I'm staying with Kieran tonight. We want to study for history first and then play a PC game. His parents are okay with it."

"Shall we drive you there or will you take the bike?"

"Bike. There's school tomorrow."

"But don't go to bed too late."

"Mom, I'm not in 13 years old anymore."

"And no alcohol!"

"What do you think of Kieran's parents?" I grin.

"Don't be like that," Dad says. "We're glad you've made friends here so quickly."

Mom takes out her wallet. "Here, a twenty. In case you fancy a spontaneous pizza," she winks.

"You're the best," I reply habitually and honestly, grabbing the bill and scurrying out of the house with my school bag and gym bag packed with a change of clothes.

First we go through Kieran's house and check all the windows. Then we agree that the foil on his room window is not enough and nail two more boards over it. We inspect our work with satisfaction. While we clean up the tools, Kieran explains to me what is dangerous for werewolves. Of course, that includes a lot of what I call *weapons* used against vampires. Holy stuff, silver bullets and so on. In the end, the only effective weapon left is the bow with the prepared silver arrows. However, I have a sharp knife and a small pair of pliers.

"What do you want with them?"

"During the day, I can use it to cut through the necklace with the stone. Without it, the vampires crumble to dust."

"You've seen the power they have. You have no chance, James."

"It doesn't matter. At least I feel safe."

As we await our fate and Oloisiu's, I tell her about Riley and how proud she is of us for wanting to help her. I mention that

Mom gave me a twenty for pizza and Kieran is already holding the phone. "Speed dial three," he says. "I'll have a large pepperoni and shinken. I'm ravenous."

"Sounds silly coming from you," I laugh. "Ravenous, hahaha."

Kieran snarls in amusement. "Grrr!"

"Is a big pizza enough for you?"

"Werewolves can really chow down, but at *Village Pizza* the large pizza feeds a whole family. It's enough for me," he grins.

We order and play GTA to pass the time. When the pizza guy rings the doorbell, Kieran opens it and I stand behind it, armed with a bow and arrow.

"That's right," he says and my twenty is gone.

"Are you crazy? I could have gotten three dollars out of that!"

"It wasn't your money and your mom can afford it."

"Hey, three dollars!"

"You're going out for pizza. This is a shitty job and the guy here is a really nice guy."

"And probably a werewolf, too, right?"

Kieran carries the boxes into the kitchen. Small holes have been punched in the corners. Small, faint wisps of steam come out of them, spreading a wonderful aroma. It smells like melted cheese and a mixture of something spicy and something grilled.

"The pizza guy always delivers to us first when he goes out. The pizza is really hot. That has to be rewarded."

Kieran puts the pizza on the table and pushes a box over to me. I sit down and lift the lid. What I see, combined with the smell, makes me immediately forget the princely tip. "If it tastes like it smells, I'll stop complaining."

"Then take a bite."

I pick off one of the pre-cut triangles, taste it, and decide not to mention the money again as soon as the pizza touches my palate. "Super tasty!"

Ding dong.

Someone rings the doorbell. My gaze meets Kieran's and our eyes wander to the bow and arrow at the same time.

"Who could that be?"

"The pizza guy because he's embarrassed to take so many tips?" I speculate.

"Nonsense, be serious, we're both supposed to die today. I'm not really in the mood for jokes at times like this."

"We're only supposed to die if Oloisius knows we were in the hut."

The bell rings again.

Ding dong.

"I'm not answering!"

"Especially not me. I don't live here."

Tock, tock, tock.

Loud knocking is heard. Someone is banging on the front door.

"Who shoots the vampire? You or me?" I ask, pointing at the gun.

"Keep your voice down. Someone's calling for us."

"I don't hear anything but knocking."

"Human ears aren't that good. Keep it down."

My buddy pricks up his ears and turns his head toward the hallway. Suddenly Kieran's features relax and he stands up. "Hey, buddy, what's going on?"

"It's Cassie."

"Don't fuck with me."

"I recognized her voice."

I follow him. We go to the door together and open it. Cassie's standing there, staring at us.

"Well, finally. What took you so long?"

"We're eating pizza. Do you want some?"

"I'd be hungry, but my dad's still in the car. I changed my mind and don't want him to wake up at home. I'll lock him up in the blood camp in the forest. There he can think in peace about what he wanted to do to you."

"Then why are you coming to us?"

"Because you must help me, you fools. I can't take him there alone."

"But let's eat first."

Cassie goes into the house. "We have plenty of time. He won't wake until morning."

Kieran looks outside once more before closing the door. "It's gone dark."

"And it's starting to rain," Cassie adds.

She sits down on an empty chair in the kitchen. She immediately notices who brought us the pizza.

"Yum, pizza from the Village. It's my favorite."

"Kieran can't handle his big pizza anyway," I say, cutting the top off my pizza, then plucking a slice from Kieran's giant pizza for Cassie and sliding it over to her on the cardboard top.

Kieran sees it as he comes in and mumbles something like "I'll just eat less then".

We are enjoying the best pizza in the world. When we're done, Cassie looks at me.

"Riley called me and filled me in on everything. She told me that she trusts you and that with Kieran's help and yours, she can break the curse. I'm part of the team, there will be four of us fighting from now on!"

"Cool!"

"Hey, nice!"

"But first we have to get Dad away before he wakes up."
Ding dong.

We look at each other at the sound of the doorbell. We look back at the bow and arrow.

Ding dong, ding dong, ding dong.

"What kind of fool rings the bell?" asks Cassie.

"Who the hell's coming again?" says Kieran.

"The pizza man, and he's bringing back my three dollars," I blurt out.

"You're repeating yourself, James."

We remain silent and listen. Suddenly Kieran jumps up and runs to his bow and arrow. "Someone's tampering with the door lock. I can hear it very clearly!"

"I don't hear anything," Cassie whispers.

"Typical werewolf. He's really showing off today," I reply, also in a whisper. Then I jump up and say to Kieran:

"I want your ears," and run to the light switch.

Click.

It is dark. The three of us step into the hallway. Now I also hear scratching and levering. Then someone swears.

"We should call the sheriff. What have we got here ..."

"Shh!" Cassie interrupts, putting her index finger to her closed lips to indicate that I should be quiet. "It's too late for that," she adds.

"Up!" Kieran urges, placing a yellow fletched arrow on the bowstring.

Click.

"Finally!" someone croaks in a hoarse voice that immediately sends shivers down my spine.

The door is pushed open. Standing in the doorway is none other than Oloisius. "Ha, ha, ha, ha," he laughs loudly and contemptuously. "Did you think I'd forget you?"

We turn and start to run.

"Where to?" I yell.

Cassie pushes me from behind. "Faster!"

Rumble

"Ouch!"

A sharp pain shoots through my body as my shin hits a chest.

"Turn left!" Kieran yells.

I turn to face him. I can dimly see him draw his bow, aim at Oloisius, and fire. The arrow whizzes towards the vampire. But Oloisius has already registered that Kieran is aiming at him as he enters the house. I've never seen anyone move so fast. The vampire makes a lunge, twisting his body to the side, and the tip of the arrow whizzing past only tears the fabric of his cloak before it lodges in the door frame with a loud thud.

"Good shot. Was your first and last attempt at the same time," the vampire mumbles. "You just made me a little angrier!"

Kieran climbs back up the stairs, pulls another arrow from the quiver and places it on the bow. Oloisius reaches for my friend and a cat-like growl comes from his mouth. I recognize large, white vampire fangs.

"Kieran, watch out!"

Kieran draws his bow, quickly aiming the arrow at his target and firing immediately. A split second before Oloisius can grab him, the tip of the arrow pierces the vampire's thigh. He stumbles and curses. "Ouch, you cursed brat! If you think that will stop me, you're wrong!"

I can tell by the color of the arrow that it wasn't a silver-tipped arrow. Damn it!

Kieran uses the time advantage, turns around and runs up the last few steps. He sits down at the top and gasps: "After me!"

Then he pushes open a door. We scurry into the room. He slams the door and turns the key. Then he turns on the light.

"That door will stop him for less than ten seconds," Cassie says matter-of-factly. "He's a vampire and he has tremendous powers."

"He shot him," I say, pointing at the bow.

"Wrong arrow. Oloisius is wounded in the thigh, but that wound will heal in less than a minute. We have that long to think of a battle tactic or to flee."

"A minute? It's already over!"

I look for the window. Kieran clumsily pulls a yellow-feathered arrow from his quiver, walks to the end of the room and takes aim. "I'll hit him this time."

"Give me an arrow, too," Cassie demands.

I can't let you do that, I think and warn: "It's too dangerous. If it breaks in the fight or you hurt yourself with it, you'll die."

"Better give me an arrow."

"What will you do with it?"

A plan matures within me. "Just give in to me!"

Footsteps. Oloisius approaches the door.

"Quickly! He's coming!"

Kieran pulls another yellow-feathered arrow from his quiver and throws it to me. I catch it and stand behind the door. Cassie goes to Kieran.

"One for all, all for one!"

"These are the Three Musketeers."

"We're better, smarter and braver. The Musketeers didn't have to fight degenerate vampires," Cassie intones, leaving no doubt about her fighting spirit.

I look at Kieran. "Are you okay? Or are you turning into a wolf?"

"I can control myself."

"If you have a problem, say so before the vampire kicks down the door."

"I told you, I'm fine!"

Oloisius seems to be enjoying the game of death. He calls out to us. "Boys, where are you? Are you playing hide and seek with me?"

This time his voice sounds like that of a madman. I'm terrified and can't stop my knees from shaking.

"One, two, three... I'm coming!"

Steps. He stomps hard on purpose. The vampire behaves almost like a cat playing with its prey before killing it. "And the two boys have also called for reinforcements. Little Cassie is with them. Ha, ha, ha."

"Uncle Oloisius?"

"Yes, my little niece."

Wham

A kick against the door and it flies out of the lock and hinge. It lands on the floor with a loud thud. Scared to death, I press myself against the wall. My right fist clenches around the arrow with the camouflaged silver tip.

"I saw the car outside the door. My brother's in the back seat, dead. What happened to him?"

"What do you want from us, Uncle Oloisius?"

Kieran aims at the vampire.

"Put that thing down or I'll..."

Oloisius makes no move. As he speaks the warning, Kieran lets the arrow whirr from the string. It whizzes towards the vampire. He jumps up, does a somersault and comes to a stop right in front of Kieran and Cassie. He grabs the bow and snatches it from the werewolf's hands. The arrow Kieran shot has missed its mark. I am shocked. Even though I've experienced how fast and powerful vampires are, I hadn't expected anything like this.

"You little shit thought you could defeat me? Me, the mighty Oloisius, the guardian of the gate to the vampire world? You dare to challenge me and kill me? You are nothing but weak little creeps! And, my dear Cassie, I will kill you and your father as well. Then my power will grow! It's not him, it's me who's responsible for the people who were killed. But I made it look like he was responsible. I've been blackmailing him ever since. He has to do certain things so that nothing happens to you and your mother.

The vampire laughs loudly and opens his mouth. I'm still standing against the wall. My knuckles are white from gripping the arrow so tightly. I see Oloisius grab Kieran by the shoulders and pull him towards him. I'm afraid my shaky knees will give out, but I gather all my courage. I push myself away from the wall and run to my friends.

"One for all, all for one!" I yell, raising my right arm and ramming the arrow into the vampire's back.

"Ahh... ahhhhhh... ahh!"

The scream is bloodcurdling. I cover my ears. Oloisius turns to me. He lets go of Kieran. The vampire's eyes sparkle yellow, then blood red.

"Ahh! This hellish pain!"

He rattles. Heavy smoke billows from the wound, then from his ears and nose. He collapses. He writhes on the floor and suddenly hisses and bubbles. Hardly anything is recognizable. Everything is filled with corrosive, foul-smelling smoke.

Kieran runs to the skylight and opens it. Plumes of smoke rise to the ceiling, drift toward the window, and disappear into the dark night.

There is only a small pile of ashes on the floor in front of us. Oloisius is dead.

"James! James, you saved my life!" Kieran cheers.

"Me too. I'm still in total shock," Cassie whimpers.

I stare at the pile of ashes. I actually managed to kill a vampire.

I, James Allington, am a vampire slayer.

"You can stop shaking," Kieran laughs, pointing at my still shaking knees.

"Knees shaking or not, you're a hero!" exclaims Cassie, her voice a little firmer. "Tell me, guys, how did all this happen? I mean, we vampires have been living normal lives here in Greenfield for umpteen years and as soon as you move in," she points at me, "our world falls apart and all hell breaks loose.

"Long story," I say.

"It can't be as long as my life. So go ahead and shoot," Cassie says.

"Never mind," I say.

"Nothing matters!"

"Well," I begin, "it wasn't me, it was you who started the mess. It started with all the deaths. Kieran and I were naturally curious and wanted to snoop around the crime scenes. We found this cabin in the woods."

Cassie nods. "The entrance to the vampire tunnels."

"And we also found a contract there."

"What kind of contract?"

"Between Oloisius and Astrigo."

"Astrigo?"

"Yes."

Cassie frowns. "Astrigo was an old vampire. He died a long time ago. Well, we don't live forever either, although we do get a little older than humans."

"Yes, it's been a while since the treaty. That was a good 200 years ago," Kieran interjects.

"And you suspected it and that's why you ran away," I say bluntly to my friend.

"That's right. My instincts drove me away and I couldn't talk to you about it then either."

"That's why you were supposed to die, you discovered the entrance. Uncle Oloisius wanted to eliminate you because of that, I know that. Anyway, he had been behaving abnormally for many years and was becoming more and more dangerous. He was frightening. He was scary for me. But why is my father angry?"

"Was he in cahoots with your uncle?"

"I can't imagine that. I don't think he's one of the renegades. And my uncle just admitted that he blackmailed my father with something. But aside from that, you were both dangerous to all

of us because you discovered the blood camp. And our civilized
life depends on it. Daddy had to make a choice."

"Anyway, I'm going to get a broom and a shovel and get rid
of your uncle."

Less than an hour later, the house is back to normal. Oloisius has found his final resting place. In the trash can. The rain
has stopped and I'm looking forward to a leisurely game of cards
when Cassie stands in front of us and puts her hands on her hips.
"Let's go!"

I look at her, confused. "What do you mean, let's go? Are
you playing?"

"Stupid! My dad is in the Mercedes waiting to be taken to
the camp."

"Oh shit, I completely forgot about him."

"That's why I came here."

"You can have a pair of rubber boots from me, James. What
shoe size?"

"Kieran, you don't think I'm going to get into your cheese
kicks, do you?"

"Then you'll ruin your sneakers. It's muddy in the woods
after that rain."

It takes me about three milliseconds to think and change my
decision. I answer very quickly : "Give me those things. And I
hope, they do not smell like cheese."

Kieran laughs. „I hope they will fit.“

I waddle like a duck and feel like I'm walking on eggs. The
rubber boots are at least two sizes too big for me, but they do the
job.

Cassie opens the driver's door and wants to get in. "I'll sit
up front!" I call and run quickly to the passenger side of the Mercedes. The faster I run, the stranger the squeaking sounds as my
feet slide out of my boots and back in again.

Squeak, squeak, squeak, squeak.

"Wrong! I'm in the front," Kieran replies, starting to laugh out loud. He points at me and yells: "You're running like you shit your pants!"

He holds his stomach and squirms. Cassie looks at me and starts laughing too. I give them both a disdainful look and stop.

"Funny," I say with a straight face. "We've got an unconscious vampire to transport and you're making fun of me."

Then I try to walk normally, which of course doesn't work. *Squeak, plop.*

"Hahahahaha," I hear now from the front and the back. "Oh, lick my ...," I call, making a dismissive gesture with my hand and seconds later I'm infected by laughter.

Kieran shamelessly seizes the opportunity, overtakes me and sits down in the passenger seat.

"Hey, that's my seat!"

"Too late."

"I'm not sitting next to a vampire."

Cassie looks at me. "So you're not sitting in the passenger seat either?"

"That's not what I meant!"

"Trunk?" asks Kieran.

"You guys are so stupid."

Of course I'm sitting in the back, listening to Mr. Anderson snore. His head is on my lap and I don't feel good at all.

"When he wakes up, he likes to be cuddled behind the ears," Cassie giggles and steps on the gas.

"I don't think that's very funny."

"Then sing him a lullaby!"

"Stop making fun of me," I say.

You have to have friends like that, then you don't need enemies.

Of course, they don't stop teasing me. It's only when we park at the edge of the forest that I'm left alone.

Kieran and Cassie grab Mr. Anderson's arms and pull him out of the Mercedes. I take his legs.

"We can make it," I say.

We start walking, but we have to stop every ten meters because the guy is as heavy as two bags of cement. I think about asking Kieran to switch places with me, but since it's pitch black and I can see next to nothing, I decide to stay put.

After what feels like two hours, we arrive at the blood warehouse. Cassie opens the trapdoor. "You go first," she says.

"Why?"

"Because it's easier."

I bite the bullet and take the stairs first. It is easier than I thought, and I have to admit that Cassie was right.

We look at Mr. Anderson and are satisfied. Cassie writes a few more lines on a piece of paper and puts it next to her father.

"What does it say?"

"That he should come to his senses and that everything is okay. And that he should talk to me and Mom before he does anything stupid. Oh, and that I turned Uncle Oloisius into dust."

"That was me!"

"I think it's better that my dad thinks it was me."

"Agreed," Kieran and I say at the same time.

The rest of the evening goes by quickly. Cassie drops us off at Kieran's. We're both dead tired and instead of playing on the sofa we fall into our beds. We look at the clock. It is almost one o'clock at night.

A few last thoughts go through my head.

I really have to see Devon again. First of all, I've removed his embarrassment, shall we say? Second, I'd like to find out some other things from him. Like how Oloisius knew Kieran and I were in the hut. Also, Devon's knowledge might be helpful in lifting the curse from Riley.

My thoughts turn to school.

Tomorrow I'll be really exhausted at school, I think, and then I'll be gone.

https://pixabay.com/de/service/license-summary/

ai-generated-8565191_1280

Chapter Seven

I immediately put yesterday's plan into action. I put my school bag in the corner, changed my clothes and quickly stuffed a piece of toast into my mouth. Salami, cheese, olives and ketchup. My favorite when I'm in a hurry or don't know what to eat. I also enjoy a sip of Diet Coke.

Kieran's parents are home by now. So of course he's home and I have to go through my plan alone. I deliberately don't take Cassie and Riley with me. I haven't told them about Devon yet.

That would be too much information at once, I think. *They would never understand.*

As soon as the last bite of toast is in my mouth, I slip on my shoes and leave the house. I grab my mountain bike and ride into the woods. I feel the coolness of the trees and smell the uniqueness of the forest in early fall. The colorful leaves enchant the landscape. I don't stop, I ride almost to the cabin. I push the last few meters and park my bike in the bushes just off the trail.

Not everyone needs to see my bike. After all, Mr. Anderson just comes along and wants to take revenge on me. No thanks. Better be careful.

I watch my target for a good minute, then I head for the little wood house. As I stand in front of the door, I feel queasy. I think about turning around and running away. My idea is daring and very dangerous anyway.

Coward!

I overcame my fear and entered the hut. It still smells old and stale. I shut the door behind me. If Anderson or anyone else comes by, everything must look normal from the outside.

My eyes quickly get used to the diffuse light. I look around and use my cell phone light as well. The cabin has never seemed so mysterious as it does now.

Don't think about it! Do your thing and get out as soon as possible, I admonish myself.

The contract between Astrigo and Oloisius lies on the desk. I walk over and pick it up. Suddenly it catches fire. I drop it as if by reflex. Within two seconds, the old parchment paper was completely reduced to ashes. Startled, I run to the door. I stop and turn around. The ashes are scattered all over the desk and the floor. My hand is on the doorknob.

Don't run, James. Think about it.

I try to stay cool. It occurs to me that Oloisius has turned to ashes, so it is possible that the contract will turn to ashes as well. The vampire died by my hand. When I picked up the contract, it caught fire. It all sounds a bit silly, but it would be a logical explanation for me. I let go of the doorknob and walk back to the desk. I lean against it and push it aside. The hatch is free. I just have to open it.

I remain calm and take another look around the cabin. Suddenly my attention is drawn to two books. They were on the shelf, but they were the only ones in the row. There are more above and below, but these two are separated from all the others. I approached them. One of these books is quite thick and has a red cover, the other is much thinner and bound in brown leather.

I remember Kieran leafing through the thick one. I open them both and realize to my horror that one work is written in handwriting, quite illegible to me, bound into a book and the other book is printed in an old font and language I don't know. It could be German or something else European. I put the books back and go back to the hatch. Now I push the latch aside and open it. Just when I thought the hut smelled of stale air, I am immediately reminded that the tunnel corridors stink much worse.

I take a deep breath before descending. I get my bearings, look at the map app on my phone, and find the right path. The flashlight app helps me find my way.

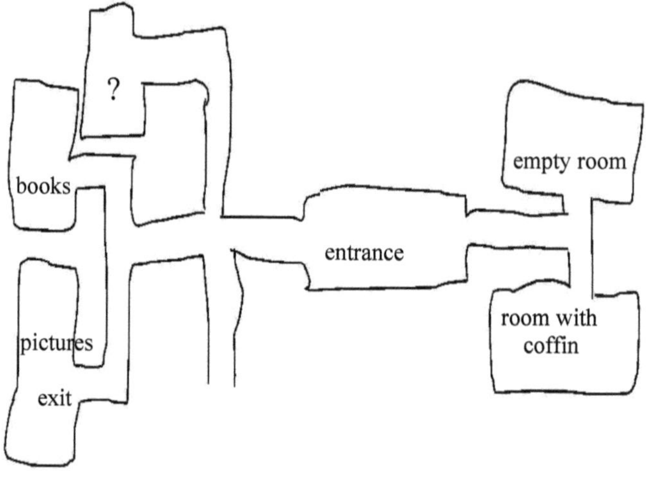

I think Devon is in the room with the coffin, so I go there purposefully. Only now do I notice the silence in the tunnels. There is really nothing to be heard here. Everything seems so unworldly. I am overcome by a kind of fear. It's that feeling you get when you're watching a horror movie and you're afraid to go to the bathroom alone. Or when you get something out of the basement and you think you're being watched or something is reaching for you. Just a really stupid and creepy feeling.

I wonder if I'm alone with Devon here in the tunnel system or if there are more vampires around. After the motto: First shopping in the blood store and then a whole afternoon stroll through the tunnel system. An idyll for vampires.

Nonsense. Stop thinking so much, James. Just go to Devon.

The crossroads is coming. With the help of my drawing app, I make the right turn. I just can't stop thinking.

What if it was Devon who betrayed me to Oloisius? I'm down here alone with him. If it was him, he'll probably suck me dry.

Goosebumps. I feel more and more uncomfortable. Today it seems to me that the air down here is particularly foul and stuffy. I wonder if I should turn back.

I can still run away.

I dismiss the thought and keep walking. After only a few steps I almost freeze. Someone calls from behind me.

"Oloisius, are you here? You idiot left the hatch open again!"

My heart skips a beat. I run faster.

Damn it, there's someone else!

Whoever it is, I can rule one out: Anderson. It wasn't his voice. I know it only too well now.

I think feverishly about who the stranger could be. Then I remember I've seen a third vampire.

It must be him. He's probably in the tunnel by now. I have to hide. But where?

The decision whether I can trust Devon or not is taken away from me at this moment. The only place I can hide from this guy is in the coffin in Devon's room.

I've been in there before, so I can do it again. I run and try to be as quiet as I can. I check my phone as I run. It's not far now. The cone of light from my phone light sweeps over the wall. Then it hits a door. I am there. My pulse is racing, my heart is pounding. I open the door, rush into the room and close it behind me. I am relieved. The coffin is in front of me.

"Devon, are you here?" I whisper excitedly.

My chest rises and falls quickly. No answer. I walk over to the coffin and slowly push the lid aside. Just far enough so it doesn't fall off and I can crawl inside. The coffin is empty. I climb inside and push the lid back. The confinement almost drives me crazy. I try to breathe shallowly, which is not easy for me. I am afraid. The feeling of helplessness increased when I heard the squeaking and creaking of the door.

He enters the room.

My body is shaking.

If only I had brought an arrow like that. But I'm rarely stupid.

I listen intently, trying to detect if the vampire enters the room and moves around. I hear nothing.

Is he standing by the coffin? Is he still in the room?

I can't estimate the time. I just lie there and wait. Nothing happens. The moment I think about checking my cell phone, I am scared to death. The vampire knocks on the coffin.

"Devon? You can come out!"

This is my certain death. When I open the coffin, he grabs me, and when he opens the coffin, he grabs me too. Goodbye world, goodbye life! It was beautiful and short.

I clench my hands. I won't die without a fight. I'm preparing for the final battle when I feel movement. Expecting the lid to be pushed aside, I close in on my life. But except for a jolt, nothing happens.

Strange. What's happening? Has the coffin been pushed aside?

My thoughts turn to the coffin.

What does he like?

I hear a second voice. It's Devon's. Suddenly I realize that the coffin stands on a grave and serves as a distraction. So Devon isn't living in this coffin, he's living *under* it.

Wow, this is my chance to live on after all.

I can hear them talking.

"Here, I brought you your blood ration." "Thank you."

"Was Oloisius here?"

"No."

"Hm, he left the trap door in the hut open. That's very unusual."

"Maybe something came up. Or maybe he's just confused. He's been acting a little strange lately anyway."

"Shut up and don't talk so disparagingly about the Keeper of the Tunnel!"

"That's all right."

"See you tomorrow."

I hear footsteps and the door creaking again. I wait a little longer, then call out: "Devon! Devon, can you hear me?"

"Sure. I know you're in the coffin. You can come out. It's gone."

I try to open the lid and find it's not so easy to lie down. "Man, this is hard. Give me a hand!"

It's no problem for Devon and he pushes the coffin lid aside with ease. "I thought it was you when Jackson said the hatch was open."

"I hope you're full," I say, pointing to the empty bottle Devon is holding.

He laughs. "That's enough, and besides, I belong to the generation of vampires who never drank human blood."

I climb out of the coffin. "That was close."

"In the coffin?"

"That too, but I mean because of this Jackson. I wanted to see you," I answer.

"Why is that?" he asks.

I climb out of the coffin. "Because I want to know how Oloisius knew my buddy Kieran and I were in the cabin."

Devon ponders. "If you were in that cabin a week ago and you're still alive, something's wrong."

"What do you know about it?"

"Take it easy, pal. It's easy to explain about Oloisius. He's set up game cameras around the cabin and checks them every day. If you've entered the hut, he'll know."

"Why didn't you tell me that the other day?"

"Because he told me four days ago. And unfortunately, I can't get out of here. I don't have a Tembolus Stone. How could I have warned you?"

"What thing?"

"Tembolus Stone. They are the protective stones of vampires."

"Thanks for the information. At least now I know what these things are called."

Devon's argument makes sense to me. I continue to trust him.

"Is he hunting you? He has to kill you."

"As you can see, I'm still alive."

"You have to watch out for him. Oloisius is not to be trifled with. He'll be very angry that he didn't manage to kill you in time. Or is your buddy dead?"

"No. Kieran is alive and well."

Devon scratches his head. "You're hiding something from me, aren't you?"

"Oloisius is in vampire heaven, if there is such a thing."

"He's what?"

"I turned him to dust. He's dead, no longer exists. *Puff* did it, and he crumbled into dust and ended up in the trash," I explain, first making a circular motion with my arms, then imitating the sweeping motion of a shovel and broom, and finishing with a lid up and in gesture.

"Oh dear, vampire poop and a thousand gallons of blood, that's good news! You'll have to tell me more about that," he exclaims in amazement.

I tell him in detail what happened, but hurry up and end the story: "And now your tormentor is dead and you can get out of here."

"If I had a Tembolus stone, I could. Oloisius smashed my stone. If I don't get a replacement, I'll be trapped here in this tunnel system for the rest of my life."

"I can help you. Where can I get these things?"

"I know two places. One is in Mexico. There is a small town called ..."

"Stop!" I raise my hand. "Mexico is a few thousand miles from here. I can't get there. Where is the second place?"

"In Vermont, about 90 miles from here. Right between Killington and Rutland in a wooded area. There's a hunting lodge there. It's on the private property of a wealthy vampire count and is safe from curious visitors. If you go 200 paces north from this hut, you will see a large old red oak surrounded by maple trees. You can't miss it. There is a cellar sunk into the ground. Similar to the one where our blood supplies are stored. The trapdoor is ten paces from the oak. The Tembolus Stones have been stored down there for many decades."

"And how am I supposed to get there?" I ask, thinking about it. "The camp will be guarded. Are there vampires there or are there any barriers or traps?"

"I don't know exactly. Just go and have a look. You are smart. You'll think of something if you can't get there easily."

I think about it. "Okay. I promised to help you, so I'll go and have a look. I could pretend that I'm on a weekend trip with my friends. But I'll tell you one thing right now. If it's life-threatening to organize one of those stones for you, then I'm out of here."

"Sounds fair!"

"And you really think I can just go over there and get a rock?"

Devon pushes around a bit. "Well, you shouldn't get caught right away. Otherwise, the vampires there might..."

"I don't want to know."

"Will you do it for me?"

I take a deep breath. "Yes. I'm a man of my word."

"If you can do this, I'll be your friend forever!"

I laugh. "Hahaha, I won't live as long as a normal person. But it's enough for me if you don't suck me dry and protect me from other hungry vampires."

"You have my word on that, James."

Devon offers me his hand. I clap my hand. Then he gives me the exact coordinates of the cabin in Vermont. I write them down in the memo on my phone.

"Okay, I'll find the thing with this. I'll get back to you."

He raises his hand in a goodbye salute. I turn and walk a-way.

Devon walks with me a few feet to the exit. I walk the last few feet alone. Jackson has closed the hatch, of course. I hope he didn't push the desk onto it, climb the stairs and push against the trapdoor. It opens easily. I look through it, see no one and leave the tunnel. Then I look through the window. The air is clear, I can go. I have an uneasy feeling until I reach the edge of the forest. Only when I get on my bike and start pedaling do I feel safe again.

My plan matures on the way home. I hurry home and arrive without incident. Before I even enter the house, I pull out my cell phone and start chatting with Kieran. He's online and ans-wers right away.

Me: Hi.
Kieran: Hi.
Me: What are you doing?
Kieran: Playing, you?
Me: Nothing, I just came home. I was just clearing some-thing up with Oloisius.
Kieran: What?
Me: How did he know about us, about going into the hut.
Kieran: Well?
Me: Cameras.
Kieran: Awesome, dude. Where did you hear that?
Me: From Devon.
Kieran: The tunnel vampire?
Me: Right.

Kieran: What's the next step?

Me: We have to get a stone like this for Devon.

Kieran: What kind of stone?

Me: Don't ask such a stupid question, just the vampire stone.

Kieran: Oh, and where?

Me: Either in Mexico or Vermont.

Kieran: Are you kidding me?

Me: Nope.

Kieran: When are we actually going to do this with the coins?

Me: As soon as possible, but first we need the stone for Devon. I wanted to ask you if you could help me.

Kieran: Get a stone for a vampire? Dude, that's mega rad.

Me: I need to get Devon a stone so he can see the light of day. He can still be very useful to us, he's a good buddy. Will you help me?

Kieran: Nope.

Me: Come on.

Kieran: Why should I?

Me: Because you're my buddy.

Kieran: That doesn't mean I have to help you with everything.

Me: Yeah.

Kieran: Dude, do it yourself.

I send the turd emoji with eyes.

Kieran: Wait.

Me: What else is there?

Kieran: Sure, I'll help you, I was just kidding.

Me: Really?

Kieran: Yeah, just tell me when and where.

Me: Great, we'll do it this weekend. Maybe Riley and Cassie will come too.

Kieran: Cool, see you at school tomorrow.

Me: Bye.

Finally I send the power upper arm and a grin - the smiley face.

If anyone is brilliant at organizing classes, it's our music teacher. The guy is really relaxed and walks around like a colorful peacock. There are students who make bets on his clothes. You can bet on the color of his shirt, the style of his pants, and again on the length. Sometimes he comes with a colorful shirt, jeans and suspenders, then again with a plaid long-sleeved shirt but three-quarter pants. Either way, Mr. Mandon's outfit takes some getting used to.

The shirt faction loses today. He is wearing a sweater. Whoever chose *pink* scores points. Mr. Mandon also wears brown corduroy pants, green striped socks and yellow sneakers. This man is wonderful.

At first I smiled at him and asked Kieran if he was gay because he looks so gay. But my buddy didn't have to give me an answer. Nobody knows anything about Mandon's private life.

Over time, I came to admire him. Mandon just does his thing. And he's mega cool at it. He also plays seven instruments and has a voice that can sing anything from hard rock to soul. I like him.

We have to stand up at the beginning of every class. He loves to be greeted the old-fashioned way. After we sing, "Good morning, Mr. Mandon," he grins cheerfully.

"Thank you. Let's get started. I was inspired by a radio song on the drive here today. Why don't you get the songbooks out of the back?"

The books have seen better days. They look old and sometimes a page is missing. It is also possible that it has been torn out to serve as a lyric sheet at some campfire.

"Please turn to page 102," the music teacher asks, grabs an electric guitar, plugs it in and starts plucking the strings. I recognize the tune immediately. It's *Yesterday* by *the Beatles*.

I don't really like the band. Somehow the music is just outdated. I can't imagine how anyone could be into that kind of music anymore.

What were their names? John Lennon, Paul McCartney, ... I can't remember the other two. Why would I know them? It's been half a century since they were at the height of their careers.

The warbling sounds bland. No wonder. Only the girls sing. And only some of them.

"What's the matter with you?" shouts Mr. Mandon. "Don't you like the sound?"

Suddenly he starts to play a reggae rhythm. We look at each other in amazement. Then he suddenly continues singing in reggae style.

"Hey, that sounds *weird*. Kind of weird," says Kieran and claps along.

Mandon changes the sound again. "Or how about hard rock? But then I'd like to hear the boys' voices," says the teacher and lets loose a great riff. He conjures a great sound from the electric guitar and screams the lyrics better than any living hard rock singer.

And that's how he gets us. We sing and scream various Beatles songs for an hour and almost miss the gong.

"And in the next hour, I want you to tell me all the top ten hits of *the Fab Four*, as the Beatles were also known," he says in a good mood.

During the break, Kieran, Cassie, Riley and I hang out together. We finally agree to meet at Luigi's for ice cream and talk about our next steps. I want to use this opportunity to tell them about Devon and the location of the Tembolus Stones. I secretly hope that Cassie and Riley will come with us. It could be very useful for us to have the two vampires with us.

On my way home I notice a dark Mercedes. It drives slowly behind me the whole time. I get suspicious and take a shortcut. I cycle against the traffic into a one-way street and turn around to see what the Mercedes driver is doing. He kept going. I'm pretty sure it was Mr. Anderson's car. Cassie didn't talk at school about whether her father was still at the blood camp or had come home.

Never mind. He's gone.

Anyway, when I get home, I text Kieran on WhatsApp and tell him about the experience.

Kieran: Take it easy, dude. We'll ask Cassie about it later. Maybe she can tell us something.
Me: We will, but be careful.
Kieran: Always.
Me: See you later, dude.

Kieran shuts off. Now he knows. That calms me down a bit, but I'm still a bit scared. After all, Mr. Anderson tried to kill us. I'd be surprised if he doesn't want to now.

Will Cassie be able to talk to him and change his mind?

I really hope so. At this moment I realize that I really need a weapon against vampires. I'm determined to discuss everything with Luigi tonight. Cassie also has to come clean and tell us what she knows.

My parents come home and we sit down to eat. We have sandwiches. I make myself a mega piece. I only toast one side of the bread at a time. Then I put some ketchup and mustard on it and garnish it with slices of pickle and fried onions. Then I add salami and cheese. I put jalapenos on top and close the sandwich. It is delicious!

Mom and Dad talk about work. Dad avoids talking about the current investigation, so I find the conversation very boring. I'm not interested in whether Mrs. Goldman's cat climbed a tree and was too stupid to get back down, or whether fat Mr. Sandermark has broken the 250-pound mark. So I wolf down my sandwich, check my watch, and get up.

"Do you have any plans?" asks Dad.

"I'm meeting the others at Luigi's for ice cream."

"That's how you make friends," Mom grins.

"Different people live here than in the cow town."

Dad laughs.

The doorbell rings.

"Who could it be? Someone from the sheriff's office?"

"I don't know, honey," Dad answers and starts to get up.

"I'll get it," Mom says.

I put on another T-shirt and start up the stairs when Mom opens the door.

I recognize two men. They look like a cross between Jehovah's Witnesses and the Blues Brothers. Black suits, sunglasses, white shirts. One is really burly, almost six feet tall, and the other is much shorter, but very broad-shouldered. They both smile. I'm just waiting for them to say whether we believe in God and know how to read the Bible correctly, when the big one introduces himself.

"We apologize for our unannounced appearance. Sheriff Allington lives here, doesn't he?"

"Yes, that's my husband."

"My name is David Forster and this is my colleague Michael Goog. We are vampire hunters from San Francisco. And when we heard from the media that bloodless corpses were being found here, we immediately traveled here."

Dad goes to the door.

"I'm Sheriff Allington," he introduces himself and looks at the boys, who start the whole game over and introduce themselves for the second time.

"Well, well, vampire hunters," Dad says smugly.

"Yes, sir, may we come in? We'd like to ask you some questions."

"No."

"But we could..." the big one starts to object when Dad cuts him off.

"*I'm* in charge of the investigation. If anyone wants access to the files, it has to be either the prosecutor's office or the FBI. And the latter only if they are investigating in accordance with the law. Since neither of you is one or the other party, I will not speak to you. Goodbye, gentlemen."

The boy tries again. "Sheriff Allington, we believe that you and the people of Greenfield are in great danger. Vampires are living among us. We'd like to explain this to you."

Father's look becomes more serious. "Goodbye," he says, slamming the door in their faces.

"Such weirdos," he adds, going back into the kitchen with Mom.

I was horrified to hear the news that there were vampire hunters in Greenfield.

We have to be really careful, I think, and get dressed.

That evening at Luigi's, Riley and Kieran immediately notice that something is wrong.

"Babe, what's wrong?" Riley asks bluntly.

"Dude, don't hang your head like that," Kieran says, getting all wide-eyed as Luigi brings our sundaes over.

"Two great couples. Bella!" he says, putting the best ice cream in the world on the table with a big grin.

"So, guys," I start, "just so you all know what I know, I'll tell you the story from the beginning."

"Just make sure your ice cream doesn't get cold," Kieran jokes.

Cassie laughs like a fool and slaps her thigh.

"Very funny," I reply and demonstratively shove a fat-filled spoonful of ice cream with a dollop of cream into my mouth. A gigantic taste spreads. For a split second, I float in ice cream heaven.

"Listen."

Everyone's ears perk up as I begin my story.

About ten minutes later I finish, "And that's why I'm asking you to help me get a Tembolus Stone for Devon."

Cassie and Riley look at each other in amazement, then at Kieran, and finally at me.

"Oh yeah, before I forget..." I add, telling him about the two vampire hunters.

Horrified looks.

"That too!"

"Those who hunt vampires also hunt werewolves. I know this type of headhunter from various stories," Kieran whispers.

Riley clears his throat. "So we have a few problems to solve. First, we have to find the coins, get them and put them on the character at the end within the allotted time to avert the curse from my family. Then we have Cassie's father breathing down our necks. Then we have Cassie's father breathing down our necks who still wants to kill Kieran and James and may be involved in the sinister murders. Next we have to get a Tembolus Stone for Devon. This is not as easy as he told you, but there are some risks involved. And last but not least, there are two vampire hunters named David Forster and Michael Goog."

Kieran scratches the back of his head, Cassie exhales loudly and I nod. "Yep, baby, it's the same."

"We're so dead!"

"Riley, what the hell are you talking about?"

"It's true. Watch this."

Cassie sits down. Kieran audibly slurps the last of the melted ice cream with the straw, whereupon Cassie elbows him in the side.

"It's dangerous as hell to get the coins to break Hostang's curse."

"Wizard or not, we can do it. We're one human, one werewolf, and two vampires. If Devon joins us, even three." "That's the next problem. Devon."

"Do you know him personally? He claims to be Oloisius' stepson."

Cassie cuts in. "No, I don't know him personally, only from stories. But he's not stuck in the tunnel for nothing. Oloisius told me that Devon was one of the first rebels in Greenfield. If you get him a Tembolus Stone, he'll start hunting people."

I get goose bumps. "Slow down a bit. He could have killed me and drained me a long time ago."

"He needs you. He can't get out of his prison without a rock," Riley confirms.

"Yes, during the day. But what does he do at night?"

"That's what the gatekeeper is for. He has to be careful. There are only two ways in and out of the tunnel. One is the exit right inside the hut, and the other is the escape route through the air shaft - where you came out the first time," Cassie explained. "I learned that from my dad once."

"Guarding is fine, but why doesn't he just go through the shaft if the hut is guarded?"

"There are silver, consecrated crosses nailed to the end. They are all around the tunnel exit. It's like an invisible prison wall. This work was done by humans at that time. No vampire would risk crawling through it voluntarily. And most importantly, when he goes out, he has to remember the way back. That's not so easy."

"Who is this Devon anyway?" Kieran wants to know.

Cassie comes closer and we put our heads together. "Devon is not Oloisius' stepson, but the third brother. He, my dad and Oloisius are brothers."

"I don't understand. If your father and Oloisius are involved in the murders and are also among the revolutionaries who want to go manhunting again, why are they holding Devon prisoner?"

"I don't think my father is a revolutionary. He is just trying to protect his family. As for Devon, he is said to be a hothead and therefore very dangerous. He knows no mercy and endangers the whole vampire world with his behavior. He was the one who came close to starting another war between werewolves and vampires. He had to be locked up."

"Why didn't the two older brothers kill him?" I ask.

Kieran frowns. "Maybe sibling love?"

"Something like that."

"I was a fool to trust him."

"You were very lucky, sweetheart," Riley says, squeezing my hand.

"Does Devon know you know all this?"

Riley and Cassie look at each other and shrug. "Probably, but it's not certain."

"What's the problem?" asks Kieran. "Devon is perfectly safe down there. He can't be a threat to us."

"Oh yes, he is."

The young werewolf looks at Cassie. "Why is that?"

"Because he can break out at night! In less than five hours it could cause chaos the likes of which the world has never seen."

"Kiss my ass! He's completely insane," Kieran groans. "This is all getting to be too much for me. The bloody curse, your villainous uncle, the murders in Greenfield. I'm afraid we're not going to get a handle on it all," Riley breathes. Tears shoot into her eyes.

"Stop it! I may be a werewolf, but I can't see the curse."

"Honey," I squeeze her hand. "I have an idea."

Hope arises.

"An idea?"

"Yes, and it's a really good idea."

"Let's hear it!"

"Devon wants me to get him a Tembolus Stone."

"Yeah, so?"

"I saw a billboard the other day. It's the Mineraly Days and an exhibit in Greenfield right now."

Riley shifts nervously. "Come on, don't make me pull this out of my butt!"

"When I was researching vampire stones on the Internet, I noticed a lot of mineral stones that look exactly like this one. What if we got an ineffective replacement stone? Devon won't recognize it in the darkness of the tunnel and cave system if I gave him a fake Tembolus stone."

Cassie's eyes widen. "You're trying to plant a fake rock on Devon?"

"It's worth a try."

Kieran grins broadly. "And when he goes out in the daylight, it goes *poof* and he's gone."

"It's not that simple," Riley interjects.

When Kieran then makes his famous scratching motion with the back of his head, I'm immediately reminded of a small dog scratching its ear with its back paw.

"You think he'll know the difference?"

"He'll smell the difference."

"Huh?"

"The magic stones have an unusual smell. They smell of something, let's say, *forbidden*."

"Riley's right," Cassie says.

"Crap!" I curse.

"What if we make the stone smell like something forbidden?" Kieran suggests.

We look at him. "How?" comes almost in chorus.

"Well," he says, scratching himself again, "church and holy water is probably *too forbidden*, isn't it?" he asks, overemphasizing the word.

"That's not possible."

"But what if we rolled the mineral stone in sacred ground?" I thought of the old Indian burial ground. There's something sacred about it, and yet not too bad, hm, in terms of weaponry, it should be close to holy water, only not as bad. Just a weak dose."

Cassie and Riley look at each other questioningly, then nod in agreement.

"That might work."

I pull my phone out of my pocket and start surfing the net. "The mineral show closes in 30 minutes."

"Where do we have to go?"

"To the museum of our industrial heritage."

"And after that?"

"Across the Connecticut River to the old Indian cemetery," says Kieran.

"We'll never make it on the bikes," Riley interjects.

"But with the taxi."

We pay and step out of the restaurant. As I desperately search for a cab app, swiping frantically at the screen of my smartphone, Kieran snaps his fingers and yells: "Here!" I lift my head to see him waving to a passing taxi. Next thing I know, the brake lights are on, then the tail lights, and in no time a taxi pulls up beside us. We get in.

"To the Museum of Our Industrial Heritage," Kieran says.

The driver nods and answers politely: "Okay, sir." He waits until we are all buckled in, drives off and turns on the taximeter.

"Are we going to make it?" Cassie asks, looking at her watch.

"The exhibition is closing soon," the taxi driver interjects: "Do you still want to go in?"

I notice his Spanish accent and look at him. He's an old Mexican. He grins at me. I see some gaps in his teeth. His hair has long since changed from its original jet black to a silvery gray.

"We just need to get a rock there fast. Can you drive a little faster so we can get there?"

"I can do that."

"And would you wait for us?"

"Where do you have to go after that, hijos?"

"Hijos?"

"That's Spanish for children," he grins.

"To the old Indian cemetery."

The grin disappears from his face. His eyes are no longer smiling and he stares silently down the road.

"Are you waiting?" Riley asks.

Silence.

"He suspects something, is he one of you?" Kieran whispers into Cassie's ear.

She shakes her head. "I'd know right away."

"He's not a werewolf either."

From now on, there is an icy silence in the cab. No one speaks. Ten minutes later the Mexican stops. "Here we are."

"Are you waiting?" Cassie repeats.

"What are you doing there?" he points questioningly at the museum. I take a deep breath. "We ... just want to do some quick shopping there, then stop at the Indian cemetery and then back to Luigi's ice cream shop. Could you wait, please?"

"Something is wrong here, my friend. I can smell trouble a hundred miles away."

The others have gotten out and are calling me. "James. Come on, come on!"

"Will you wait, please?" I ask again.

The Mexican takes a deep breath. "You're normal, the others aren't. They are..." he doesn't say it.

"What do you mean?"

"I'm old, my boy. I've been through a lot."

"James, where are you?"

Annoyed, I turn around. "You get the rock, I'll stop the driver here, okay?"

"Yes, good!"

My friends run into the museum.

"What are they?" I want to follow up on the Mexican's statement and point to my friends who have just entered the building.

"They're with the others."

I nod. "I don't know what you mean."

"You know very well, and so do I. I'm married to one of them."

That makes me salivate.

Is that good news or bad news? I wonder silently and add, "Interesting."

"Do you know the story of old Jack Blood?" "Never heard of him. Was he a pirate?"

The cab driver laughs. "Haha, pirate? Well, he swam a sea too, but it was a sea of blood. Jack Blood was and is the most feared vampire in all of North America. One person still disappears every day because of him. He is said to drain every last drop of blood from his victims and has been doing so for hundreds of years. He moves from town to town and country to country. He owns the continent. Only one of his many victims has ever been found. And that was right here in Greenfield on October 13, 1928. That was the last time he was in town. The bloodless body was discovered by the side of the road, right next to the Connecticut River. Just where Montague City Rd crosses a bridge over the river. That's the way we have to go to the cemetery. It all happened the day I was born. For my fiftieth birthday I got a newspaper from that time. It says everything. When they went to bury the body, it was gone. They believed in body snatchers."

The Mexican coughs.

"I'm almost 100 years old now."

"You're making fun of me."

"No. My wife had to give me a blood transfusion once. The doctor was one of them ... You know," he winks, "since then I've aged more slowly. She's afraid I'm going to die, but one day I will."

"What happened to James Blood?"

"His name is Jack Blood."

"Yes, that's right. Jack Blood."

"I once tried to pick up his trail and collect the missing persons cases, but it's endless. You might as well count the grains of sand on the seashore."

"Will you drive us to the cemetery?"

"I'll drive you, but only because my gut tells me you're doing the right thing. I can feel the change in Greenfield. I read about the murders and I suspect that Jack Blood is here again. If someone else is responsible, so much the worse. There'll be more crazy vampires."

"Why don't you tell the sheriff?"

"Because no one would believe me."

"And why should I believe you?"

"Because you, like me, are with one of them. I saw it in my rearview mirror. You were holding hands. I'm old, but I'm not blind."

"So you're driving us?"

"Yes. And I'll give you another hint."

"What's that?"

"Jack Blood always eats at the same place. If he drained his victim at the bridge over the Connecticut River umpteen years ago, he will eat his future gruesome meals there as well."

"And how can I recognize this vampire tyrant?"

"Don't take it lightly, boy. Call him by his name and be on your guard. Jack Blood is a handsome figure. He is said to be exactly 190 centimeters tall and always wears black suits. He never travels alone. Blood always has a servant with him. On his right hand he wears the signet ring of his European guild. On his left ear is an earring. Simple, made of gold. In addition, his entire right arm is or was tattooed."

The others return. The Mexican reaches into his briefcase and pulls out a small metal flask. It looks like a miniature hip flask. "Here, put this in your pocket. It's very special holy water. It comes from Europe. More specifically, from the home of vampires. It is extraordinarily effective and you will need such a remedy to save your life one day."

I take the bottle and put it in my pocket. "Thank you very much." The passenger side door opens and Kieran gets in. "Old buddy, it might be dusty in there. Mineral collectors are more boring than synchronized swimmers!"

The girls squeeze into the backseat with me.

"We got it," grins Cassie.

"Just three dollars," Riley says, opening a small paper bag.

I see a mineral that actually looks a lot like the Tembolus stone.

"To the cemetery, amigo!"

The Mexican starts the Chevrolet and turns around. "We'll be there in half an hour."

As we cross the river, he points to the right. "That's where I told you before."

I look around and can't see anything out of the ordinary. We cross the Connecticut River and finally arrive at the Indian cemetery.

"You have to do that," Riley nudges me.

I don't hesitate long, take the paper bag and go. The cemetery looks like an old field. A half-ruined wall separates it from the surrounding area. I entered the area and felt a little uncomfortable. I don't go far and kneel down right between the first two graves. I took the stone from the bag and pressed it firmly into the ground. Then I shovel dirt over it, pull it out again with my fingers, and when I hear the call of an owl and the crowing of a raven, I start to run.   There it is again, that feeling of a hand reaching out to grab you from behind. I'm glad I chose a grave right next to the entrance and breathe a sigh of relief when I'm back in the back left of the cab.

My new friend is winking at me. I can see it in his rearview mirror. "All right, amigo?"

"All right," I reply.

"Please take us back to Luigi's," Kieran says, staring at the meter. "Guys, the meter is already at 17 dollars. I've still got three or four dollars in my pocket. How about you guys?"

The Mexican turns off the meter. "Don't thank me. Just give me a dollar each, then I'll have my gas money and the rest is on the house."

"Wow, you're nice," Riley says happily.

"You should do one good deed a day, my wife Jodie always says. And that's what I did."

Back at Luigi's, we say goodbye to the cab driver and thank him for the almost free ride. "Take care, kids."

We slam the doors, hear the hum of the Chevrolet and it's gone.

"Nice guy."

"Yeah, all right."

"What did you tell him when we bought the rock?" asks Cassie.

"Oh, nothing really. We talked about this and that," I fib. Explaining is too complicated for me right now. The girls get on their bikes. "I'll see you tomorrow. We'll figure out what to do next."

Riley gives me a kiss on the hand, Cassie waves.

As Kieran and I enjoy the setting sun and the balmy Indian summer temperatures, I let him in and tell him about Jack Blood, whose gruesome story is as blood-red as the autumn leaves on the trees in New England. Finally we say goodbye.

At home, I make ham and cheese toast and retire to my room. I don't feel like watching TV with my parents. Too much has happened and I need to think. I want to work on my plan and not make any mistakes when I hand over the stone to Devon.

It's getting dark. I turn on the light and pull down the shade.

"What's that?" I say softly to myself.

There is a stain on the window pane.

Has someone smeared something on the outside?

I look closer and see that the stain is on the inside of the window.

A dark spot.

I take a paper handkerchief from my pocket and wipe it. Then I get scared.

Blood!

Thoughts race through my mind. I reach into the other pocket. I pull out the small bottle the Mexican gave me. It's silver, and there's an emblem and some characters on the front. They resemble the runes of the Vikings or ancient Germanic tribes. Feeling a little safer, I look around my room.

Has anyone been here? Where did the blood come from?

The thought of someone else in the house gives me goosebumps again. Fear creeps up and runs through my body. My right knee starts to shake and I grip the bottle in my hand so tightly that the white of my fist knuckles starts to show. I'm on the verge of telling my parents everything.

Not a good idea. They'd think I'm crazy and that I'm only telling them this because the two vampire hunters were here today.

I wipe the stain away, look at the window and see a small lever mark and some wood splinters sticking out. This is where the guy came in and where he hurt himself, I realize. I think about telling my dad. He would call a deputy and have a burglary reported. But there was no break-in here, just snooping.

Who would be interested in finding something here?

I immediately get the idea that it could have been the two vampire hunters. Maybe they wanted to get their hands on my father's documents about the murders.

Yes, I say to myself, *that is a plausible explanation.* I check everything once more and walk through the house unobtrusively. Everything is in perfect order.

The blood wasn't too old either. I guess he wanted to come in when it got dark. But then apparently my parents came home and the burglar fled.

Yes, I'm sure that's what happened, I decide, I'm going to wash up and go to bed.

https://pixabay.com/de/service/license-summary/

ai-generated-7801493_1280

Chapter Eight

The next morning, I deliberately lock my window and place a few cloves of garlic on the windowsill as a precaution. If the burglar really was a vampire, he won't like it if he does it again. And if it was one of the human vampire hunters and he tries it again, my father will catch him sooner or later.

I decide to scare the hell out of the guy, and search my Halloween box for the real-looking Bird Spinner dummy. I grab one of its eight legs, pull it out of the plunger, and am satisfied. I tie the spider to the window so that it will fly down when the window is opened. I secretly laugh at the thought of a burglar falling backwards over the roof, frightened by the spider's smile. I look at my work with satisfaction and walk to school with a calm heart.

Classes go on as usual. During the big lunch break I meet up with Riley. Cassie hangs out with the cheerleaders and Kieran with the boys from the football team. They have to talk about tactics for the next game.

That's fine with me, because it means I can flirt with Riley and make out a little without being annoyed by stupid comments.

"Come on, let's go to the cafeteria," my friend suggests.

Holding hands, we walk through the school building. I see three guys standing in front of the cafeteria entrance. Their names are Toby, Harry and Luke. Three parade assholes who feel very much part of the clique and can't open their mouths on their own. They go to a parallel class and are generally quite unpopular.

"Oh la la, who have we got here?" asks Toby, who really makes a fuss when he sees us coming.

"Kiss, kiss," mimics fat Harry, smacking his lips.

"The little sheriff and the pretty bitch Riley," Luke chimes in.

I immediately feel uncomfortable.

"Just ignore them," Riley mumbles, squeezing my hand tighter.

"So how does that little ass feel?" Toby asks when we're at her level. He stands in front of us, standing up and blocking the entrance to the cafeteria. Toby is about half a head taller than me.

"Which ass do you mean? The one in her pants or the one she's holding by the hand?" fat Harry laughs, and the other two start laughing out loud too.

I get angry. Although I wanted to avoid an argument, I spontaneously slip out: "Bacon cheek, you must have spent the night in the cabadose."

I quickly realize that this was probably a mistake. The grins disappear from the faces of the three half-siblings and Toby clenches his hands.

"You're taking this pretty hard, you victim. Why are you hurting my buddy?"

Riley intervenes. "Toby, you're an ass. Harry, you lazy fatso, why don't you stand up to James on your own? You got your pants full, don't you?"

"I ... I ... you stupid cow!" Harry snorts.

"*Shut the fuck up* goes for you too, Riley, you bitch."

That's enough for me, I take a step forward, lunge and punch Toby right in the face. Direct hit! Immediately blood shoots out of his fang and he screams loudly. "Ouch, shit, that hurts!"

I walk over to Harry. "Do you want one too?"

"N-no," he stammers.

Then I feel a bump from the side and stumble. Luke pushed me. At the same moment Harry takes a step towards me. "Now you're scared!"

Luke follows and grabs me from behind. Harry lunges at me and is about to hit me when Kieran yells, "You bastards can only hit one out of three. Now it's time for a good threesome!"

"Fuck, it's Kieran," Harry groans.

"Come on, let's get out of here!" Luke turns to my buddy and moans, "Oh man, him of all people!"

Riley slaps his face.

Slap

Luke holds his cheek, which immediately turns bright red. "You ... you!"

"Say it and I'll give you a big nose, too."

Kieran is almost there. All three of them quickly turn around, run through the cafeteria, and disappear out the other exit.

We laugh.

"Wow, my hero," Riley beams at me.

I grin proudly, but really I'm just glad that I got out of that number unscathed, thanks to Kieran and Riley's help.

"You got Toby good. He won't take it. You'd better keep an eye out for him in the near future."

"Thank you, Kieran. I'll do that. But maybe he's had enough because he knows I'm struggling."

"Coffee?" asks Riley.

"Sure."

We're sitting there talking when Mrs. White suddenly stands in front of us. "I saw that. Fighting is strictly forbidden here at school."

"The three of them started it," I reply immediately.

"I saw you hit Toby." "That was self-defense," Riley interjects.

"The three of them were going after James," Kieran says.

"You three will spend an hour in detention today to think about your behaviour. Toby is in the first aid room. He's got a nosebleed. You're lucky, James, his nose isn't broken."

"That really was self-defense."

"One hour after the official lesson, you will come to room mer 17K. There, under the supervision of our new substitute teacher, Mr. Hools, you will learn about respect and give a little talk about it next week."

"Mrs. White, that's not fair!"

"I can talk to your parents if you prefer."

Kieran raises his hand. "An hour is fine." I don't want to. "It was just me. It was just me hitting. Why don't you leave my friends out of this?"

"All three of them!"

"It's okay, James," Riley says.

Kieran nods. "That's fine. I don't have anything planned anyway, and 17K is like the ultimate punishment, I can't leave you there alone," he loosens up a bit. "Besides, it looks good on my cool list. Get the football boys to respect me more." Mrs. White turns and leaves. All three of us immediately have an appropriate name for the teacher.

"Stupid cow."

"Snipe."

"Nasty hen."

Every school building in the world probably has its own unique flair. This is the third school I have visited, and the flair of this building is guaranteed to stick in my mind in a special way, thanks to the obligatory visit to room 17K.

The room is located in the basement at the very back. You have to walk through the entire corridor to get there. Just getting there is pure punishment. I am reminded of scenes from the psychological thriller *The Sixth Sense* and can easily imagine that ghosts are just waiting to scare some poor students. I'm glad there are three of us. And now that I think about it, I'm even happier that my friends are a werewolf and a vampire lady. There's no safer way to be accompanied.

Crazy world, I think.

A world that until recently I had relegated to the realm of fairy tales.

The room is not exactly spacious and quite dusty. Apart from a few chairs and desks, Room 17K is mostly filled with skeletons and other models used in biology classes. It is the school's storage room. Now I understand why many students affectionately call this room the torture chamber.

When we go there, it somehow reminds me of the vampire tunnel system. It smells almost as musty and the ceiling light comes from old light bulbs. Half of them flicker like candlelight in the wind.

The door is open. Kieran turns on the light. We go in and sit down. The only window in the room is a skylight with a lot of cobwebs hanging in the shaft.

We talk and don't hear Mr. Hools approaching. He suddenly stands in front of us and stares at us.

"How did he get in here?" whispers Kieran. I look at the substitute teacher. He looks familiar, but I can't place him.

"My name is Hools. J.B. Hools. Mr. Hools to you," he says in a dark, raspy voice that sounds dark and black.

As a dubbing actor, he would only do horror roles and would give me goosebumps right away.

Hools wears a black suit and a hat with a wide brim that shades most of his face. The sight of this teacher takes our breath away. You don't want to mess with this guy. He's scary. No. Worse. He's terrifying.

"What are we going to do?" asks Riley.

"Study on our own, or do you have an assignment for us?"

"You will speak only when I ask. The first thing you must learn is respect!"

Hools turns, goes to the old-fashioned blackboard, takes a piece of chalk and writes a word on it. The chalk squeaks with each letter. The writing looks as antique as the blackboard itself. It reminds me of the old book in the cabin.

Suddenly it hits me. Now I know how I know this guy. Mr. Hools is one of the two vampire hunters who came to our house. I'm pretty sure, but I can't swear to it. Not yet.

"I think I know him," I whisper into Kieran's ear.

"Quiet!" Hools replies immediately and I fall silent instantly. *He has ears like a lynx. Damn it, how could he hear that?* When the teacher turns around again and points an arm at the blackboard, his sleeve slides back and I see a lot of tattoos. Then I noticed the glitter on his ear.

An earring. Tattoos. That's Jack Blood.

I almost feel sick with fear. Sweat pours down my forehead, my knees start to shake slightly. Kieran and Riley don't move, they both stare into Mr. Hools' eyes in awe. His gaze can be hypnotic. I have to force myself to stop looking at him and close my eyes for a moment. Then I read the word he had written on the blackboard.

Silence!

"You will sit quietly and not make a sound. Not a single syllable will pass your lips. For one hour. If you can do this, you will be allowed to leave. If not, you will spend another hour in silence!"

We no longer dare to speak. We don't move at all. Even when Hools leaves the room, we remain silent. We look at each other but don't say a word. It was the longest hour of my life. I forget any sense of time, and looking at the clock becomes a guessing game.

How much time has passed? Will I be able to look at the watch again in exactly three minutes?

I think about everything and nothing. Just before the lesson ends, Hools comes back. He looks at each of us for about a minute, then makes a hand gesture and says, "The lesson is over. You can go now.

We get up without saying a word and walk out of the room. Mr. Hools, alias Jack Blood, radiates an icy cold. I can still feel his eyes on my back in the hallway. When we reach the large auditorium, I put my arms around my friends' shoulders and pull them toward me.

"Guys, that was him. That's one of the men who introduced himself to us the other day as a vampire hunter. He's the vampire calling himself Jack Blood."

"Jack Blood?" Riley asks, her eyes wide.

I nod and tell them about the taxi driver and his story. They are breathless. They listen to me in rapt attention.

"This is insane. What's going on, guys?" replies Riley.

"One more thing, guys," I say in a serious voice. "If Hools is not Hools but Blood, then where is the real Mr. Hools?"

Kieran has an idea. "It could be an alias. After all, he needs an identity to live and also to register somewhere."

Riley frowns thoughtfully. "And what if he takes on the identities of his victims?"

Kieran takes a deep breath. "We're starting to outgrow this thing."

"Werewolves don't scare," Riley jokes.

"Are you kidding me? That guy was beyond disgusting. I'm getting anxiety pimples just thinking about him."

"Anyway, we need to act as soon as possible and take care of the curse. Then Riley and her family will be out of danger for now."

"Good idea," Riley says and gives me a kiss on the cheek.

"All wright, you lovebirds, I'm going to make some quick deliveries in the toilet and then I'll meet you at the bikes, okay?"

"You could use a little more discretion in front of a lady, Kieran," Riley winks.

"Right, in front of a lady, but not in front of you, Riley," he laughs and heads for the toilets.

"See you soon."

At the bikes we meet Toby, Harry and Luke again. I'm annoyed when I recognize the three guys, but I'm not afraid. My punch to Toby's nose should have been enough to make him respect me.

The closer we get, the more I have to grin. There are two cotton buds in Toby's stitches. But when I see Harry playing with a baseball bat, I sense danger and the grin immediately disappears. When they see us, all three of them stand up. "Allington, we have a score to settle."

"It's all right, boys. The lesson was for nothing. I'll give it to you as a present," I reply coolly, admiring myself for saying that on the spur of the moment.

"You heard me," Harry says aggressively and raises his baseball bat threateningly.

"Bacon cheek, don't hurt yourself with that."

"I'll hit you right in the mouth, you ass!"

Riley pulls me back. "Don't tease them. I wouldn't put anything past them."

"I could also see you paying me $100 in compensation," Toby suggests with the meanest look I've ever seen on a student's face. I could kick his ass for that alone.

"And I could see myself finishing what I started before," I reply, pushing Riley aside and clenching my hands into fists. "My fist and your nose could be good friends."

"You're full of it, Allington," Luke hisses.

I concentrate on Toby.

What did Dad teach me once? When someone is angry and irritable, they react spontaneously and don't think.

I tease Toby even more by pointing to his nose and saying, "Toby, are you on your period? You have tampons up your nose."

That was enough. He's seething with rage and signals to his two buddies. The three guys spread out and try to circle me.

"Kieran!" shouts Riley. "Kieran, hurry up!"

"I think your friend got locked in the bathroom," Luke laughs. "He just went to pee at the wrong time."

Since I was secretly counting on Kieran's help, I feel a little uncomfortable after this statement. I'm just thinking of the right words to say when I hear a loud crash. It comes from the school building and sounds terrible.

Wham, clap.

All eyes turn to the school.

"What was that? Did something explode?" Harry asks his friends, looking rather puzzled.

The answer comes less than 15 seconds later when a wing of the large glass door is pushed open and Kieran comes out. He sees our three opponents and yells: "You bastards are back. He comes towards us. "By the way, one of you has to pay for the toilet door. It just broke."

"Luke, you ass. I told you to lock it!" Toby yells.

"I did!"

"You must not have done it right. Look, there's Kieran," Harry points with the bat.

Luke is now barking at Harry. "Fatty, shut up. I wonder how you got this far without repeating a grade."

The overweight teenager grins. "I'm a great storyteller!"

Kieran is with us. He stands next to Harry, picks up his baseball bat and slaps him on the back of the head with the flat of his hand. "I guess you can't play sports because you had an accident once?"

"It was something like that, Kieran," he answers in a shaky voice. You can really hear the fear he has of Kieran.

"You're not only stupid, you're also a liar and a shyster."

"I'm not afraid!" Harry snorts. His head glows bright red.

"Then I'll show you what you can do with a baseball bat," Kieran replies, taking a swing.

"No!" Harry shouts, turning and waddling off at a fast pace.

"Harry, come back! We want to show Allington who's boss in the ring," Toby shouts.

"Kiss my ass. I've got no problem with Allington! That is your thing."

"Me neither. He asked for it," Luke says, pointing at Toby and leaving. "Ciao, guys."

Toby stands alone. I come very close to him. "So, Toby? Do you have a problem with me?"

"Well, if you ask me so directly, not really."

Kieran pulls his smartphone out of his pocket and hits record. He points it at Toby. "Toby, who broke the bathroom door?"

"You did!"

"Pardon? I didn't hear you right." Kieran says.

Toby swallows. "Not you. It was me. I broke the toilet door."

"Thank you. You'll say exactly that at school tomorrow and pay for the damage. And if that doesn't work, or if I see your face again when you attack my buddy, I'm going to shove this baseball bat up your ass! Right in the face!"

"No problem. I'll pay for the damage. It was my fault. Allington, you're really okay. What time is it? I think it is late." stammers Toby, looks at his watch, turns around and runs after his buddies. "Hang on, guys. I'm coming with you!"

Riley laughs uproariously, holding his stomach. "Those wimps! You did a great job, Kieran!"

We joke around for a few more minutes, repeating the sentences of the three losers. Then we say goodbye with tears of laughter in our eyes and drive home.

When I get home, I check the windows and doors. Everything is in perfect order. I leave the tarantula up. I like my little fear trap.

I think again about my plan with Devon and the coins, try to find out more information about Jack Blood on the Internet, and then prepare dinner.

After I've set the table, Dad and Mom come home one after the other.

I am amazed as I eat.

"Guess what, the sheriff's office has been broken into."

"What?" Mom and I yell at the same time.

"I looked just as stupid when they showed me the crime scene this morning."

"How could this happen?"

"There were three deputies. Two of them went to the Millers' house. They were having another big fight. Arthur Miller, who was completely drunk, had to be taken into custody. When they got here with the rioter, Hutter, the third deputy, was sitting at his desk, completely distraught, babbling something like *vampires of the night*. We tested him for drugs and alcohol. Negative. He is..."

"In the psychiatric ward of my hospital," Mom adds.

"Is he injured?" I ask.

"No."

"No punctures or anything?"

"What are you getting at? Don't get me started on vampires being up to no good in Greenfield."

"No, Dad, absolutely not. It's so illogical," I wave.

"So?" I ask Mom. "Does he have bites on his neck now?"

"James," Dad reminds me.

I laugh. Mom and Dad laugh with me.

If only they knew, I think, trying to figure out how to get more information from my parents in an inconspicuous way.

"What did that vampire look like that scared Deputy Hutter so much?"

"The poor guy didn't say a word. He just sits there, staring and babbling something like *blood*."

"Blood?"

"Could be. You don't really understand him. Anyway, the guys who broke in did a lot of damage. They broke into all the filing cabinets. Apparently they were looking for very specific documents. I guess at some point there was a mafia investigation or something and a private detective is desperate to find evidence. Either to hide it or to make a lot of money from it."

"Dad, maybe someone wants to get the documents for the murders."

"But he was unlucky. I left them in my car. I was going to put them together and send a copy to the FBI office in Boston."

"Is anything missing from the sheriff's office?"

"Nothing. Absolutely nothing. The guys could have taken guns and ammo and even confiscated some marijuana. Everything is still there. They were looking for something specific."

Dad takes a sip of beer and puts the can down. "And I'll get that out, too."

"And how was your day, James?" asks Mom, "Nothing special."

"The FBI is sending a man over. I wonder why, but I still prefer that to having to give up the case altogether. I guess the FBI would like to take the case, but they picked the wrong sheriff."

"Just one man?" I ask.

"The FBI usually sends whole teams."

"You and your TV knowledge. It's often different in real life, James."

"All right, Dad."

Back in my room, I type my news into the new chat between Kieran, Riley, Cassie and me. We immediately realize who broke into the sheriff's office. Jack Blood. The only thing we discuss is the reason. In the end, Cassie says that he wanted to take all the evidence with him because things had become too conspicuous here in Greenfield.

Kieran: That's right! He always works in silence. Silence is his profession. That's why we had to be as quiet as mice when we were in room 17K.

Me: Oh man, don't remind me.

Riley: He has to cover up something his helpers screwed up. So he's probably pretty pissed.

Cassie: I'll see what I can find out about him. Maybe my dad has some notes or something. He's going hunting in an hour and making new blood reserves.

Me: All right, everyone, we'll all try to get as much information as we can. Tomorrow we'll gather it all together and plan when and how we're going to proceed.

Riley: Yep. Kieran: Okay.

Cassie: Agreed. Good n8.

I have a bad feeling about this night. I know now that it was either Jack Blood or his helper who broke into our house. I wonder if he's really going to be scared off by a tarantula or some garlic and pull the blanket up to my chin.

Jack Blood, I'm going to beat you, I think, reaching for the bottle of Mexican under my pillow and falling asleep.

I wake up in the middle of the night, drenched in sweat. In my dream, I was running through the woods. Jack Blood was chasing me. I stumbled and fell. Blood knelt over me and said: "You can't escape me. You're my next victim!" I felt his sharp teeth and I felt my blood leave my body. I was getting weaker and weaker.

"Fucking dream," I say out loud and instinctively grab my neck. Everything is fine. I am unharmed. I shiver a little and cover myself up again. Suddenly I freeze like an icicle.

The window.

It is open.

James, you're dead, it runs through me. Jack Blood is here in the house, and my dream must have been some kind of veiled perception in half-sleep.

My knees shake. My hand goes under the pillow. I look for the bottle. It's gone. I panic and turn on the light. Luckily it's next to me.

Flash of inspiration.

Is this why Jack Blood couldn't kill me or drain me? The bottle is silver. The contents, the very special holy water and the runes with the emblem are surely magical.

Thank you, Mr. Mexican, I call out.

I stand up, take the bottle, go to the window and close it. Then I tiptoe to the door. It's only ajar. I listen. Except for my father's sonorous snoring, I hear nothing.

Just as I'm about to close the door and go back to bed, I hear a rustling in the office.

He's here.

"Dad! Burglars in the house!" I yell as loud as I can and turn on the light. Then I run down the stairs. I unscrew the bottle and am about to pour the contents over Jack Blood when I hear a loud clink.

Dad rumbles out of the bedroom behind me. "Get out of the way!" he yells, overtaking me. We hear the sound of an engine outside. Someone is driving away quickly. The desk in the study had been ransacked.

"The guy jumped through the closed window, but there's no blood anywhere. He must have been wearing really thick clothes." I look at the tracks.

"James, call the sheriff's office right away and tell the deputies to set up a roadblock through dispatch. I need two men to come out here right away and have them alert the others."

An hour later, our house is swarming with police officers. The forensics team searches for anything they can use, but finds almost nothing. Mom is desperate and wants to move away immediately, Dad is furious and swears that he will hunt down the burglar until his last day in office.

I am sure that the bottle with the runes saved my life. That reassures me. But I'm also sure that Jack Blood is hunting me, and that scares me. I watch the investigators and specialists at work, sip a hot coffee and hear the odd remark from the police officers. It's a stupid, flippant remark from a detective that makes me think. I'm going to put my father on the trail of Mr. Hools. So I turn the tables. Then I have the advantage, because I know that Jack Blood is after me, but Jack Blood doesn't know that I am after him.

Word quickly got around the school that something had happened at the Sheriff's house. So it's no surprise that I have to go to the principal's office. Mr. Saunders is an odd little guy with nickel glasses, but he has complete authority. Many of the students like to call him *Grandpa*.

The secretary glances up as I enter the office and waves me through with a smile. "He's waiting for you." Mr. Saunders' office is rather bare. A large desk, a cabinet, and a yucca palm in one corner. One wall is covered with framed photographs, and on the opposite side hangs a replica of a Van Gogh. It is a painting of sunflowers.

"Sit down."

I follow the instructions of the director, who strikes up a friendly conversation. Now I understand why he is called Grandpa. Saunders smiles in an incredibly sympathetic way that takes some of the awe out of it.

"Are you okay?"

"I'm fine."

"That's amazing, what I've heard..." and the questioning begins. On the one hand he's curious, but on the other hand he lets me know that he really cares about me. I play along for a while, then I start to put my plan into action.

"Mr. Saunders, I have a question."

"Then ask me, James."

"What does Mr. Hools look like? Do you have an application photo or anything of him?"

"You mean our substitute teacher?"

"That's exactly what I mean."

Saunders' gaze changes. I can see that something is rattling under his skullcap.

"But of course. Why do you ask?" he replies.

"I'm not quite sure, Mr. Saunders, but I have my suspicions. I'll tell you in a moment, but may I see the picture first?"

"Wait a minute."

The headmaster gets up and walks to a filing cabinet. He opens a drawer, pulls out a file and flips through it. "Ah, here it is, the photo of Mr. Hools."

Saunders comes over to me and shows me a passport photo of a man of about thirty with a full beard and glasses.

"Did the substitute teacher introduce himself to you personally when he started?"

"No. I was at a conference. As I can see from the schedule, Mr. Hools started his shift on time. He was assigned by Mrs. Myers. However, he called in sick the next day."

Saunders sits back in his chair. "And I can tell you why."

Saunders squints his eyes. "Why is that, James? What do you know that I don't?"

"Because the man who claims to be Mr. Hools is not Mr. Hools. I got detention for a stupid thing. Mr. Hools was in charge. He looked completely different. The man who pretended to be Mr. Hools was definitely not the man who applied to be Mr. Hools."

"Are you sure about that?"

"Sure as the Amen in church."

"How did you get detention? Who arranged all that?"

Now I tell the story of the three fools and how Mrs. White reacted. Mr. Saunders listens intently. At the end of my explanation he sighed: "Oh, dear!" He reaches for the intercom on his desk and has Mrs. White paged. "Have her come to my office immediately," he adds, standing up and patting me on the shoulder.

"James, of course the lecture has been canceled, even though violence is not the answer!"

"I know I overreacted," I admit ruefully. The headmaster smiles graciously. "I'll talk to Mrs. White about it. Thank you for letting me know. I'll write up a report immediately and send it to the school administration in Boston. A copy will be faxed directly to your father at the sheriff's office. Thank you very much."

"You're welcome, Mr. Saunders."

I'm a winner and Mrs. White can go to hell! And when the report gets to my dad, he'll go after that phony Mr. Hools. We've gained valuable time and increased the pressure on Jack Blood.

Classes are a minor matter today, and as soon as the long lunch break begins, my friends and I disappear into the cafeteria. We reach the final stage of our planning and lay all the facts we have gathered on the table.

"Oloisius was the keeper of the tunnel. Devon is trapped inside. Your father," I look at Cassie, "will probably succeed him and take that position."

"Or that Jackson," Kieran throws in.

"Right, we can't ignore him." "Then there's Jack Blood, aka Mr. Hools, and his unknown helpers."

"And the curse," Riley adds.

"When my father receives the report from Mr. Saunders, he will hunt down Jack Blood."

"Then your father is in danger. He doesn't stand a chance against a vampire. And Blood is a very dangerous opponent. He is brutal and ruthless."

"True, but Blood isn't stupid. He won't fight in public. That would cause too much trouble, and he can't draw the attention of the vampire world to himself with such an action. He may be one of the strongest among us, but he doesn't stand a chance against all the others on his own. No matter how much fear and terror he spreads, if the peaceful vampires unite, they will defeat him," Cassie interjects.

"Okay. That means we can buy some time to get the coins and break the curse," Kieran sums up.

Toby, Harry and Luke come into the cafeteria. All three look at me. Then they crouch down in the far corner of the cafeteria. From there they keep looking over at me. Riley rolls his eyes. "Oh God, those three guys already like her."

"I thought I made myself clear the other day. I'm going over there," Kieran says and starts to get up.

"Stop, stay seated. You reported the broken toilet door and said it was you. I think they understood," says Cassie, laughing as we tell her about the last incident.

"Okay," Kieran replies, giving them the finger and sipping his Coke.

I actually enjoy having a mate who is tall and athletic. In other words, who has the strength of a werewolf. So I raise my

Coke with a grin and toast Toby and his buddies. They whisper, get up and leave.

"What are we going to do about Devon?"

"I'm going into the tunnel today and bring him the fake rock."

"Too dangerous. I'll go with you," Kieran says immediately.

"Then he might get suspicious. After all, he is a vampire."

"Honey, I don't think you should go alone either."

"I'm not afraid of Devon. He needs me. I'm more worried about Jackson. If you can keep him away from me could help me a lot. Cassie, don't let your dad show up either."

"I can easily hold him off for an hour. I tell him to take me to the hairdresser and pick me up. He always does that and waits in a bar in the meantime."

"Do you have an appointment?"

"No, but my dad doesn't know that."

Riley high-five her. The hands clap together. "Good idea! As for Jackson, I can stand outside the cabin and ask him for something if he comes."

I don't know," I reply.

"Because I'm one of the vampires, that's quite normal. My family is also taken care of by the blood camp."

"Okay, let's do it like this then."

"And me?" asks Kieran.

"You'll come too, but you'll stay hidden in the forest as a wild card."

"Boring."

"Important!"

"Really?"

"Sure. You're the cavalry and will jump in if anything goes wrong."

"All right. That's how we do it."

"And when do we take care of the coins?"

"As soon as I convince Devon to help us."
All four of us chime in.

After school, I come home for pancakes, maple syrup, and applesauce. Mom tells me that Dad is hot on the trail of an impostor and has already raided his boarding house. The guy calls himself Mr. Hools and unfortunately wasn't in the room, but one of the deputies found more than 20 passports with different names. A manhunt has been launched and he doesn't like the fact that the man from the FBI is also coming today. Dad is afraid that the feds will want to take credit for the successful search.

I meet Riley and Kieran at the edge of the forest. We wait for the news from Cassie and go over our plan one more time. The smartphones vibrate almost simultaneously when Cassie's message arrives.
"Green light! She's with her dad." Kieran laughs. "She says he grumbled. He's driving her anyway."
Riley just says, "Typical dads." "Let's go!"
I know the way now. It won't take us four hours to get to the clearing. I pull the fake Tembolus stone out of my pocket again and hold it out to Riley. "Does it really smell like a real rock?"
She sniffs it. "It smells magical. That's all Devon can smell, too."
"All right then."
Kieran disappears into the thick undergrowth. Riley sits down on the grass at the edge of the clearing and I enter the hut. "Shit!" I yell.
Riley comes running to me. "What's wrong?"
I point at the desk and the hatch. "It's open. I have to assume Jackson's in there."
"Do you want me to go?"

"No, because they would accuse you of treason and kill you!"

"Then you won't go."

I swallow. My Adam's apple is moving up and down. I feel my right knee start to shake. I have to make a decision. "I'll go in and you stay outside the cabin. Zen. You come out as soon as you hear or see anything dangerous."

"Take care of yourself!"

We kiss each other. This time the kiss is long and tender.

Wow, I love this vampire girl.

I can't help but think of the Mexican. It works. He's married to a vampire too.

I smile.

"Riley, now I'm going to take the first step towards breaking the curse. You will soon be free."

"Take care of yourself."

"Always," I answer and climb into the tunnel. Riley looks after me.

"Get out," I say.

She disappears from my view. I switch on my phone and search for the drawing app. Then I turn on the flashlight.

"Devon, my friend. Now we'll see if you're good or bad. I hope I can get one or two important secrets out of you," I mutter to myself.

I'm probably trying to encourage myself. I look at the screen of my cell phone, orient myself, and start walking. The musty smell is still strong. You could probably air out this place for fifty years in a row and it would still smell awful. I turn right at the first intersection. I am extremely careful and stop again and again to listen.

Nothing. Silence. An eerie silence.

I get goose bumps just thinking about the word silence. It reminds me of Jack Blood and detention.

Keep going, I urge myself mentally and continue on my way. I reach the first intersection and choose the right tunnel. Again I wait a moment.

Has it always been so quiet here?

Pure goose bumps. They seem to cover my entire body. It tingles from my neck to my heels. Fear comes up. Something inside of me is reluctant to go on, but my love for Riley and not least a certain thirst for adventure and the need to defeat Jack Blood drive me on. With every step I take, I can feel the unease growing.

Something is different today.

I'm already in the corridor that leads directly to the room where Devon's coffin is. Suddenly I know what's going on and what's changed from my previous visits. It's the smell. It is much more pungent than usual - somehow foul and dirty.

When I was a kid, I found a dead raccoon. It had been nibbled on by other animals. The carcass smelled like this. It's a smell you never forget. It creeps into your nose, settles there, and you never get rid of it. It's a mixture of sweet decay and stale, damp, musty air. It smells like death.

The closer I get to Devon's room, the stronger the stench becomes. Suspecting evil, I turn off my smartphone. I am immediately enveloped in endless darkness. Not a ray of light, not a glimmer, nothing. Absolute darkness. I immediately feel blind.

"This is not the solution either," I whisper to myself and turn the phone back on.

I walk very slowly. My senses are tense. Unfortunately, this includes my sense of smell. It smells so bad that I pull my T-shirt over my nose. But this filter has almost no effect. The stench gets worse and worse and it smells even worse than after a break in the boys' bathroom. And that's saying something. I've seen tests of courage where you have to endure five minutes in the toilet before you're accepted into a clique. I would imagine that one of the stinkers is fat Harry.

The door to Devon's room is ajar. All is quiet. "Devon?" I whisper, pushing the door open. It squeaks and creaks inward.

"Devon, are you in there? Tell me, boy, did you dump a bunch of vampires? It smells worse in here than..." I fall silent for a moment.

The coffin is pushed aside and I can see the entrance to Devon's crypt. This is unmistakably the source of the wooden stench. I walk over and shine the light inside.

The light from my phone wanders into the dark hole and touches something that makes my blood run cold. Devon and Jackson are on the ground. Wooden stakes have been driven through their bodies. Worms are crawling out of Jackson's decomposed and mummified body.

He's rotting, it runs through me.

I'm startled when Devon moves. "You're alive?" I shout.

"I...am dying," comes the faint voice. "He held us and his aide staked us. The stake was driven through Jackson's heart. My heart was only grazed, but that's enough to make me die slowly. I will leave this world.

I overcome my disgust and climb down. Devon has been salted. He looks like an old man, but I recognize him. "Who was that?"

"Jack Blood."

An icy shiver runs down my spine. He is here. We are in mortal danger. "Jack Blood?" I ask anyway.

The dying vampire speaks softly and with a broken voice: "He wants to seize power and sit on the throne of the vampires as sole ruler.

"Devon, is there anything I can do to help?"

A barely discernible shake of the head, followed by an exhaled word: "No."

"Are you good or evil? Did you want to drink human blood and that's why you were locked up?" I want to know and ask the question directly and bluntly.

Devon looks at me. His eyes glow blood red. "I made a mistake a long time ago. And I paid for it for many years, but I'm not a bad vampire. I was inclined to follow Jack Blood's call, but in the end I turned against him. James, you have to stop him."

"How?"

Devon rattles.

"Damn it, stay here. Don't die. I've taken care of the stupid stone," I fib.

Devon smiles. "Thank you. You're a real friend." I feel guilty, after all I would have sent him to his death with that stone if he had gone to the light of day.

"You must get the coins. When the curse is lifted, Jack Blood will have a harder time.

"Why?"

"Too many opponents."

"What about Anderson?"

"He's fine. Oloisius blackmailed him and Anderson is afraid of Jack Blood."

"Are they your brothers?"

"Yes."

One of Devon's legs is obviously disintegrating. Between the shoe and the pant leg, I can see bones under the disintegrating, leathery-looking skin.

"Devon! Where do I go? Are the coins behind the locked doors?"

"No. There are burial grounds and emergency camps for vampires set up there. Anderson has a map. It's real. I know it. The coins are in the marked places. At least I'm pretty sure about two of the coins. They are old caves. They are both old caves. They used to be the hideouts of the vampires," he coughs.

"James, you can do it. Defeat Jack Blood!"

"Devon, don't die!"

"It burns like hell. Make him pay! Defeat his helper and you will defeat him."

He closes his glowing eyes. A pale breath of stinking air comes out of his mouth, then Devon is dead.

A mixture of rage and sadness spreads through me. Jack Blood is dangerous. Jack Blood is treacherous and kills even his own kind. Jack Blood must be defeated.

I get out of the tomb, leave the room and walk thoughtfully towards the exit. I realize that we have to fight this murderer immediately. I have no idea how far this sorcerer Hostang's power reaches and what will happen if the curse he cast on Riley's family is broken, but I do know that it will weaken Jack Blood in some way. We can't wait any longer. We're going after the coins. Tomorrow! It's Friday and we can tell our parents that we're staying with each other. That way we have all the time in the world.

As I climb out of the hatch and leave the cabin, Riley waves happily. "Finally! We were getting worried. You were down there for a long time," she calls to me.

I walk purposefully towards them.

Kieran comes out of the woods and runs over to us. "Are you all right, mate?" he wants to know.

Riley stops about a meter in front of me. Kieran doesn't come any closer either.

"What's wrong?"

"Did you make out with a dead moose? You smell like a skunk's butt after you shoot the stinky liquid," Kieran says, laughing and holding his nose.

"You ass."

"Maybe you should change your deodorant," he shoots at her. "Dead baboon is out!"

"Cut the crap, Kieran. I want to know what James found down there."

As we walk back, I talk about my walk through the tunnel, leaving nothing out. By the time I'm done, we've reached the edge of the forest.

Kieran claps me on the shoulder. "Good job, buddy! And tomorrow we'll do what you suggested. I'll say I'll sleep at your place and you'll sleep at mine. Riley and Cas- they'll do the same."

Chapter Nine

All my clothes go straight into the wash. I don't just take a shower, I take a long, long bath. Only then do I feel normal again.

Later I have dinner with mom and dad. Dad is restless. He hasn't seen the man from the FBI yet, but he knows he's already checked into the hotel and wants to meet him tomorrow.

"The agent's name is Ted Harper. He contacted the office as soon as he arrived. I know a Ted Harper, but I don't know if that's him."

Mom puts hot chicken wings on the table. They come with a tomateo salad and baguette. "Tastier and better than Kentucky Fried Chicken, and the chickens lived happier, too, I guess."

"No fries?" asks Dad.

"Not today!"

"Is it good or bad that you know him?" I ask.

"It doesn't matter. If it's the Harper from back then, I just remember that he was a nice guy with high aspirations. We went to the police academy in Boston together. Harper graduated second in his class. I noticed at the time that he joined the FBI right away."

"Who was number one? You were?"

Dad takes a big gulp of beer. "Nope. But today I'm the sheriff of Greenfield, Massachusetts, and that's better than being an ordinary FBI agent."

I grab the second wing. I remember the Mexican at the bridge saying that Jack Blood comes back there all the time. "By the way," I say with a full mouth to make it sound casual.

"Swallow before you talk," Mom grumbles.

I swallow the bite and wash it down with water. "Riley told me she saw Mr. Hools twice on the bridge over the Connecticut River. It's on the west side of Montague City Rd."

"Interesting. I'm going to send some people over there right away. I might even have the bridge watched. This Hools has made himself invisible."

"Do you think he's involved in the murders?"

"James," Mom warns.

"I'm not ruling it out. At least he's a big number. The IDs are barely recognizable as forgeries, some are even real. I'm checking all the data right now. I've already got one report back. He has a passport of a Mr. Jonathan Lawinski. This Lawinski has been missing for 29 years, but the passport was issued only last year. In person!"

"Where?"

"In California."

"The two vampire hunters said they were from San Francisco. That's in California too," Mom says, confused.

"Don't worry about it. Our house is guarded by a patrol every hour. The off shifts have been canceled, and we have twice as many patrols on the street as usual. We'll get him."

"And now I'd like to talk about something else. How do you like the food?"

"Yum, Mom!"

"Excellent," Dad winks and reaches for his beer. After dinner, I discuss the idea of staying overnight and my parents agree. Dad even likes the idea and suggests that Mom could pay a long overdue visit to her sister, who lives in New Hampshire and Mom could stay there for the whole weekend.

So we put it in our family planner. Everything goes according to plan.

Nothing happens that night. Everything is quiet and I even sleep very well and a little too long.

"You're not leaving without breakfast," Mom nags, and I quickly stuff myself with toast, wash it down with fresh orange juice, and jet off.

Fit as a fiddle, I jump on my bike and ride to school. It annoys me that I'm a little late. I wanted to talk to Riley and the others about this afternoon. That will have to wait until the break.

My friends' bikes are already there. I look at my watch and hurry. The lesson starts in a minute. As I put the lock on the frame and turn around to enter the school building, I can't believe what I see. Toby, Harry and Luke are sitting behind me.

"Finally we've got the big mouth alone."

There are days that start off really bad, and there are days that start off really more bad. Today is one of those days. I'm standing here alone in front of the three bagpipes and they probably want to beat me up. My friends are in the classroom. I assess the situation in fractions of a second.

First of all, there are three of them, I'm alone. Second, they are stronger and will beat me up. Third: Last but not least, I will be scolded for being late for class. "What do you want?" I ask, trying not to show any fear.

"What do we want?" Toby laughs.

"What do we want?" Harry repeats, laughing too.

"Harry, did you have a good breakfast?"

"Uh, yes. Why do you ask?"

"Because half of it is on your shirt." Harry looks down. I use this moment to jump up to Luke. He's so surprised that he just stares at me. I push him aside. He stumbles. I start to run, but I get caught on his book bag and trip and fall. All three of them immediately surround me.

"Allington, you owe us about $100 and a big nose," Toby yells at me.

"And the bathroom door," Harry adds.

"It's already there," Luke improves.

"Really?"

"Take that!" Toby pushes after me, swings his right leg out and tries to kick me.

Expecting the worst, I put my arms over my head and turn to the side. Suddenly I hear a "Ouch!"

I turn my head to see a man. He has grabbed Toby by the ear and is pulling him up. "You lousy little bastard! You don't kick people when they're down."

Harry waddles off again at a duck's pace. "I have to get to class."

"Me too," Luke gasps, hurrying after him.

The man has to pull hard on his ear. Toby screams like a banshee. "Aahhhhh!"

"Next time I'll break every bone in your body!" he roars, letting go of the half-elf. "Not today, but tomorrow, or next week, or a month from now, I'll visit you in the night, drag you out of your beds, and do things to you that you wouldn't even want to do to your worst enemies."

That was it. Toby starts to cry and mumbles: "No more, I promise!"

The man feigns a quick forward movement and yells: "Buhhhh!"

Toby flinches and runs after his buddies. "Wait! Help!"

I sit up, wanting to see who my rescuer is. The man looks familiar, but I can't place him. He's strong, but not tall. He's well dressed, but the outfit doesn't suit him. I stand up.

"Thank you."

"Thank Jack Blood."

It comes to me in an instant. I know who this guy is. He's the companion of the horrible killer vampire. Instinctively, I take two steps back.

"Don't worry. If I'd wanted to, those three yokels would have beaten you up and all I had to do was pick you up."

"Why did you do that? What do you want from me?"

"You'll find out soon enough. Come with me."

"No," I say, looking around for help. I never see anyone. I'm alone with Jack Blood's helper.

"You don't need to be afraid. Just follow me."

"Just tell me here."

"Don't get on my nerves, boy! Jack Blood wants to see you. Come with me or don't!"

"To kill me?"

The man begins to laugh out loud. "I or he could have done that a long time ago."

"Like you killed Devon and Jackson?" I answer, feeling less and less afraid the longer I talk to him.

"Jack still needs you."

"For what?"

"You'll find out soon enough," he says and walks away briskly. I run after him.

"I just have one more question."

"I'm not going to answer it."

"Are you the one who always does the dirty work for Blood? Did you break into our house?"

"I said I'm not going to answer your question."

"Why not?" I ask, stopping when I notice that we are getting further and further away from the school grounds.

"Because I don't like questions," he says, walks over to a black van with no writing on it, gets in, starts the engine, rolls down the passenger window and asks: "Are you coming or not?"

"What's your name?"

"Edward. Well? Are you coming now?"

"No."

He lifts the window again, joins the traffic and disappears after a short while.

I stand there and watch him. I'm irritated. A strange guy.

I go back to the school.

Why did he do that? Why does Jack Blood want to see me and what does he need me for?

I knock on the door of my classroom, apologize for being late and sit down.

The lesson goes on forever. I can't keep up with the stories during the short breaks. Kieran says he's going to intercept Toby and his gang of bullies and beat them up. I wave him off. "They're not worth it."

Cassie and Riley feel confirmed in how stupid boys can be. "Guys, let's take care of the coins and the blood. Toby and company will have enough for sure. They're in for a few sleepless nights."

In the early afternoon, the time has finally come. I'm standing outside Kieran's door with my backpack packed. His parents have left again and he's saving himself the trouble of spending the night at my place.

Lucky bastard. I'd like to have a storm-free place every now and then, too.

Cassie and Riley arrive five minutes later. They both look really good. Tight jeans, t-shirts, a little makeup.

"Really great girls," Kieran says as he looks out the window after they ring the bell.

"Riley's mine. You can hit on Cassie."

"Let's see," he grins and heads for the door.

I look at the window frame and the glass. "Good job! You can't even tell it was broken."

"An uncle of mine is a glazier. It was a special price. But the window will be deducted from my allowance," he shouts back.

Riley is already in the room, gives me a quick kiss, reaches into her backpack, pulls out a map and spreads it out.

"Let's get right to it. I'd rather we get the first coin while it's still daylight. These things are hidden several miles apart."

"Sounds good."

"Cassie, I think it's really cool of you to steal your dad's map."

"I think he knows, but he doesn't say anything."

"What makes you think that?"

"He has a really bad conscience since the other day."

"Listen, he wanted to kill us! He can have a bad conscience about that."

"He wanted to get rid of you. That doesn't mean he wanted to kill you," she counters.

"At least he scared me a lot."

"I don't trust him either," Kieran adds.

"Guys, I overheard a conversation he had with my mom. He confessed everything to her. Jack Blood was blackmailing him. Devon was a Blood supporter from the beginning and Uncle Oloisius was until the end. Devon backed down and so did Dad. But Oloisius wanted to implement Blood's ideas and become one of his leading lords once Blood put on the vampire crown of his own invention. Then Papa was threatened. Or rather, Blood threatened to kill my mother and me. Dad bowed. That's all he did. Deep down, he's a supporter of peaceful vampires."

"So we would have died a martyr's death?" I ask.

"Forget it, James. You can't change what happened. You can learn from it and do better in the future."

Riley chimes in. "Forget it now, guys. We are running out of time. Let's get to work."

"Anyway, he gave you this card. That's a step in the right direction," Kieran ends the discussion.

Cassie laughs. "At least it was clearly visible on his desk."

Riley is already deep into the subject. "I've analyzed all the comparative material from my family's research and marked the locations of the coins on this map here. If you take a look, you'll see that two of the coins are in exactly the same locations as marked on Cassie's map. There are some minor variations in the location of the third coin, but we'll take care of that once we find the first two."

I look at the location. "Kieran, do you have a pencil and a compass?"

"Logically."

"Forget it, James. We've already tried everything mathematically, compared the coordinate data and linked all the numbers to the alphabet. There's nothing we can do. The location of the third coin can't be pinpointed," Riley interjects. Kieran scratches his head again. It looks as if he's thinking hard. "This Hopkins..."

"Hostang?"

"Yes, Hostang then. So that wizard."

"Wizard," Riley interjects.

"Fine by me. Well, this wizard put the coins there 200 years ago and was sure you wouldn't find them."

"Right."

"We need a map from that time," he says, getting up and going to his bookshelf. "Where is it?" my buddy mumbles, then reaches for a historical atlas and pulls it off the shelf. "Fire up the PC, James."

I get up and walk over to Kieran's desk, turn on the PC and sit down.

"Internet!"

I start the browser.

"Find a map of New England from 1818 and open it beside Google Maps."

Meanwhile, Kieran is drawing something on the map in his atlas.

"What are you getting at?" asks Cassie.

"Just an idea. I used to do puzzles as well as American history."

"Just let him do it," Riley says.

"I got it," I say as the Google Maps map pops up.

"The first coin is in a hiding place about 50 miles from here in a wooded area near the small town of Washington. Hostang refers to the nation's capital, but not to it."

"That's right."

"Let's look at the second coin. It's in a cave in the Flume Gorge in Lincoln, New Hampshire. It names a president. That's a reference to Washington, and the distance is about 150 miles, three times the distance. You say the coin is in Salem. That makes sense, because that's where the witch burnings were, and Hostang certainly lost familiars. But Salem doesn't fit the distances. We have 50 and 150, what's missing?"

"A hundred miles?"

"Right."

I zoom in on Google Maps, search around, and find a small town that might fit the bill. I immediately fire up the route planner. "I've got a town here called Salem. To the south. It's 100 miles from here."

"That's the Salem we're looking for. He put up a mirror, you know? Washington, the President, and then a misdirection with the known Salem. I say you're both wrong about the third coin. We have to go to Salem, Connecticut."

"The river," I interject, "Jack Blood drained his victims at the Connecticut River."

"He gave clues. To Hostang, it was nothing more than a game."

"And the price of this game is the life of my family and me."

"Who benefits?" "Jack Blood."

"That sounds convincing. I say we get the coin in Washington today. We can do it in time. We can discuss enough on the way there about which Sarem we're looking for the third coin."

"Bingo! That's exactly what we'll do. Then let's go and get the first coin. Man, I've never been so excited," I say.

"This moment is historic. Two vampires, a werewolf and a human working together. Let's take a selfie and capture the moment forever."

"Kieran, this takes time."

"We're making history, people! You have to document it. Come here," the werewolf grins, emphasizing the word "must. "I don't bite," he adds with a laugh.

We all laugh and move closer together. Kieran takes a picture. Cassie, Riley and I do the same. We take a last look at the map. Kieran looks around. "And how do we get there?" Cassie grins broadly, opens her purse and pulls out a paper. "Surprise! I'll drive you. My license, brand new. I passed my test yesterday."

"You little sweet bitch didn't tell me!" Riley exclaims in amazement.

"I was afraid I was going to fail - well, I've already failed once and I thought I'd wait until I had the rag in my hand."

Kieran and I clap. "Great!"

"Yay, we drive Mercedes!"

"Not quite."

Kieran and I look at each other questioningly. "Did you get your own car?"

"No, but Dad says I can only drive Mom's old Toyota. I can pick it up from home in half an hour. She'll be home and won't need the car anymore."

"Better than walking or taking the train," Riley says.

"Or a stolen Porsche," Kieran nudges me and winks.

"You ass," I whisper and laugh.

Half an hour later, we're in a white Toyota Corolla, rolling down Main Street toward MA 9.

"The GPS says we'll be there in a good hour."

The trip goes smoothly, and after a pee break for the girls, we arrive in Washington, Massachusetts, an hour and a half later.

"Can someone tell me exactly where to go?"

Riley reads from her notes. "There's got to be a church or a chapel somewhere. We park there and walk into the woods behind it. We have to walk about 500 meters into it and look for an old cabin."

"You vampires seem to have a soft spot for old forest huts," Kieran observes.

"Probably goes back to the good old days when people were afraid of the deep, dark forest. That's where we got our peace and quiet."

"That's what my grandparents say," the werewolf agrees.

We park at St. Andrew's Chapel, get out, stretch and start walking. Kieran hangs back a bit. I wait for him. "Scared?"

"No, flatulence. I just dropped off two smelly farts. I didn't think the girls would notice." 7

Riley turns around. "We vampires have good ears!"

Kieran blushes.

"But I think it's nice that you kept your distance," Cassie adds, laughing.

"Ha, ha," Kieran mimics. "Then I won't take that into account in the future."

"Can I call you a fart wolf instead of a werewolf?"

Kieran takes a swing and hits my upper arm with his fist. It pulls pretty hard. "Ouch!"

Then we both laugh and run ahead to the girls.

Cassie stops at the edge of the woods. "Guys, isn't there a trail or something? I'm going to ruin my new shoes," she stammers when she sees the swampy, muddy ground.

"Just cry," Kieran says.

"Do you know what they cost?" asks Cassie.

"Money?"

"Jesus, Kieran, I mean, how much?"

"Do you want me to carry you or what?"

Cassie considers. "Good idea."

"Stop bitching. Where exactly is this cabin?" I want to know.

Riley looks at her notes. "Go inside and turn left. Can't be far. And you, Cassie," she snaps at her friend, "could have worn different shoes. Getting the coin is different from going shopping."

"Oh," Cassie sighs, "my dad will just have to clean it."

"Jump up," Kieran suggests, standing in front of the vampire. "But don't bite me!"

"Don't worry, I'm kind of a vegetarian."

She actually jumps on Kieran's back. He takes Cassie's backpack and leaves. I take Riley's hand and we follow. "Another cute couple," I whisper. Riley only nods briefly. She's too focused to joke.

After about fifty meters, Kieran sets Cassie down.

A long scream follows. "Ewwwww!"

"What's wrong?" he asks.

"This place is crawling with ants!"

"Sorry, I didn't mean to."

"That's disgusting!"

"They won't eat you."

"Yes, they'll crawl everywhere!"

Cassie takes a few steps aside, stomps the ground until the last ants fall off, and says, "I'll walk alone, at least I know where I'm going.

After another ten minutes, we stop again.

"We're wandering through the forest like fools.

We can't find that damn hut. Are you sure it still exists?" asks Kieran, who is getting tired of walking through all the underbrush.

"Yes, it must be here somewhere," Riley answers.

"Keep looking, I have to pee and find a tree," my buddy says, turning right into a dense thicket of leaves. Less than ten seconds later he shouts in our direction: "Over here!"

"What's the matter? Can't you hold him by yourself?"

The girls laugh.

"James, you idiot. I found the cabin!"

We fight our way through the underbrush and finally stand in front of an almost completely overgrown house.

"This looks really creepy," Cassie says.

Kieran walks around the outside. "When I open the door, the whole box collapses. The boards are only held together by the roots and the plants.

I understand the concern. Arm-thick vines twine along the wood, crawl over the roof, and wrap around an oak tree standing next to the hut.

"But at least it looks stable," I say after taking a closer look at the rustic structure.

Ferns have grown almost as tall as a man in front of the windows. A few cobwebs don't make it any easier to enter.

The four of us stand in front of the door. We read a sign with faded letters. It warns against entering.

Danger of collapse and no trespassing! Private property!

Riley pushes a fern aside and grabs the doorknob. "Locked."

"So what do we do now?" asks Cassie.

"I can knock," Kieran suggests, walking to the door and slamming his shoulder against it.

Boom - crack

The rickety hinges are ripped from the rotten wood with a clatter and the door falls in. "See? If you knock hard enough, they'll open the door for you." He looks around. "It's cozy in here."

Cassie and Riley roll their eyes. "Typical werewolf."

I follow Cassie's gaze. "You're looking at Kieran's ass."

"James, I'm not."

"And if she is," Kieran says, "at least she'll see a bubble butt."

We laugh.

The furniture is more than sparse. A chunky wooden table that could actually be from 1818 and a matching chair stand in front of a small window. Opposite is the frame of a bed, with a slatted frame but no mattress.

"There must be an entrance to a cave. The coins are in caves whose entrances are protected so that only the hands of vampires, werewolves and humans can open them."

"Riley, I don't see anything," Cassie says in a disappointed voice.

"Are you sure we're in the right place?" I ask.

"We must be right," Kieran supports Riley's theory.

"It all makes sense. This Hostang is playing with us. We just need to know the rules, then we can play along."

"What do you mean?"

"Stop chatting and concentrate. There must be an entrance to a cave here in this shabby hut with a single room that isn't 20 square meters."

"I don't see a hatch."

"Neither do I."

"But I see a wooden floor, and there must be something hidden under it."

"Kieran, do you think we need to rip up the floorboards? We don't have any tools."

Cassie puts her hands on her hips. "That's what you think. Mom still has a spade and other stuff lying around in the back room. She wants to plant a new hedge next week and she bought a few things for it. I was too lazy to unload them and she forgot."

"Cassie, that's fantastic! Give me the car keys and you wait here. I'll be quicker on my own," says Kieran, taking the key to the Toyota and disappearing into the woods.

While he's gone, we look at Riley's notes and compare them with Kieran's theory. "I think Kieran's right and the third coin is in this little town called Salem, Connecticut. I've been to Salem on the coast before and I honestly wouldn't know where there's supposed to be a cave," I say.

"That's what we vampires thought, but we're convinced it's under the church and that there's something like catacombs there. We found records to that effect. Of course, none of us have ever gone into that church to find a cave entrance."

"What is the source of the clues?"

"I don't know."

"What if we go into the wrong cave? I mean, the three of us. Werewolf, vampire and human."

"I have no idea. We're losing time, what else is going to happen?"

Cassie clears her throat. "And maybe lives. Hostang will surely have set traps. It's impossible to bring these three kinds of creatures together. But if one of them dies, there will certainly be no new attempt to get the next coin, but everything will degenerate into a new battle between werewolves, vampires and humans. Each will blame the other."

"Sounds plausible."

"Okay, we'll look for the third coin in Connecticut first," Riley agrees. "Kieran's way of thinking is logical."

Rustling in the woods. Hurried footsteps. We look to where our friend disappeared into the dense green a few minutes ago.

"Let's go!" we hear Kieran yell before we even see him. He's holding a spade and an axe. "Tell me, Cassie, did your mom want to dig a grave and use the hatchet to cut your dad into quarters?"

We laugh.

"No, she wanted to remove a bush and its roots and then plant a new hedge."

"Anyway, thanks to Cassie's mother, we have the right tools. Move over."

We make room. Kieran looks at the floorboards. Finally he goes to the bedstead and takes up the spade. "This board first." He heaves the edge into the gap between two planks and lifts it up with a belt. "Give me a hand," he gasps.

I grab it, then Cassie and Riley help, and with the loud cracking of the old floor, we heave the plank out with our combined strength. We repeat the process a few more times. Shortly after we have removed the third board, we can see the entrance to a cave. The entrance is just big enough for an adult to squeeze through. It reminds me of the exit of the tunnel system in our forest. We break three more planks out of the ground and the entrance is completely exposed. We shine three cell phone flashlights into the cave.

"No ladder."

"It goes in flat. We can slide through."

"There's no way I'm going first," comes from Cassie.

"Worried about your clothes?" laughs Kieran.

"No, but critters of all kinds," she admits.

"I'll go first," I say, giving Riley a kiss on the cheek. Then I slide into the cave, lying on my back with my legs out in front of me. It goes down a narrow hole for about three meters at a slight angle, then the cavity widens and I can turn around and sit up. I can hear Kieran sliding down behind me. The air is stuffy and smells of musty earth. I crawl forward two meters, then I can stand in a crouched position. After about ten more meters I stand in a larger cave. Kieran arrives. We illuminate the ceiling. Old Indian drawings are visible. Men, fish, boats, horses and other animals. Everything is only faintly visible, but it still looks very impressive. Riley and Cassie catch up to us and look up at the ceiling in awe.

"Wow, this is really nice," my friend says while Cas wrinkles her nose.

"But it smells awful."

"Not as bad as your vampire tunnel in Greenfield," I explain.

Cassie shrugs. "Could be."

Kieran finds what looks like an entrance to a side cave. But the entrance is blocked by a heavy stone. On the wall next to it are two hands and an animal paw. "That must be me," Kieran realizes.

We put our hands on the drawings. Nothing happens. "We need to look for something else."

Even before we look around, Cassie has spotted something and shouts: "Here! Look at this."

She is standing a meter behind us next to a small, waist-high pillar with a stone on top of it. "I see indentations under the stone."

Kieran lifts the stone and places it next to the pillar. "It has covered the imprints of three hands," he gasps. We stand around the pillar.

"Shall we?" I ask.

Riley and Kieran nod. Each of them places a hand in the imprint. My heart is pounding with excitement as I'm the last to place my hand in the appropriate recess. Nothing happens.

"It's not going to work. We're doomed," Riley says as the pillar suddenly starts to move.

Kieran grins broadly. "Keep your hands on it!"

The column vibrates and lowers. At the same time, it rumbles loudly and the large stone blocking a side passage of the cave slowly rolls to the side. As we stand by the pillar, Cassie shines a light into the now clear cavity.

"There's a box. It looks like wood. I see gold fittings," she describes her observation. "The thing is on some kind of altar. Should I take it?"

"Wait a minute! I don't trust that Hostang," Kieran warns.

Meanwhile we crouch down so we don't take our hands out of the notches.

"When I think of Indiana Jones, I imagine there will be quite a rumble if we take our hands off here."

"I'm convinced this is the trap. The three of us are tied to the pillar. If one of us leaves, the whole thing will collapse. The box can only be retrieved by a vampire. Without Cashe, we're really screwed," Kieran says.

"We have about thirty seconds left, then this pillar will have disappeared into the ground. I suggest that Cassie grabs the crate, sees if the coin is inside, and then immediately runs for the exit. We'll follow as soon as possible."

"Should I take it now?"

"Do it!" Riley blurts out.

Cassie reaches for the box, takes it and opens the lid. "I've got the coin!"

"Get out!"

Cassie runs to the exit. "You can come!"

The pillar stops moving. We get up and start running as well. The moment our hands leave the notches, there is the same rumble as before, and the stone that originally rolled to the side moves again. This time in the other direction.

"Faster!" Kieran gasps, pushing Cassie up. Then he crawls through the opening himself. Riley follows. I look back and see small chunks of earth and stone falling from the ceiling. Cracks appear, widening, and more and more rocks and dust trickle down. The cave is collapsing.

Getting out of the cave goes very well. Cassie is already outside. So is Kieran. The werewolf turns and offers his hand to

Riley. First he pulls her out of the cave, then he offers his hand to me. We hear a loud thud. The ground vibrates.

I can feel Kieran's strength as he pulls on his clothes. "Now get out of the hut," my buddy urges. I just made it with his help. I breathe a sigh of relief.

"Faster!" Riley admonishes.

I get up. We set off, leaving the cabin and running away from it. We are barely a few meters away when the ground beneath the old log cabin collapses and it slides thunderously into the gaping hole in the ground. A thick cloud of dust rises.

"We did it!" we cheer.

"That was close," Kieran laughs.

"I think we make a good team."

"I'm so grateful to you!" shouts Riley, looking at the coin.

"Let's go home. I'm starving," Kieran groans.

"How about Burger King?"

"I'd love to, but the one in Greenfield."

"Home, then," laughs Cassie.

https://pixabay.com/de/service/license-summary/

book-7431063_1280

Chapter Ten

Cassie, Riley and I each had a Set Menu, Kieran had a Menu and an extra Double Whopper. While the others were already on their way to the parking lot, I was still in the bathroom. Of course, I spilled ketchup on myself again and I wash the stain out. I look down at my work and am glad that no one else is here. It's too embarrassing. The door opens. Someone enters the bathroom. I am annoyed.

"What a load of crap," I curse, spreading the red stuff all over my t-shirt instead of getting it off.

"Well, doesn't it work?"

That voice. I jump and turn around. Jack Blood is standing behind me.

I am so screwed.

My mind is racing. I need a quick solution to get out of this number in one piece.

"Hi, Mr. Hools," I say quickly. I think that was good, but I don't get the desired reaction.

"James Allington. I know exactly what you've done." "Please? What are you talking about, Mr. Hools?"

"Stop taking me for a fool. You know who I am." "The substitute teacher."

The blood comes very close to me. My right hand slips into my pants pocket as inconspicuously as possible. I reach for the bottle as the vampire grabs my upper arms and squeezes them together.

Fuck, I can't get the fucking bottle out.

"You're Jack Blood, right?"

"You can do it," the guy breathes into my ear. His breath really stinks. I have to suppress a gag.

"What do you want from me?"

"You're in my way. You snoop around too much. I'm surprised you're still alive. Any human who discovers the tunnel of the vampires of Greenfield is doomed to die."

"Times are changing."

"I don't care."

"Vampires and humans live together in peace."

"You are so stupid. This is nothing but the calm before the storm."

"What do you want from me?"

"Just the coin! You must bring it to me. I cannot take it by force. The coin is magical, and it is predestined. So, James, give me the coin."

"I don't have a coin."

I'm secretly glad about the information Jack Blood probably gave me by accident. He can't take the coins by force. That's a small advantage for us.

"Bullshit! Edward followed you. I know you were in Washington."

"What's in it for you if the curse is fulfilled?"

Laughter. Disgusting, foul breath hits me. The vampire's eyes begin to glow. "Riley's family has a claim on the title of prince. I must eliminate them to ascend to the vampire throne. Hostang, my late wizard friend, created a wonderful curse. When Riley's family is dead, I can make my appearance."

"And if the curse is lifted from the family? Then you can also become king - or whatever that means. Why don't you become the ruler of a peaceful vampire kingdom?"

That ugly laugh again. Again, stinking breath flows towards me. "You good-for-nothing, you pathetic weakling! I will seize power and bathe in blood! First human blood, then werewolf blood!"

If only I could get the bottle out of my pocket.

"First I'll take America, then Europe, and then the whole world!"

"So you need my help?"

He suddenly looks at me as if he's going to suck me dry. Jack Blood opens his mouthI recognize the long, pointed vampire fangs.

"I demand the coin. You will bring it to me immediately or ..."

He lets go of me and raises his arms threateningly, as if he were a bird of prey about to swoop down on me. I take the opportunity to pull the bottle out of my pocket, hold it in front of my face and unscrew the cap with my other hand. Blood immediately takes two steps back, holding his hands protectively in front of his eyes. I see pure fear in his eyes.

"Or what?" I ask. "I think you'd like to get to know the contents of this bottle now."

Blood turns and flees from the toilet. The next moment Kieran comes in.

"Dude, did you fall in the toilet? What's taking so long?" My whole body is shaking. Kieran immediately realizes that something is wrong and starts to think.

"Say, wasn't that just Mr. Hools coming out of the toilet?"
I nod.

"Oh you fat egg, you were in the toilet with Hools - or should I say Jack Blood? That's just so disgusting! What did he want?"

I calm down a bit. "The coin. He wants to use force to prevent us from breaking the curse."

"Tell me."

"In the car, so the others can hear."

After I've told my friends everything in detail, Cassie and Riley are stunned.

"What a bastard! We'll stop this."

Kieran does his famous scratch-think move again. "The way you told it, Jack Blood is also responsible for the curse. That Hostang was friends with him."

"He is!" Riley clarifies. "I realize a few things now." We stare at her. "What do you know that we don't?"

"I can only guess, but it sounds logical from what you've just told us, James."

"We're all ears."

"We vampires don't live forever either. We can live to be quite old, but we don't have eternal life. One of my ancestors joined the revolutionaries. As a young vampire, he traveled the world spreading fear and terror. He was ostracized and hunted by the vampire lords. Eventually he disappeared and was never seen again. Shortly thereafter, according to the vampire history books, a wizard and a vampire set out. They joined forces. From then on, the name Jack Blood appeared everywhere. He wants to come to power, but even he cannot override the Vampire Law. He can kill and spread terror, but he can never take the throne as long as there are vampires who have senior rights. This is my family. We have spoken out against vampire rule and in favor of coexistence with humans, but if we were all dead, our lost relative could claim the throne and all their vampires would have to follow him."

"Jack Blood!"

"That's right. He used to be called William McCallan."

"A Scot?"

"My mother's family is from Scotland. I suspect he hid out in the Scottish Highlands for decades before he went out into the world as Jack Blood and began his mischief."

"Okay. Now we know that. And we also know that James has a weapon that Jack Blood is afraid of. So he's not invincible. Now we just have to decide how to proceed."

"Simple," I say. "We stay together and get the next coin."

"By *stay together*, do you mean all night?"

"If that's what you want, no problem. But you girls will have to sleep in my parents' bed. The couch already belongs to James."

"No, no," Cassie dismisses. "That's not possible. I have to take such good care of myself and have a full bath. Then I need a body scrub to get the stench of the cave out of my pores. I think it will be good for Riley, too. We'll have a really nice girls' night at my place and come back to yours at eight in the morning."

Riley smiles. "Sounds fantastic."

Kieran's eyes widen. "At eight o'clock? In the middle of the night?"

I interrupt. "That's a great time. We have 150 miles to go before we reach our destination. There must be a lot of tourists on their way to Flume Gorge this time of year. They all want to see Indian summer in all its glory, and the national park is a great place to do that."

"I'm convinced, but you're making breakfast. A man's breakfast with eggs and bacon and stuff," Kieran says.

"You're a really great guy," I joke. "You invite me over and I'm supposed to serve you and cook for you.

We laugh.

The night passes quietly. Neither Jack Blood nor his helper, the same Edward, show up. I lie awake for a long time, but eventually sleep catches up with me and I sleep until seven in the morning. My dreams are only interrupted when my cell phone wakes me up. We prepare the men's breakfast that Kieran wants and have a lot of fun.

At eight o'clock on the dot, the horn honks. I look out the window and see Mrs. Anderson's car. Cassie and Riley are standing next to it, fooling around in a good mood. They've been shopping, too. As we drive away, we see *Slim Jims*, *Coca Cola* and *Mr. Peppers*, some candy bars and four bottles of water.

"The gas tank is full and Daddy slipped me an *50 Bucks* extra. We're ready to go."

The drive is fun. We joke and laugh a lot. I think we are actually pretty cool considering the situation. I keep looking back at the traffic behind us, but I don't see anything.

"You want to know if Blood or his helper Edward are following us, don't you?" asks Riley.

"Right."

The miles roll by and I begin to enjoy the scenery. New England in the fall is really worth a trip. I start to rave. "We live in a beautiful part of the country, don't you think?"

"James is getting romantic," Kieran laughs, listening to the next song and turning it up. "Wow, rock 'n' roll!"

"Another 20 miles. Do you know where we have to go in the Flume?" I interject and almost have to shout to be heard.

"*Highway to Hell*!" Kieran belts out, playing air guitar. Then he uses a *Slim Jim* as a microphone and finally he keeps on singing even though there are no lyrics.

We roar with laughter.

"Now it's another 15 miles. Do you know exactly where we are going?" I repeat my question.

Cassie sees a sign for a parking lot and turns on her blinkers. "Another one for little girls," she says.

We pull into the parking lot. There's another camper next to us, but the owners don't seem to be with their vehicle. They are also sound asleep. Cassie parks in front of the camper and gets out.

"Shit, no bathroom here. I wonder why they're building a parking lot here," Cassie grumbles.

"Come on, let's take the big one," says Riley, who has also gotten out of the car and points into the woods.

Cassie makes a face. "All right."

Behind us, a red Dogde rolls into the parking lot, followed by a light blue old Ford. Both stop right at the beginning of the lot. The driver of the Ford gets out and scurries off into the woods.

He's got a lot of pressure on his bladder, I think, and tries to see who's driving the Dogde. No chance. Darkened windows prevent everything.

Kieran distracts me. "Would you like a Slim Jim before we go? Who knows when we'll get another meal."

"No, thanks," I say, getting out and walking to the dog. I take a deep breath. It smells like fall. The sound of engines drifts over from the highway. But you can't see any cars because of a thick strip of green. I move slowly, expecting everything. I hold the Mexican bottle tightly in my hand, ready to use it in an emergency. Finally I reach the vehicle. I can't see anything, so I get very close and look inside.

Empty.

I am amazed. The driver must have gotten out while I was talking to Kieran. I don't see anything suspicious inside the vehicle and calmly walk back.

"Aaahhhh!", a shrill, prolonged scream suddenly sends adrenaline coursing through my bloodstream.

Kieran and I immediately run into the forest.

"Cassie?"

"Riley?" we call worriedly.

We run deeper into the undergrowth and call out again. Riley answers. Her voice sounds worried. "Here! We ... we're trapped!"

We run in the direction of the voice and find the girls. They are both kneeling on the ground. Behind them is Edward. He is holding a revolver in his right fist. "This one is loaded with consecrated silver bullets, friends. So think twice about what you're doing."

"Edward!" I groan.

Blood's helper looks at me and grins viciously. "James, you should have come with me before school. Jack Blood was willing to offer you money then."

"You miserable scumbag!"

"Well, who wants to be rude? Give me the coin or I'll pull the trigger. First this little doll will get it, then the cheeky brat. Or I can put a bullet in your gluttonous friend first. Or you too, you big mouth."

"My father will hunt you down and suck you dry, you bastard," Cassie threatens.

"Shut up, you stupid bitch! You're pissing me off!" Edward loses it and points the barrel of his revolver at Cassie. "Say goodbye to your friends!"

"Stop! Don't shoot or you'll never get the coin!"

Edward cocks the hammer. With the barrel still pointed at Cassie, he looks at me. "This is where I give the orders, you little runt."

"Are you a vampire?" I ask him.

Edward laughs. "No, I'm Jack Blood's partner and he promised to make me the most powerful person in the world. I'll drink from golden taps and I can buy whatever I want."

"Put the gun down. I'll get the coin," I calm the guy down.

"I'll give you two minutes. And you," he points the barrel of the gun at Kieran, "come over here, put your hands up and kneel down next to the two chicks!"

Kieran looks at me questioningly.

"I'll think of something," I whisper.

"Hopefully something good," he replies, raising his arms. I haven't taken three steps when I hear something. Instinctively, I turn around. I know vampires and werewolves are fast, but I'm afraid they're slower than a bullet fired from a handgun. My fear that Kieran will go crazy, lunge at Edward and catch a bullet is unfounded. He stands just as rooted to the spot as I am, watching the spectacle unfold before our eyes. Everything seems to be happening in slow motion, even though it only lasts a few seconds.

Suddenly, a young man emerges from the undergrowth and runs straight at Edward. Startled, he turns to the side and raises his revolver. He crooks his index finger. The hammer clicks and strikes the firing cap of the inserted patron. The shot breaks and the silver bullet leaves the barrel of the pistol, framed by an orange-yellow muzzle flash.

With a deft, quick turn to the side, the assailant dodges the shot, performs a huge somersault, and comes to a stop right next to Edward before he can flex his right index finger for another shot. Edward's wrists are grabbed. The revolver falls to the ground. Although the gangster is well-built, he appears to be inferior to his unknown and much slimmer opponent. He makes a powerful grab, turns and bends down in one motion, throwing Edward through the air. The criminal hits hard on his back and gasps for air. The young man is already sitting on Edward's chest and grabbing his neck. "You rotten bastard! You want to kill my sister? I'll show you what it means to mess with vampires!"

"Ian! I've never been so happy to see you," Riley exclaims.

Edward gasps. His face turns blue. I take the revolver, open the cylinder and pull out a cartridge.

"These are actually silver bullets. I can still use them against Jack Blood," I say and shove them into my waistband.

"Don't shoot your balls off with that, mate," Kieran warns.

The werewolf quickly regains his sense of humor.

Cassie watches the fight anxiously, worried that Ian might overreact. "Don't kill him," she urges him.

Ian loosens his grip. Edward coughs wildly, struggling for oxygen. He knows he has lost.

Riley says forcefully, "We have to tie him up."

"I'd better kill him," Ian thunders and lets his fist fly forward. He stops just before it lands on Edward's nose. Only millimeters separate the knuckle and the tip of his nose.

"Please don't," Edward whines. "I can help you!"

Cassie stands over him. "What did you say to me before? Would you like to repeat it?"

"I'm so sorry!" Edward feigns.

"I'd like to shove an earthworm down your throat, but I don't touch those things. Your loss."

Kieran kneels next to Edward and pulls his car keys out of his pocket. "Let's see what we can find in your car," he says, running to the Dogde. There he takes a quick, safe look inside the car. He finds nothing dangerous. Kieran opens the passenger door and gets in. He looks around carefully. He flips the sun visors down and up, then opens the glove compartment. He finds what he was looking for, takes it and gets out. Now the young werewolf walks purposefully to the trunk and opens it. Kieran rummages around a bit, finds something again and finally comes back with a broad grin on his face. "Handcuffs! I knew our comrade here was well equipped," he says triumphantly and lifts up the handcuffs for all to see.

Ian stands up. He points warningly at Edward. "Turn over on your stomach and put your hands behind your back!"

The defeated man immediately complies. We put his own handcuffs on Edward. As he lies in front of us, handcuffed and free to defend himself, a heavy weight falls from my shoulders. I'm really relieved.

"Look what else I found. This was in the Dogde's glove compartment."

"Like what?"

Kieran holds up a driver's license and vehicle registration. "It's all made out to a Mr. Hools." Jack Blood's assistant groans. He just realized that he's going to jail for a very long time. Maybe forever.

"Edward, you are so fucked," Riley laughs.

"I had nothing to do with this!" he tries to explain in a panic.

"Save your lies. You can tell them to the police." Riley looks at Ian. "Ian, how the hell did you get here?"

"This is Ian?" I ask.

"Yeah, that's my big brother," Riley explains.

The vampire puts his hand on his sister's shoulder. "I'm worried, little sister. That's why I filled up my Ford and spent the night in the car outside the Andersons' house and followed you. Even before we got to Kieran's, I noticed the Dogde. He was following you at a great distance, so I attached myself to him. When you both disappeared into the woods, I immediately followed. You know the rest of the story."

"What do we do with him?" I ask, pointing at Edward.

"Eat him?" Kieran suggests.

"Suck him out," Ian says.

Edward starts to cry and shakes like a leaf. No, please don't,' he cries.

I release him. "We'll turn him over to the New Hampshire police, say the owner of this car is missing in Massachusetts and this guy is a prime suspect and definitely has something to do with it," I suggest.

"Okay, not bad. Besides, he stinks. I think he peed his pants," Kieran teases the prisoner.

"Yes, I admit I helped Mr. Blood, but I didn't kill Hools. Blood did. I just buried the body."

"Like I said, you can tell the police all about it."

"And if he changes his mind, I already recorded it with the smartphone," Cassie says.

I look at my watch. "We have to get going."

"That's fine. I'll call the police and wait here. I'll tell them what happened, tell them to meet with Sheriff Allington, and then I'll follow you."

"You know the destination? We're looking for the cave in Franconia Notch State Park, right in Flume Gorge. Cassie got a good map from her dad."

"Great. I'll take a quick picture of it. Then I'll have no problem finding you in Flume Gorge."

A few minutes later we give Edward a last disdainful look, get into the car and drive off.

"You have a really cool brother, Riley," I say.

Her look is proud and satisfied and also a little mischievous. "You mess with me, you're going to get in trouble with him."

"Now I understand why you haven't had a boyfriend in so long," Kieran laughs, turning up the radio. "Twelve miles to go!"
"What?"

Kieran turns around. "I can't hear anything, the radio's so loud!"

We laugh. Then we fall silent.

"Exit 34a, we have to get off the highway," Riley finally says.

Cassie puts on her blinker and slows down.

"I never thought I'd come back to Franconia Notch State Park. The last time I was here was five years ago with my parents," I say.

"The gorge alone is worth it," Kieran says and starts raving about Flume Gorge.

The natural granite gorge lies at the foot of Mount Liberty and is a tourist magnet in New Hampshire.

We park not far from the entrance to Flume Gorge. The number of visitors is probably limited due to the announced regens, but there is still a lot going on.

We go to the ticket office. A woman chewing gum looks at us amused. "Regular or Discovery Pass?"

"Four regular tickets, please," Cassie says.

"Sixty dollars."

"What, how much?"

The woman behind the glass doesn't seem to like Cassie's tone. She stops chewing, narrowing her eyes like a cat about to pounce on its prey, and repeats in a sharp tone: "60 dollars. 15 dollars each."

"That's okay," I interject before Cassie can answer, because judging by the look on her face, there would have been at least one insult in it.

Riley nudges Cassie. "That's money well spent."

Cassie stares at her friend open-mouthed. Kieran grabs the bill from Cassie's hand, places 10 Dollar on top and slides the two bills to the cashier. "Here. That's right!"

"You've got to be kidding me," grumbles the chewing gum aunt.

"Only if..." Kieran starts, but I play it safe and interrupt.

"Thanks for the cards."

The woman shakes her head, puts the money in the till and gives us four tickets. "Always stay on the paths."

"Of course! Thank you."

We skip the shuttle bus that would take us to the entrance of the gorge and take the footpath instead.

"Where exactly are we supposed to go?"

Riley pulls out her notes. "To one of the waterfalls, and it's the biggest one."

"And where is this waterfall?" asks Cassie, who is still angry because the gum aunt gave her such a stupid look. "Man, that bitch! Next time I'll pull it out of her till".

Kieran laughs. "Now, don't get mad. We got what we wanted."

"Sure, with my fifty dollars."

"We'll pay you back," I interject.

Cassie looks at us in turn. "That's not what I meant. I'm just upset about the high price of the ticket. Of course I'll donate the fifty."

"Cassie, you're the best friend a girl could ever have," Riley says happily and gives her a hug.

Kieran rolls his eyes. "Is the General going to cuddle now or can we move on? My stomach will be back soon."

"Kieran, what do you think about when you're not thinking about food?"

"Why?"

"Oh, never mind," the two girls laugh.

Riley spreads out a map, studies it and points to a spot with her index finger. "I think this is it," she says. "If we're going cross-country, it shouldn't be too far."

"That chick said not to leave the loop."

"Cassie, I think this chick is a stupid cow. Are you listening to her?"

"Me?" she points at herself and shakes her head. "Never! We'll get off the trail and go where we want. For a $60 entrance fee, we own the whole park here."

"Seriously, guys. Look here," Riley reminds us and we all look at the map to memorize the way.

"Check! Follow me, guys. I know where we have to go," Kieran says and starts walking purposefully. We hurry to follow him when he disappears into the forest after only a few meters.

I enjoy the walk. We hardly speak. The air is cool, clear and feels really good. Unfortunately, dark rain clouds have been hovering over us for some time.

"It is really beautiful here," Riley says after a while.

We agree with her.

"It would be even nicer if it didn't start raining," Kieran grumbles and pulls on the hood of his rain jacket as the first drops fall from the sky.

It doesn't take long for the rain to come down in torrents. We wait under a large tree until the first heavy downpour has passed, then we continue in light, steady rain.

90 minutes after our arrival at Flume Gorge we are standing at a beautiful waterfall. Not in front of it, but above it. The water rushes past us, squeezes through the gravel, and finally plunges deep into the gorge.

"That's it," Kieran says proudly. "And we saved at least half the time by cutting it short."

"True, but we're standing over the waterfall. We need to get down," I point to the natural wonder.

Cassie looks down. The water roars down about 20 or 30 meters.

"See that wooden bridge over there, the one the tourists walk on?" Kieran points to the other side of the gorge.

"Yeah."

"You can't go down from there. There's no ledge, no path. Just bare rock. The only way down is from this side. We'll have to climb a bit, but it's not too hard. We can make it."

"Riley, where exactly are we supposed to go? We're at the waterfall and now? What's the next step?" I ask.

"There's a cave behind the waterfall.We have to go in there."

"Well then, guys. Let's climb," Kieran grins and spits into his hands.

The werewolf looks for a suitable descent and turns to us. "Come on now! It's not that hard." "It's so deep," Riley says worriedly, grabbing my left arm.

"We'll make it," I encourage her. "Just don't look down."

"I can't. I'm not free of dizziness. I'm sorry," Riley moans.

"I'm getting really dirty," Cassie complains.

"Dirty suits you," laughs Kieran.

"I don't want to go down there. I'm staying with Riley," Cassie says firmly.

"What the hell? We need a human, a werewolf and a vampire!"

Kieran is furious.

"You guys go ahead. We'll see if the descent works. I'll text Ian and send him our position. If we're lucky, he won't take too long and can climb down to you," Riley suggests.

"And if he can't, I'll follow," Cassie adds.

"All right, we can do it like this, but have Ian bring some sandwiches," Kieran replies, looking at me and saying, "Let's go!

The girls stay at the top and we climb down into the gorge. The first part of the descent is easy and I can hold on to branches and logs that grow further down the slope. From the middle of our route, however, you have to look for cracks to hold on to. It's not like free climbing on a steep wall, but it's going in that direction.

The descent is quite good. Only once it gets tricky. While holding on to a bush that seems to be stuck, I'm looking for a good foothold with my right foot. However, I dislodged a loose rock and for a moment I only had the bush to hold on to as it detached from the rock. I barely managed to grab hold of a crevice. I finally find my footing and take a deep breath.

Kieran grumbles as a few small pieces of rock fall on his head. "Careful, old man! That hurts."

"Everything is so slippery because of this stupid rain."

"Then be twice as careful!"

My hands are really shaking from the effort. I make sure I step safely and look up from time to time. Cassie and Riley haven't noticed a thing. That's good, I think. They're chatting and seem to be having a good time.

"Sorry," I call to Kieran as another small stone rolls down.

He dodges it and thanks me with a thumbs up. "Fits!"

I keep climbing.

"Boys!" the girls call. "Ian's already at the front of the parking lot. It all worked out and this Edward has been arrested. Ian's coming as fast as he can."

"What are they saying?" Kieran wants to know.

The sound of the water is so loud that he can't understand what is being shouted at us. I have to shout loudly. "I'll tell you in a minute!"

He puts his thumb up again, indicating that he has understood. Kieran is almost there. Just a few more steps and he's there.

A few minutes later I am also safely on the ground. The background noise is enormous. I have to shout loudly to talk to Kieran. We use a lot of hand gestures to communicate.

A few people have stopped at the tourist jetty to watch us. Thankfully none of the park rangers are there. They shake their heads and move on. Kieran points to the waterfall. We go there. I hope, that the entrance to the cave is not on the other side of the river.

"If we have to cross, we won't make it. The current is too strong," I call.

Kieran doesn't hear me. He walks along the shore, approaching the rock face over which the water falls. I look back at Riley and Cassie. They wave. I wave back and turn to Kieran. He's gone.

Damn it! Where did he go? I hope he didn't fall in. I panic and search the surface of the water. There's no sign of Kieran. Suddenly he reappears. He's standing behind the waterfall and waves at me.

"Come here!" he seems to be shouting, but I can only make out his mouth and hand gestures. I don't understand a word. I looked back at the girls. They are waving again.

What is this?

Now I understand. They are pointing at their smartphones. I pull mine out of my pocket. They have written to me. I open WhatsApp and read the message.

Riley: Hold on a second. Ian's going to be here in a few minutes.

Me: Okay, we'll wait. Then I go to Kieran.

It doesn't take long until Ian climbs down the rock face towards us. I watch him fascinated.

He's as agile as Kieran, I think.

The vampire clears the slope easily and comes over to us.

"We can do it," he says and points to the waterfall. Then he offers his hand to Kieran. Kieran takes it.

"Thank you from the bottom of my heart. I never thought that a werewolf would help us. Besides, I don't know any werewolves on purpose. Kieran, you've done a really good job for me!"

"I noticed."

It is an indescribable experience to stand in a cave whose entrance is covered by a roaring waterfall. I have only seen these pictures on television or in the movies. We took off our hoods and walked a few meters into the cave. Almost at the same time, we turn on the flashlight apps on our smartphones.

"Expansive."

"Do you know how far in we have to go?" I ask Ian.

He shakes his head. "No, but we'll find what we're looking for."

We start walking. The beams of light from our cell phones flit from the floor to the ceiling, along the walls and back to the floor. It is warm and damp and smells slightly musty. But not as wild as the vampire tunnel system.

After about twenty meters, the previously extremely high ceiling becomes significantly lower and the corridor narrows. A junction leads to the right and steeply upwards.

"Keep going straight," Ian says.

I start my drawing application.

Again we see two junctions. One goes to the left, the other to the right.

"It's like a crossroads. What do we do?"

"I'll go a few yards to the left, one of you to the right," Kieran suggests.

"Wait here," says Ian and continues straight ahead. After about three minutes he comes back. "We can't go straight on. The cave passage narrows and becomes a dead end."

"Then turn right," says Kieran.

We turn into the right cave passage. I follow. After another twenty meters the cave branches off again. This time we go right first. When it turns out to be a dead end, we go back and take the left fork.

Kieran is at the top. "There was something," he says, shining his light down.

"I felt resistance."

At the same time we hear a whirring noise and a dull thud.

"Ahhh, damn it! Auaaa!"

"What's going on?" shouts Ian.

I shine a light on Kieran. There's an arrow in his thigh. "Holy shit! How did that happen?"

"Trip wire. Watch out, it's set up like a self firing system!"

I search for the trap in the light of my cell phone and spot the wire. "This is where it happened!"

"Is it very bad?" asks Ian.

"Not that bad," Kieran groans and sits down. He grimaces. "I hope I don't get blood poisoning or something. At least it wasn't a deadly silver arrow."

"That reassures me."

Ian pulls out a Swiss Army pocket knife and carefully cuts a hole in Kieran's jeans around the arrow. Kieran flinches at first, but quickly realizes that his new friend is being extremely careful and holds still.

"You're lucky you're wearing jeans with rivets, mate. The arrowhead hit one of those rivets, dulling it and breaking it off. The thing is only superficially stuck in the flesh. It probably hurts a lot, but you won't have to deal with it for long.

Kieran fights back a smile and tries to stay cool. "I was going to throw these jeans away, but I thought they'd come in handy for a trip like this."

Ian examines the wound and feels carefully around the arrow. "I'm going to have to pull it out. There's no way around it."

"Do you have to?"

"Yes, absolutely. I need to disinfect and close the wound. If bacteria get in, it could end badly."

Kieran groans. "I won't be spared either. I feel like I'm in the Wild West already."

"I'll draw on the count of three."

The werewolf nods and closes his eyes for a moment. "I'm ready."

"One..." Ian begins to count, holding the shaft of the arrow just below the tip and pulling it out of the wound with a jerk. Kieran, who has been waiting for the second number, opens his eyes and screams: "Auaaaa!"

Ian grins and lifts the arrow.

Relieved and yet a little annoyed, the werewolf says: "I thought you weren't going to draw until the count of three!"

"Changed my mind," Ian grins. "It's an old doctor's trick."

"Are you a doctor?"

"No, not yet, but I'm studying to be one. I've already done my first internship. I worked at Greenfield Hospital."

The vampire fumbles around in his backpack, mumbling: "It's got to be here somewhere," and pulls out an emergency kit. "I always carry this with me when I go hiking," the medical student explains. "It even has some iodine for disinfection."

Shortly after, Kieran is dressed, the wound disinfected and bandaged, and the skin cleaned of blood. He stands and limps a few feet back and forth. "That's all right. I can keep walking."

I am astonished. "Doesn't that hurt?"

"It's all right. Werewolves are built a little differently than humans."

"But this time we shine the light on the floor, walls and ceilings," Ian advises, taking a closer look at the shaft of the arrow. After a while he says: "Guys, I don't think this trap is more than a year or two old.

"Nonsense, the curse is a good 200 years old," I say and go over to Ian to inspect the arrow as well.

"It's carved from beautiful wood and the point is made from a soft material, maybe a lead-zinc mixture or something like that, but it's not from that time. The feathers are real, but the person who made the arrow used modern nylon string. So he made a mistake."

"And the tripwire is made of fishing line. I know that. I go fishing with my dad sometimes," I say. "So it wasn't Hostang who set us up, but..."

"Jack Blood," Kieran interrupts Ian in a deep, grim voice.

Ian thinks about it. "Then Blood knows where the coins are, but he can't get to them, otherwise he would have hidden them somewhere else by now," Kieran summarizes.

"And he wants to keep us from getting them. That's why he set traps."

Ian tosses the arrow aside and straps on his backpack. "You're really going to make it?" he asks Kieran.

"Of course I am! I have to make it. For Riley," he looks into Ian's eyes, "and for you and the whole vampire clan."

Ian holds out his hand. "We are making a start and I hope that this peace and friendship between werewolves and vampires will last forever."

"And with us normal humans too, of course," I laugh and put my hand on his.

We continue, but more slowly and with more caution. We follow the cave passage. After fifteen minutes we reach another crossroads. Kieran scratches his head. Ian and I look at each other questioningly.

"We've been walking in circles. My grandmother's ass. We've been here before," Kieran spits out. I look at the drawing application. "That's right. Then let's take the other cave passage this time."

"Left or right, from my point of view?" asks Ian, entering one of the two passages.

Kieran pricks up his ears like a wolf and warns in a flash. "I heard something, get out of there!"

Ian reacts immediately and not a second too late. At the very spot where he was standing a second ago, a granite boulder plummets to the ground, its shape reminiscent of an oversized hand axe - or rather, a guillotine axe. The thing misses Ian by a hair's breadth and crashes heavily to the rocky ground. Dust and stone splinters are thrown up. A chunk the size of a pebble whizzes past my ear. White as a sheet, Ian stares at the death trap.

"Now you look like a real vampire. Pale as a corpse," Kieran jokes.

I admire him for being able to joke in the face of such mortal danger.

He must have a lot of gallows humor, I smile in style.

"There-there-thank you," Ian stutters.

"Kieran, I love your wolf ears. You can hear really well," I say and add: "Guys, we have to be really careful.

I go to the only possible path and point into the cave passage. "Shall we?"

Ian goes first, I follow close behind and Kieran goes last. We light up meter by meter and don't make as much progress as in the beginning, but we feel much safer.

Undisturbed we reach a larger cave with a gate at the end. Before entering the cave in front of the gate, we scan everything three times. We have a lot of respect for the traps and want to make sure that we don't fall into any of them. To the right of the iron gate is another stone that reminds me of a menhir. A prehistoric boundary or standing stone that has been set upright by human hands.

"There's another one of those stones," Kieran says, pushing forward.

Nothing happens. Ian and I follow. Again there are three handprints on the top of the stone. We look at each other, nod wordlessly and each of us places a hand in one of the prints. It takes about thirty seconds, then we feel the waist-high menhir move. Like the stone in the first cave, it sinks into the earth. There is a loud rattling and rumbling. The gate is pulled up like the protective gate of a castle.

"The stone releases the lock on the counterweight of the gate. We have set off a mechanism. Just like yesterday, it lowers. This raises the gate. We have to be careful as we go through the gate to see if the mechanism reverses and before especially how fast it reverses, otherwise we'll be trapped in there. Forever," Ian says immediately.

I shine my free hand into the space behind the gate. "It doesn't go in very far. About a meter or two," I say.

Kieran also looks into the cave behind the gate. "I see the box. It's the same size as the last one. Only it's not brown, it's red," he says.

"I'm going to run and get the box," Ian exclaims, wanting to sprint away.

"Stop!" I yell.

Ian stops. His hand is still in the menhir's imprint.

"The last time we let go of the stone and clawed at the box, the damn cave collapsed. There's another trap, I'd bet my uncle's Porsche on it. And if the car is gone when he gets home, I'm dead! I mean, we've got to be really damn careful."

"James, I can't see anything. I'll run over, grab the box and, poof, we're gone. Kieran should go first, he can't run that fast."

While I talk to Ian, Kieran lights up the cave. His cone of light creeps across the floor, walls and ceiling of the cave. Finally he says dryly: "I think the box is blocking a spring or a counterweight or something." "Huh? What?" Ian and I ask almost simultaneously. "What makes you think that?"

"Simple. There are a lot of spearheads on the ceiling above the box. I think they fall down when you pick up the box."

Ian and I follow the cone of light from Kieran's cell phone light.

"Bloody hell!" I blurt out.

"We're so screwed. How are we going to get the box?" asks Ian, sounding desperate.

"Maybe I'll run back and get the fishing line. We could make a lasso with it..."

"Forget it," Kieran interjects. "The line is way too light to throw like a lasso. It won't work."

"How far is it from the cave entrance, the gate, to the box?" Ian wants to know.

"About one and a half to two meters," I estimate. "The ground is not rocky, but covered with wooden planks.

"I think I know how to get to the box," he answers quite firmly.

"And how?"

"I'll take my hood, throw it in, and pull the box down with the hood. When the spears come hurtling down from the ceiling, they'll only make a few holes in my sweater."

"What if the rocks start falling again and this whole cave thing collapses?" asks Kieran.

"I don't think so," I counter immediately. "This isn't a small cave like the first one, it's a huge labyrinth of caves and it's ancient. Only the iron gate and the menhir here were built by human hands."

"Or by a witch's hand, James," Ian corrects me.

"Or something like that. Either way. We can't stand here for hours, the three of us holding a stone. Shall we do it with the hoodie now?"

"Sure!"

We concentrate. Ian is the first to take his hand off the stone, pulls off his backpack and slips out of his hoodie. Kieran and I take our hands off the stone as well. I stare respectfully at the menhir.

"It doesn't seem to be moving. Everything's fine," I say as a warning.

Ian stands with the hoodie in the entrance of the gate and forms it into a throw. Kieran limps towards the tunnel where we have to run quickly in case of danger.

At the same moment Ian throws his sweater forward, the stone moves up again. The scratching and grinding doesn't sound very good. Especially when you know that your life is in danger.

"Ian," I warn in a worried voice "I think we should hurry."

The vampire misses the box with the first throw and kneads the hoodie together for the second. "It's good," he mumbles intently and pushes his right hand forward. The hoodie unfolds and stays on top of the crate. "Yay!" he triumphs.

"Hurry up, the menhir's going up again!" shouts Kieran, who was already aware of the dangerous situation when I first warned him.

Ian turns around. "What's going on? Keep it down, I need to concentrate.

I point at the stone. "Then concentrate faster. The menhir is coming up again!"

Ian stares at the menhir. "Why don't you say something? You have to tell me something right now!"

"I did! Now get the damn box!"

The vampire turns his head to the box. "Fuck it," he spits out and yanks the box towards him with a jerk.

The box falls to the ground and actually gets caught in the capsule. Ian is about to pull it towards him when at least twenty spears come crashing down from the ceiling, their sharp tips digging into the wooden floor. As if by a miracle, the crate is spared, but the hoodie is nailed to the floor. Ian reacts instantly, jumps into the room, grabs the crate and runs out.

Rumble

The gate slams shut. By a split second, Ian has once again managed to defy certain death.   He can still feel the pull of the closing trapdoor on his neck.

"Get out of here!" I yell.

We run and rush to Kieran who is standing at the entrance to our escape route. The werewolf waves us off. "You can slow down, the cave - or whatever this is - isn't going to collapse. The trap was in the gate this time."

I turn around. My friend is right. No rocks are falling from the ceiling, the ground isn't shaking and no stone is rolling towards us. We can make our way back without haste. Ian opens the box. The coin looks ancient.

"That's number two!"

We pat each other on the back.

"Go to the girls, they'll be nervous."

Thanks to my drawing app, we quickly find our way back to the exit. We are guided the last few meters by the sound of the roaring waterfall. As we stand behind the rushing water, I pause for a moment to admire this small wonder of nature.

Ian nudges me. "Go on."

We step outside. Our first glance is up at the girls. They both throw their arms up in the air and cheer as we demonstratively hold up the wooden coin box. Riley and Cassie applaud and shout something at us, but we don't understand a word. Kieran has been limping along bravely the whole time, not making a face. But when he sees the steep slope, I can tell he is wondering if he can make it up. Another problem is the rain. It's no longer just dripping from the sky, but pouring down in torrents.

"Hardly different from the waterfall," I remark smugly.

Ian takes over the decision from Kieran. "We have to walk along the slope in the gorge and find a better way up. This steep wall is deadly in the rain. The rock is soaking wet and slippery, as is the ground."

I nod. Kieran nods too. He seems relieved. Ian gives his sister and Cassie a few hand signals, then walks away. We follow without a word. Normal conversation is still impossible. The noise of the water is enormous.

I point to the rocks and shout to Kieran: "Watch out, it's slippery as hell!"

As soon as I have spoken, I slip out with my left foot, row with my arms, and find myself completely in the river. As I tip backwards, Kieran's arms catch me. He supports me. I regain my balance.

"Smooth as an ass, right," he laughs.

"Thank you."

I pay more attention to the path now. We walk slowly, but make good progress. After a few hundred meters we've made it. You can talk again. Your ears still ring a little, but at least you don't have to shout anymore.

Ian points ahead. "That's the path the workers used to carry the wood for the footbridge through the gorge to set the supports. We can easily get up there."

When we reach the first trees, Ian immediately looks for two larger branches and quickly finds them. He breaks off a few overhanging branches and hands the poles to Kieran. "Here! These are your walking sticks now."

"Cool idea."

The path snakes through the forest up to . The route is about five times as long as the direct ascent, but much easier to manage.

My rain jacket is starting to leak and I can feel the wetness seeping in. "I hope this pissing rain stops soon," I grumble.

"I hope we get there soon. Even if it's just a flesh wound on my thigh, it hurts like hell."

"Won't be long now," Ian gasps, warning of a sausage tent sticking out of the ground in the middle of the path.

"Guys, my muscles are going to be sore for a long time. I can already feel my thighs," I groan after another ten minutes.

"I could use a little break too," Kieran groans. Then we hear two girls giggling and talking.

Carrie and Riley are in high spirits and stomp towards us. "Guys, why didn't we take this path earlier? We could have gone into the cave."

"Riley, you're lucky you weren't there," Ian replies.

Cassie sees Kieran's injured leg. "Oh no, what happened?"

Worry lines appear on the foreheads of the two friends.

"Not too bad," Kieran says, playing it cool. "It was just an arrow."

"What?" Riley groans.

"Someone is using violence to keep us from finding the coins. At least one of the traps was new and disguised as old. We suspect that Jack Blood had a hand in it," Ian explains and gradually tells the girls what happened in the cave.

Kieran is now supported by Cassie and Riley and feels very comfortable.

By the time we reach the car, the rain has stopped and a few rays of sunshine are peeking through the gray band of clouds.

"The weather's screwing us too," I grumble. Cassie presses the button.

Click

The door lock unlocks. Riley opens the passenger door. "Sit down."

Kieran sits down. The bandage has turned red. Riley calls to her brother. "Ian, you should take a look at this."

"I'm fine," the werewolf tries to deflect, but Ian pushes Riley aside and dabs at the wound with his index finger.

"Ouch!"

Ian looks at Kieran. "We should get to a hospital. It's better if we get it stitched up."

"Werewolves have the best healing flesh. That's what my grandfather used to say."

"If the wound gets infected, they might have to remove your leg."

"What?"

Ian laughs. "No, of course not, but we also don't know if there are small splinters in the wound. If there are, they have to be removed, otherwise it can quickly lead to purulent complications."

Kieran snorts hard. "What a load of crap."

"No argument," Cassie says. "I'll go to the nearest hospital, we'll get the wound treated and then we'll go back. We still have to get another coin. The sooner we get back home, the sooner we can plan. So let's get going!"

"And I have to get out of my wet clothes," I add.

"You can ride naked, then they won't bother you," Kieran teases me.

They all laugh.

"The wound can't be that bad. If Kieran can still make fun of people, then he's fine."

"What if they have to remove his leg because Jack Blood put some nasty poison in it?"

"Riley, don't joke about that," Kieran snaps at her.

"Sissy!" I say.

"Sissy!" comes back.

"Is anybody hungry?" asks Cassie.

A chorus from Ian, Kieran and me: "Yeah!"

"Then get in my mom's car. I'm going to the nearest burger place and then to the hospital."

"Does the hospital thing have to be real?"

"Of course! You heard about it from Ian, and he's studying medicine."

"Oh my god."

"Chill out, dude."

"Chill, chill, chill. You're always supposed to chill. Hello people, that gets my goat!"

"I don't think the burgers are a bad idea. Whenever the little wolf gets hungry, he gets grumpy."

Everyone laughs again.

"Guys, I'll meet you in Greenfield at Kieran's," Ian says goodbye and gets into his car.

"Yo, man," Kieran replies, in *Breaking Bad style*.

Cassie starts the engine. "Close the door, Kieran."

Clack

She drives off. We are glad we have the coin.

We have come much closer to our goal, and we have become even closer friends. Even more. We have shown that the impossible is possible. Vampires, werewolves and humans can live together peacefully as friends. I'm proud of them all, and even a little proud of myself.

Chapter Eleven

Four cheeseburgers later, with a large Coke and XL fries of course, Kieran is back in high spirits. The doctor at the nearest hospital has given us the all-clear and assured us that his leg will not have to be amputated. He winked at us. It was right to take another look at the wound. Using a magnifying glass and tweezers, the doctor removed two tiny splinters and then sewed up the flesh wound with three stitches.

"You've prevented a serious infection, young man. The stitches will come out in a few days," he said goodbye and gave us directions back to the highway.

Of course, we took a wrong turn, and when after thirty minutes there was still no sign of the highway, Cassie turned on the GPS.

"Turn left in 200 meters," the clumsy navigation voice crackles out of the box, sparking a discussion about how great navigation voices can be. We come up with singing and parodies of celebrity voices or different dialects. Then silence returns and we listen to the latest charts on the radio.

We drive through extensive woods. It seems to me that the country road we are driving on at 55 miles per hour leads into a forest with no exit.

"We're in the right place, aren't we?" I ask. "It's like Hansel and Gretel. The road leads into the forest, but not out of it."

"The navigation system says everything is okay."

"How much longer?" Riley finally wants to know.

Kieran looks at the navigation system's display. "A good hour. We missed the highway and are rolling home on country roads."

"It's cozy," Cassie beams, enjoying the ride.

Riley shifts nervously.

"What's going on?" I ask.

"I have to pee."

"Really?" comes from Kieran, almost reproachfully. "Typical women! You could have gone to the bathroom in the hospital."

"But I didn't have to go then," the vampire snaps back.

"I could even pee," I support my girlfriend.

"Usually it's the girls who have weak bladders," Cassie laughs at me.

"And the wimps," Kieran says.

"Dude, what was that back there?"

"What?"

I mimic Kieran: "Doctor, is it possible I'm losing my leg?"

Riley laughs, Kieran struggles for a nonchalant answer, and Cassie desperately tries to stop herself from laughing. She finally concentrates on driving. "Can you make it a little longer or should I pull over to the shoulder?"

"I still have a few miles to go," I say.

"If I have to, but not much longer," comes from Riley.

"I'm just saying. I really don't want you peeing in my car."

"Hahahahahaha!" Kieran roars.

"You never know with you guys," Cassie adds.

We have to laugh too, which makes the feeling of having to empty our full bladders even worse. Riley still tries to hold back her laughter but it's hard. Finally she gives up. "Either you pull over or I'll build you a swimming pool back here."

"Hang in there," Cassie says, her expression suddenly changing from funny to deadly serious. She slows down, looking for a way to stop. As a precaution, she turns on her blinkers.

Five minutes later the car is parked, we jump out and head off in different directions into the woods. Kieran follows me.

"If we're going to take a pee break, I'm going to use it," he says, standing next to me. "Ahhh," he says after relieving himself. "This is almost as nice as eating."

We joke around in a good mood, go back to the car and wait for the girls.

The trip continues without complications and the information on the navigation system is almost to the minute. When we pass the town sign of Greenfield, I feel at home.

Yes, I say to myself, *this place is my home. I have arrived here. I have made friends here, and even if the whole world conspires against us, I will always stand by them.*

Cassie drops us off in front of Kieran's house. "We'll be back in an hour."

We dawdle at first, see how quickly the time passes, and finally hurry to be ready on time. Kieran goes upstairs to the bathroom, I use the guest shower downstairs. The hot shower does wonders. When I slip into fresh clothes, I feel like I've been reborn. No sooner do I button my jeans than the doorbell rings.

"Can you get the door?" Kieran calls from upstairs. "I need to get dressed."

I go to the door. It's Ian. Kieran comes downstairs, stuffs his t-shirt into his pants, and an unmistakable grin crosses his face when he sees the pizza boxes in Ian's hands.

"Keep them warm. We'll eat when the girls get here," Ian says, handing the boxes to Kieran.

"Can I try a slice?"

"Kieran, if you keep eating like that you'll soon be so fat we'll think you're not a werewolf, but a werewolf."

"Just kidding," the teenager grins. "I can wait another ten minutes."

As Kieran puts the pizzas in the oven and turns the temperature control, the doorbell rings again. It's Cassie and Riley.

Ian is surprised. "I didn't think so. You usually spend what feels like ten hours in the bathroom," he greets his sister.

Riley rolls her eyes. "That's in the morning, Ian. And it only seems that long to you because you occupy the throne for hours on end."

Ian quickly changes the subject. "I've got pizza. Shall we eat?"

Later we sit in front of the map and plan the route for the next morning.

Ian is engrossed, running his finger along the route. "Really simple. We're on Highway 91, and we're just going through town. The only intersection is Springfield, but there will be less traffic than usual, even on the weekend. We're sure to make it through. It'll take us about an hour and a half," he estimates.

Riley chimes in. "We have to be prepared for anything. Let's say Jack Blood hid the coins with Hostang. Then of course he knows exactly where they are."

"Why doesn't he just go get them himself?" Cassie asks the group.

"We've been through this before. The *vampire-werewolf-human connection* thing works for him, too. That was completely unimaginable back then," Kieran explains.

"Guys, this Hostang just didn't trust Jack Blood. It's as simple as that. Also, it doesn't itch. We're probably the only team in the world that can get those coins. We did something nobody thought possible.

Everyone looks at me and nods. "That's right, James."

Ian is still pressing his index finger on the map where Salem is located. "Back to our task tomorrow," he says. "Where in Salem is the coin hidden? Where exactly do we have to go?"

Riley pulls a notebook out of her purse and flips through it. "I made some notes. Ah, here it is. Wait a minute." She clears her throat, then reads a short passage. "The rivers of the land are like the veins of the people. They are the lifeblood. Not far from where they flow into the sea, on the shadowy side of the blood, hidden deep in the green." Riley lifts his head. "That's all that survived. This text is from an old letter that Hostang left behind as a clue. The bottom part is missing. It says that about 100 years ago there was a fight between one of our ancestors and Jack Blood. Blood stole the bottom part."

"So it could be anywhere," I groan.

"How do you get to Salem and especially to that Salem in Connecticut?" Cassie wants to know.

Kieran has been listening intently the whole time. "Well, as you know, we've deduced the location of Salem and the hide-out from everything we've learned so far. For me, what you read is definitely further proof that we are right."

"What?"

We ponder. "What makes you think that?" Riley wants to know.

Ian is also surprised and looks at Kieran questioningly.

The werewolf is puzzled. "Have you never solved a puzzle?"

"You mean like Sudoku and stuff like that?"

Kieran shakes his head. "Vampires and humans," he says with a grin. "How could I get involved with you?" Then he laughs out loud.

"Just watch out, or else..." I raise my fist threateningly, but I can't keep up the serious look for long. We laugh again.

"Okay, then watch out. Here comes my werewolf logic."

Cassie: "Wow!"

Me: "Uhhh!"

Ian: "I can't wait to see it."

Riley: "Come on, you show-off."

Kieran clears his throat and explains his thesis: "River of the land and veins in humans are references to vampires and locations at the same time. The mouth of the Connecticut River is near Salem, or at least in New London County. It flows into the Long Island Sound and out to sea. They are the lifeblood of the country and the population. So that means life. That also applies to the hidden coin. For me, the dark side of the blood is the clear reference to Salem - the famous Salem where the witch burnings took place. Hence the reference to the blood. The dark side of the blood is Salem in Connecticut. Shadow because it is not the real Salem and the shadow side of the blood as a clue that it is Salem. There is a hint of forest in the deep green, but that was almost everywhere back then. That means we have to focus on the deep green. This could mean that the coin was hidden deep in the forest, which would be a problem. Then we would need old maps and would have to define a radius to search. Or," now Kieran raises his index finger and looks a bit like the *Brainy Smurf*, "there's also a cave there, in a wooded area, and that's why the coin is hidden deep in the green."

"I'm stunned. I would never have thought of that," I praise him.

"Nice, but you wouldn't think of something like that," Ian grins.

"Kieran, are you still hungry? Do you want a fried egg or something - what?"

The werewolf looks at Riley. "Well, that's nice. Of course I'm still a little hungry."

"With ham or bacon?" Cassie wants to know.

Kieran is surprised by the girls' politeness and takes advantage of the situation. "Very happy to do both!"

"You get it as a reward."

"But that doesn't mean I'm greedy. The pizza was just a little too small. You know, if I'm on the road all day..."

"We know, Kieran," we all agree.

Only Ian is brooding. "I bought big pizzas," he says quietly, and I poke him in the side. "Shh!"

He grins.

While Riley and Cassie are in the kitchen, the boys sit in front of the PC and search for caves near Salem. The first hit is negative. After a few minutes, however, we come across a promising clue on . A hobby hiker had published a hiking tip on his homepage and included a route for us along the Connecticut River. Among other things, he tells us about a largely unknown and hidden cave near Salem. We follow the trail virtually and decide to try our luck there tomorrow.

Cassie honks her horn three times, even though Kieran and I are already sitting on the randa, waiting. We've prepared our rucksacks and packed five bottles of water and everything we need to help us: flashlights, a long, strong rope, pliers, a screwdriver, a sharp knife, and a bow and arrow with silver tips.

"Stupid cow, stop honking! The neighbors will hear me," scolds the werewolf.

"What a lovely greeting," grins Cassie. "Are we a morning grouch, Mr. Wolf?"

"Stop teasing me at the crack of dawn."

We get into the car. Ian is in the passenger seat, Kieran, Riley and I in the back. Cassie drives.

"How's the leg?" asks Ian.

"I'm a werewolf. These things heal overnight. The stitches are already out. I did it myself. This morning."

"I didn't think so," Ian marvels. "I guess the wound wasn't as deep as I first thought."

I laugh: "And we didn't have to amputate the leg!"

Kieran grimaces. "Could have been. You never know."

Cassie chimes in: "I already filled the tank and Mom made us sandwiches."

"Sandwiches?"

"Yes, I told you. Or did I not make myself clear?"

"No. It's just that, well..."

I interrupt Kieran. "He ate the eggs he wanted for breakfast yesterday. Now there were only two slices of toast and some peanut butter. Not enough for a glutton."

"I need energy when I have to think!"

"Ah," Riley laughs. "Now I know why you sometimes can't keep up in school. You haven't eaten enough and you don't have the energy."

Kieran looks at my friend questioningly. "I hadn't thought of that. Maybe that's true."

"Mate, if you keep eating like that you'll soon be giving Harry a run for his money!"

Kieran takes a deep breath and looks down at himself. "Cassie, we can eat the sandwiches later. I've lost my appetite."

"Are you hungry Harry, sorry, Kieran?" asks Cassie.

"No! And now stop comparing me to that pudge!"

"Next time I hear *stupid cow*, I'll call you *Harry*."

"Sorry, it just slipped out before."

"Apology accepted. My mother made ham and chicken sandwiches. Three for each of us and five for you, Kieran," she winks in the rearview mirror.

My buddy leans back in satisfaction. "Now we'll drive a few more miles and then we'll have a nice lunch break!"

The trip is without incident. Kieran gets his food break, the girls pee as usual, and about two hours after we set off we see the sign *next exit Salem.*

Cassie pulls off the highway and into the next gas station. We fill up the Toyota. Ian pays and comes back with a big smile on his face. He gets into the passenger seat, Cassie starts the engine and drives off.

"Do you have facial paralysis or something?" Riley asks her brother.

"I talked to the guy at the gas station. There's a cave near here. He says if we take the next road to the right, go straight for three miles, and then turn left, we'll come to a dirt road. You can drive on this road. I don't know how to drive, but the county sheriff is out with his people today for a big parade. He made me do it."

"Or did he just wink at you because he thought you were gay?" Riley teases him.

"No, not that."

Break – silence for some seconds.

"Or was it?" Ian ponders.

"If the route the guy described to you takes us straight to the next men's meeting, I'm not getting out," Kieran grumbles.

We roar with laughter.

"Fooled! No, the path leads us to the exact hiking route we found on the Internet. We can drive a good distance, but then we have to continue on foot.

"And if it goes down here like in the *Wrong Turn movies*, we're screwed."

"How do you know those movies? They're R-rated."

"Well," Kieran grins.

Cassie turns off. "Then I guess I'll have to come in here."

We follow the directions and come to a gravel road. Cassie drives slowly. Behind us, a cloud of dust rises, swirls in the light wind, and finally dissipates. The gravel road leads directly into a forest. Cassie slows down. Ian tries to remember the exact words of the gas station attendant. "Just pull over. The guy at the gas station said this road was still passable," he finally says.

Obviously the road was only made for forest workers and their vehicles. The treetops above the road are very dense. Nevertheless, the sun manages to peek through the red foliage. We roll slowly along the forest road. Cassie thinks about turning on the headlights, but decides against it.

What's the point, there's no one out there anyway.

A few things occur to her. One of them is a story that gave me goosebumps at the time. "I think of a story I once read," I say.

"Which one?" comes the curious question from all sides.

I lower my voice and speak slowly. I make the text sound threatening and sinister. "It was dark and raining, so a woman had to drive home through a wooded area. Suddenly there was an injured person lying on the road in front of her. She stopped and looked at the situation in her headlights. Finally, she decided to help and got out of her car. In the cone of light from her vehicle, she saw that it was a doll, and she quickly pushed it aside. Then, because of the heavy rain, she ran back to her car, got in and slammed the door shut. Really hard, aren't you standing there?

Nod.

Riley says, "Yes.

Kieran is glued to my lips. "Hey, tell me more, man!"

Ian seems to be considering whether this is possible. His nod comes late. "Okay," he mumbles.

I continue. "She heard another scratching noise, got scared, hit the gas and drove straight home. When she got out, two fingers fell to the garage floor. They had been caught in the door and ripped off by someone who had probably tried to grab the woman. Scratches from a hatchet or something were found on the roof of the car. On the next news, she heard about a *madman* running around beheading motorists.

"Stop it, I'm already getting goose bumps," Cassie grunts.

Riley moves closer to me. "Yeah, James. This place is scary."

"Oh my gosh, strong, dude! Did they get the guy? The old lady got lucky. He was just about to pull her out and probably play beetroot when she cut off his fingers."

"That won't work," Ian interjects. "I think it will. If the edges of the door are sharp and..."

"Quiet now! Someone's there."

Cassie slows down. We stare down the path. A slightly older gentleman walks toward us, sees us, stops demonstratively on the path with us, and gives us a fierce, almost sinister look. I am immediately reminded of the movie series *Wrong Turn*.

"I wonder if it's some kind of cannibal. The guys in the movies always had those country lumberjack outfits and the same crazy look. The only thing I don't remember is full beards. He looks like some old trapper they left in the wilderness 100 years ago."

"Stop with your horror stories," Riley pokes me in the side.

Cassie is now driving at walking speed and stops about two meters in front of the guy. He waves us over.

"I'm getting out," Ian says, reaching for the door opener.

"The window's fine," Riley suggests, looking worried.

"Okay," Ian says and lowers the side window. He leans out a little and says he: "Hello."

"What are you doing here?" a deep voice thunders at us.

"We, uh, we want to hike."

He looks at us and we look at him.

"Hiking," he repeats in a way that suggests he doesn't believe it.

"Ian, you always were a terrible liar," Riley whispers.

"Wandering, by car?" the man repeats questioningly.

"Uh, yeah. We'll find a good parking spot, then we'll go."

"What are you looking at? You look like I'm from another world. Have you never seen an old man with a full beard?"

Ian reacts quickly. "Yes, of course," he replies.

"It was a rhetorical question. Anyone who answers that doesn't seem to have much of a brain under their cap," the stranger replies, looking at our license plate. "Massachusetts. This state is either home to horns or people who are too curious," he says shortly afterwards and asks: "Which are you?"

"He suspects something," I breathe to Riley and Kieran.

Ian is on the same level as the guy. "Why did you stop us? Here you're either a sheriff or a bum when you stop a car. Which one are you?"

The bearded man bursts out laughing. "Ha, ha, ha, ha!"

"Why did you stop us?" Ian insists again.

"Why did you stop?" the man asks, taking a step closer.

"I'm afraid of this guy," Cassie says.

"If he pulls a gun, step on the gas and run him over the pile," Kieran suggests.

"Do you have Alzheimer's or something?" asks Ian. "You're in the middle of the road. We had to stop."

"Do you have Alzheimer's?" the man repeats.

"You seem a bit confused to me."

"You seem a little confused to me."

I don't like the game. I call from the back of the car: "Tell me, why did you get in the way and stop us?"

"I wanted to see who was driving through my beautiful forest when it's forbidden."

"We just don't know our way around."

"I wish you a good day. Good luck and have fun. Maybe we'll meet again. Goodbye," says the chemical guy, steps aside, looks at us all again and disappears into the woods.

Cassie continues immediately. "I have goosebumps, guys. That guy gave me the creeps. Did you see his eyes?"

"Why did he stop us?" asks Riley.

"Because he's deranged," says Kieran. "Just a retarded country bumpkin."

I turn around. "He's back on the path, staring at us."

"Weird guy. I think Kieran's right and it was just a cranky tawny owl," Ian says, ending the discussion.

We roll slowly through the forest for another ten minutes or so. The road gets more and more uneven and there are a few potholes that shake us up. Cassie drives very carefully. The springs of the old Toyota Corolla squeak, but they do their job. I think Cassie drives really well for a beginner.

"Ian, what did the guy at the gas station say about how far we have to go down the forest road?" she asks.

"He said something about a creek with a little bridge over it. We have to cross it and follow the dirt road on the other side. Not far from there is supposed to be an old, abandoned mill. It is known here as the *Wood Mill*. We should park there."

"A mill in the forest? That's pretty silly," says Kieran.

"Who knows where the farmers came from. Maybe it was centrally located. Besides, where there's a stream, there could be a mill," Cassie says, adding: "There's the bridge. I can see it now. It looks stable too. I'm going to drive over it."

She is right. The bridge is very strong. A few minutes later we arrive at *Wood Mill*. Cassie parks and we get out. The wooden structure looks ancient. The former water wheel that once powered the millstone lies rotting in the grass. I also see two disused and broken huge millstones. The mill itself looks good from the outside, but you can tell it has at least two centuries under its belt. The wood is gray. The paint on the windows has long since flaked off. Some panes are broken. Or rather, I can only see two panes that are still intact.

"The guy from before could live here and be the former miller. He looked as old as this shabby mill," Kieran jokes.

We get out and take a closer look at the building. Then we go to the trunk, open it and grab the two backpacks with the equipment. I also take the bow and the quiver with the arrows.

"Do you want to go hunting?" asks Ian, pointing to the weapon.

"There are some special arrows. Silver tips."

Fear is obvious. The vampire instinctively steps back a meter. "Just be careful with that."

Cassie locks the Toyota with the remote.

Beep, clack.

Then she looks around. "Let's get down to business. Where do we have to go? Where do we find this hidden cave?"

Suddenly, the door of the mill opens with an unmistakable creak. I am startled. We all stood rooted to the spot. A very unpleasant man comes out. You can see right away that he's looking for a fight. His look alone is aggressive enough to start a mass brawl. It's the kind of person that makes you change sides of the sidewalk when they come at you. An estimated 100 kilos of fighting weight. Not a muscle man like a bodybuilder, more of a bouncer. Big belly, big flabby upper arms, tattoos, bald head.

"Well, well, well," he grunts, clenching his fists. "No parking here."

A fist flies clapping into the open other hand. He rubs it with glee. Behind this guy, a second guy pushes his way out of the mill and into the open. Same category. I feel immediately that we're in the greatest danger. My legs start to shake.

"Oh dear, I think they're up to no good with us," Kieran whispers. "And I also smell danger. They're not humans. They're vampires!"

I see the necklaces with the Tembolus stones hanging from them. At the same time, I reach for my quiver and pull out an arrow.

"I wish you a good day, sir. Is this your estate? We didn't know. We were just going for a walk. Can we park here?" Ian begins a conversation in an overly polite manner.

"Unfortunately, you've already gone too far. My brother and I don't want that at all. We'll probably have to teach you some manners."

"Slow down, friends," Riley's brother warns, raising his right hand in warning.

"Ohhh," the guy in front cackles to the others, wiggling his hands and knees in a deliberately contemptuous manner. "Look, I'm scared."

They both laugh out loud. Suddenly everything happens in a flash. They look at us with dark eyes and start to run. The one in front crashes into Ian, the one behind has chosen Kieran as his victim.

"Greetings from Uncle Jack," one of them shouts, opening his mouth wide. That is when I recognize his vampire teeth.

Ian falls to the ground from the impact, rolls over, and immediately jumps back up. He staggers for a moment, catches himself and is ready for the next attack. This one comes in the form of a powerful punch. Like a skilled boxer, Ian makes a side step. The bald man's fist whizzes past Ian's head by millimeters. The attacker follows, pushing his massive body forward. Ian, backpedaling even further, drops his left leg and hammers his right fist twice into the side of his attacker's face. He falls to the ground, grunting like a pig at the impact. Despite his portly frame, he spins around nimbly and jumps back up. "You rat, wait a minute!"

The second guy grabs Kieran's collar and tries to headbutt him, but the werewolf kicks his knee up several times at the speed of an arrow. He hammers it into the vampire's stomach three or four times. The vampire opens his mouth in pain. The eyes glow blood red. The headbutt becomes a headbutt and Kieran is able to wriggle out of his grip. He begins to transform and growls aggressively. His opponent snorts a few times. "Look at you, a werewolf. I'm going to eat you for dinner!"

The vampire jumps at Kieran again. He leaps into the air as well. The two bodies collide in mid-air. Kieran has no chance. The fat vampire has so much mass that the young werewolf literally bounces off and hits the ground hard.

The girls have gotten over their initial shock and want to help.

"Kieran!" Cassie yells, preparing to attack the vampire.

Riley opens her mouth and bares her teeth in a snarl.

"Step aside!" I yell at them and put the arrow on the bow. I pull the string, aim at the vampire standing in front of Kieran and let go. The arrow whizzes forward, whirring through the air, and the point bores into the back of the bald mountain of flesh. Nothing. No reaction. It's like a mosquito biting him.

Crap! That was one of the practice arrows.

I am very nervous and scared. My hands tremble as I search for one of the four remaining silver-tipped arrows. I reach for the colorful feathers and pull the arrow out of the quiver. Placing and cocking the bow is a single movement. I aim the arrow at the target.

Ian and his opponent surround each other, assessing each other. Both raise their fists. Their gazes seem to attract each other like magnets. They weigh advantages and disadvantages. Any blow could be fatal. Meanwhile, Kieran gasps and struggles to catch his breath. The blow was too hard even for the practiced football player. The vampire takes advantage and throws his massive body at the wolf. Then he grabs my friend's neck and squeezes. Kieran has no chance.

"First I'll squeeze the air out of you, then I'll suck you dry! I'll roast your wolf body over a fire and hang your skull on the wall as a trophy.

I'm ready for the shot, giving Cassie and Riley a warning look to make sure they don't run into my path. I'm ready to kill the vampire with a silver-tipped arrow. Suddenly, Riley screams.

"Ian! He's going to kill Ian!"

I immediately turn around. Ian's opponent seems to be an experienced fighter. He fooled the student with a body twist. Ian's punch went nowhere. The bouncer has grabbed Ian's arm, literally spun the student around, and is now standing behind him with his head in a headlock. Ian gasps, unable to move. "Now I'm going to break your neck, you wretch," the bald man laughs.

Without thinking, I make a quick movement to the right with my bow. The tip of my arrow points at the vampire. He looks at me and grins. "You can scare small children with that, but not me. If you shoot the arrow and annoy me with it, you'll be next. Now watch your friend die!"

I have to be very careful not to hit Ian and aim extra high.

The shot has to be right. Take a shallow breath, James. Do it like Daddy taught you when you were shooting. Breathe shallow, stay calm, it goes through my head.

Despite the hustle and bustle, time seems to stand still for a split second. My target is in sight, I am completely calm. The arrow flies off the string. It whizzes through the air in slow motion. The vampire watches me and seems to weigh how to react. He hesitates a second too long and the silver tip pierces his neck. Instinctively, he lets go of Ian. His hands grab the end of the arrow. He opens his mouth and a bloodcurdling scream follows. Birds flutter and fly away. Ian rolls to the side and struggles to find fuel.

At the same time, Riley and Cassie jump on the back of the second vampire, pulling him away from Kieran. While Cassie wraps her hands around her opponent's neck and grabs the Tembolus Stone necklace, Riley tries to bite. Her attempt fails. The massive man makes a kind of flinging motion, similar to a dog coming out of the water and shaking itself dry.

Both girls are thrown to the side and land in the grass. Suddenly the fighter screams and gasps. He lets go of Kieran and gets to his feet. Wisps of smoke rise from his body. Small flames twitch from his shoulders, thighs and head. "NO!" he shouts in a scary voice.

I look at Cassie. She is holding the necklace from the Tembolus stone. When she was thrown, she didn't let go of the chain. The force of the throw was so great that the chain broke. He lost the vital stone. The foul smell of burnt flesh fills the air and pierces our noses. The sun burns the vampire within a short time. A pile of ashes remains. A black cloud hovers above us, billowing in the gentle wind, becoming a transparent veil and finally dissipating.

Ian's opponent also dies. The effect of the silver arrow has taken effect before he can grab Ian again and kill him. Like Oloisius, he crumbles to dust.

Kieran turns around. He and Ian are sitting on the grass, still gasping for air. They rub their necks. "Thanks," Ian struggles to say in a husky voice.

"Hey, that was close," Kieran gasps.

Riley runs to her brother and gives him a hug. "I was so scared for you."

The student hugs her. "Weeds don't grow back, sister. You have a nice *Robin Hood* for a boyfriend, by the way. You have my blessing," Ian says with great relief and stands up. He looks down at his body for a moment. "Uninjured. Lucky you," he says and walks over to me. "Respect, great shot! You can handle a bow and arrow."

My knees are still shaking. "Man, I was afraid I was going to miss or hit you."

Ian's eyes widen. "What, you were unsure?"

Riley winks. "Don't worry, bro. James always has everything under control."

Ian pats my shoulder. "Thanks," he repeats, pointing at Cassie and Kieran.

They are standing close together.

"Cassie, I owe you one," Kieran says, looking the vampire in the eye.

Cassie doesn't hesitate for a moment and hugs him. "I was so scared!"

"It's okay."

"You make a lovely couple," I call out.

Kieran grunts something unintelligible and winks at me. Cassie looks at me first, then at Kieran in a way that any complete idiot would understand immediately. "If you don't do it, I will," she says and gives him a kiss. "I don't give a fuck what my parents will say, I like you, Kieran."

I check my watch and look around. It's quiet. A little too quiet. Well, frighteningly quiet. No birds singing, nothing to be heard. Scarey. I feel uncomfortable.

"Hey, lovebirds, now is not the time to play *Romeo and Juliet*. We should hurry. I don't want us to run into any more of Jack Blood's relatives. I've only got three of the effective arrows left, five bullets in the revolver chamber and the flask from the Mexican. But I'll save that for Blood himself,' I call the team together.

We stand in a circle.

"What's next?" asks Cassie.

"Let's check the mill first. Maybe we'll find some useful clues," Ian suggests and heads for the entrance corridor without waiting for an answer.

"Wait a minute! I don't know," Riley hesitates. "What if there are more of those bastards in there?"

"They would have stormed out by now."

We agree with Ian and follow him to the entrance of the mill. Ian pushes the door open. Only a little light enters the room through the small windows and the open door. There is no furniture. I can see wooden beams and another old millstone.

"There's no one here," Ian says.

We go in. It takes a while to get used to the dim light. Through the frosted glass of one of the back windows we can see that the two guys have arrived on motorcycles.

"They parked their Harleys back there," Cassie tells us.

"We already saw them, thanks for the info," comes from Kieran.

"Here's their stuff. Two helmets and definitely no sign of other people. There were only two of them," I add.

Riley has stopped at the door and is paying attention. "We should hurry. My gut tells me they weren't the last ones to try and stop us," she warns, urging us to hurry.

Kieran and Cassie stay downstairs, Ian and I go upstairs. We quickly search for clues about Jack Blood or the third coin, but find nothing. Finally, Ian suggests that we break off and look for our real destination, the cave.

"The two bikers were just using the mill as a hideout. I think Blood has set up his posts at every access route to stop us."

"Okay, let's go," Kieran confirms.

"Bloody hell!" Riley curses.

I've never seen my girlfriend run down the rotten stairs in such a panic. "What's wrong?"

Crack

A step breaks. I feel strong arms under my armpits. "Watch it, brother-in-law," Ian breathes into my ear, holding me tight.

I pull my foot out of the hole in the stairs and walk down carefully.

Riley points first to the path and then to the edge of the forest. "There are vampires coming at us from all directions. I counted five of them."

Kieran pushes his way forward. "Shit, they saw the smoke from their burnt buddy! No wonder, he was fat enough for a lot of smoke."

"Are you sure they're vampires?" asks Cassie.

"They don't exactly look like friendly boy scouts," Riley comments.

I instinctively grab the arrows. "Three of them," I repeat what I said earlier.

"We need to get out of here! Come on, everyone in the car," Riley pushes out and wants to start running.

" No! First, we can't make it, second, the way to the bridge is blocked, and third, we only have this one chance to get to the third coin. If we leave now and don't fight, we're dead!" Ian drowns them all out.

"He's right," I agree.

"Say, what are we doing?" asks Cassie.

"I'm starting to hate vampires," Kieran growls, looking at Riley, Cassie and Ian, and adds, "But not all of them, just the ones out there."

Ian took charge. "Quick to the first floor," he orders. "And watch out for the stairs, they're rotten."

We go upstairs and cover all the windows.

"Here's one!"

"Two on this side. One in civilian clothes, one in a suit."

"And two more guys coming from the front," Riley adds. "They match the rocker types in their clothing."

"Five men."

"I can count too, Kieran. Use your head. You're a first-rate puzzle solver. I ask you, how do we get out of here?"

The werewolf looks at me. "Mate, if these guys get the idea to set fire to the mill, no way. It'll be our grave."

"That's exactly the answer I didn't want to hear!"

I pull one of the silver-tipped arrows out of my quiver. "I really need to save one of these deadly weapons for Jack Blood. Without a weapon we have no chance against him. He's a powerful vampire," I tell the others. I want them to be aware of our situation.

"Do they know we're here?" Cassie asks hopefully.

"I think so."

"If all they saw was smoke and fumes, they might as well think those two bikers killed us."

"Good idea, but that gives us a time advantage of about three seconds if the guys are here," Kieran says dryly.

"And they'll be here in less than 30 seconds. Hide behind the beams," Ian whispers.

I press myself against the first of the many beams, put the arrow on the bow, but don't pull the string. If I move my head a little to the side, I can see the stairs. A good tactical position for an archer.

"Bloody hell!" Riley curses.

"What's going on?"

"When I took a big step over that broken step, my cell phone fell out of my pocket. It's on the bottom step. I'll get it quick!"

"Too late! Stay down, the first one will be here soon," Kieran pulls her back.

We are quiet. Quiet as a mouse. Beads of sweat roll down my forehead. I hardly dare to breathe. I can feel my palms getting damp.

I hope I can draw the bow without it slipping.

We hear footsteps. Someone is at the door. "Carl, John? Are you here?"

Ian puts his outstretched index finger over his mouth, indicating that we must not make a sound.

Footsteps again. Judging by the noise level, there are at least two men among us now.   I make eye contact with Ian. He points to two with his fingers. I nod.

"Carl, John?" the other one calls now. His voice is deep and rough. "Where are you hiding?"

"Their machines are behind this dump," the first one says.

"Two of them got here! There's nothing left but ashes," someone shouts loudly from outside.

"And who?" asks one of the men in the mill just as loudly.

"You can't tell. Everything is completely burnt and disintegrated."

"I guess they grabbed some of those pants-eaters and barbecued them. The others took off into the woods and Carl and John are chasing them," the vampire with the deep voice speculates.

I hear one of the men approaching the stairs. To get a better look, I peek out from behind the beam. My knees are already weak again and begin to shake slightly. I realize it is the man in the suit. He's standing in front of the stairs now, bending down. I'm sure he's found Riley's cell phone. My suspicion is confirmed. He picks it up and puts it in his jacket pocket.

"Did you find anything?" the vampire with the deep voice asks. "No, my shoelace was untied."

I am astonished.

Does he want to steal the cell phone and not share his booty, or why is he lying? Or has he spotted me and wants to lull me into a false sense of security?

"They're not here anyway," grumbles the one with the deep voice. "But let's look upstairs. Jack hates mistakes, and if we make one, we'll be the next ones he turns to dust."

He comes to the stairs as well. I tighten the bow slightly.

"Just stay downstairs. This thing looks pretty ramshackle. I'll go up and have a look around."

"I prefer it anyway. I'll wait outside. It smells better here than in a coffin."

Footsteps.

He goes out.

"Did you find anything else?" I hear from outside. The suit comes up slowly. I draw the bow further and am ready to swing around the beam and shoot immediately.

"Stay calm!" I hear a whisper. "Don't panic, nothing will happen to you."

I hesitate. Ian looks at me and shrugs. I go with my gut again and move quickly around the bar. I aim for the man in the suit. He raises his hands, but doesn't stop. He continues to move slowly toward me.

"You can trust me."

"Kill him!" Kieran hisses.

I wait.

The man in the suit turns his head to the side and shouts down: "There's no one up here either. Everything is empty. Niente, nada, nothing!"

"Shit! Then we'll have to go to the forest and find their trail there," replies the one with the bass voice. "Come down, Ted. We keep going."

This *Ted* looks at me and makes a slow downward motion with the flat of his left hand. "Be careful with that arrow, boy."

I hesitate.

"What's wrong?" whispers Kieran. "Why aren't you shooting?"

My eyes are on the vampire. The suit has stopped on the last step. He stands there, smiling at me in a friendly way. "Here," he says, pulling the cell phone out of his pocket, "you dropped this."

I lower the tip of the arrow, no longer threatening him. He bends down and puts the phone on the ground. "I won't betray you. Stay here for a while. I'll distract the others," he says quietly and goes back down the stairs.

I don't know why, but I trust this man. He leaves the old mill and calls to the others: "I have searched everywhere. There's absolutely no one here. It's probably what you think. The boys will go after the last three survivors.

"Then Carl and John can prepare for something. I told them to stay here no matter what! Man oh man, Jane is going to be really pissed."

"It's hunting fever. I don't blame them," the suit replies. "Mrs. Huckings will have to overlook this. These two men mean well."

Despite the loud bass voice, the reply is barely audible. Scraps of words like: "Blood... daughter... punishment," still ring out, but can no longer be put into a sentence that makes sense.

The voices become fainter and fainter and soon we hear nothing at all. We stay there for a while, then I see all five vampires disappear into the woods. We breathe a sigh of relief.

"I was so scared I almost peed myself!" Kieran groans in relief.

"Really?" Cassie asks.

"I was just joking. Werewolves don't do that," Kieran grins, obviously relieved.

"That was close."

Ian ponders. "Guys, why did that Ted guy help us?"

I'm sure I've heard the name before, but I can't place it. "Maybe he's a moderate vampire and hates Jack Blood?" I say.

Riley looks around. "Another question. What do we do now?"

Cassie replies: "Stupid question. Leave, of course."

Everyone stares at Cassie after this statement.

"What's wrong? Do I have spots or something?"

"No, but we need the coin. Otherwise it's all for nothing!"

"Oh man, that damn coin. I totally forgot about it, I was so scared."

"Would you like to wait for us here in the car?" asks Riley. "We wouldn't blame you. I totally understand."

"Are you crazy? Of course I'm coming with you. Someone has to take care of Kieran."

Kieran is still thinking. "What is this guy, this Ted? Well, he's seen us, so at least he's seen you, James. What if it was just a trick and they're waiting outside and lurking until we come out of the mill?" Kieran is suspicious about the whole thing.

"It could be," Cassie agrees. "Maybe it was just a tactic because we would have had a chance in the mill."

"The fact is, if they come back and we're still here, they'll burn the place down. I'm pretty sure of that," I counter.

"Fire is deadly to us vampires. You're afraid of fire," Ian throws in.

"I can understand that," Kieran says.

"Fire kills all of us, not just vampires. Just for your information. We need to get out of here. We don't have much time. The clock is ticking, the curse will kill you," I warn urgently.

"He's right," Riley confirms.

"Do you really think so? I don't trust all this peace," Kieran still doubts.

"What other choice do we have? We can't stay here forever," Ian finally agrees and goes down the stairs first. "Watch your step," he reminds us.

On the first floor of the mill, we take a long look out of all the windows to make sure that all the vampires are really gone or that one has stayed behind to keep watch.

„It´s okay. Nobody is here!"

We step outside.

"You know we have to follow them, right? They took the exact same route to the cave," Ian says. "Apparently the tank has had to give that information a couple of times today."

"What are we waiting for? Let's go to the cave!" I play the brave hero and am rewarded with a kiss on the cheek from Riley.

"Let´s follow them, straight to the cave?" Cassie yells, slapping her forehead.

"Walk into a trap like those bastards? No way."

"And what do you suggest?" I want to know. "We should go another way."

"I had that idea too, Cassie," Ian throws in. "But we don't know our way around here. We have to follow them."

I try to convince Cassie. "Where would you least expect us?"

"The Australian outback?" Kieran replies.

Cassie and Riley roll their eyes, Ian grins, I give Kieran *the finger.*

"Behind them. They never dreamed we'd be right on their heels."

Cassie wrinkles her nose and nods. "Sounds plausible and crazy. Since I'm pretty crazy anyway, you talked me into it. So, kids, let's go!"

"Why the stinky finger?" Kieran wants to know. "They'd never suspect us in the outback."

"Give Kieran a cookie. It'll be hollow again," I laugh.

"Just kidding," he laughs and pats me on the shoulder. A second later he asks: "Did we really bring cookies?"

I look at him with a grin.

He shrugs. "You know wolves have to..."

"Yeah, I know. Now come on."

Ian looks at his watch. "I don't mean to rush you guys, but the ultimatum expires in seven hours and I don't want to know how the curse works."

Kieran and I look confused. "What?" we ask in shock. "*When* does the ultimatum expire?"

"You heard right."

"Why are you telling us this now?"

"So you won't be so hyper-nervous and can think clearly."

Cassie puts her hands on her hips. "One for all!"

We answer in chorus: "And all for one!"

I set the timer on my phone for 6 hours and 58 minutes.

Chapter Twelve

Up until the moment we enter the forest, I have a bad feeling. I just feel like I'm being watched. It's like someone else is close by and watching us.

It smells like leaves, wood and moss. This is unmistakably the much-praised and indefinably good forest air. I take a deep breath, filling my lungs and exhaling consciously. I repeat this process two or three times. I feel strong in the company of my friends. I look around.

No trap, no lurking vampires.

I am reassured.

"This way," Ian says, staying in front.

We follow the only path that leads into the undergrowth in single file. I walk close behind Ian. My thoughts keep circling around this vampire in a suit.

This Ted doesn't seem to have betrayed us.

I conclude that Ted is with Jack Blood's people, but not one of them. For whatever reason. My theory seems to be confirmed, because when the path splits, I see a paper handkerchief lying on the ground at the fork to the left. It looks like it has been deliberately discarded, as a small piece has been stuffed into the ground with a finger.

To keep the wind from blowing it away, I realize.

Ian stops and hesitates. I can tell from his posture that he wants to keep going to the right. "Left," I say, pointing to the handkerchief. "Trap?" Kieran asks in one word.

I shake my head, but think about it anyway. Of course, it could be a handkerchief that was thrown away by accident. But what speaks against it is that it's unused and stuffed in the ground. Cassie takes a few steps forward and looks at it.

"No, I don't think it's a trivially discarded rag. I think this Ted is leaving us signs. He itself is like a riddle and therefore a task for you, Kieran," she says.

"My mind is like a machine. It needs to be fed and lubricated. It's like a car. It won't run if the gas tank is empty. I need food, then it will work with the thought ken".

I take a deep breath, almost a little annoyed. "Why don't you give this ravenous werewolf something to eat," I say.

Kieran points at me. "Backpack."

I don't know what he wants. "What about the backpack? You've got one on too."

"I put some *Slim Jims* in yours this morning."

"What did you do? Put *Slim Jims* in my backpack? Why not in yours?"

"Because the stuff would be long gone if I carried it myself. So it's left for emergencies," he grins.

"For an emergency? We're not in an emergency."

"Yeah, my stomach says *this is an emergency*."

Riley whines: "Give him something to eat."

Kieran comes over to me and grabs a *Slim Jim* out of my backpack. "Anyone else?"

No one answers.

"Great, then I'll take another one."

He pulls out another and closes the backpack. Then he rips open the wrapper of the first *Slim Jim* and bites into the meat stick with relish. "Mmmh, delicious. I can feel my brain starting to work."

We walk on. The path narrows and turns into a book trail. At regular intervals we find objects left behind. Despite the small meal, Kieran has no idea what's going on with Ted. But he seems to be showing us the way.

After a good hour we stop at the next sign - it's the packaging for the tissues. It turns out we were wise to pack a water bottle for everyone. Drinking thirstily of us. It's good how the liquid flows down the throat and makes you feel good. I hate thirst. After I've drunk about half the bottle, I close it and put it back in my backpack. Then I look at the display on my smartphone. The timer shows 5:49 hours.

"Let's keep going, please. Time is of the essence."

Branches continue to hang in the path. Some of them have been accidentally broken by the vampires that have gone before us, and some of the branches hang far into the path and have to be pushed aside. Every now and then a branch has been deliberately broken for us.

Ted, every single one of these shoots through my head. The mystery surrounding this man is getting more and more exciting. *Do we have an ally in the ranks of Jack Blood?*

After another ten minutes, Ian stops and raises his hand. "There's a red handkerchief hanging there. Guys, that's the clearest sign so far. I think we're here," he points ahead. We all catch up with Ian. Kieran lifts his nose to the wind. "They're on our left. Let's go there."

"You and me," Ian says in an unmistakable tone of command and taps Kieran on the shoulder.

They both take off. As they disappear into the undergrowth, I look at my watch for the first time. The waiting is cruel. Every minute seems like ten. Doubts arise in me.

Should I have told Dad a long time ago? Nonsense! He would never have believed me.

When my friends finally return, they sit down with us. Ian wipes the leaves off the floor, takes a stick and carves something into the ground. Without further ado, he begins to explain: "The terrain is getting a bit hilly. If we go about 80 meters in that direction," he points in that direction, "we can see the cave. The five vampires we know from the mill are there, and there must be five more. One of them is a woman who everyone respectfully refers to only as *Mrs. Huckings*. Kieran can tell you more about her."

The werewolf now continues. "I set up my cuddly wolf eavesdroppers and overheard two of the vampires talking about this lady. She's Jack Blood's daughter!"

"Fuck, that guy has a daughter? How did he manage that?" I ask.

"Since her last name is *Mrs.* Huckings, he could also have grandchildren and thus a larger family clan behind him," Cassie concludes. "And his daughter is probably married. Because of the other name," she adds.

I clear my throat until everyone is looking at me, then I say quietly: "Let's put all the hard facts on the table. They're standing like guards at the entrance to the cave. But we have to get in there, right past them. If we don't, you'll both die."

Silence.

Ian swallows. His Adam's apple moves up and down. "I don't have a choice anyway. I'm going to die anyway if I don't go in and find the third coin. So I might as well die if I fight to get into the cave."

"Me too," Riley says and looks at me.

I feel hot and cold at the same time. Tears well up in my eyes. My stomach cramps and at the same time an indescribable rage that is growing inside me against this Jack Blood opens all the adrenaline floodgates. I'm getting something like a fighting spirit. Just a few weeks ago, I was a lonely kid in a farm town whose biggest worry was not having an Internet connection, and now I'm sitting here in the woods of Connecticut, ready to risk my life for my girlfriend. Not only that, but I'm also willing to risk my life for my girlfriend. And not only that, but I've realized that there are wizards and witches and vampires and werewolves. It's a crazy world. Much more colorful and bizarre than I ever imagined. I think carefully about my next sentence and place my hand in the middle of our circle. I do it like the famous musketeers in Alexandre Dumas' novel. "If I were to get up and walk away now, I wouldn't be able to look in the mirror for the rest of my life. One for all!"

One by one, everyone joins in, finally shouting in unison: "All for one!"

A shadow falls over us. We flinch, startled. "That's very brave, boy," someone says.

We jump aside, spread out. Kieran and Ian assume fighting positions, clenching their fists. I stand in front of Cassie and Riley. The shadow is gone. I'm confused.

"Where did that voice come from? Who was talking to us?" asks Kieran.

"Me!" comes the answer and out of nowhere a man steps out of the forest. I recognize him at once. It's the bearded lumberjack who blocked our way on the way here.

"You're all we need," Ian groans.

"For God's sake, that lunatic," Riley whispers.

Leaves rustling, hurried footsteps. I turn around. The suit is coming at us through the woods. "That Ted's coming up behind us," I warn the others, grabbing an arrow.

"Don't be afraid and leave the arrow in the bag," the guy with the beard yells.

We move closer together again, standing back to back. I'm still confused.

"Who are you two?" I ask.

Ted is almost with us. He slows down for the last few meters and greets us, slightly out of breath: "Very good. You found my signs."

"Damn it, I want to know what's going on here," I blurt out. "Why did you leave us little signposts and who the hell are you?"

"Shh," Ted points to his mouth with his index finger. "Keep it down! They can't hear you."

"Who are you two?" Kieran repeats the question.

The old man approaches. "I apologize for my rudeness this morning. I wasn't sure you were up to the challenge. But after watching the fight at the mill, I was sure you could. Allow me, my name is Zachory Smith. I am a sorcerer and have lived for a long time here. This is my land, and I don't like old spells tainting my kingdom. Besides, I am a moderate, good witch. I would like to help you break the Hostang's spell."

Ted, the vampire in the suit, also introduces himself. "And I'm FBI Agent Ted Harper."

"FBI?" asks Ian in surprise.

"That's what he said," Kieran pokes him in the side.

"Ted Harper?" I ask, remembering my father's words. "Then you're here on a special assignment?" I add.

"You must be James Allington," Harper says, looking at me. "You look like your father. I remember him being a determined, stubborn man in training. I met him at the police academy."

"That's right, he told me about that."

The spell seems to be broken. I trust Harper and therefore also this magician Mr. Smith. The tension eases. Now my friends introduce themselves to our new ally. Then the wizard takes the floor. "And now you want to go into the cave to get the third coin?" he interrupts the group. He looks deeply into each of our eyes.

I could hardly escape his hypnotic gaze. Deep black eyes captured me. It's as if he's penetrating my brain and reading it. "But you don't know how to get past the guards," he finally says. "You have absolutely no plan, and yet you would rather die together than give up?"

I think for a moment and confidently agree. "Yes, it's something like that."

"You're fools!" he laughs, but then his face turns serious again. "We have a plan for you. Would you like to know what it is? Shall we tell you?"

What a stupid question. Of course we want to know. None of us wants to die, I guess.

I would have liked to say the same thing, but instead I get, "It would be very nice of you to tell us your plan.

At the same time I think to myself: *James, we need to practice this a little bit more. You need to be more direct and more casual.*

"My plan is working. But you have to follow it to the letter. One deviation and everything goes wrong!"

On the one hand I'm annoyed by the beard, but on the other hand he really seems to have a solution ready.

"What's the plan? We're all ears," Ian interjects, looking nervously at his watch.

"Yeah, what's the plan?" asks Riley.

"Come on, dude," Kieran shoots off, immediately regretting using the word dude. "Well, *dude* isn't meant personally, it's just a figure of speech and..." when he realizes that the wizard isn't listening to him, he immediately shuts up.

"The plan starts with you shutting up and listening carefully."

We remain silent. Ted Harper grins.

"The last thing we need right now is a couple of cheeky guys who don't know anything, don't remember anything, and get it all wrong afterwards."

"It's all right. We'll be quiet," Ian reassures us.

"In exactly 25 minutes and 23 seconds, Jane Huckings will call the vampires to dinner. All but one. That one vampire will stay behind as the last guard. The dinner break will last exactly five minutes."

"How do you know that?"

"From me," Ted Harper interjects. "She called in a helicopter with blood bags. The flight plan is pretty precise."

"And what about the remaining guard?"

"That's me," Harper explains.

"Wait a minute! Why should we trust you? Maybe this is a trick by Jack Blood. He wants to use you to lure us into the cave and we're trapped there," Cassie snaps.

"I went to police school with James' dad. Now I am a FBI Agent and we've been hunting a serial killer for a long time. And this killer's name is *Jack Blood*. I was introduced to Blood's circle of followers about two years ago. Now we are very close. You have two choices. You can either trust me or you can go down there and fight the vampires."

Riley grabs my hand. "James, what do you think?"

"I trust him."

"Me too," Ian says firmly.

"And I always stand by my friends," Kieran says clearly.

This sentence makes me incredibly proud. It is a very nice feeling to have found such friends.

"Okay, Mr. FBI Undercover Agent or whatever you're called. I trust you too, but if you play dirty with us, you'll be the first one I grab in a fight," Cassie threatens.

"20 minutes and 13 seconds," the wizard says.

"If we're in the cave, then what?" I push forward. "There were traps in the last cave."

"Not here. I went as far as the wooden coffin at the front. There is a stone there that looks like a menhir, and it has three notches in it," Ted Harper explains. "There is no trap until you get there. That means the only danger is getting lost in the little maze, but that danger is very easy to avoid."

"How is that? Is there a tunnel system?" I ask.

"Two questions at once is one question too many," the FBI man grins. "Well, yes, there is a tunnel system with branches that are like a labyrinth, but if you always go right when you go in and left when you go out, nothing can happen."

"We know the one with the stone and the hands carved in it. As soon as the three of us put our hands in there, a gate or something like that opens and the coin comes out. At the same time, the cave collapses or some shit happens," Kieran suggests.

"I can stop any spell. The question is for how long. The stronger a spell is, the shorter the time of my shield I can put over it. I figure I can do it with which is the strongest spell I know. And I can block it for a maximum of five minutes. You have five minutes from when you enter the cave to when you come out, maybe a little less."

"That's a damn small window."

"I can't change it. Hostang was a great master. His traps are magnificent, worked then, work now, and will have the same powerful effect in 500 years."

"Comparable to German craftsmanship, so to speak, let's say Porsche," I interject and get stupid looks.

Only the witcher nods and says: "Yes, comparable to German workmanship.

"I'm in," says Ian emphatically.

"Me too," comes clearly from Kieran.

"And I'm in too," I add.

Cassie and Riley also agree.

"18 minutes, 17 seconds."

The agent has to go back to the vampires. "I'm counting on you!"

We get ready and lie in wait. "Where can a helicopter land, please?" asks Kieran.

The wizard answers: "Not at all, but behind the cave, on the opposite side, there is a small clearing. It is large enough for him to stand in the air and take the supplies or even lower a passenger or two. The walk there takes about five or six minutes. A normal vampir will suck out a food bag in a good minute, followed by another five to six minutes for the return trip. This gives you a window of about 11 minutes. In that time, you have to run down there, go into the cave, get the coin, and come back. Can you do that?"

"Yes."

"Sure," Kieran agrees and I nod, too.

"What are we girls going to do?" Cassie asks.

"Very simple. You two cover the way back with Agent Harper. If there are any unplanned incidents, like one of the vampires isn't hungry or one comes back earlier than expected, then you'll have to fight!"

"Then I'd better stay outside and Riley can go into the cave," Ian suggests.

"Can she run as fast as you? If you don't make it in five minutes, my spell will break and you might not make it out of there."

Ian thinks. "Damn!"

Riley reassures her brother. "It's all right, Ian. Cassie and I make a good team. And if we each take a silver-tipped arrow, we'll be well armed."

"Young men!" the wizard's voice now sounds deeper and more serious than before. "You have exactly one chance. You will run in, follow the path, place your hands on the stone, and when the gate opens, a certain boy of yours will grab the box."

The wizard turns in a circle. He spins faster and faster and suddenly stops in front of Kieran.

"It must be the werewolf. The last box can only be taken by a werewolf. This is how I interpreted the spell of the great Hostang. This is the final trap. If a human or vampire were to grab it, the container would begin to glow and melt the coin stored inside, rendering it useless forever."

"I'll do it," Kieran says. "No problem."

Zachory Smith reaches into his dirty jacket and pulls out a pale, transparent stone. "You must not touch or take anything, absolutely nothing, that you see on the way to the stone. Do you understand?"

"Yes."

"Then get ready. The helicopter will be here in 12 minutes and 36 seconds!"

We make our way as far as we can to the cave. We crawl the last few meters and stay in a line. Protected by the bushes of the forest, we can see all the way to the entrance of the cave. The witcher lies in the middle behind us.

The hiker is right. The landscape is a feast for the eyes. This part is really worth a trip.

There is a small plateau in front of the cave, which gives it the appearance of a Stone Age dwelling with a terrace. "Mr. Smith, what happens after the five minutes you said?" Cassie wants to know. "You said you could stop the spell for five minutes."

The wizard lowers his eyes. "My child, every spell has an effect. It can be good or bad. My spell will stop all evil for a maximum of five minutes. After that, however, all the traps will be triggered simultaneously. The cave will collapse and hide the coin in the rock forever. If your three friends don't make it, they will die."

"Thank you for that information," Kieran says worriedly. "You didn't have to make it so clear right away."

"Ian, James, Kieran, we're afraid for you."

As upset and thoughtful as Kieran was a moment ago, he feels cool now. "Babe, we can handle this. I'm just worried about James and Ian. I can do this myself with ease!"

"No time to be a cocky hero, mate," I bring Kieran back to reality.

"And the sign?" Ian asks the wizard. "When will we know that we can go into the cave without worrying and that the counterspell will work?" "My magic will make this stone glow so brightly that you can see it. The glow is my shield. The countdown begins at this moment."

Waiting for the helicopter to arrive makes my nerves fray. I'm already questioning everything when I suddenly hear the sound of a rotor.

Flop, flop, flop, flop.

"There it is. Get ready," says the magician and stands up.

I can feel every pulse and heartbeat inside me. My knees are weak and shaky, my palms damp. My breathing is shallow and rapid. In short, I'm more excited than I've ever been in my life.

"Look out, guys! If I jump up and start running, follow me immediately," Ian takes command.

I turn around. The wizard has stood up. He holds up the white stone with his hands and speaks incomprehensible gibberish. His eyes are jet black and his piercing gaze is fixed on the stone. I can also see the stone begin to flicker in the center. The light is brighter than any light I have ever seen in my life. I have to force myself to look away.

"Done," Ian whispers.

I look into the cave. The first vampires begin to move. Ted Harper talks to another vampire. That Jane Huckings joins them. The three of them keep talking.

Get lost, you bitch. Get lost, we need to get to the cave.

The last doubts arise whether Harper is playing a false game. Then the Huckings and the last vampire leave and follow the others to the clearing the FBI agent told us about. Behind us the light gets brighter and brighter. I don't dare turn around. The wizard seems to be in a complete trance. He keeps saying the same spell over and over again.

Huckings and the last vampire disappear from sight. Ian jumps up. "Go!"

We follow him. I pull my right leg up, brace myself and quickly go up. Now I'm behind Ian and Kieran. I'm glad that my weak knees don't give out. The excitement disappears as I run. I watch the ground, I don't want to trip over a root or a stone. Ted Harper turns and waves to us. My mental carousel starts.

How much time has passed? Has the shield been effective since then? When did it reach its full strength? Watch the ground! If you fall, it's over. Then it was all for nothing.

I try to suppress my thoughts and feel a slight sting in my side. We're almost there. We arrive at the cave. Harper looks to the edge of the forest. I look back as well. The bright glow of the stone is gigantic. I want to ask if this light also attracts the vampires, but I can't make a sound. My chest is rising and falling like crazy. I am literally sucking in oxygen. Kieran pulls a flashlight out of his backpack and runs into the cave. Ian follows close behind. The girls arrive. They line up beside Harper. Each holds an arrow.

"Good luck," Harper says, patting me on the back. "I've been counting. All the vampires are gone. The cave is clear!" I nod wordlessly, take a last look at my Riley and enter the cave. I quickly catch up. It's pleasantly cool at first, but then it gets downright cold.

The cone of light from Kieran's flashlight wobbles along the walls and floor. The cave passage was built by human hands. Solid floor, worked walls. The ceiling is almost two meters high, as is the width of the passage. The werewolf slows down at the first intersection.

"Always to the right. He said to always go right!" I shout at him.

Kieran takes the right direction and runs ahead again at high speed. Ian is still close behind. I also manage to stay close to my friends, even though they are running at a tremendous speed.

Damn it! I didn't stop the time, I suddenly remember. Another thrill I have to push out of my mind.

How long are five minutes? Think of something else.

At a crossroads with three junctions, Kieran immediately chooses the right corridor. He slows down a bit and the flashlight flickers over various pieces of equipment hanging on the wall. There are weapons and tools of all kinds. Kieran finally just walks along. "We could use a weapon or two in the need to fight the Guardians," he says, reaching for a Morning Star with a silver-tipped iron ball.

"Hands off!" warns Ian. "The wizard said to take nothing, absolutely nothing!"

Kieran immediately withdraws his hand.

"Go on!" I urge. "Time is running out."

We hurry through the tunnel and come to a dead end. Panting, we stop and look around. "Where is this stele we are supposed to lay our hands on?" I ask.

"There," Kieran points and walks over.

The menhir Harper was talking about is in the middle of the room. Kieran hesitates. "Something's wrong here!"

There are some notches, but they are not like the other two. We are perplexed. Perplexed, we look at each other.

"Is there another stone?"

We look around feverishly. Nothing. No stone, no pillar, no stele in sight.

"This is definitely the wrong stone," Kieran insists. "It's definitely a trap."

"Then what?" I ask hastily.

Time is pressing.

"Quick, light the walls," Ian suggests.

At the same time, the cone of light flies along the walls. It stops at three indentations. All three look like little grottoes. We go there and Kieran shines his light into the three grottos. They are all about 50 centimeters in diameter and about an arm's length deep. Each one contains exactly the same wooden crates. The box in the right grotto contains gold coins. The one in the middle is on a treasure chest, and the one on the left is on a block of rock.

"Shit!" Ian grumbles.

"Which one is it?" asks Kieran.

"How am I supposed to know?" I hiss in panic. "That forest rascal didn't say anything about it!"

"Guys, time is running out. We have to make a decision," Ian urges.

"In any case, there are three hand prints at the very front of each of the grottos. That means we each have to place a hand in one of the caves," Kieran begins to summarize.

"Think faster, mate!"

The werewolf looks at all three caves and the crates. Then he says, "If we wait too long, we'll die here, so I'll make a decision."

"Finally meet her!"

"The witcher said that only a werewolf can get the box with the coin. That means I have to choose a grotto. Then you have to place your hands in the imprints of the other grottoes. I think that will set off a mechanism that will release a lock so I can grab the right box.

Ian becomes visibly nervous. "We don't have much time, Kieran."

"Okay. Here's a puzzle. This Hostang is an ass. How do you know a donkey? Easy!" says the werewolf finally. "Ian, you're a vampire. They say you have a cold heart. Cold as a rock. Put your hand in the cave with the rock. James, you're a human. Humans are greedy. Put your hand in the cave with the gold coins."

"And you?"

"I reach for the box with the treasure chest."

"Why? That's greed too!"

"No, friend. It's something hidden. We werewolves hide and transform. This box points to the transformation."

"If that's true, you get ten free meals at Burger King," Ian groans.

"Boy, I'll eat you poot," Kieran snorts, winking at Ian.

"Hands in!" yells Ian.

We do exactly as Kieran instructed. When all three hands are in the prints, Kieran sticks his second hand into the grotto and reaches for the box. He manages to touch it with the tips of his fingers, maneuvers it forward in his direction, and finally grabs it completely. He pulls it out and opens the lid. "The coin!" he rejoices.

"Get out of here!" Ian and I yell at the same time, pulling our hands out of the caves, turning and running.

Kieran has taken the lead again with the flashlight.

"Left! Always left!" I call to him.

"And leave the weapons hanging. We don't need them," Ian warns.

We run for our lives. I've lost all sense of time and think the cave could collapse at any moment. We turn left again. I feel the ground start to shake. "Did you hear that, guys?" I gasp. "Hell, yeah! And I thought it was my legs because I'm out of shape," Ian replies.

"Run!" Kieran yells.

I give it everything I've got, ignoring my body, which is already telling me that I've reached the end of my tether. Left again. I see daylight. We hurry to the exit. I recognize the girls and Harper. They have their backs to us.

"We're coming!" Kieran yells.

Where does this guy get the strength to yell so loud while running, I ask myself. The best I can manage is a *thud* or something. I'm definitely at the end of my tether. I feel completely flat.

Now the ground is shaking noticeably. The bright light at the end of the tunnel fades. This again gives me a last burst of energy.

I can make it! Why is the ground shaking? Damn it, the Wizard's shield is losing its power!

I see the freedom and feel how close I am to the finish line, but suddenly I am overcome by strong doubts about victory. I stumble. Our three friends in front of the cave fall back.

"Out, not in!" warns Kieran. He's about to reach them.

Oh no, they're taking up fighting positions, it shoots through my head.

I make out movement. Several people are visible. A group of vampires is setting up at the entrance to the cave in front of my friends.

"Get out of the cave!" Ian shouts now.

We seem to be lost. A fight breaks out at the entrance of the cave. One of the vampires lunges at Harper. He dodges, reaches under his jacket, pulls out a revolver, and fires two shots. The attacker is hit and falls to the dust with a choking scream.

Riley and Cassie raise their arrows protectively in front of them. Kieran and Ian make it to the exit. Kieran tosses me the coin box. I almost stumble when I catch it.

The werewolf and Riley's brother immediately stand next to Harper. Now I also come to the cave exit and realize the journey. Five vampires and Jane Huckings are standing in a semicircle around my friends. All of them have their mouths open in warning. Harper keeps them at bay with his revolver. I can still hear the end of his warning: "You've seen it, it's loaded with consecrated silver bullets!"

"You traitor! My father trusted you. You and your friends will all die!" Jane Huckings spits hatefully. "I have the box," I breathe to Riley, looking over to where the witch is standing and handing her the container.

The light of the magic stone is fading. With every second it fades, the ground beneath us shakes more and more.

"Move your backs towards the witch and keep the vampires on the opposite side of you," I say, pulling a silver-tipped arrow from my quiver and drawing the bow I have slung around my neck. I aim at the vampire standing on the far left.

"Give us the coin and we'll spare you," Huckings suggests. Her voice almost cracks. Her eyes are wild and deep red.

"Screw you," I say, drawing the bow so everyone can see I'm ready to shoot.

The vampire I'm aiming at takes a step to the right. That's exactly where I want him.

"Get her!" Blood's daughter hisses, giving the order to attack.

Harper cocks the hammer of his revolver. "Come on over here. Which one of you wants to be the next to turn to dust?" he warns.

The vampires take a step back. I turn to face the wizard. The light is barely visible. "One shot, then we run for our lives to Mr. Smith. All hell is about to break loose," I urge Harper and the others, now aiming at Jane Huckings.

I hear a loud rumble from inside the cave. The first small cloud of dust shoots out. Ted fires a bullet at the first vampire, hitting him in the shoulder. Flames flicker from the wound. The victim falls to his knees and dies. I let the arrow fly from the string. Jane Huckings is distracted for a split second as she keeps her eyes on the wounded vampire. My arrow pierces her chest. The vampires realize their leader has been hit and back off.

"You bloody bastard!" Jack Blood's daughter groans, grabbing the shaft of the arrow. At first she thought it was a normal arrow, but now she wants to pull it out of her body and attack me. "You're going to die slowly for this, boy!"

Clouds of dust shoot out of the cave, the ground beneath us cracking.

"Run!" I yell.

Jane Huckings coughs. Tongues of fire blaze from the wound around the arrow. She realizes she is mortally wounded and tears open her mouth to scream.

We turn, dust enveloping us, and run away. The plateau in front of the cave collapses, taking with it the dying Jane Huckings, now on fire, and two of her men. The other vampires retreat. My plan has worked.

"The rest of Blood's helpers are cut off. To follow us, they will have to go around the outside of the collapsing cave. That will probably take more than an hour," I gasp, feeling a weight lift from my shoulders. When we reach Mr. Smith, the witcher is lying on the ground.

"Mr. Smith? Are you all right?" Cassie asks worriedly and runs over to him.

The bearded man lifts his head and smiles. "You did well. Very well."

"I'm worried about you."

"Everything is fine, my child. The spell has only weakened me a little. I need a few minutes. I'm not the youngest anymore."

We form a circle around the wizard. He sits up. "Don't worry about me. You must now complete the last part to lift the curse. Place the coins on the statue."

I look at the timer on my phone. "4:13 hours. We'll never make it!"

"Did you bring the statue?" Kieran wants to know.

Ian and Riley look at each other. "No."

"And now?"

"Daddy has to meet us," Cassie suggests.

"Mr. Anderson? Oh, dear. If he sees James or me, he might..."

Cassie tries to reassure Kieran, but her friend is quicker. "Stop! He knows he made a mistake. He was under a lot of pressure," Riley interrupts the werewolf. "And besides, it's about time he found out who he's getting for a son-in-law," Cassie grins.

Kieran blushes, then swallows and now his ears start to glow red. "No, you can't do that. We have to break it to him gently, Cassie. Otherwise he'll eat me alive."

Cassie laughs. "Don't worry, I was joking."

"Your schedule's not going to work," Ted Harper interjects.

"Yeah, it will be tight," Ian admits.

"But I have a way out."

Everyone stares at the agent. "A way out?"

"Yes. We fly back."

"Are you kidding us?"

Harper looks around. "You duelled with me earlier. We fought together and gave Jack Blood a good beating. We won a fight against him. You are important witnesses for me in a possible trial, and as an FBI agent I can request a helicopter in such cases. Like I said, we're going back! The helicopter can be here in twenty minutes and then we can make it to Greenfield within the required time frame without any problems."

"That would be very nice of you," Riley says.

Harper pulls out his smartphone. "You'll have to get lucky. One bar of reception."

While the FBI agent is on the phone, Cassie asks, "And who's going to drive my Toyota back?"

Smith sits up. "I can do that."

Cassie looks at the witch and grimaces. "You're a really nice guy on the inside, but, sorry, on the outside you look like you haven't washed in a while. I mean, my car will smell like you for months."

Harper ends the call. "The helicopter and some men are coming. We'll get your car back, Cassie. We can all fly together."

"Lucky you," Riley whispers.

"No offense, Mr. Smith."

The wizard laughs. "No one's ever told me so plainly that I should take another bath. Well, maybe I will. It's going to be fall, and the last time I had a bath was in the spring..."

The girls stare at the Wizard. "Ugh!"
Smith laughs again. "That was a joke."
A sigh of relief.
"We thought so."
"I bathe once a month."
Everyone stares again. Smith raises his right arm and sniffs his armpit. Then he wiggles the tip of his nose. "Hm," he says. "The fabric of the shirt might be a little..." He waves it off as Cassie and Riley put on their ugly faces and says, "It doesn't matter how often I bathe, the important thing is that I get you to a place where a helicopter can land."

https://pixabay.com/de/service/license-summary/

man-7861536_1280

Chapter Thirteen

Some people, maybe a lot of people, might think that flying in a helicopter is great and adventurous. I, on the other hand, feel uncomfortable and struggle with nausea. With my eyes closed, I listen to what Harper explains during the flight.

Some of the bodies found in Greenfield can be clearly attributed to Jack Blood and others to Oloisius. The FBI agent will soon discuss this with my father and together they will present the mysterious series of deaths to the public as solved.

Things look good for Mr. Anderson. Agent Harper does not want to arrest or charge Cassie's father. He considers the aiding and abetting to have been done under duress. Besides, it was Mr. Anderson who finally contacted the FBI and their *office for secret, mysterious cases* or something like that. According to Harper, he is on some kind of leniency program. However, the FBI agent will have some more serious, personal words with Mr. Anderson.

Despite the euphoria of having solved the case, the helicopter ride is one of the most terrifying things that has happened to me in my life, and I am relieved when the pilot finally lands near Greenfield.

We get out of the car dazed. The whirling rotor blades were still creating quite a bit of wind. When I finally get back on solid ground, I breathe a sigh of relief. I'm glad that I didn't throw up during the flight and I'm glad that the queasy feeling in my stomach is visibly disappearing. Riley looks at me and says that I look gorgeous and beautiful.

Pale as a corpse. Typical vampire taste, I think and take her in my arms.

I see two cars in the countryside. A blue Buick and a red Chevrolet van. Three men are standing beside them. Harper walks straight towards them, we follow. They are unmistakably FBI men. One opens the passenger door and the rear sliding door of the van, the other two nod wordlessly to Harper and get into the Buick. The driver of the van walks around the red Chevrolet and gets in.

"I thought the FBI vans were all black," Kieran muses.

Ted smiles. "Typical Hollywood. Of course, we have different cars." He points to the Chevy. "Get in!"

We are about four miles out of town. The blue Buick turns onto Highway 91, and our driver signals and follows. The man's eyes keep wandering to the rearview mirror.

"Sir, I think we're being followed," he says in a monotone voice.

Harper turns around. So do I.

"Which one?" the FBI vampire wants to know.

"The dark van. Behind it is a Ford with some pretty daring passing maneuvers. That could be one of them."

Harper reaches for a hidden radio in the glove compartment. He contacts the helicopter and the team in the Buick.

Moments later, the speaker crackles. The pilot's voice comes in rather nasally. He confirms the information from the driver. "This is Hawk 3. We have both vehicles in visual range and were able to read the license plates with the camera. We are sending the data to Central Control for verification."

"What's the current situation?" asks Harper, as our driver has passed a truck and is moving back into the right lane in front of him. The view to the rear is blocked.

"The Ford has caught up and is now level with the dark van. They are traveling side by side at the same speed."

"Stay with them!"

"Sorry, but we have to turn off. We're running out of fuel. We only have twelve minutes of flying time left. We must return to base."

Harper angrily slaps his flat hand on the armaturing board and acknowledges the radio message: "Crap! Roger, Hawk 3, have a nice flight home."

The driver keeps an eye on the traffic behind him. Harper speaks directly to the two agents in the Buick: "Blue team, fall back. We have two hostiles in the rear," followed by descriptions of the vehicles.

The radio transmission is confirmed. "Blue team understands. We are about two miles ahead of you and are now exiting the highway. Take the next exit. We'll wait there undercover and then stay behind the pursuit."

"Got it!"

A female voice now comes over the loudspeaker: "Central calling Greenfield - Red Team. Red team, come in!" Harper confirms. "This is red team."

"The two license plates transmitted by Hawk 3 have been reported stolen."

Harper confirms, Blue Team as well. The driver of the van flashes his lights. "We're about to take the exit and leave the highway."

Harper immediately relays the information to the second team.

"We have you in sight. Stay on the road and stay in front of the candle store. There, turn onto *W. Mountain Rd* and then speed down *Eden Trail* to the first possible drop-off. Turn off to the side and go behind the bushes and trees. If our pursuers come by here at high speed, they won't see you.

"Roger that, blue team!"

The driver squeals the tires, twists the wheel, and presses the accelerator. "Hang on, guys," he warns us.

We are pushed left and right in the car. I've never been so glad in my life to have seat belts. Except for my grandfather, of course. He always drove like a madman - even though he was almost blind. It was pure *kamikaze driving*.

"Yeah," Kieran cheers. "I've always wanted to do that! Makes Disneyland look like a pipe compared to this."

The next thing he knows, his head hits the window. "Ouch!"

"Go away," Cassie says, squeezing Kieran's hand anxiously.

We're already speeding down the *Eden Trail*. After a curve or two, where I thought the van would break loose and we would end up in the grass, the driver warns us again: "Hang on!" I'm thinking what's worse, another helicopter flyover or this ride, when the driver slams on the brakes immediately after his warning.

We are thrown back and forth. The enormous centrifugal force literally presses us into our seats. The speedometer needle suddenly jumps from right to left. The driver turns the steering wheel in a flash, leaves the road and performs a fantastic slide. We come to a stop behind a tree.

"Wow, that was awesome!" beams Kieran. "You really have to teach me how to do that. That's how I'm going to park in front of the movie theater when I get my license."

"Well done, Jason," Harper praises.

I see he has his revolver in his hand. He's expecting the worst.

"Team Blue, are you all right?" the FBI agent asks over the radio.

No answer. Instead, we hear shots. There are two or three bangs in quick succession. I can see a little of the road. A dark van roars past us at high speed. "Blue team, come in!"

Harper lets go of the transmit button and listens. Still no response. The driver presses two buttons on the door at the same time and rolls down the side windows a little. "This way we can hear what's going on outside," he explains.

Gunshots whip through the air again, then tires screech. The Ford speeds past us, the Buick close behind. Shots are fired from the Ford at the Buick, the Buick's passenger fires at the Ford.

"Cover!" Harper warns.

Then it happens. I can just make out the brake lights on the Buick. The sound of screeching tires reaches us again, but this time it's followed by a loud crash. I stretch to see better. A jet of blazing flame shoots upward. I see orange-yellow light surrounded by thick, dark smoke.

"Red team, red team, come in," comes a rush over the radio.

"We can hear you fine. Please talk!"

The send button is pressed. At first there's just static on the speaker, then I hear a wheeze, and then the FBI agent from Team Red speaks: "The Ford is disabled. The vehicle is on fire. It looks like none of the occupants were able to escape. Drive back to your destination. We'll take care of the situation here and call for assistance."

Without waiting for a sign from Harper, our driver starts the van's engine and drives off. The side windows are rolled up again.

"Got it," Harper replies. "Have Sheriff Allington or his deputies take over here with you. Is the APB out on the dark van yet?"

"Yes, sir. The manhunt is on all channels. With the FBI as well as the local police, highway patrol and neighboring departments."

"Thank you and over."

Harper puts the radio back in the glove box. He turns to us. "Let's go to your house, Riley and Ian."

"Too bad, I would have loved to see the action there," Kieran grumbles. "It's much more awesome in real life than on the big screen. Maybe I'll be a stuntman too. Danger is my second name.

"You're out of your mind, dude," I say, and Kieran just shrugs his shoulders contemptuously.

"That's just the way it is. I'm just an action guy."

Cassie adores him, I shrug, and Riley squeezes my hand. I don't say anything back. The next ten minutes go by quietly. We're driving at a moderate speed toward a red light when the driver suddenly gives another warning. This time, however, he is desperate, almost panicked: "Two motorcycles. One with a pillion. This one is armed with a submachine gun!" he shouts, and immediately presses the accelerator. The van lurches forward.

There must be a lot of horsepower under the hood of this Chevy, I think.

I see the needle on the speedometer. It immediately moves up, easily reaching 30, 50, and 70 miles per hour. We all stare at the traffic light, which is still red. "Stooooooooooopp!" we scream desperately.

I press myself into the seat, close my eyes, feel Riley's firm handshake, and promise myself that if we survive this, I will never do anything wrong again. I open my eyes. The light is still red. A truck with a trailer is making a U-turn. It's right in front of us and, barring a miracle, we're going to hit it.

In a split second, pure fear spreads and paralyzes me. The feeling of certain death in front of my eyes is much, much more unpleasant than flying in a helicopter.

Rrrrrrrttt

The sound of a machine gun scares us to death. A motorcycle passes next to us. The man on the passenger seat points and shoots at us.

Tock, tock, tock, tock

There are bullet holes in the side of the van. The bullets whiz diagonally upward through the vehicle and pierce the roof. My heart almost stops. Adrenaline is released. "That was close," I exhale and squeeze Riley's hand as tightly as I can. "Don't be afraid. I'm here with you," I tell her. It probably helps me more than it helps her. It calms me down when I talk. The only one of us with a real sense of gallows humor is Kieran.

"Guys, this is mega awesome!" he says, staring at the bullet holes. "You don't even need air conditioning anymore. I can feel the air on the street. It's amazing!"

Jason slams on the brakes and spins the wheel. This time it's our tires that lock up and squeal loudly despite the ABS. The motorcyclist can't react as fast. His bike passes the van and is level with us for a moment. Jason turns the steering wheel like crazy. We swing from left to right and back again. With this sideways swing the van hits the Kawasaki.

"Not with me, you son of a bitch," Jason grumbles.

The bike crashes, rider and passenger are thrown up and fly through the air. Meanwhile, we keep going and are about to collide with the truck. Now Jason jerks the steering wheel around again. We slide towards the truck, but don't touch it. The vehicle, which weighs several tons, passes us with less than three millimeters of clearance. Jason's *stop and go* continues. When the truck has passed us with a loud, continuous honk and I feel the life in my veins again, frozen with fear, the FBI agent presses the accelerator again and pulls the handbrake while still accelerating. The rear of our car skids around and slides right behind the truck. Two more daring maneuvers with near misses follow, and then we are through the intersection. Of course, our heads immediately spin. The truck driver is still honking and braking his monster. The crashed Kawasaki slides under the wheels of the truck and is crushed. A motorcyclist has crashed into the trailer of the truck, the shooting pillion rider has hit the road more than rudely. Both lie motionless.

"Knocked out," Jason says dryly.

I'm glad to see that he and Harper also have beads of sweat on their foreheads.

"Are you okay?" the FBI agent asks worriedly.

"Everything's fine," I say.

The girls nod, Ian snorts in relief: "Yeah," and Kieran grins: "Better than any roller coaster ride! That was the coolest,

I have ever been on. Guys, do you need a new generation? That would be a job for me. FBI agent just pushed in front of the stuntman."

"Good," Harper says and picks up the radio again. He announces what just happened and calls for police and emergency vehicles. Then he turns back to us. "I hope we can continue our journey without further incident."

"Our needs are covered for today," Ian groans.

Shortly after, we hear the first sirens of emergency vehicles. Sheriff's deputies, fire trucks and ambulances race through Greenfield.

"We're almost there. Just one more cross street," Riley says.

"Pull over," comes Ian.

The driver flashes his lights and pulls over. Harper turns around. "What's going on?"

"Ted, did the FBI put people outside our house too?" The agent shakes his head. "No. I don't have any more people. My department is very small. Besides Jason and the two guys in the Buick, there's just Emma. She sits in the control center and runs the missions from there."

"And the pilots?" asks Kieran.

"They don't ask questions. They're up in the air and don't know what's going on down here on the ground."

Ian returns to the topic. "Let's stick to the point. The countdown is on. Time is against us and for Blood. We have to get to the statue and drop the coins, otherwise it's all for nothing. And when I think that there's another van full of Blood's people, I feel sick. Because then the question arises, where did the van go? Do you think they're waiting for us at home?"

Harper summarizes very astutely. "As a matter of fact, I'm very sure they're expecting us. I also suspect that Jack Blood will be there in person.   He won't miss the opportunity to enjoy his triumph."

Silence.

We think about it. Riley speaks first: "And how are we supposed to get there? Just stop in front of the house and march in, for nothing?"

"Give me a gun and I'll shoot your way out," Kieran suggests. "I think I'm in the best shape possible after this performance here."

Harper shakes his head. "No, I was imagining us getting out at the intersection and Jason driving by your house in the van. The windows are blacked out and they can't see if we're in the van or not. They will follow the van."

Cassie objects. "It's way too dangerous for Jason."

Kieran squeezes her hand. "Don't worry, honey. Jason is a genius driver. You'll never catch him."

It is Riley who now steps forward and makes a decision. "That's not a bad trick. Jason doesn't have to drive right by the house. It's enough if he rolls past the intersection. They'll see him and give chase. We'll set off on foot from here at the same time and approach the house from the back through the neighbors' yards.

"Brilliant," Ian agrees. "The Bakers' yard is right next to ours. That's great. From there, we can get to the fence without being seen, and if we climb the big cherry tree, we can also jump over to our roof."

Ted Harper frowns. You can see it rattling and working behind him. "That sounds good."

"I even left my window open."

"That doesn't matter. I can open a window like that in less than 30 seconds," the FBI agent winks. "And so can Blood's people, by the way," he adds warningly.

"Me in less than five seconds," Kieran says, showing his elbow. "Clank, windshield out, us in," he laughs. "I should join the FBI. You teach me how to drive a car and I'll show you how to get into houses."

"Kieran," Cassie admonishes.

"How much money does an agent make anyway?" he adds.

"Later, Kieran," Harper waves him off. "Let's get going."

We head straight for the next house. Ian squeezes through the narrow passage between the garage and the house. "It's narrow here, but we can get through easily. I used to walk here almost every day when I was a boy. It was a shortcut to my buddy's house." Jason rolls down the passenger side window. "I'm going to wait exactly five minutes, and then I'm going to leave. In exactly six minutes, I'll be rolling slowly down Pine St. They'll definitely see me if they're in front of the house. If they're not there, I'll make sure they see me.

Ted gives the okay with a thumbs up, turns and starts to leave.

"Just a minute," Jason calls to him.

Ted turns back to his colleague in the van. The Agent reaches behind him and tosses some folded jackets out the side window. "Put these on. This is an official operation, and I want the neighbors to know who's sneaking through the yards. Don't get into trouble with them and have someone shoot at you with a shotgun."

"Very good, Jason. I hadn't thought of that."

Ted picks up the jackets and passes them around. "You're not FBI agents, but put the jackets on anyway."

We take the blue windbreakers. The back says *FBI* in big yellow letters.

Kieran is very proud. "Look, this looks really good on me. I think I'll take the job offer."

I give my buddy a dirty look. "What job offer?"

"The one the FBI is going to give me. They can't get a better agent than me," he grins and gets in line behind Ian.

We climb over a low fence into a yard, cross it, and climb over the next fence. Ian waves to an elderly woman drinking tea on the back patio of her house. "Hello, Mrs. Saunders."

"Hello, Ian," comes the reply, followed by a look I only know from the farmer's hut. When someone walks by, they stare until the person is out of sight.

After another garden, we finally stood in front of the big cherry tree that Ian had told us about. The student raises his hand and whispers: "Stop! Slow down, guys."

Cautiously, everyone closes up. Ted Harper pulls out a small pair of binoculars, no bigger than an opera glass. He seems to be looking at every corner of the house, lingering a little longer at the windows.

"What are you..." the curious gardener asks and is immediately interrupted by Kieran.

"Get inside! Can't you see this is an FBI operation?" He points to his back. "That's what it says. I'm an FBI agent. Man, oh man, what kind of blind neighbors do you have?"

The neighbor immediately closes the window.

"I saw movement. Someone's definitely in the house. Are your parents really gone for the weekend?"

"No one's home," Ian confirms.

"We don't have any pets either," Riley adds. "Except for a few fish in the aquarium."

Kieran looks at Harper. "And they barely run around the apartment."

The FBI agent puts down the binoculars. "How much time do we have?"

I look at my phone. "52 minutes!"

"What if Blood's people stole the statue and hid it?" Kieran asks.

"If they had the statue, they wouldn't be in the house," Harper counters. "They're looking for it. That's why they're still here."

"They have it, don't they?" I ask.

Riley looks at me. "Of course, James. It's simple, but it's still so well hidden that I guarantee people have walked past it in there umpteen times and always missed it."

"How is that possible?"

"It's in the aquarium. It's set up like a sunken city. It was Ian's idea when he was twelve years old."

"I'll go in alone and you surround the house," Ted Harper decides.

"Alone? That's too dangerous. I'll go with you. Besides, you don't know our house," Ian argues.

"Absolutely not. I can't be responsible if..."

"If we don't make it, we'll die! So I might as well go in with you."

"I don't want to rush, but in about a minute Jason will show up with the van," Kieran calls in between.

"Oh, do what you want," Harper angrily waves off and climbs up the cherry tree.

A strong branch leads to the roof of Riley's house. Ian follows Harper, then Kieran and I climb the tree and wait at the branch that leads to the roof.

"Riley and Cassie, you should stay here with the bow. If one of Blood's vampires actually runs out with the statue, you will be the last barrier."

At first there is a scowl, then Ian agrees to the suggestion. "He's right, sis. You are our life insurance."

"All right," she replies, showing one of the arrows that are dangerous to vampires.

Kieran points at the house. "They spotted the van. There is life in the house."

We see two or three people inside the house jump up and run out. Moments later, a powerful engine hums. Tires squeal.

"The plan is working. We're storming the house," Harper says, sliding the last bit along the thick branch and jumping onto the roof.

We follow. Ian pushes past Harper and gets to the window first. He peers in cautiously.

"Room's clear," he whispers, pushing the window up. Harper climbs in first. He waits until we're all in the room, then he scurries to the door and puts his index finger to his mouth, indicating that we should be quiet. He reaches for the doorknob and turns it.

Click

He opens the door a little. We hear footsteps and muffled voices. Harper raises his hand and shows us two fingers. We nod. Then he indicates with his fingers that the two men are downstairs. We again indicate that we understand. The FBI agent holds his revolver in his right hand and opens the door with his left. He walks into the hallway. We are close behind him. While he secures the stairs, we are to search the upper rooms. One goes left, two right. ner goes left, two right. All three rooms, including the shower, are empty. On the first floor we hear two vampires talking.

"I hope they catch that van, then we'll all have a chance to catch all together."

"I hope so too. The boss is getting uncomfortable."

"Uncomfortable? That's much too harmless. He's already angry and there's no end in sight. I listened to the phone call between Billy and the boss earlier. That's when Blood found out about his daughter's death. He's going to rip the head off that traitor Harper."

"Back to the point. I don't think the damn statue we're supposed to be looking for is here. We've already searched the whole house. I bet the brats took it."

Harper raises his hand and counts backwards on three fingers, folding them together. Three ... two ... one!

With the snap of his last finger, he runs down the stairs at lightning speed, aiming his revolver at the two vampires and yelling: "FBI! Hands in the air! Freeze!"

The vampire in front is startled and throws his hands up. The one behind him reaches to his side and pulls out a gun. Harper fires once.

Bang

The sound is deafening in the house. For a split second, there is a muzzle flash on the barrel of the revolver. The vampire who tried to pull the gun grabs his breast, then smoke and fumes hiss from the wound.

"Silver bullets, my friend," Kieran shouts, holding out his middle finger.

The victim's skin turns ashen and wrinkled. He collapses and dies. I see the aquarium and look for the statue. At that moment, the vampire across from me follows my gaze, looks into the aquarium, and makes a lightning combination. I can see the light in his eyes as he recognizes the statue. "Nora, she's in the aquarium! Get her and get out the back!"

"There's three of them!" warns Ian, trying to push past Ted Harper.

Blood's helper takes advantage of the moment of inattention and leaps at Harper. A shot is fired, but the silver bullet hits the ceiling. Harper falls, the assailant holding the FBI agent's gun with one hand and pressing against his throat with the other. Kieran grabs the vampire's shoulders and tries to pull him away. He defends himself by turning his head and trying to bite my friend's arm.

"Watch out!" I warn Kieran, grabbing a nearby candlestick and shoving it between Kieran's arm and the vampire's head. His bite hits the metal candlestick. A tooth breaks. The vampire hisses in pain. Harper gains the upper hand and manages to escape the chokehold. He rolls around once. The vampire jumps to his feet, opens his mouth to bite, and is about to lunge at Kieran

317

when Harper fires. The bullet pierces the vampire's back. It immediately begins to steam. As before, smoke creeps out of the wound and the victim ages in a matter of seconds. He collapses and turns to dust.

Ian sees Nora. The vampire has discovered the statue in the water of the aquarium. She reaches in, grabs the stone figure by the head and pulls it out of the tank. Before Ian can reach her, she runs and jumps through the window of the patio door.

Clang

She rolls in the pile of broken glass, jumps back to her feet, and starts to run when Cassie and Riley block her path.

"You have something that belongs to me!"

The vampire opens her mouth to reveal pointed teeth. "Out of my way, you stupid brats!"

Riley has drawn his bow and is aiming the arrow at the vampire. "I won't warn you again."

"Die!" yells Blood's helper and jumps at the girls.

The arrow whizzes off the string and pierces the attacker's body. She flinches and falls to the ground like a felled tree. The statue rolls out of her hand and comes to rest at Cassie's feet. She picks up the stone figure.

"No!" comes a last word from the dying woman's mouth, then her body turns to ash.

Cassie looks at the statue, seemingly unfazed by the fighting around her. "It looks like an ugly Buddha with three arms for tea lights," she says.

Riley is relieved. "It's unharmed. Thank God!"

Ted, Ian, Kieran and I stand on the patio and look at the two girls.

"Well done!" praises the FBI agent. "How much time do we have?"

"Just under half an hour," I answer after looking at the timer on my phone.

Ted's smartphone rings. He sees the caller's number and picks it up. "Harper."

"This is Jason. I drove out of Greenfield and lost the boys. They should be out on the highway somewhere looking for me by now. Is everything okay with you?"

"Yes, everything is fine. We have the statue and the coins. We'll start the ceremony to break the curse right away."

Cassie puts down the statue. Ian, who has the coins with him, takes them out of his pocket. "Come here, Riley," he says, his voice cracking. Tears of joyful relief are visible. "We can break the curse thanks to your friends."

They each place a coin in the statue's hand. "Now the last coin," Ian says, turning around. "James, would you be so kind and place the coin on your hand?"

"Stop!" Kieran suddenly interrupts. "What's going on?"

"Take one of the coins back."

Cassie pokes her friend in the side. "Why?"

"Because it was always supposed to be three of us. A vampire, a human, and a werewolf. Why should this be any different? If the curse is to be lifted, it will be the same here. Each of us must place a coin on the statue. Only that makes sense and would obey the order of this sorcerer Hostang. This is the last deadly trap!"

"He's absolutely right. Man, we almost blew it at the end," Ian says and takes back the coin he put on the statue's hand. "Here, Kieran. This is yours!"

"Why this one exactly?"

Ian grins. "Because it has a wolf on it!"

Kieran takes the coin and carefully kneels down in front of the statue. Then he places it on the open palm of the statue. "Now you, James."

I take the last coin and look at it. I recognize the image of a human being. Then I look at the timer. "We have 17 minutes left."

"Put it on!"

A shot rings out. I feel a sharp breeze pass my head.

"You're not going to make it!" we hear the deep voice of Jack Blood. He's standing on the roof of Riley's house with a gun in his hand. Harper pulls out the revolver and fires at Blood.

"Hurry, James!" Kieran urges, standing in front of me.

"You're protecting your friend with your body to save our lives? You're a real hero," Riley shouts.

Blood fires another shot. But he can't aim accurately as he runs along the roof to avoid the FBI agent's shots.

My pulse is racing, my hands are shaking. Once again, I'm in mortal danger. I try to remain as calm as possible and raise the coin demonstratively. "Blood, you've lost!" I shout loudly, showing him the last coin and placing it on his free hand.

The statue's eyes begin to glow green, then orange, then red, then the stone figure begins to glow, the coins melt and the figure breaks apart. Smoking, they lie in the in the grass. The coins have dissolved. The spell is broken, the curse banished.

"NOOOO!" Blood roars, firing wildly at us.

"Take cover!" warns Ted, who has to reload.

I stare up at the roof of the house and feel anger. Indescribable rage. My right hand goes to my waistband. I feel the grip of Blood's buddy's revolver.

"I've been saving this thing for this moment. This is for you, you murderer!" I yell, standing up, aiming at the vampire and pulling the trigger. The hammer strikes the patron twice, three times, four times, sending silver bullets flying from the barrel.

Blood takes cover behind the chimney. Every time I shoot, he ducks. I only missed him once. I see the bullet hitting the chimney and sending small stones flying.

"Well done, James!" shouts Ted Harper, pulling back the loaded barrel of his revolver and firing again at Jack Blood.

He is cornered. "You won't stop me. I'll be back!" the vampire yells, jumping up and running over the gable to the other side of the house.

Ted also jumps up and runs forward through the house. He won't let the criminal get away. Just as the FBI agent opens the front door, he sees Blood get into a small car and speed away. Ted immediately grabs his cell phone, but puts it away when Jason arrives with the van. Ted opens the passenger door and jumps into the Chevrolet. "Blood's on the move, follow him!"

Kieran, Ian and I are close behind Ted, open the rear sliding door and jump into the van as well. Before Harper can protest about us coming along, Jason steps on the gas and chases after Jack Blood's van.

Ted turns around. "What the hell are you doing here? This is an FBI operation, you need to get out! This is life-threatening!" he yells, gesturing wildly.

Kieran points at our jackets. "We're FBI, buddy! And if you think we're going to miss this ride, you're wrong."

"Should we throw them out?" asks Jason.

Harper looks down the road and waves him off. "It's no use. Step on it! These guys are stubborn. Besides, we'd just lose time and Blood could get away."

"Yeah! Give me five, buddy," Kieran says happily, holding up his hand. I punch in.

The van shoots through the streets of Greenfield, literally chasing Jack Blood's van. Even the most daring driving maneuvers are useless against the fleeing vampire. Jason is a fantastic driver. I check the load on the drum of my rifle. There is still an intact bullet in the chamber. "This is reserved for Jack Blood. And then I'm going to throw the contents of the Mexican's bottle in his face and grin," I say angrily. I hate Jack Blood.

Ted has called for backup on the radio. Police cars from all over have responded. The radio traffic is almost indecipherable, so many patrols yelling at each other, telling each other where they are.

"He's heading for the main road. He probably wants to get out of town," I say.

"It's going to be tight," Jason announces.

We keep our eyes on the road ahead. A tanker pulls out of the gas station. Blood heads straight for it. Jason slows down. "He's not going to make it. No way!" The truck accelerates, putting more distance between us and Blood.

Jason slams on the brakes. The centrifugal force pushes us forward and back into our seats.

"He's crazy," Harper blurts out.

The small car slams into the back of the tanker and flips over. A jet of flame immediately shoots upward. The pressure of the ensuing explosion shatters the windows of the surrounding houses.

We come to a screeching halt and stare at a huge ball of fire. People are running around. The driver of the tanker jumps out of the cab and runs away. The gas station employees also flee. Harper gets on the radio and makes an emergency call.

A good hour later, the street is still filled with emergency vehicles and police cars. Blue and red lights reflected in the windows.

Miraculously, there were no fatalities and no serious injuries. The fire department has put out the fire. Thick smoke billows over the wreckage. Ted Harper and my dad approached the burned-out little car with their guns drawn. The driver's side door is open. They both stand in front of it and look inside. Then they shrug and look at each other questioningly.

"It's empty! Jack Blood either burned up or escaped."

"Was he thrown out?" asks Dad.

"Maybe. I didn't see it. I could have sworn he was in the vehicle when the fire started."

"We will search the scene as thoroughly as possible." "I hope the worst opponent I've ever had is no longer alive. If Jack Blood survived this accident, he'll come back one day and make good on his threat." My father puts his right hand on Ted Harper's shoulder. "If that's the case, Ted, old friend, then we're ready. Now we know our enemies."

The next day we are all sitting at Luigi's enjoying the house cup. Mr. Anderson invited us. The guy isn't as unpleasant as I thought, and he can even laugh and tell good jokes. Well, I still don't fully trust him, but I'll keep that to myself.

Before that we had a meeting with Kieran's parents, my dad, Riley's parents, the Andersons and Ted Harper. We don't know exactly what they discussed, but it seems that we have taken the first step towards what we hope will be a long lasting peace between the different creatures.

Mr. Anderson taps Kieran on the shoulder. "I'll be keeping an eye on you. Always be careful," he winks at him. Kieran swallows and looks at Cassie who grins at him.

My father stands up. "I am proud of the youth of Greenfield. They have shown us how to put prejudices aside and what it means to help each other. Let's use this as an example. Let Greenfield be the cradle of a common future. I quote our former president, Abraham Lincoln, who once said: *"Will I not destroy my enemies by making them my friends?"*

Everyone applauds.

Of course, we are still not allowed to talk about the fact that there are werewolves and vampires among us, but that hurdle will surely fall one day.

In the evening I lie contentedly in my bed and let the day pass by.

Man, this was the greatest adventure of my life. How to start again?

My brain immediately starts rattling and the memories come flooding back. Actually, I just wanted to show off a little at the new school and make new friends by being cool.

I was very lucky. Nothing bad happened to me while I was driving without a license and I wasn't stopped by the police. I learned a lot from that stupidity. I'm definitely not going to do something stupid like that again. It can ruin your whole life.

As for friends, the Porsche didn't help anyway. I've made great and close friends because no matter what your background is, we just stick together. We're a team and it would be nice if everyone could get ahead would think and act like that without any foundation. It doesn't matter where you come from, what you look like, or how much money you have. It all depends on your character.

Now I have a really cool werewolf as my best friend and my girlfriend is a charming vampire. Cassie is always good for a good line and I think we make a great quartet. Unfortunately, I also have a nemesis now, and I don't know if he's alive or dead. All I know is that if Jack Blood comes back one day, I won't have to fight him alone, because I have friends with a bite.

End